I0771753

Steele's Battalion:
The Great War Diaries

Also from John D. Beatty

Fiction

Crop Duster: A Novel of World War II
Sergeant's Business and Other Stories
The Liberty Bell Files: J Edgar's Demons
The Past Not Taken: Three Novellas
This Redhead: The Dialogues

The Stella's Game Trilogy

Stella's Game: A Story of Friendship
Tideline: Friendship Abides
The Safe Tree: Friendship Triumphs

Non-Fiction

The Devil's Own Day: Shiloh and the American Civil War

Why the Samurai Lost Japan:
A Study In Miscalculation And Folly

The Fire Blitz: Burning Down Japan

Steele's Battalion:
The Great War Diaries

John D. Beatty

JDB COMMUNICATIONS, LLC
WEST ALLIS, WISCONSIN

Copyright © 2025 by John D. Beatty and
JDB Communications, LLC

All rights reserved, including the right to reproduce this book or any portion thereof in any form or by any means, electronic or mechanical, including photocopying, recording, or by any information retrieval system without permission in writing from the publisher. Direct all inquiries to JDB Communications, LLC at jdbcom@gmail.com.

1ˢᵗ Edition Paperback ISBN: 979-8-9860169-8-6
1ˢᵗ Edition E-book ISBN: 979-8-9860169-9-3

This is a work of fiction. Actions of the characters, living or dead, are products of the author's imagination. The events described, historical or not, are also products of the author's imagination. The author strictly intends any resemblance to the actual past to further the story, and not to impugn the reputations of any persons, places, or organizations.

*Behold, their brave men cry in the streets, The
ambassadors of peace weep bitterly.*

Isaiah 33:7

For My Maternal Grandparents,
Helen Wilmington and John Benjamin Tramer
Who survived the Great Influenza and World War One...

Introduction: Volume XI 1916-1917

6ᵗʰ April 1905. Dearborn, Mich.

I got this diary today for my ninth birthday. Mama

says I should write and practice every day to

improve my penmanship.

We saw a flying machine at the fair park today.

Papa's truck can carry 7 of us in the back if we don't

sit. Helen and Irving sat in front with Mama and

Papa when we went to the park.

THIS WAS THE *FIRST* ENTRY IN THE *FIRST* DIARY—VOLUME I—OF Edmund Archer "Ned" Steele, born in Crawfordville, Michigan on 6 April 1896. Most of his subsequent volumes started on his birthday, with notable exceptions.

My name is Curtis H. Durand, and I am the Jensen Endowment Professor of American History at Crest University. I am also the Curator of the Steele Collection of Ned's diaries and papers, part of the Crest/Jenson Archives. My son-in-law, Michel Klein, found these diaries in an old steamer trunk in 1996.

What you will read are diary entries extracted from Ned's Volumes XI through the beginning of XIV, which document his experience in World War One from Mexico in January 1917 to France in May 1919. His papers, three unpublished memoirs entitled *With the AEF, From Corporal to Lieutenant General,* and *The Brownshoe Army*, and assets in other collections and archives, helped to fill in Ned's story.

As the transcribers, researchers and verifiers of the diaries, myself and my daughter, Ms. Maria Durand, provide footnotes to explain terms and concepts that may be foreign to some readers, and bracketed descriptions [] to describe anomalies in the texts which are, after all nearly a century old at this publishing (1997). We also removed vulgar [expletives] found in the diaries, which became more numerous over time. Gaps in the timeline either follow diary gaps or jump over uneventful periods.

Researchers can consult the microforms or the original Steele documents used to create this narrative, and photostatic copies of other original documents in the Steele Collection at Crest University.

We hope you enjoy and learn from Ned's story, which starts in Mexico....

January

1st January, 1917, Mexico.

I have neglected my diary for too long.

No celebration of any kind for the New Year. The cold desert is surprising. We have been in Mexico for nearly three months. I have not taken a bath of any kind in nearly five weeks and I [expletive] reek. We are all out of razor blades and soap. I borrowed a cutthroat and sliced myself up pretty badly. We see no bandits, no action, but we hear it sometimes. One fellow's Kodak has filled up, but I don't know what he's taking pictures of, in this featureless [expletive] desert.

20th January, near the Texas-Mexico border.

Welding two different metals is tricky, but with proper flux and heat…Met Gen. Pershing…I am glad when officers have a sense of humor…An officer with an unpleasant voice wanted my view on something military… My invention invoked a great deal of curiosity at HQ, but I doubt we will ever see it used since we are ordered out of [expletive] Mexico.

I have reduced my profane entries, but not eliminated them. I must strive to do better.

The Machine-Gun Section of the US Army's Provisional Division slogged down yet another dusty trail in the cold, bright afternoon desert sun, the mules tired and saddle-sore despite the packer's care. The bouncing and bumping machine-gun carts, the swearing of the tired men pushing the carts back onto the rocky track, and braying and kicking of the long-suffering mules pulling the carts broke the primeval quiet of the desert.

This fifty-five-man section detached several machine gun teams (in their only touring motor cars) that had skirmished with bandits over the past weeks, but it had yet to see any "major" action—"major" being *anything like* what they had heard was happening in Europe. *Detachments* had fired at bandits and received fire from other small-caliber weapons a half-dozen times…and *that* was *it*.

Some in the section believed they were missing out on *something*.

This rough trail ended at a *wide* north-south *track* and a parked supply column of motor wagons[1] at the side of the road. Men transferred crates and bags between vehicles while others stood guard. Civilians from a nearby village stood mute, watching.

Locals called roads by their start or end point, as in "the road to *this place*" or "the road to *that place*." The few available maps did no better, *if* they mapped the roads at all. *This* one, in particular, was only called a "road" because it was *wider* than a trail and *higher* than the surrounding countryside. *Here* it was a "highway" because it was General John J. Pershing's main supply route the Americans called "Pershing's Highway."

"Damn *paesanos*," one man in the column grumbled. "Steal us *blind* whenever we stop anywhere for over five minutes."

"*Campesinos*," another corrected. "But…say, want to *sell* your mules, boys?" The speaker spotted the Machine-Gun Section.

"Sorry, fellers," Lieutenant Lucas shook his head. "*These* mules are for machine guns."

"*Yeah*," a bandy-legged Captain said. "Machine guns, eh? *We've* got one of them damn *useless* things."

"Useless," Lucas repeated. "Why…?"

---

[1] Early term for a *truck*.

"Take too long to set up," the Captain said. "We got raided last night. Our machine gun was on *one* side of the road and the bandits attacked the *other* side. By the time we got it moved and back in action, them bandits were *long* gone."

"Well, poor deployment was the problem," Lucas declared, his lean face twisted into a scowl. "Not…"

"Sir," a Corporal interrupted, "they need some way to mount the gun to cover *both* sides of…"

"Steele," Sergeant McTee said, "That's an *officer* you're…"

"Let him *talk*, Sergeant," the Captain declared. "I want to hear what he's got to *say* about how to *mount* a *machine gun*…."

"Go ahead with *another* of your ideas, Steele," McTee sighed, hitching a thumb over his shoulder with a knowing glance. "He's got a *million* of 'em, sir. *College* boy, ya know." The tall, lean, NCO, like many of his long-serving type, was of an indeterminate age—a fair guess would be thirty-five to forty.

"Sir," Steele started. "I've been *thinking* a pedestal mount for vehicles would be an excellent way to do just what Captain…excuse me, sir; I didn't get your name?"

"Stilwell, Corporal. Go ahead."

"Sir. We need a post *strong* enough to resist the recoil but *high* enough to increase the visual arc. What we'd *need* is…the rear axle of *that* motor wagon," Steele pointed to a vehicle pushed off the steeply sloped road. "*She'll* never run again…"

"How do you *know* that?" Stilwell frowned.

"Someone's looted the radiator and the wheels. *That* firm went out of business in 1910, so we'll *never* get parts for it."

"Huh," Stilwell sniffed. "You seem *certain* of yourself, Corporal…"

"I helped my father clean out the factory after he *bought* it when the owners went bankrupt, sir. The radiators in *those* motor wagons were *very* complex; *too* expensive. Makes the *Ford* version cheaper by *half*."

Stilwell stared, looking back and forth between Steele and the vehicle. "What's your *name*, Corporal?"

"*Steele*, sir. Edmund Steele," he answered.

"Uh-huh," Stilwell said sourly. "So that axle's a *post*. What about a *base*?"

"Weld the *chain drive sprocket* to cross-rods from the motor wagon's *steering axle*. Sir."

Stilwell stared at the truck, then back at Steele, then at Lucas, with a quick glance at McTee, who raised his eyebrows and gave a slight shrug. "If we had the *tools*…"

"Up *there*, sir," Steele pointed. "There's a *gas welding* rig in *that* motor wagon."

"Yeah," Stilwell nodded. "Nobody *here* knows how to…"

"*I* do, sir," Steele declared.

Stilwell, sour-faced but curious, glanced at Lucas. "Lieutenant, will you allow the Corporal to, ah, *try* to build his invention?"

"Yessir," Lucas nodded. "*Most* of his ideas are sound."

"Sir," Steele saluted his Lieutenant briskly. "By your *leave*, sir," he said to Stilwell. "Sergeant McTee, we need to get that axle off; I can show you how."

Stilwell and Lucas watched the Machine-Gun Section and several of the supply column's men move into action, securing the great squared logs under the truck while others moved the welding motor wagon closer. "Ever see the like, Lieutenant?" Stilwell asked.

"*More* than once," Lucas answered. "Steele can organize *worms* in a *bucket*."

"Might be handy to remember Corporal Steele, Lieutenant," Stilwell nodded. "We might *need* that kind of talent soon."

Several minutes later, as Steele put the machine gun pintle on the axle, they heard a gruff voice ask, "who's in *command* here?"

"*I* command the Machine-Gun Section, sir," Lucas said, saluting.

"*I'm* the senior officer in the Supply Column escort, sir," Stilwell declared, saluting.

Steele's working party stopped and turned to see two officers on horseback—The General and a Lieutenant. "What's the *meaning* of this, Sergeant McTee?" the General asked.

"We're making a machine gun mounting to…" McTee answered,

"I can *see* it *wants* to be a machine gun mounting, Sergeant.

I'm *enquiring* why, ex*actly*, this Corporal is *doing* it?"

"Ah, sir," Steele said, coming to attention. "If I may speak."

"Yes," the General answered, annoyed. "Go *on*."

"This is a pedestal mount for *that* motor wagon, sir; just designing it on-the-fly. We welded these cross-rods to the drive sprocket for a base. It will provide all-around observation and a complete field of fire for..."

"I *see*," the General said. "Those...*things*...*where* did you *find* them?"

"*That's* a rear axle and other parts from *that* motor wagon, sir," Steele answered, pointing at the cannibalized vehicle. "We *just*..."

"You disabled *one* motor wagon to arm *another*," Pershing sniffed. "*Hardly* a satisfactory..."

Steele explained why the vehicle was unrepairable. "So Captain Stilwell said we could..."

"Very well, Corporal Steele," Pershing said. "How long will it take to complete this *project* of yours?"

"A few more minutes, sir, and the quartermasters will have an *armed* motor wagon..."

Pershing heaved a sigh. "Whose idea was this *project*, Sergeant McTee?" Pershing's horse scuffed at the ground.

"Ah, it *was* Corporal Steele's initiative, sir," McTee said.

Steele interrupted. "*This* pintle is for a M1914 Benet-Mercier gun chambered for the 8 mm French..."

"Are you *also* an *expert* in automatic weapons, Corporal?" Pershing *seemed* interested in Steele, fixing him with a flinty gaze.

"Sir," McTee said loudly, "Steele *reads* everything he can get his hands on about machine guns and everything *else* mechanical. Knows *all* our manuals forward and backward, can field-strip *any* of our guns in his sleep. He's got to *college*; gets *Scientific American* of his own accord and learns about *foreign* guns. He can teach a *horse* to read and a *mule* to do sums."

"I see," the General declared, affecting a doubtful grin. "Carry on," watching as Steele and his helpers went back to work.

"Sir," McTee stepped towards Pershing and cleared his throat as Steele and the rest worked. "I was *so* sorry to hear of Mrs.

Pershing and the girls…"[1]

Pershing nodded. "*Thank* you, John; I know that's heartfelt. Frankie thought a *great deal* of you." He looked curious. "You're a Platoon Sergeant…*again?*"

"Force of *habit*, sir."

Pershing grinned, shifted in his saddle. "And a *bad* one at that, John. How many times is *this?*"

"Ah…*second* only, sir," McTee answered, grinning.

"Mind you don't *retire* a *Corporal*, John…" Pershing chuckled, leaning down on his saddle. "This *Steele*, John: might I have *heard* of him?"

"He's *got* a reputation as a go-getter, sir," McTee said.

"Sir," Patton interrupted. "The *staff*…" Patton had a somewhat unpleasant voice to listen to; high-pitched and yet somewhat graveled.

"Yes, Lieutenant," Pershing sighed, nodding to McTee. "Duty calls once again, John." He turned again to Steele and his party. "The President has ordered me to *end* this expedition. The quartermasters no longer *need* an armed motor wagon."

"Does *that* mean…?" Steele started.

"I want to *see* the final product when you're *done*, Corporal." The general turned to Patton. "Lieutenant Patton, make certain that the Corporal completes his, ah, *project.* Sergeant McTee, bring it to the headquarters this evening."

"*Yes*sir," Patton nodded, watching the general ride away. As Patton dismounted, Steele saw that his boots and breeches, not to mention his overcoat, were elegant, expensive and well-cared for. "Corporal, carry on."

"Sir," Steele said, and continued with his work, adding two braces to the pedestal base.

Patton watched Steele work, fascinated, without offering comments or asking questions. When Steele mounted the gun, chambered a round and fired a long burst, Patton nodded appreciably as the animals started and bucked in alarm. "Good

---

[1] Pershing's wife and three daughters were killed in a house fire at the Presidio of San Francisco on 27 August 1915.

work, Corporal."

"*Thank* you, sir," Steele said, stooping to check on his welds. "Held up under the recoil, looks like."

"You seem pretty handy, Steele," Patton said. "Where'd you learn to *do* all that?"

"My father is a blacksmith-turned-auto-tinkerer, sir. We all learned to pitch in on his inventions."

"Eh," Patton nodded. "I sometimes wish *I* were better with my hands than I am. But I *didn't…never* mind. Your father *has* many inventions?"

Steele pointed to a touring car being used by the Supply Train. "Invented the suspension for that Cadillac, sir," he said. "*I* forged the clips for the first two springs."

"Indeed," Patton said, his voice pitching upward. "So, *what* are you doing *here?*"

Steele grinned widely. "If I may be frank, sir, when I joined the Army, it was the first time I had a *bed* to myself." Patton smiled, chuckled. "And my brother Charlie said this was a *better* career than beating iron."

"I see. Your father is still with us?"

"Making suspensions for motor cars in Detroit, sir," Steele answered.

"Well, get your contraption up to HQ when you're done," Patton sighed. "I understand what machine guns have done to horse cavalry in Europe…"

"Yes, sir," Steele said. "Shrapnel-firing artillery *and* machine guns simply *shredded* them at Audregnies…"[1]

"Well," Patton balked. "I suppose that will be the *last…*"

"Perhaps sad, but true, sir," Steele agreed. "I believe the day of the mounted charge is done."

"You're probably right, Corporal," Patton agreed. "I had a *little* mounted action, though, in motor cars…"

"Yessir; we were just around the bend."

"Do you reckon the military usefulness of the horse has finally

---

[1] 14 August 1914. The first British cavalry charge on the Western Front, it cost them 800 of 1,000 men.

ended, Corporal?"

"I do, sir, or it *will* soon enough," Steele answered confidently. "Motor vehicles are getting more reliable all the time. From a strictly *technical* standpoint, I feel there will come a day when ammunition will outweigh fodder in the Army supply train."

"Oh," Patton replied, remounting his horse and gazing about; Stilwell and Lucas listened with curiosity. "*When* will that day come, do you think?"

"It already *has* in France, sir," Steele answered. "For the *American* army…" He shrugged. "Do you imagine we'll get into this war, sir?"

"I *do*, Corporal." Patton sighed, adjusted his ivory-handled revolver as he settled into his saddle. "President Wilson certainly recalled us for a reason, though I'm not *privy* to its specifics. We'll be *in* this war soon enough."

* * *

Steele and McTee stopped their motor car short of the "front gate" of the headquarters camp. At minimum, they half-expected to see a shack or a one-room adobe and stone *casa*, but….

Pershing's Provisional Division HQ personnel roster comprised four officers and twenty-six enlisted men. The camp comprised two rows of tents, a mess-tent fly, and two latrine flies. Horses, picketed on the other side of the road, cropped at the thin brush. A blacksmith wagon under a fourth fly nearby rang with the sound of a hammer striking iron. Two motor cars parked nearby were having tires changed. Near the mess fly, a detail peeling potatoes sang:

> *Someone's in the kitchen with Dinah!*
> *Someone's in the kitchen, I know!*
> *Someone's in the kitchen with Dinah!*
> *Strumming on the old banjo!*

As they approached, a Private stepped into the road, raising his hand; Steele stopped. "State your business here," the sentinel drawled.

"We're delivering a machine gun pedestal to the General," Steele said.

The Private blinked, glanced at McTee, looked at the back seat of the flivver,[1] then back at Steele. "A *what?*"

"Machine gun pedestal," Steele repeated. "It's for mounting machine guns on vehicles…"

"And how'd you *get* it?" the Private asked, puzzled.

"We built it," McTee said.

"Uh-*huh.*" The Private, still mystified, said, "stay *here,*" and walked to a scrap of canvas suspended from a scraggly mesquite. Soon, a Corporal who'd been lounging under the canvas slowly rose and sauntered over to Steele's vehicle, dusting himself off as he gave it a suspicious once-over.

"*Help* ya?" the Corporal asked.

"We've got this machine gun pedestal…" Steele explained…again.

After listening patiently, the Corporal pursed his lips. "Well, if you were Mex spies, I reckon you're some of the *best* there *is* with *that* story, so you might as well go on through. HQ tent's the double on the far end, there."

They drove the two hundred yards to the far end of the camp, stopping in front of a pair of large wall tents end-to-end, with a sign that read, "HQ, 1st Provisional Division; J. Pershing, Comdg."

A Sergeant in a too-clean uniform walked out of the tent to the car as Steele rolled to a stop. "Help you, fellas? *Oh,*" he added. "McTee! Where *you* been? Ain't seen *you* since Peking."

"Here and there, Kips; here and there…" McTee answered, grinning slightly. "Still got that doxie in Manila?"

"Hell, ain't heard from *her* since…goin' on two *years,*" Kips answered. "Reckon she's found *another* poor bastard to pay her squeeze…"[2]

"We've got this pedestal for the General," Steele interrupted.

"Pedestal," Kips nodded, looking in the back, glancing at McTee. "What *for?*"

"Machine guns," Steele sighed.

---

[1] Popular nickname for the Model T..

[2] In this case, payments for services rendered.

"And the General *wanted* one?"

"This is the *first* one," McTee said. "He wanted to *see* the prototype."

Kips smiled. "Ah," he said at length, "well, *haul* it out of there and I'll *get* him."

"Well," Pershing declared as he approached while they wrenched the weldment out of the back of their motor car. "This is…as I imagined it."

"Pretty simple, sir," Steele said, snapped to attention. "As Lieutenant Patton saw…"

"He reported it works as you *said* it would," Pershing nodded, looking the object up and down. "Works well enough for the Benet-Mercier…"

"Bigger guns would require bigger bases, sir, and probably bigger posts," Steele said. "I wouldn't *want* to mount a Maxim or a Vickers on it."

"No." Pershing, hands on hips, nodded appreciatively. "Very well. Sergeant Kips: tell Captain Quinn he can sign for this."

"Yessir," Kips said.

In the fading twilight of the desert night, the quartermaster handed Steele a hand-written receipt:

> 20 JAN'Y. '17
> REC'D FROM CORP. E. STEELE: ONE (1) PEDESTAL FOR MACHINE GUNS.

Volume XII
1917-1918

HOLDING THAT RECEIPT IN MY HAND AND CORRELATING IT TO HIS diary entry gave me confidence in the contents of the trunk, but *confirmation* came later. After an exhaustive study of Ned's handwriting and its contents, I determined that this find, the only known diaries of a US Army enlisted man before WWI, was not an elaborate forgery. His memoirs confirmed my judgement.

We (Maria was thirteen when we began) saw our biggest hurdle: aligning Ned's notes with matching events and other documents.

In the summer of 1996, we decided on this transcription project. We had to take it on faith that, mostly, we could trust his entry dates.

We join Ned's story now at the beginning of Volume XII (1917).

April

6ᵗʰ April 1917, Jefferson Barracks, Mo.

I start Vol. XLI with some apprehension. I was told to report to Lieut. Lucas this afternoon. This good man, this model officer, provoked someone's ire. He's probably close to forty, waiting for Simple Semple to kick off so he can get promoted[1]... I somehow __like__ being a Corporal...A fellow doesn't turn twenty-one every year...

"Corporal Steele reporting as ordered, sir," Steele said, coming to attention in front of the acting company commander's desk. Lucas was in command only until Captain Semple came back from his leave-of-absence.

Lieutenant Lucas returned Steele's salute and said, "Please, be seated."

"Sir," Steele said, lowering himself gingerly into the proffered side chair.

"Steele..." Lucas looked resigned, handing Steele a typed sheet. "*This* is from the Bureau of Personnel."

The paper read:

> YOU WILL INFORM THE AFOREMENTIONED NON-COMMISSIONED OFFICERS THAT THE BUREAU OF PERSONNEL WILL IMMEDIATELY APPROVE THEIR APPLICATIONS FOR COMMISSION. THIS OFFICE WILL COUNTENANCE NO DELAY IN THIS MATTER. TRANSFERS TO OFFICER SCHOOL WILL BE FORTHCOMING AS SOON AS THIS OFFICE RECEIVES APPLICATIONS. LOWER HEADQUARTERS WILL APPROVE ALL APPLICATIONS.

---

[1] Not unusual for the time, since rank belonged to the unit, not the individual. The wait for promotion was called "waiting for dead men's shoes."

The letter listed all the Corporals and Sergeants in the battalion who served in the Machine-Gun Section except McTee. "Congress will approve a declaration of war on Germany by this afternoon," Lucas sighed. "Saw *this* kind of thing when we went to war with Spain: they needed officers in a hurry and they *got* them."

Steele handed the memo back to Lucas. "I'm to *apply...*"

"Sergeant McTee will help *all* of you," Lucas sighed.

"Ah, can I *decline...?*" Steele asked.

"I would *not* advise that," Lucas declared. "You'll *retire* a Corporal if you *do*. The Bureau of Personnel has a *very* long memory in these matters."

"Um...if I may be so bold...*voice* of *experience*, sir?"

"*Very* astute, Steele. Now," Lucas continued, "I'll speak to *all* of you this afternoon, but..." He handed Steele a copy of another memo:

> 15TH MARCH 1917, FT. BLISS, TX
> FROM: GENERAL J. J. PERSHING, COMDG 8TH BRIG.
> TO: COMMANDER, 89TH INFANTRY REGT.
> IT HAS COME TO MY ATTENTION THAT CORPORAL STEELE OF YOUR COMMAND HAS THE TECHNICAL EXPERTISE AND LEADERSHIP POTENTIAL TO MAKE A USEFUL OFFICER IN THE COMING CONFLICT, ESPECIALLY IN THE FIELD OF MACHINE GUNS. YOUR HEADQUARTERS IS TO AFFORD HIM EVERY ASSISTANCE IN HIS COMMISSIONING. ORDERS TO THAT EFFECT SHALL BE FORTHCOMING AND ACTED UPON AT ONCE.
> PERSHING

"*So...oh, yes, and...*" he stopped, took a paper out from under his blotter. "Many happy returns." It was typical in the 89th to grant a pass a three-day pass on birthdays *if* duty requirements allowed. "You'll have to spend part of the *weekend* filling out your application for commission, I'm afraid."

"Yessir," Steele answered. "And *thank* you, sir..."

8th April, Riverfront Hotel, St. Louis, Misso.

I didn't think filling out paperwork for Officer's

school was so detailed. Why do they need to know all

of that? I remember the birthdays; Irving's birthday was eight years and a day after mine. The rest are just days. I had to calculate just when Al was born: 1888. Dad would have been twenty-five, since _he_ was born a month after Ft. Sumter.

My three-day pass to St. Louis began the moment I turned in my forms this morning. Caught the omnibus to town, going to see a picture show if I can. The Rose Hotel had rooms for servicemen as long as we don't mind sharing. Riverfront Hotel has a private room for a dime more.

Saw "Joan the Woman" this evening. Joan of Arc with a British officer dreaming about her. The newsreels were more interesting.

I still have five dollars left to my name and I have to buy uniforms. Wired Dad for money fpr the first time.

PLEASE WIRE $75 HERE FOR OFFICER UNIFORMS[1] STOP HOPE FOR HOME LEAVE JULY STOP MORE IN NEXT LETTER END

9th April, Riverfront Hotel, St. Louis, Misso.

Last night, I had my first _legal_ drink in a saloon. Whiskey from a bottle, not a jar like they pass around

---

[1] Officers in US services have to buy their own uniforms and meals. Newly commissioned enlisted men were given an allowance to buy uniforms, but it was often slow in coming. So was the higher pay.

in the barracks, is much better tasting. However, I noticed no significant change in effect. Experimenting further, I had several more drinks and found that walking was not easy. A girl named Dotty helped me to my room, I am told. It is a very uneasy feeling waking up, not knowing how you got where you are. Fearing the worst, I found my possibles[1] unmolested and my four remaining dollars in my hat where I left it.

10th April, Pioneer Park, St. Louis, Misso.
Met a Corporal acting as MP this morning at breakfast. Satisfied by my pass, I asked him where I could find a shower-bath. He pointed me to the YMCA that offered them for five cents.
Riverboats pass the park about three a minute. I wonder where they are going. I wonder where I will go after Officer's school.
I got Dad's wire and his very generous $100. Now I can buy what uniforms I can get before I have to ship out. Took a chance and bought another three diary books; I might not have a chance later.

15th April, Jeff. Barracks, Misso.
Diane is divorcing her husband of only two years.

---

[1] Property.

Don't know what happened, but she's moving back in

with the family. Mom's note sounds as if Di's got

grounds. None of my business, but I have to feel for

Buddy Di.

Since the regiment and War Dept. already approved

our applications, they tell us we will depart at the end

of the month. The Army has only two gears: 1st and

4th. Sometimes the clutch slips, but it is always in one

or the other.

May

6th May, Jeff. Barracks, Misso.

I leave the 89th with some regrets but great

excitement...

"Corporal Steele," Lucas said, offering his hand in the orderly room, "you depart this regiment, having done it the *honor* of being a member."

"Sir," Steele said solemnly. "I will take care to *not* sully the honor of the 89th."

With that, Steele shouldered his barracks bag....

7th May, Ft Leavenworth, Kan.

I arrived at Officer School with the other fellows

from the 89th last night, and I am excited at the

prospect of being an officer and going to war.

My new uniforms fit me better than my issued enlisted

uniforms, possibly because I had to pay for them.

One reason I enjoyed being an enlisted man was I

<del>don't</del> *didn't have to* [expletive] *pay for everything.*

A day full of marching, of filling out papers, of

answered questions...

They issued us our horses this afternoon. We must

care for them daily. Mine is a roan mare, about three

or four years of age, a gentle creature that takes the

saddle well. I imagine she has had many riders in her

time. She is called Number 934...

Our instructors mean for us to [expletive] *fail our first*

homework assignment...

"Fall...*IN, in four ranks*," Captain Sterling intoned, standing stock-still in the hollow center of the square building as Steele's class of fifty-five *former* enlisted men scrambled to comply. "C'mon; *you* know *how* as well as *we* do…"

"Class 12 of the 27th Officer's Candidate Company," Sterling began, his face an inscrutable mask, "*I* am Captain William Jennings Sterling, your company commander and primary instructor, and *you* are the most contemptible creatures on *God's Earth: Third Lieutenants*. For the next ninety-one days you will *remain* the most contemptible creatures unless you *fail*, are *ejected* or *quit*, at which point you will revert to whatever enlisted *slime* you once *were* where you will remain until you *die* or muster out. *Do you understand?*"

"Yessir," the class answered discordantly. On the other sides of the square, *other* classes formed up, giving similar responses to the same question.

"You sound like a *cow barn!* SOUND OFF like you've got a pair! DO YOU UNDERSTAND?"

"*YESSIR!*" the class shouted; other classes did the same. For whatever reason, Steele's class included no one from the 89th.

"Better," Sterling said, almost in a whisper. "Not good *enough*, but *better*; I don't want to be standing here all day waiting for *men* to show up. Now," Sterling declared, pointing to two Lieutenants standing to the side, "*they* are my assistant instructors, Lieutenant Harris Freeman and Lieutenant Michael Jason. When they speak, you will regard their words as if *God* etched them in *stone* on *Sinai*. When *I* speak, you will regard *my* words as if I just carried those very words *off* the mountain. Am I *clear?*"

"YESSIR!" The students shouted, unable to stand stock-still as required, but still tried as they got used to their new uniforms, especially the Sam Browne cross-chest shoulder belts that made them stand so straight.

"All *right*, then," Sterling nodded. "We *understand* each other. Class, *right…FACE*," Sterling shouted, and as one, the formation turned. "At the DOUBLE…*MARCH!*"

And off they shuffled to their breakfast of porridge and bacon with coffee and milk, jostling each other and the three *other* classes for the few seats available in the mess.

***

"And *that* is the end of the lesson on basic Army structure," Sterling said. "Any questions?"

"*Sir*," an aquiline-faced candidate stood, "permission to speak to the Company Commander."

"Talk," Sterling answered.

"Sir…" he started…

"*Who* gave you permission to *croak*, cockroach?"

"*Sir*, I…"

"You've gone *deaf*, cockroach? *Your* name?"

"Brick, sir…"

"*Sit*, Candidate Brick! Now, *any* questions?"

"Sir," a red-haired candidate stood. "Permission to speak to the Company Commander."

"Speak," Sterling nodded.

"Sir, I wish to ask…"

"If wishes were ponies, then beggars would ride, wooden-head. You *wish* nothing! Assert yourself clearly and in the correct format. *Your* name?"

"Grimes, sir…"

"*Sit!* Anyone *else?*"

"Sir," a blonde candidate stood up, "permission to address the Company Commander."

"Speak," Sterling said, distracted.

He remained silent.

"*Talk,* mutton-head!"

He remained silent.

Sterling grinned slightly. "Figured it out already? Name?"

"Ishim, sir."

"Permission *granted,* Candidate Ishim," Sterling nodded.

"Sir," Ishim began, "can the Company Commander expand upon the distinction between the field artillery and the coast artillery in terms of organization and administration?"

Sterling looked surprised. "*That's* a *better* question. We cover *that* distinction later in this course of instruction; especially since Candidate Ishim can probably *teach* the subject since he has experience in *both*. Are there questions within *my* competence?"

"Sir," Steele stood, "Permission to speak…?"

"Granted."[1]

"Sir; some men have wondered…we *know* we have to pay for our meals, but not *all* of us have enough…"

"*Good* question," Sterling said. "You will be paid the same as a Staff Sergeant[2] for your duration here, *unless* you were of a higher rank before you *got* here; then you get *that* pay. You will draw $10 a calender week for your expenses while you are *here* and will draw your *first* $10 this evening. We will catch you up on your pay upon graduation or termination, because you do not need *that* much money while you are here. You have nothing to spend it on and we will not *allow* you to lose it all in the first poker game you happen upon…or that *crap game* that runs between the buildings every night. Does *that* answer the question?"

"I believe it does, sir," Steele said. "But, *sir*…?"

---

[1] This is a typical exchange in OCS or any other such rigid instruction. The idea is to inculcate a sense of form, of obedience to routine.

[2] As a Corporal with under 4 years of service, Steele would have been making $54.00 a month. In OCS, $84.00 a month.

"*Yes*, Steele?"

"When will we, ah…?"

"Get a pass to *spend* your *excess* cash?"

"Yessir…"

"Your first pass will be in a *month*…providing you *deserve* it. Anything *else*? No? Ten minute break before the class on the chain of command…"

***

"Um…you're Brick?" Steele approached his classmate at noon chow. The food was palatable, if unrecognizable.

"I *am*; you're Steele?" Brick offered his hand. "Call me Mike." The cooks packed the mess hall with more tables and benches since breakfast.

"Call me Ned, Mike." Steele took the offered hand; a confident grip just strong enough to let Steele know there was more to it. "I don't know if we're supposed to address each other by our Christian names…"

"Nobody said we couldn't," Brick said. "We shouldn't need permission to be civil."

"I would hope not." Grimes hovered nearby; Steele cocked his head. "Join us."

"I think I *will*. Gary Grimes," he offered his hand. "Minnesota National Guard. *You* guys?"

"Regular Army; call me Ned," Steele said. "I was a *Corporal* a few days ago…"

"Long Island Militia," Brick said, "I'm Mike."

"Never *heard* of a Long Island Milita," Steele answered.

"Nobody *else* has, either," Brick replied. "My college classmates and I formed it after our second Plattsburg camp[1] last summer.…"

"They *had* a camp in Minneapolis last summer," Grimes said.

---

[1] Outshoots of the Preparedness Movement in pre-1917 America. Plattsburg camps, named for the New York town where they were first held, were originally organized and sponsored by private citizens to train potential Army officers.

"But I had to work in Grampa's store. Ned, where do you come from besides the Army?

"Detroit."

"If *only* we knew what this *was*," Grimes said, stuffing a large forkful of brown *something* into his mouth.

"We may not *want* to know," Brick declared.

"Gentlemen," Ishim said, sitting next to Brick, "I presume this isn't an *exclusive* club."

"It is not," Grimes said. "We were just discussing what *we*..."

"First, your *Christian* name," Steele said, extending his hand. "I'm Ned."

"Corey," Ishim answered. "I *was* a year in California Guard field artillery," Ishim answered, "but I've been in the *coast* artillery for the past three months."

"We have diverse backgrounds, then," Steele said, adding, "we'd better get *moving*."

"So much for a leisurely lunch," Brick groused.

"Be a long while before we see one of *those* again," Steele grinned.

***

"As you familiarize yourself with your mounts," Freeman announced, "raise your hands if you have never been *on* a horse... *Corporals*..." Several older Corporals stepped forward to the raised hands. "If you don't know how to *saddle*...? And...*Sergeants*..."

The class unsteadily got on their respective mounts. Steele managed the McClellan saddle easily. "Your horses must be groomed and exercised *every day*," Freeman went on. "An hour every *morning* and every *evening* is dedicated to your *horse*. You will *care* for it, *brush* it, *wash* it down when needed, and *muck out* its stall *daily*."

Gradually, the class mounted their horses. "Today is familiarization. Every *Tuesday,* we hold a mounted drill parade. You will learn to ride in formation like *proper* officers." Freeman, astride a red stallion, pointed in front of him. "Now, line up in front of me *here*."

***

"Any idea what they *want* to see?" A dour New Yorker named Sternberg asked Steele.

"I can only guess," Steele answered, staring at the spirit-master map, barely legible. "Ever *make* a route march?"

"Plenty, in the Cavalry," Sternberg sighed, looking at his own map.

"*Could* it be that they *want* us to make the plans we're *used* to?" Steele wondered aloud. "You, for the Cavalry; me for the Infantry…huh," Steele answered. "Hey, Corey?" he called across the bunk room aisle. "If *you* were to plan a route march for the *Field* Artillery, *how* would you…?"

8th May, Ft. Leavenworth, Kans.

I was correct in my judgement about the route march assignment: they wanted to see how many ways there were to do it and how fast it would take us to figure that out…what have they got against me? What have they got me into…choosing between new friends…?

"*Well*," Sterling said, somewhat nonplussed. "You…huh." He looked up from the sheaf of papers. "All right: *today's* first order of business is the election of a Class Leader. Can be any of you, but we have *our*…"

"Sir," Ishim stood and, after the preliminaries, "Candidate Ishim nominates Candidate Steele as Class Leader."

"Hear, hear," someone in the back of the classroom answered.

"*Who* was that?" Sterling asked. "*Who* spoke without permission?"

"*I* did, sir," Brick raised his hand, "Candidate Brick, sir."

"Brick: Ten demerits for your outburst; five *merits* for your integrity. Now, who *else*…?"

"Sir," Grimes rose. "Permission to address the Class."

"Permission granted," Sterling said.

"Thank you, sir." He strode forward, faced the class and said, "I believe I can speak for the entire Class when I *declare* Candidate Steele Class Leader."

Sterling crossed his arms sternly. "And *what* did Candidate Steele do to deserve this, ah, confidence in all of you so quickly?"

"Sir," Sternberg stood. "Permission to answer frankly."

"Granted."

"Well, sir, Steele figured out that route march problem pretty damn quick, got us all to just do what we'd *always* done. *That* made it easy."

Sterling's normally stern face grinned as he looked around the class. "Candidate *Steele, on* your *feet*."

"Sir…"

"Candidate *Steele*: your classmates have declared you their Class Leader. Do you understand?"

"*No*, sir," Steele answered.

"*Good*, Steele; *very* good. *First*, Class Leader, sit by the door. That's where you will *always* sit. Your *second* duty will be to call the room to attention when an officer of superior rank to any others in the room enters or leaves. Is *that* understood?"

"Yessir," Steele answered.

"Very well," Sterling declared, then, *sotto voce*, added, "*we'll* talk later. Now, candidates, today we talk about the *duties* of command…."

***

"Have a *seat*, Steele," Sterling pointed to a padded chair in the Officer's Lounge, a small room attached to the mess hall. They forbid the candidates to *sit* in the Lounge, but that they had to *clean* it. "Like some water?"

"Sir," Steele nodded, parched from the day's grueling close order drill in the baking sun.

Sterling poured water out of a glass pitcher into a ceramic tumbler, handing it to Steele. "Steele, as Class Leader, you are the liaison between your classmates and the rest of the world. Like…"

"Like an NCO is," Steele ventured.

"*Yes*, but the difference is you get *paid* more," Sterling glanced up at Freeman as he entered. "And, the responsibilities of command as their senior are greater because you really *are* life and death to them."

"Command as an *officer* means you also *lead* more men, *get* more orders, *make* more plans…" Freeman offered.

"*Original* plans," Steele said, noting Freeman's piercing-yet-haunting blue eyes.

"Privilege and *duties* of command," Sterling agreed. "As Class Leader, you will march your class wherever you go; you showed this afternoon you've got *that* down pat…"

Steele said, "NCOs usually handle that kind of thing. They taught us in leadership class…"

"You *had* leadership classes?" Sterling looked surprised.[1]

"Yessir. The 89th Infantry *is* unique in that respect, I understand."

"Certainly *is*," Sterling agreed.

"But, yes, the NCO leaders *are* troop handlers," Freeman said, "and troop managers. When *I* was a Sergeant…"

"*How* long ago?" Sterling asked with a grin.

"Before the *Flood*," Freeman said. "Point is, the difference between NCOs and officers is a very thin *line* but a very wide *gap*. The difference is *command* versus *management*. Officers lead; NCOs get the men moving. Officers show *where*; NCOs *get* them there. Officers *sign* for everything; NCOs *maintain* everything."

"Officers are the drivers; NCOs are the motors…" Steele started.

"*Yes*," Sterling said, startled. "I can *use* that. Your duties will include acting as middle-man for any problems your men want to address to us. In all matters, we will expect you to carry out our policies. *You* will conduct the *daily* inspections of footlockers and living areas; *we* will conduct the *weekly* inspections on Saturdays. Here," he handed Steele a typewritten list. "Pick four squad leaders."

"Sir, Candidate Sternberg's name is not…"

"No, and it *won't* be."

---

[1] *Formal* classes for NCOs were rare.

"Neither is Candidate Brick..." Nor were any of the friends he had made already....

"Four squad leaders from *this list...*" Steele named the first four. "They'll *do*. Now, your *assistant*."

"Candidate...Brick?"

Sterling smiled, an odd grimace. "I *win*."

"*Sir?*"

"We placed bets on who you'd choose..."

"Bets?"

"The first week, we do a *lot* of betting around here," Freeman added. "Right now, we're drawing up odds on which candidates will drop out first."

"Seems...mercenary, sir."

"It *is*, but it's also instructive," Sterling said. "We learn to see the signs of who will *last* and who *won't* very early. Now, assign the *squads*." Steele simply lined up the roster alphabetically.

"*Exactly*. You learn fast, Steele," Sterling nodded. "Expedience is easily the *best* solution when you don't *know* who you're dealing with."

Steele and his two instructors talked well into the evening.

***

It was ten o'clock that night before Steele got back to his barracks. The fire guard, Hughes, walked around the building with a bamboo stick, symbol of his office. As Steele mounted the steps, Hughes called to him. "Say, brother Steele; what's the news?"

"Not a great deal...ah, Hughes, is it?"

"Yes...where've *you* been?"

"Learning what I'm supposed to do as Class Leader. When's your shift up?"

"I..." Hughes consulted an alarm clock on the stoop, "when the hands are on eleven and twelve." He looked at Steele. "Just learned to *use* that thing."

"Tell *time?*"

"Yeah. I can *read*, but I never needed to tell time on the farm. Even as a Guard Corporal, I didn't..."

"*How* did you…?"

"My grampa is the regimental adjutant."

"Hughes, do you know how many *other* men in our class cannot tell time?"

"I'd allow as *ten* never *saw* a clock before they got here.[1] Just respond to the bugles and the roosters."

"Ah." Steele sat on the barracks steps; Hughes sat with him. "Hughes, I need you to do me a service…."

"Whatever I *can* do…"

9th May, Ft. Leavenworth, Kan.

Leadership is part courage, part knowledge, and part

recklessness…

"All right, everyone," Steele shouted as the class fell in for breakfast formation ten minutes early. "All right; fall in, there. C'*mon*, fellows…"

"Early, ain't ya, Ned?" Brick growled. "We've still got…"

"All right; you *chowderheaded yardbirds* made *me* Class Leader, now dress and cover…*At* close inter*val*, *dress* right…*DRESS! FRONT! COVER!*" Steele walked along the front of the formation, observing how each man in the back ranks stood behind the one in front.[2] "All right, we have squad assignments." He consulted his list. "*First* Squad Leader is…*Abernathy*. Step forward and take your place." A former cavalry Sergeant stepped to the far right of the first rank. "*Second* Squad…*Allen*. Take your place….*Third* Squad…*Avarlenstevich*? I pronounce that right? OK…*Fourth* Squad…*Axelrod*. Now…*First* Squad members are…" Men jostled and hustled into place. "And *Second* Squad…*Third* Squad…*Fourth* Squad…"

Finally, everyone but Brick and Steele were in the formation. "Candidate Brick will be my assistant…*Gawd* help him…" A

---

[1] Until about 1910, more than half the US population was rural. They might have been able to tell time by sun position, but there was little perceived need to tell time with a clock.

[2] Called *covering*.

ripple of laughter rose. "Candidate Brick; I believe your position is back center…where the platoon sergeant would…yes. Now…" Steele cleared his throat. "Stand *at…ease.* We have to work together, men. Work together as perhaps we never have *before* to make this the very best class to *graduate* from this school. Several of you will have more to learn than others. But I'm just as sure that some of you have much to teach the rest of us." He let the murmuring subside before he continued. "I'm *serious*. Not all of us have been soldiers for very long. I've been in uniform since the spring of 1914, but I'll wager that's *not* as long as, say, Bradley here…"

"I signed on in 1910," Bradley declared.

"Took the oath in '06," Axelrod said.

"Very well, then; we have a wealth of experience right here. Let's take advantage of…" Steele saw Sterling approach out of the corner of his eye. "Class, *A*-ten-*SHUN!*"

"Carry on, Candidate Steele," Sterling said quietly, "*double-time* your class to *chow*."

***

"Anyone know *how* this…*what* this is?" Steele held the class alarm clock up. They gathered in the barracks after evening chow, pondering the stack of books they had to share and, ultimately, all *read*.

"My *first* guess is a clock," Allen ventured.

"That's right," Steele said. "And everyone knows how to *read* it, right?" Silence. "Fellows, look, I know for a *fact* some of you cannot read this thing. There's no shame in it; it's just something new you gotta learn 'cause you can't always depend on roosters and bugles. Just…raise your hand if you *can't*." Eleven hands went up, timidly. "All right. How many of you can speak *some* German?" Three hands, including Steele's, went up. "Good. French?" Four hands, including Brick. "Excellent. Spanish?" Five hands, including Grimes. "How many of you can milk a cow?" Perhaps two dozen hands shot up. "Shoe a horse?" Ten hands, including Steele's. "My father was a blacksmith. A mule?" Four hands. "Never *had* to, myself; *seen* it done. All right," Steele sighed. "As you all can *see*, we have a tremendous well of resources here. First, we'll all learn to tell time on this clock. Second, we'll make sure everyone can get to these books at least long enough to get the gist of what's *in* them. Then we'll have language classes. If we've got time, we'll talk about how to *milk* a *cow*, shoe a horse *and* a mule…"

10th May, Ft. Leavenworth.

I find it odd that officers are expected to ride while enlisted men, except in the Cavalry, are expected to walk. "Officer and Gentleman" seems to belong to another century, another country…

12th May, Ft. Leavenworth, Kans.

A brutal inspection this morning left most of my men with demerits…I gather church call is part of our course of instruction…there shall be no day of rest for us tomorrow…I refer to the class as "my men" already. I haven't been their leader for a week yet and already they look to me for guidance…

"*Can*didates," Sterling declared as he strode down the center aisle of the barracks; the center aisle the cadets could only tread upon when they were *cleaning* or *waxing* it. "*This inspection has been a disgrace!* I have never *seen* such *filthy* and *unmilitary* areas in *all my life! You* couldn't maintain a *Manila whore-house! Washroom* looks like a *vomitory* after a *Roman feast!* You have *sinned* against the Army! *Sinned, I say!* You shall repent your sins against the Army by walking punishment tours around the company square *prior* to cleaning your washroom. He who does *not* partake in *this* penance shall have his demerits *doubled. All* you sinners *desiring* to repent fall out on the class street. Those angels among you who are miraculously *without* sins shall *polish* these *windows*; they are *filthy!*"

Minutes later, Sterling stood before nearly the entire class outside. "A punishment tour, candidates, works like this: you march *alone* as if you were in formation around this square. You march sixty inches behind the man ahead of you. You will square each corner, and as you pass myself or an instructor *here*, you sound off with your name. The supervising officer will then announce how many *more* tours are needed to absolve you of *all* your sins. And *speaking* of sins, tomorrow is the Lord's day, and *here* you will observe the Lord's day by falling into formation *here* at 11 o'clock in the morning, whereupon we will *march* to chapel. *And*," Sterling paused, as if for effect, "neither *I* nor the Army *care* if you are Christian, Jew, Mohammedean, Buddhist, atheist, Druid or anything *else*, you *will* fall in for church call *every* Sunday at eleven unless you are *dead* or *dying*. Is that *clear?*"

"YESSIR!"

"Then you will begin your punishment tours. *Right…FACE! Steele: stand* fast. *First* man, *first* squad…forward… MARCH!…Second man…*"

As his class began marching around the square, Steele stood stock-still, waiting for Sterling. After the last man began marching, Sterling walked calmly up to Steele. "By my reckoning, your five demerits rank among the lowest in your class. Care to tell me why your *men* got so *many?*"

"Sir, the candidates did not appreciate that *razors* needed to shine, nor that the *bottom* of shoes needed blacking…."

"No, indeed, they did *not*, Steele." Sterling watched the class marching around the square. "And every *other* inspection shall be as bullshit-picky for at least the first month. This is a bullshit-picky profession, our profession of arms. Absolutely *every* detail *must* be seen to. As a leader, you must *anticipate* what your, ah, opponents will do and communicate this to your people. Your instructors are, in this sense, your *opponents*. Understand?"

"*Yes*sir."

"I certainly hope so. This is as much a learning experience for *them* as it is for *you* as their leader. Now; *you* have five sins to seek penance for. Get ye to *seeking*."

"*Yes*sir."

13ᵗʰ May, Ft. Leavenworth, Kans.

There is no exemption for anyone on Sunday church

call…

"Officer Candidate Classes 11, 12, 13 and 14 of 1917," Sterling intoned from the pulpit at the front of the chapel, "today we introduce you to the United States Army's approach to organized religion. Chaplain Morse?"

A somewhat husky man of perhaps fifty with silver hair took Sterling's place at the pulpit. "Gentlemen, I'm Chaplain Herbert Morse, and I'm the *post* chaplain. Don't bother saluting me because I'm *not* a commissioned officer...."[1]

✳✳✳

"Well," Steele sighed, settling on his footlocker, boot polish in hand, "*that* was enlightening." After Morse told them about the services he and his fellow chaplains provided, the men could stay for an ecumenical service or retire to their barracks or whatever amusements they could find within *their* bounds on the post...which for *them* was the barracks, the stables, and the mess hall.

"In all your time in the Army, you never knew the chaplains could give almost any service they wanted?" Ishim asked. "Even in the *Guard*, we knew *that*."

"If you've never had the opportunity," Grimes chimed in, "you never know, do you? The kinda stuff we're gettin' doesn't get taught to enlisted men. Hell, I've been in the Guard for three years and I never..."

"I'll bet no one ever saw a chaplain outside of church call," Brick pronounced. "We had one at one of our camps who spent most of his time drunk."

"Plattsburg?" Ishim asked.

"The very one," Brick said. "But he wasn't *from* the Army, so..."

"There's..." Steele looked up. "Hey, ah, Bailey, yeah?"

"Yessir," the artilleryman said. "I've, ah, I've got this...truth is, I don't *read* that well. Can someone help me with this...?" He held out a manual.

"Don't call *me* sir," Steele said. "Sure...."

---

[1] Military chaplains weren't commissioned until 1942.

"Bring it here," Brick volunteered.

16ᵗʰ May, Ft. Leavenworth, Kans.

Today we start a two-day class on dancing and deportment. Learning to waltz in the Army-prescribed fashion[1] is, I believe, meant to further humiliate us. Dancing with other men, (of course), fills <u>what</u> military function? Deportment simply means acting like a civilized [expletive] gentleman.

22ⁿᵈ May, Ft. Leavenworth, Kans.

What they call a terrain ride yesterday familiarized us with cross-country mounted movement. I am not unfamiliar with horses or riding off the road and trail, but riding up steep hills on an unfamiliar mount seems dangerous. Number 934 takes steep slopes as if she knows them, and well she might. During the same class, we learn how to "read" terrain ~~prepatory~~ preparatory to movement and to deployment. We bivouacked at the end. Of course, it rained all [expletive] night, my shelter tent collapsed, and I lost my good razor in the mud. We had to wash the horses and saddle-soap our tack before we put them

---

[1] Most people had at least *some* exposure to the waltz in the early 20ᵗʰ Century, but the military had certain proprieties to be observed. This meant no skin-to-skin contact; both parties wore gloves and moved to the music at arm's length. Only experienced persons made it look like "dancing."

"You *realize* you're making the *rest* of us *look* bad, Steele," the big, dark Infantryman named Palmer said seriously. This first Class Leader Conference with the instructors was Steele's idea, which the faculty readily embraced.

"That's *not* my intention," Steele protested. Palmer, who Steele knew vaguely, had been a Sergeant in another 89th Infantry company. "I'm trying to help the *classes*..."

"And he's doing a *fine* job at it," Sterling nodded. "Academically, they're..."

"But he can't *keep* doing it, sir," Palmer protested. "There's nothing worse than a smartass college kid taking *all* the honors for *himself* when there's fellas been in this man's Army since..."

"*This* school runs on *merit*, Candidate Palmer," Sterling chided. "Regardless of how your *last* unit works, but *here*," he emphasized with a raised finger, "you *know* your job, you *do* your job, and you help *others* do *theirs*."

"That *ain't*," Palmer demanded. "*That*..."

"It's how it always *should* have been, Palmer," another Class Leader, Simmons, declared. "Do the *job*, *not* just lick the CO's boots."

Steele didn't know Simmons at all, but appreciated the defense. "Simmons, *I* can..." he started.

"You'd better not find yourself *alone*, Steele," Palmer grumbled.

"*Enough*, Palmer," Sterling shouted. "You're *done* here. Pack your bags. *You* shall be returned to your *unit*..."

"But...*SIR*," Palmer protested.

"No *ifs, ands or buts*. You and everyone *else* were told on your first *day*: threats *of* or physical violence *towards* another man in this outfit gets you the *boot, no exceptions.*"[1]

June

4th June, Ft. Leavenworth, Kans.

This week we begin on cartography. My drafting skills come in very handy for this. I thought only the engineers were mapmakers, it turns out that officers make a lot of them, including overlays. This shows us the practical merge between our route march plans and the terrain rides.

11th June, Ft. Leavenworth, Kans.

After a week of mapmaking, we learn landscape drawing. This is a much more interesting subject, because it's helping to make sense of our <u>weekly</u> terrain rides.

Having learned the supply system, knowing how to recognize, map and traverse unfamiliar terrain becomes an essential planning skill vital to our success.

15th June, Ft Leavenworth, Kans. Today we had classes on morale, football, soccer, boxing and baseball.

Morale begins with hope, hope for the future. Sports, organized or not, are about keeping soldier's minds off

---

[1] Physical violence was a way of life in *some* Army units. Fighting ability and friendship earned rank and privileges in many.

what they need to do, now and in the future.

Thus, maintaining morale includes providing chow, rest, recreation and, most important, caring for casualties.

Lessons for us all.

16th June, Leavenworth, Kans.

After nearly six weeks, we have a 24-hour pass to go where we like after Saturday inspection and punishment tours. Because most of us only have a little money, we can't go far. There is not much in Leavenworth but saloons and brothels...our dance classes came in handy...

"You write down everything you *do*, Ned?" Ishim asked.

"*Most*, not *all*. It helps to organize my thoughts," Steele answered, distracted. Steele and Ishim, Grimes and Brick sat in a small, uncrowded restaurant, glad of their patronage.

"Like *you* need any more organized *anything*," Brick mused, stretching. The four drank *splendid* coffee after a sumptuous-yet-inexpensive repast, consumed at a polite pace instead of the chew-it-outside frenzy of the mess hall.

"My *mother* kept a diary; I never got the habit," Ishim sighed.

"*I* keep a diary from time to time," Grimes said. "Sometimes there's a month between entries; sometimes a year. Haven't *been* keeping it here."

"Gents," Ishim sighed, "it's six o'clock on a Saturday night and we are four soldiers sitting in a restaurant without *women*..."

"There're women right over *there*, Corey," Steele observed, nodding at a table not far away.

"*They* are with escorts that look like husbands," Grimes said. "We should find a *house*..."

"Indeed," Brick grumbled. "Have *any* of you ever been *in* a house of ill-repute?"

"Didn't *before* I got married; ain't *thought* of it since…" "Not me…" "Too *broke* most of the time…" came the answers.

"Yeah; me *neither*," Brick sighed. "Shall we take a stroll around town?"

The four paid their bills and went out into the waning sunlight. Leavenworth, Kansas, was *not* a bustling metropolis. However, like most Army towns on weekend nights, there *was* an area *alive* with activity…but *that* part of town was *decidedly not* where Ned and his companions found themselves.

"Well," Steele sighed, "what can four *clean-cut* American soldiers find to *do?*"

"Four clean-cut soldiers who have to spend *most* of their meager allowances on *polish* and *soap* and *razor blades*," Grimes grunted.

"Not to mention *puttees*. I noticed there ain't a lot *else* in that PX, either," Brick added.

"I hear music," Ishim said, cocking his head. "*Band…* somewhere…maybe we can snag a *girl* and have a *whirl…*"

"And *you* a married man," Steele chided.

"Married does *not* mean I can't *dance* with a female; in the *polite* fashion, of *course*," Ishim answered indignantly. "Married does *not* mean *dead*."

"See what we can find," Steele said, setting off toward the sound. In a few blocks, they found a park with a bandstand…and a table selling tickets. Knots of cadets and enlisted men stood around a table acting as a bar.

"Sign says, 'All proceeds to benefit the American Field Service[1] in France,'" Steele read.

"Beer's a nickel," Brick declared, pointing at the bar where *most* of the soldiers were. "Punch is free."

"Ice cream's two cents," Steele said.

"*Looks* like they let *anybody* in," Grimes said, staring at the

---

[1] A volunteer organization that provided medical and ambulance services to the Allies starting in 1914.

bar. "Huh: 'Dance, 10 Cents; Group Rates.'" A large group of sitting and standing women of all descriptions, all wearing nurse's caps near a booth selling dance tickets, watched the dance floor, where couples tripped the light fantastic.

Turning out their pockets, the party discovered that they had $34.97 between them, and the return bus fare was a quarter each. And, there was the ever-present demand for cleaning supplies…and their meals were a buck and a quarter a day…and another *week* before they got paid again…

"Gentlemen, we need to support a *worthy* cause that supports our *gallant* troops," Brick said.

"Yeah," Steele added, "we might *be* four *of* those gallant troops soon enough."

"Let us eat, drink and be merry, for tomorrow we may die," Ishim loudly announced.

"Ya *gotta* quote the Bible[1] just when we're going to a party?" Brick growled.

***

Watching from the bar/table, Steele and Brick quaffed watery lager while Ishim and Grimes spoke to a matronly woman at the dance ticket booth. "Wonder what 'group rates' means?" Brick asked.

"Beats me." Steele sipped his beer. "We *may* find out in just a few…" he added, as Ishim and Grimes beckoned to their compatriots, both grinning slightly.

"Maybe buy *three*, get *one* free?" Brick suggested as they walked to the booth.

"*Could* be," Steele agreed, holding out Grimes' beer.

"Well?" Brick asked.

"Young patriots," the matronly woman said loudly, "the *four* of you can have *all* the dances you *wish* for a dollar…*if*…" she paused.

"If, *what?*" Steele asked.

"*If* we can find *four* ladies who would be *interested* in dancing

---

[1] Both Biblical and Shakesperian.

with us all night," Grimes nodded, downing half his beer.

"Choose any *willing* lady in a nurse's cap." The woman waved to the women. "Young patriots, the ladies of Leavenworth are awaiting *your* introduction. The ladies consider themselves introduced for *this* occasion."[1]

"*Very* well; we *thank* you, ma'am," Steele said, summoning up his courage....

He was only a yard away from a raven-haired, violet-eyed beauty who raised her eyes to his...and smiled. "Hello, soldier," she said in a mellifluous voice. "Care to *dance?*"

"I *do*, Miss," Steele said, "but...my comrades over there..." he hitched a thumb over his shoulder, "*want* to, as well. We can *spare* a buck apiece between now and payday, and..."

"Melodie," one of her companions whispered. "I don't *like* it."

"Prue, *that* rate is for the *Normal School*[2] boys," the other hissed, "*not* for *soldiers.*"

"Oh, those *boys* will go *home* in another hour and a half," Melodie said, not taking her eyes off Steele. "These *gentlemen* may be here *all night*." She glanced at her companions, then at Steele's. "Stand around with *them* while *I'm* dancing, if you're *concerned* about my *honor*." She stood up and walked three paces to Steele. "*Shall* we?" She nodded. "*My* name is Melodie Wilson."

"*I'm* Ned Steele," he smiled, offering her an elbow; she took it with a lace-gloved hand.

Prue and the other girl glanced at each other, exchanging their views in the young ladies' dialect of secret conversation while several older women rolled their eyes and shook their heads; other women looked on with interest, amusement, or disdain. Whispered conversations began. After several moments, Melodie sighed, "*Now* or *never*, ladies," as she led Steele towards the dance floor.

Prue gathered her wrap and bag while the third still looked on pensively, until *she* harrumphed loudly and followed her friends.

---

[1] Formal introductions were essential parts of inter-sex relationships in the early 20th Century.

[2] Starting after 8th Grade/grammar school, empahsizing teacher training.

They caught up to Melodie and Steele in just a few paces, flanking both. "*Mr.* Steele," Melodie said, "to your *left* is Prudence Kelling; to my *right* is Sarah Adler. Ladies, *this* is Officer Candidate Ned Steele."

"*Mr.* Steele," both women chirped while they carefully eyed Ishim, Grimes and Brick.

"Ladies," Steele politely introduced the ladies to his classmates.

"I shall *join* you girls," another, older woman with eyes like Melodie's declared, taking Ishim by the arm. "I'm Adeline Wilson, Melodie's *mother*. *You* are…?"

And *dance* they *all* did…until the band played "Good Night, Ladies" near midnight.

17ᵗʰ June, Ft. Leavenworth, Kans.

Melodie said I was a wonderful dancer, but she was being kind. I'm like a hog on ice despite the lessons… made it back in time for church call this morning and to tend to our horses this afternoon…

"Ned," Brick sighed as they got off the bus at the fort the next morning, "I *still* don't *know* how you did it, but, *damn*, you found some *sweet* ladies."

"Amen to that," Ishim agreed. "And we danced *all night* for a *dollar*…"

"Don't forget the ice cream," Grimes added.

"And strolling around town after," Steele sighed. "Melodie is *such* a nice girl…"

"And her mother is *such* a fine woman," Ishim declared. "Glad she took pity on us and let us sleep in her barn…"

"And a *fine* haystack they have, too," Brick added. "Where's *Mr.* Wilson, anyway?"

"Adeline said he was off on a Four-Minute Man[1]

---

[1] Wartime orators who gave short patriotic addresses based on topics from the Committee on Public Information (CPI).

encampment," Ishim answered. "Both those women are fine cooks, as well."

"Best breakfast I've had in *weeks*," Steele said. "Gents, we have to make church formation."

"And no time to shave," Brick grimaced. "Hope there's no inspection…"

"Hasn't been *yet*," Grimes said, straightening his collar.

***

"Anyone have any saddle soap left?" Grimes asked. The four were cleaning their tack for Monday's inspection.

"*Here*," Steele tossed his block of the yellow, waxy stuff. "It's the *last* of mine."

"I've another lump," Brick said. "In my locker. Anyone *else* need…?"

"Yeah," Sternhagen called. "If you *can*…?"

"Here," Brick tossed his across the barn. "I'm done with *this* for today."

"For a rich kid, you sure do that well," Ishim said mockingly.

"*This* rich kid had to clean his *own* tack since he was *eight*," Brick replied…again. "*My* old man never let us *forget* the importance of hard *physical* work."

"Muck out your own stalls, too?" Steele asked.

"On holidays, when the staff was off work." Brick snapped his rag to shed the dust. "I've done it often enough. We'll be graduating…"

"Three weeks," Grimes interrupted. "Won't be soon enough for me."

"How's the horse blanket washing going?" Steele called outside the barn.

"We're wringing them out now," another voice called. Among other innovations, Steele made rosters for the routine chores—drawing on the adage of many hands makes light work—so they could finish quicker and more efficiently, especially with the labor-intensive horses.

Cleaning the tack, however, was a *solo* task.

July

5ᵗʰ July, Ft Leavenworth.

Honor graduate, the top of my class. I don't know what it is the Army sees in me because they made me a First Lieutenant of Infantry instead of a Second like the others, but I want to live up to that; I hope I can.

It was my honor to lead my class. I only had an average of ten demerits a week (no one gets by with none) and an academic score of 98%. I'm still uncertain how I did it.

We are the Honor Class of this cycle, the best academically, and we only lost five of our 48—three to broken limbs. As I led the commencement ride, Ishim carried the guidon between Brick and I.

My orders for Camp Dix are a mystery, but at least I can get home for a couple of weeks.

"All right, fellows," Sterling yelled after the parade. "Gather 'round and get your orders…Abernathy!"

"Here!"

"Back in the Quartermasters, I see."

And on until… "Brick!"

"Yo!"

"Infantry, Camp Dix…Butterfield!"

And on until…"Grimes!"

"Here!"

"Infantry, Camp *Dix*…Harris!"

"

And on until… "Ishim!"

"Here!"

"Infantry, Camp *Dix*…Jordan!"

And on until… "Steele!"

"Here, sir!"

"*Another* one for Infantry *and* Camp Dix…Thomas!"

* * *

As the four friends gathered their barracks bags, they glanced at each other with consternation. "Why us?" Ishim asked.

"Hard to say," Steele said. "They needed Lieutenants and picked *us*…"

"Yeah, but I *was* in the Artillery," Ishim said. "Now…not sure what to make of this…unit?"

"I'm not either," Brick added. "I keep reading these orders and I just don't *get* it."

They loaded their barracks bags and civilian suitcases on the omnibus for the train station. Steele studied his orders, hoping *maybe*, with careful thought, they would *start* to make some *sense*. Even his three years of military experience didn't prepare him for anything *this* cryptic:

> ABOVE NAMED INDIVIDUALS ARE TO REPORT TO CAMP DIX, NEW JERSEY, BY 31 JULY 1917, READY FOR TRANSPORTATION OVERSEAS. THE ASSIGNED WILL MAKE ALL NECESSARY ARRANGEMENTS FOR AN EXTENDED DEPLOYMENT….

"*I* believe we're going to Europe," Steele declared.

"What makes you say that?" Ishim, next to him, asked.

"Just a feeling. Where are *you* headed now, Gary?"

"Minneapolis," Grimes said. "Say goodbye to the folks and…" he hesitated, "ask a certain *someone* to *maybe*…."

"Huh," Brick grunted from across the aisle. "Long Island for me," he added. "Not gonna weaken *now* and get all sentimental about some *female*…"

"What was that letter *you* got a few weeks ago?" Steele asked, remembering a scented note being passed around at mail call.

"Wasn't from your *mother*…"

"No," Brick admitted. "No. It was…known *her* since we were in *nappies*." He stopped. "She *seemed*…she…"

"Wrote something you remember," Steele said, noting *that look* in Brick's eyes; *that grin* on his face.

"Yeah. She said, 'I shall wait for you while you do your patriotic duty, *my dear*.' And she *signed* it, 'Affectionately, Suzie.'" He stopped, blinked. "*She* hasn't called herself that… since we were *kids*…"

"*You're* not exactly *Methuselah* now, Mike," Steele said. "Maybe she feels *more* for you than you *think*…"

Brick stared at the ground. "Maybe it *would* be better to have someone to *write* to…"

"I believe it would," Steele said. "There's a girl I walked out with before I enlisted…"

"That's *right*," Ishim said, "you *were* in the Army *before*…"

"Yes, I was," Steele admitted, "three *years* before. Just because you blue-bloods could *finish* university and go to work for your daddies…"

"Not *my* old man," Ishim said. "University, yes, but I wasn't *about* to go into the mines…"

"I was still in school," Brick said. "Didn't *quite* finish…"

"But you both went to Plattsburg camps," Steele said; both agreed. "So you were half-officers when you got to Officer's School…"

"More like a quarter," Brick mused. "Plattsburg was a lot of rallies and rah-rah, but not much practical training like we got here." He stopped. "*Where* were you from?"

"Michigan." Steele stopped. "How little we know about each other after being together for three months…"

"Three months, and I'm not sure I knew the first names of over *ten* of my classmates," Ishim admitted. "Just no *time*…"

"Barely had time to…we got *one* pass to town," Brick lamented. "We were too *broke* to do anything…"

"Well, we'll have our chance," Steele said as the omnibus rolled up to the train station and studied the schedule. "If I read this right," Steele mumbled, "the *earliest* I can get to Detroit is…*Saturday*…I'll send a wire ahead…"

"Two days," Ishim nodded. "Eh; I can be in Los Angeles by…next *Wednesday*…a *week*…on a *train*…"

"I can't get to Long Island before…*Monday*," Brick sighed.

"Won't make Wisconsin before tomorrow *night*," Grimes declared.

"But we will be on the same train as far as St. Louis," Steele declared, "if we can get on *that* one leaving in *twenty minutes*."

"Yeah, and I wish somebody could tell me why I have to go *east* before I go *west*…" Ishim complained, picking up his bags.

"After three months of officer's school, you *gotta* ask a question like *that?*" Steele asked.

***

"A barracks bag and a portmanteau," Steele sighed, settling into the train's bench seat as it rattled out of the station. "That's all we've got in this world."

"At least we've got that," Brick, next to him, answered. "*That* and our *commissions* and all that *money* in our pockets…"

"Most I've ever had at once," Grimes, beside Brick, declared. "Feel like a tycoon…"

"I admit, it is the most folding cash *I've* ever carried," Ishim, across from them, agreed. "Dad didn't *believe* in shin-plasters; paid our allowances in silver or gold."

"A lot of that?" Steele asked.

"Enough when we were *kids*," Ishim answered. "All dried up when he passed…"

"You were *how* old?" Grimes asked. They'd heard the story before, in bits and pieces.

"Seventeen…" Ishim drifted off. "Went to work managing the family business since I was the oldest boy." He sighed. "Then Mom married Thomas and *he* took over…."

They shared small talk for four hours as they crossed Missouri…until they split up in St. Louis.

After a day, the rattle and bump rhythm of the train was becoming *almost* comfortable. Steele tried to sleep, fitfully, after a quick meal of sandwiches and soup at a water stop. He dully watched the young couple sitting across from him, crammed together with two other passengers on a bench designed for three.

"Tickets," the conductor slid the car door open again. Some held up their punched tickets; others got theirs punched; others *bought* tickets.

Around midnight, the young man watched out the window as his lady tried to sleep. Brick shrugged in his sleep, head lolling back again as he snored loudly once, waking himself. "Damn" Brick groused. "Can't *get* a sleeper…?"

"Officers take all the sleepers," the young man said. "I heard the conductor *say* that…"

"And what the *Hell* are *we?*" Brick growled.

"Lower-*ranking* officers," Steele mumbled.

"Are you going to *France?*" the young man asked.

"We *think* so," Brick sighed, disinterested. "You…?"

"I'm enlisting when…*shh*, sweetheart," he said as his lady woke up. "Go *back* to…"

"*How*, if *you* keep chattering?" she sighed. "Only train we could *get* to Philadelphia *had* to leave in the middle of the night…"

"You're going to Philly?" Brick asked. "Going to Camden myself, then to Long Island…"

"Yes," the young woman said, shifting in her tiny space. "Going to see my old Gran for her blessing and gifts."

"Just married, I take it," Steele said.

"*Three whole days* of wedded bliss," the young man said, beaming at his bride in the darkness, her face lit only by the occasional flash of moonlight through the window next to her.

"And *bliss* it *was* until we got on this train," the young woman declared. "*Now* it's just…"

"Traveling," a woman said. "Honey, would you like to *stretch* your *legs?*"

"You don't have to ask *me* twice," the bride answered, standing up. "I'm Ethel…"

"Patience," the other woman answered as they left the car.

"Anyone for poker, gents?" another male voice asked. "The club car's *bound* to be…"

"I'll pass," Brick said.

"The Army doesn't pay Lieutenants enough to gamble with civilians," Steele answered.

"Maybe not," another voice said. "Care for a *snort*, gents?"

"*That* I'll take," Brick said. After catching a whiff of the jug's evil-smelling contents, Steele passed it on to Brick, who took a quick swig before passing it on to the groom, who didn't seem to mind it.

"You young men on your way to the war?" a voice in the dark asked.

"Yes," Steele answered, tiredly.

"Well, Wilson got us *into* it all on his own; he can get himself *out* of it all on his own, that's all *I've* got to say."

"Sounds like it's too much," another voice said sharply. "You'd better watch what…"

"Or what?" the first voice asked. "What are *you* going to do about…?"

"He's got a right to say what he wants," Steele said loudly. "That's what we're *fighting* for: *his* right to say what he wants, if *we* like it or not."

"Well," another voice answered. "You've got more gumption

to say *that* than most, young man. If I were ten years younger, I'd be in uniform, too."

"Twenty for me," another said.

"Never get *me* in one of those things," said a third.

"I will be *in* one in a few weeks," the groom said softly.

"Good luck, young man," a voice said. "*All* of you young men…"

> [Date smudged] *July, North-bound train in Ohio.*
>
> *No matter where I go, it's the same damn thing.*
>
> *Most people are in favor of the war, but there's always someone who is not.*
>
> *Reached Cincinnati near 3 AM; changed trains for Detroit, parted with Mike. Weather clear and of course hot and humid. Sharing a bench with small boys thrilled by my uniform. Their mother is pretty and worried about the conscription. They'd explained the classifications to us in Officer's School. Doesn't mean they can't make mistakes, or worse…*

"My husband is going to be called," she sighed. "I just *know* it." Her three boys, aged seven, five and three, listened solemnly. Two boys shared a bench with their mother; the third on the facing bench with Steele and their luggage;[1] it was nearly dawn.

"You can't *know* that, ma'am," Steele replied, he *hoped* convincingly. "As I understand it, he'd be Category II. There're *millions* in Category I and they have to take *them* first…"

"Yes, but my *husband*…" she shook her head. "He's a dead shot. They'll come for him as soon as the draft board finds his registry and realizes *who* he is…"

---

[1] Baggage cars were for the First-Class passengers. Others had to manage as best they could.

"Is he that well known?" Steele asked. "The board…"

"Includes his hunting buddies," she answered.

"They can't override his classification," Steele said, knowing this was true…legally. "Where are you bound, ma'am, if you don't mind my asking?"

"Zanesville, where my parents are," she answered. "Byron will join us in a week."

"Your husband?"

"Yes." She smiled at the window. "We've been married nearly ten years now."

"I won't guess your age, ma'am," Steele grinned.

"You can *check* my *teeth*, sir," she giggled. Her boys smiled. "We've been traveling nearly a week," she added. "You are the first soldier we've traveled with in all that time. Don't you find that odd?"

"No, not *really*," Steele answered. "*Most* troops are traveling on their *own* trains. You might encounter the occasional officer or militiaman on his own, but not large groups of soldiers."

"*That* answers it," she mumbled.

"Where did you come from that you've been traveling for so long?"

"Cody, Wyoming."

"How did you get…?" He stopped. "Sorry, ma'am."

"Mail-order bride, sir," she said without hesitation. "Please call me Marilyn."

"I'm Ned. Dad's *first* wife was a mail-order bride. His second was her sister, came *with* her."[1]

"Well…*where*, if you don't mind…?"

"Northern Michigan, where he was a blacksmith. He made a *small* fortune inventing a motor car suspension. Then we moved to Dearborn, *making* suspensions…."

"Oh." She was quiet. "My husband is a teamster. Our business is being pushed out by the motor wagons. So, we are coming back

---

[1] Mail-order brides came just as often from families as alone. Their reasons for finding grooms that way were many.

East to…he has a plan to start a freight forwarding firm. Father is putting up some money, starting a terminal in Zanesville."

"I wish him luck, Marilyn."

"Thank you. I wish *you* luck, Ned. *You* may need it more than *we…*"

> [Date?]*7ᵗʰ July, Troy, Michigan.*
>
> *Arrived at Fort Street Union Depot at 1450; ten minutes to three civilian time. Still getting used to this 24-hour clock.[1]*
>
> *Dad's doing OK for the family…going to dinner in civvies (that don't fit) for the first time in three months…Diane seems at peace with her situation…*

"Hi, Dad," Steele said, stepping off the Pullman car.

"Son," Alan Steele Senior smiled, shaking Ned's hand. "*Good* to see you."

"Same here," Ned replied, added, "Hi, Mom!"

"*Neddie*," his mother smiled warmly and bussed his cheek.

"And…Di*ane*," Ned exclaimed, spotting his sister. "*So* glad you could…"

"Hi, Ned," she nodded, reaching out her hands. "I see *you're* well."

"Well, let's get going," Alan Senior declared. "Can't tarry on the platform all night."

They piled into a big Cadillac for a long ride out to the quiet farm community of Troy, traveling dirt roads bordered by both cornfields and factories. "Quite a change from Dearborn, Dad," Ned said as they turned, finally, off of the Telegraph Road onto Maple Road, then on a long driveway.

---

[1] The 24-hour format was *taught* to American officers as early as 1916. *Some* Army officers used it in WWI; *some* French and British officers also used it. The US Army *officially* adopted it in 1942.

"It *is*," Alan declared. "That was the point. I have a longer drive to the plant, but the children are better off out here."

***

Vanelle, the Steele's cook and housekeeper for so long she was almost part of the family, smiled at him as she served dinner, and said, "Hello, Mister Ned, and welcome *home*, sir."

"Thanks, Vanelle," Ned answered, "good to *be* back. And how's *your* family these days?"

"All well, sir, thank you," Vanelle said.

"*Opal* just had a baby," thirteen-year-old Helen said loudly.

"*That* a fact? Boy or girl, Gramma?"

"A little *boy*, sir, thank you," Vanelle answered, smiling warmly at Ned's familiarity, but glaring at Helen.

"Didn't know she was *married*…"

"Last *winter*, sir." Vanelle said.

"Indeed," Ned smiled. "Got my first girl-kiss from Opal; we were *nine*…"

"I *recall*, sir," Vanelle said. "She was all *gushy* about it until her *father*…"[1]

"Of *course*. Give her my regards, Vanelle," Ned said.

"I *will*, sir."

***

"More *air* out here," Diane sighed, sitting on the settee next to Ned on the porch. "Can't get a *draft* in there."

"Not much," Ned agreed, finishing a diary entry. "How are *you?*"

"Fine," she said, glancing at him as she opened and rolled her sleeve cuffs. "You mean…oh, *that*," she waved a hand. "*We* were *finished* before our honeymoon ended."

"I know I wasn't around, but Ted *sounded* like a…"

"A money-grubbing bounder," she said, "not to mention an

---

[1] Familiarity with a domestic's family was *one* thing, but crossing the color line into intimacy, even as children, was something *else*.

adulterer." She stretched her legs out, then curled them beneath her, flapping her skirt and opening her collar. "I found *that* out early."

"Sorry, Di." Ned took off his cuffs and stiff collar.

"It's *fine*, Ned." She brushed away a mosquito. "We were in court *last* month; we expect the decree by this time next year. The marriage will be legally over by next *Christmas*."

"Seems…fast…."[1]

"Dad's a buddy to our judge. Besides, by the time I wrote you, I'd *left* him nearly a *year*."

"What about *after*…you're…?" Ned knew little about that *kind* of thing, but knew that divorced women had few employment options.

"I'm back in school for bookkeeping." They were quiet, listening to the night sounds. "You're going to France?"

"I believe so."

"Good luck."

"Thank you. Have *you* heard anything from Charlotte?" Charlotte was a strawberry blonde Ned had walked out with in the Normal School. "I wrote her until early last year; haven't heard from her since…."

"I know *why*. Her father chucked her out after she got in a *family way* with a whiskey drummer last year. Lately she's been *seen* at The Grand on 8 Mile Road.[2] But I know a gal you might *like* and who might like *you*. Her name's Georgia Pamplin, and she's a pretty thing. I know her from church. Her father owns a tool and die shop."

"We'll see her at church tomorrow, then…?"

"*And* at the ice cream social tomorrow *afternoon*." They were quiet again. "Do you want an introduction?"

"You can *go* to church?"

"*Dad* and *Al* and *you* will be with me."[3]

---

[1] Divorce without custody fights in Michigan took about three years circa 1917. *With* custody issues could take a decade and more.

[2] A well-known brothel.

[3] Women undergoing divorce didn't appear in pubic until their decrees

Just then, Alan Junior drove up the drive and walked up to the house, slinging his coat off. "*Ned*," he cried, spotting his brother. "You got *in* all right?"

"Al," Ned said, extending his hand as he stood up. "You *working hard* or *hardly working?*"

"We've got more orders this *month* than we can fill in a *year*," Al Jr. answered, shaking Ned's hand. "What are *you* two plotting *now?*" As children, Di and Ned were notorious instigators of many a scheme.

"Plotting *against* your wedding, Al," Diane grinned. "I'm telling Alice that you snore."

"She *knows*," Al replied, tipping his straw boater back on his head. "I fell asleep at the concert last week." He planned to marry a *slightly* wealthy Grosse Pointe socialite in 1918.

"Other than swamped, how's work with Timken, Al?" Ned asked.

"*Rolling* right along," Al answered, taking a seat across from them both. Al was an engineer with the big bearing manufacturer. "Have *you* heard anything from Charlie?"

"Got a letter from him in April, just before I left for OCS," Ned said. "Says they want to commission *him*, too. 'The Philippine Department is short nearly a hundred Lieutenants,' he said."

"You wrote about *that*," Diane said. "Nothing since?"

"Just being *in* the Army doesn't give me any special wires to the rest of it," Ned declared. "There's over a hundred thousand men in the Army now. There'll be another hundred thousand a *month* by the end of the year."

"That...*my*," Al declared, fidgeting with his collar button. "I was *just* told that they have placed *me* in Category III." He shrugged. "Guess I'm too important an engineer to go fight."

"I guess," Ned said. "It's *also* possible Dad had something to do with it."

"He's still with the National Guard, though at 56..." Al shrugged. "Still, he went to Arizona last year with what *used* to be

---

were final, unless escorted by an adult male member of their family, signaling the family's support of the woman's case. Men were under no such stygma.

the 1st Michigan Light Artillery."

"*Did* he?" Ned asked, surprised. "Didn't…he never *said*…"

"Told us *not* to say," Diane said. "Didn't want you worrying."

"Is he still a Colonel?" Ned asked.

"In the *State* Guard, yes; in the *National* Guard, he's a Captain since they *abolished* the 1st Michigan," Al explained. "It's a *headquarters* now. Maybe *that* makes sense to *you*…"

"I *can* explain it," Ned sighed. "It comes down to why and how the State Guard *isn't* and *won't be* under federal control. As for the reorganization, I *believe* the old 1st Michigan became the headquarters of the Michigan Guard."

"*Greek* to me," Diane said, slipping off her shoes and standing up. "*I'm* getting some sleep. See you boys in the morning."

"*G'night*, Di," her brothers said in unison.

"I'm getting some sleep myself," Al declared, standing up. "Church tomorrow?"

"Di has a young lady she wants me to meet," Ned sighed.

"Georgia Pamplin. She's a *sweet* girl."

"We'll see." They were quiet. "I'm going off to war like Great-Grandfather…"

"*Not* like Great-Grandfather," Al mumbled. "This war is *nothing* like his." He glanced at his brother. "I *read* the *Windsor* papers for work; saw pictures of what they did at Verdun and the Somme." He paused, looked away. "I wish you *luck*, Ned."

"Oh, it won't be *that* bad, Al," Ned said. "We're…"

"Going into a *meat grinder*, Ned."

8th July, Troy, Mich.

G[1] is a sweet girl. We had a swell time listening to the band and sharing ice cream. She dances at least as poorly as I, wanted <u>close</u> dancing[2] I'd never done it

---

[1] Diarists sometimes use initials to protect the subjects from controversy. Ned's practice is uneven.

[2] *Closer* than between-strangers-arm's-length dancing in this period.

"*Dancing* with Georgia, Neddie," Betty said casually as she trimmed her pie crust while they talked in the kitchen. "She seemed more *interested*."

"Yeah," Ned said. "First time for *me*."

"*You* didn't seem to *mind*."

"Didn't want to embarrass her by saying no."

"A gal you just met wants you to rub *against* her *chest* and you worry about embarrassing *her?*"

"I'm an *officer* and a *gentleman*, Bets..."

"Yeah, but you're also my *brother* Neddie, who kissed the *maid's* girl. Is there *any* chance you'll encounter her brother?"

"Not much," Ned answered. "But it was what Georgia needed to hear." He put his pen down. "You were getting serious with Dick when you wrote last. *Did* you...?"

"He spoke to Dad," Betty said, not looking up. "We've *talked* about our future. He's pretty sure the draft will take him. So is Dad..."

"Eh, *well*," Ned said. "You'll *wait*...?"

"I've got *five years* invested in this guy, Neddie," she said. "Of *course*, I'll wait."

"Well, why *not*...?" Ned grinned.

"No; *not* before he goes. I'm not *that* desperate." She rolled her eyes, then snapped her towel at him. "If he *goes* over there...and the *worst*..."

He closed his diary. "What do *you* hear about the war?"

"Al studies the Windsor papers for sales leads," she sighed. "*Some* things he...the casualty lists are *horrid*..."

"If you'll *allow*, Lieutenant Ned, sir," the factory foreman said, whipping off his cap, "with Mr. Steele's permission, the plant took up a collection." The plant employees stood in a semicircle around Ned and Al Sr. "In honor of your service and commissioning, sir." He held out a flat box.

"Open it, Ned," Al Sr. urged.

Ned opened the leather-covered case, finding a Waltham General Funston watch with a khaki strap. "I…" Ned started.

"It's got a sentiment on the underside, sir," the foreman added. "It's dustproof and waterproof, the salesman said."

Ned turned the watch over and read the engraving: *To Lieutenant Ned Steele from the Steele Suspension Factory.* "I'm *touched*," Ned managed. "*Thank* you. I shall be *honored* to wear it and will think of you often."

"Jes' keep yer *head* down, Ned," a voice in the back of the crowd said. "Come back in one piece. That'd be enough for *us*."

"Here, here," another voice said.

"*Three cheers* for *Lieutenant Ned*," the foreman shouted. "*Hip, hip, hooray!*"

"Children," their mother called, "come in for lunch. Oh, *hello*, Frannie. Come and join us." Their big beach tent faced the Canadian end of the island.

"Mama," Francis bristled slightly at her childhood nickname, "*thank* you; I *shall*." Francis struggled to *act* older than her nineteen years, but her family's persistence in treating her like a *child* grated. Around the big round table, Vanelle served the cold broth and sandwiches just like she would back home.

"Now, if *Ned* should make a career of the Army," Nora beamed, "we shall have *four* military officers in this family *should* George get an appointment. Not quite as many as *mine*, but…"

"Yours was an exception, Mom," Ned said. The Pierces of Pennsylvania, a family renowned for its military contributions (twenty men over three generations), now consisted solely of Nora, the last of seven sisters.

"And my sister had to find your father in a newspaper advertisement," she smiled.

"We've *heard* that, Mama," Helen said. "Can *I* find a fella in a newspaper?"

"Maybe when you're older," Nora said.

"You *always* say that about *everything* I want to do," Helen pouted.

"I met a woman on the train," Ned related Marilyn's story. "You're better off with some fella you know around here, like Herman down the road…"

"They're all too immature," Helen declared. "Why, he dosen't even *shave*…"

"And we don't have to measure your *bathing skirt* yet, either,"[1] Nora declared. "He'll grow into it, just as *you* will. Don't *rush*."

"How old *is* this Herman, anyway?" Ned asked.

"Thirteen," Nora answered. "Same age; same grade as Helen…"

"But boys mature slower than girls, Helen," Francis said; Nora glared at her daughter briefly, but Francis went on. "Just…you know; *we'll* talk about this *later*…"

"Always *later*," Helen sniffed, sipping her soup. "*Irving's* got

---

[1] Bathing skirts could only be *so* far above the knee and *were* measured if they *seemed* too short. *Most* beaches started measuring only when girl's breasts became noticeable.

a *sweetheart…*"

"*Do not*," Irving protested. "She's a…a…"

"Girl, who's a friend," George put in. "*Pretty* one, too."

"I saw you back behind that piling," Helen exclaimed. "What were you doing back there if *not hanky-panky…?*"

"Not *that*," Irving said, taking a swipe at Helen. "We were building a sand castle away from the water…"

"No waves in the Detroit River," Nora declared firmly. "What *were* you doing, Irving? And *where* did you learn *that* phrase, Helen?"

"Building a sand castle where *Horrible Helen* can't find it," Irving declared with finality.

"Who's horrible?" Helen cried. "Bets and Di say *that* all the *time…*"

***

"*Beautiful* evening," Al Senior declared, puffing his cigar and staring at the lights of Windsor just across the water. He casually removed his old-fashioned wing collar, set his felt hat down.

"Yes," Ned agreed, pushing his straw hat back on his head. "Wonder where I'll be next summer?"

"I don't," Al Senior said. "You'll be in the Army wherever they send you."

"*France*, I believe," Ned said.

"And I'll be in the Navy, God *willing*," George said.

"*Yes*, my sons," Al Senior said. "You'll be serving your country just like generations of Steeles have. My father, you know, was with Reno at the Powder River. *His* father was at Antietam and Gettysburg."

"You've *said* that, Dad," Ned said. "And you were ready to fight in Cuba, but you never *got* that far. Bets said you went to Arizona in '16?"

"I went with my *battery*, except now it's a *company*." Al Senior said bitterly. "That *Congress*…reorganized *everything*, *ruined* everything."

"All for the better, Dad," Ned said. "They explained it to us in officer's school: the militias were a *mess*. Couldn't do *anything* with most of 'em…"

"My *son*," Al Senior mumbled, "you are the only man alive who can say *that* to me and *not* get a thrashing." He handed Ned a cigar. "Not for *you*, George; not *yet*." George made a disgusted face, got up, and left.

"Thanks, Dad," Ned said, biting off the end. "Got a lucifer?"[1]

Ned puffed quietly on the match, then grinned, "me *and* Charlie."

"How's that?"

"*Charlie* could tell you that and not get thrashed."

"No; I'd thrash him, *too*." Al Sr. took a long drag on his cigar. "That's *one* reason he *left*: we are too *different* and too much *alike*." The two men sat silently for several minutes before Al Sr. mumbled, "it's a *horrible* war, Ned."

"Not like any *other*, they say."

"You could get killed before you *get* there."

"And that's one reason we're *in* this war."

22nd July, Troy, Mich.

G's father gave his permission to write to her. She said she would write to me. She said more than that.

I don't know what to think about a girl I barely know who likes to dance very close in public. I don't really feel that way about her and I don't know if I will. But someone is better than no one to write to.

Morale is about hope.

Two young people sat in separate chairs next to each other on the spacious porch of her enormous house, the sweet notes of the Sunday ice cream social still resonating in their heads.

"You dance well, Ned," Georgia said.

----

[1] A match.

"Thank you," Ned said. "Not a lot of practice."

They gazed at the gold and red sun setting slowly in the west; the good old Michigan July sun taking its sweet time. Some summer days, it was quite light out as late as ten in the evening.

"Will you be in any danger?" Georgia asked. She folded her ungloved hands in her lap.

"I'm an Infantry officer," Ned said. His hands grasped the arms of his chair. "I almost certainly will be in *some* danger, depending on what assignment I get."

"I will pray for your safe return," she said. "There will be women there…if you are *tempted*…"

"Georgia, I've been *tempted* before," Ned said with a smile. "I *shall* wait for my wedding night…"

"Would you *mind* if I…" Georgia started, "if I *think* of you like *that?*"

"On a wedding night?" Ned asked, surprised. "*Our*…?"

"My *dear*, I am 21 and I have *been* jilted twice; once at the altar. I can*not* wait *much* longer." She looked at him pointedly. "*Would* you mind if I *had* such thoughts?"

"I…I suppose not," he said, nodding slightly. "Does *that* mean we are…?"

"You didn't *speak* to Father of *that?*" she asked, looking away as if disappointed, knowing the answer. "*Think* of ours as an *agreement* to *discuss* it when you return."

"You will *wait*, then?"

"Of course, *dear*."

"I am…*glad*…."

23ʳᵈ July, Gross Isle, Mich.

George has gotten good news…and I will miss this…

"You *got* the appointment?" Ned exclaimed from the cabin door. "You're going to Annapolis?" The family now stayed in several west-end island cabins.

"Class of '22, as long as I keep my grades up at the Normal School and can pass the examinations," George smiled modestly, sorting through the mail. "I should be commissioned by '24.[1] Dad got Senator Gibson to wrangle it."

"Hi, guys," Francis yelled from the boardwalk.

"George got the appointment," Ned said.

"Congratulations, Georgie!" Francis walked across the sand to the cabin, hiking her skirt up to her calves.

"Thanks, Frankie," George waved. "I should graduate before *you* finish school." Their sister Francis was one of the first women training as a doctor in the Detroit College of Medicine and Surgery.

"Rub it *in*, why don't ya?" she grunted. "I'll make more money as a doctor than *you* will as a *sailor…*"

"*Naval officer*," George corrected loudly. "And I'm *not…*"

"She's probably right, George," Ned said. "Officers of the 1st Rank, like you'll be when you are commissioned, don't make as much as those of the 2nd Rank, like me, but I can *tell* you she's *certainly* right…"[2]

"But it's not the money," George protested. "It's the service itself."

"*What* is?" Helen asked, her swim dress covered with sand, her stockings sagging below her knees as she entered the cabin.

"George is going to Annapolis," Francis declared.

"What's an apolis?" Irving asked, right behind her, his swimming costume similarly soiled.

"Not…*oh, I give up*," George declared, climbing out of his chair. "You *children* will *never…*"

"They're not *that* much younger than you, George," Francis scolded, rolling up Helen's stockings. "Helen, *don't* be indecent."

"Why do I have to wear these stockings, anyway?" Helen

---

[1] At that time, graduated midshipmen spent two years shipboard before taking their final examinations for commissioning.

[2] 1st Rank officers (Ensigns and 2nd Lieutenants) with less than five years of service, even with sea pay, made $155.83 a month in 1917. 2nd Rank officers (1st Lieutenants) with the same time in service made $166.67. A newly-licensed American physician/midwife averaged somewhat more than $250.00 a month in that same year.

asked coldly. "Those girls down the beach *don't* wear 'em…."

"Then let's let *them* lead the fashion world, but *you* shall *not*," Nora declared firmly.

"Who wants to see *your* pins, anyway?" Irving stage-whispered.

"*Mama*," Helen cried, "Irving's being *mean!*"

> *26ᵗʰ July, Troy, Mich.*
>
> *I must not think of G; it's bad luck and breaks the concentration…But, my <u>morale</u>.*

"Penny for your thoughts, Neddie," Diane sighed, settling on the divan beside him.

"Just…*last night* of *leave*, Di."

"And…Georgia?"

"I think *Georgia*…I *can't* think of *her* like *that*. Not *now*…."

"Neddie, she's had her heart broken before; I can tell."

"She *said* as much."

"She *wants*…?"

"Yes." Silence. "Can *you* speak with her?"

"For my little brother, sure."

> *27ᵗʰ July, Southbound train.*
>
> *I wonder yet again at that awkward conversation with G. Did she say those things for <u>me</u>, or I for <u>her</u>? I don't know enough about women to really know.*
>
> *There is a sense of dread, of foreboding in my heart, leaving my family behind. There is no reason to fear for any of their lives, except Dad, who is getting on in*

years. The Germans can't really attack America. So why am I afraid for them...?

"Bound for France, Lieutenant?" the man on the bench opposite asked. The Pullman club car, half-full near midnight, was glaringly lit by their tungsten-electric lights.

"My orders *say* overseas," Steele answered.

"What's your outfit?"

Steele studied the man briefly. notably older than his father, a bit on the pudgy side and sounding a little phlegmy, with wisps of hair sticking out from under his homburg and tobacco stains on his fingers. "Don't *have* one yet, sir," Steele answered.

"Huh," the man answered. "I was with the 14th Ohio Volunteers in the War Between the States. Marched with them from '61 until they mustered out in '65."

"Quite the feat," Steele nodded. "You were lucky to survive."

"Aw, *not* luck, son: good breeding." The man, eyes fixed on the window, swayed with the car's motion along a bumpy track. "And…well, I *suppose* you *could* call it luck." He reached for a cigar, offering one to Steele, who waved it away.

"I imagine you *saw* some things," Steele sighed distractedly.

"Saw things *you*…I saw my *best friend* lose his head to a cannon ball in Georgia. Saw my cousin choke his life out in Tennessee." The man's countenance steeled as he lit up from the gas match in the wall. "I did what Mr. Lincoln called for: put down the rebellion. Marched in that big parade at the end." He inhaled and sighed heavily, seeming to exude smoke from every pore. "We lost so *many* good boys so we could *have* that parade."

"Do you think it was *worth* it, the sacrifice?"

The man's facial expression changed, starting with anger, and followed by a slow transformation to benign resignation. "We have to decide what *anything* is worth to answer *that*, son. What's your *republic* worth? What's your *freedom* worth?" He looked at Steele, cocking his head. "Is freedom worth *your life?* If not, *why* are you wearing that uniform and going to France?"

"If *nothing* is worth dying for," a woman's voice behind Steele said, "then *what* is your life *worth?*"

"Ma'am," Steele said, twisting to look around. "*Care* to…?"

"I was *just* about to go to my *sleeper*, sir," she said, rising. "Good *evening*."

"Good *evening*, miss," the man said as Steele watched her walk away, an alluring figure in a sensible traveling suit with a stack of reddish hair under her unadorned straw hat.

Then she turned, smiled slightly at them, and left the car…

> *28th July, Eastbound train.*
>
> *I am sensible of what I am about to say because of my understanding[1] with G, but I have met quite the most remarkable young woman…*

"Good morning," the woman said, smiled at Steele as she sat next to him on the bench seat.

"Good…did *we*…?" he started, "meet last *night?*"

"It *was* last night, sir," she smiled again. She had fair skin and wisps of light red hair sticking out from under her hat. Her most pronounced feature, however, was her *sparkling* violet eyes. "Traditionally, a lady is introduced to a gentleman by her chaperone or family member. How*ever*," she sighed, "I don't *have* either *here*, so…*hello*; I am Angela Gibson of Washington and Michigan. And *you* are…?" She extended her hand.

"Lieutenant Edmund Steele, US Army, Miss Gibson," he answered, grasping her surprisingly firm hand encased in a light linen glove. "You're of Washington *and* Michigan?"

"Officially, we *are* residents of Michigan and I *was* born in Lansing," Angela said, and added, "but we are there *only* when Congress is *not* in session." She looked away. "*Or* when I cannot *bear* Georgetown *any* longer."

"Congress," he repeated, puzzled.

"My father is Senator Gibson."

"*Ah*," he said. "Then my family owes him our thanks for my

---

[1] An "understanding" in 1917's polite society was a step before formal engagement.

brother's appointment to the Naval Academy…"

"I shall pass it on. Where are you bound, Lieutenant Steele?"

"New Jersey, then, I am sure, France. You?"

"I'm…*maybe* I'll end up in France with the Red Cross…"

"A nurse?"

"Nurse's *aide*. Wish I *were* a nurse, but *Mother* objected to my getting the training." She looked out the window. "*She* plans for me to *marry* well."

"You *don't?*"

"I plan to *marry*, yes, but *not* for *her* reasons. I *also* plan to do *something* in this *war* Father voted *for*."

"Unusual for…" he started.

"Yes," she said, looking at him. "I suspect your family does not expect *your* young women to…?"

"My sister Betty *wants* to volunteer for overseas duty. She got Red Cross training…"

"Betty…Steele," she mused. "Can't place her name. Where did she train?"

"Fort Wayne."

"*That* would explain it; *I* trained in Lansing. That's where *I'm* coming from."

"Ah." They bumped shoulders as the train rumbled over a rough part of the track. "And *now…?*"

"*Now* I shall tell Father and Mother that I'm volunteering for France."

"You just decide that *now?*"

She smiled, glanced at him. "*Yes*." She strained past him, her hair brushing his face to look ahead on the tracks. "The next stop…I shall *wire ahead* with the news and *hopefully* get back on." She smiled sincerely, offering her hand again. "Good *luck*, Lieutenant, if I cannot re-board."

He *took* it gently. "Good *luck*, Miss Gibson."

31st July, Camp Dix, New Jersey.

Arrived here yesterday, met up with Mike and Gary

As they stood alone in a small barren room attached to an empty building, Steele asked no one in particular, "Anyone have any idea what we're *doing* here?"

"Nope," Brick answered. "I got *this*..." he held up a note, "from some Corporal to come *here* at four this afternoon."

They were in wood frame buildings isolated from the rest of the post: a mess hall where they ate three meals so far, served up by cooks who only knew what they were told, a barracks and this storehouse with a little office. Steele and a growing number of enlisted men—many of whom had been in the Machine-Gun Section—arrived at the barracks either the night before or that morning.

"Yep." Ishim held up a similar note. "Got handed *this* an hour ago..."

"Me, too," Grimes added. "Got mine this morning at breakfast."

"And *me*," Lieutenant Richard Buchalter declared, waving his note.

"Well, that's five of us," Steele mused. "There's going on a hundred enlisted men in the barracks over there. Gotta wonder *what's* going on?"

"*Quite* simple, actually," a tall man in a British uniform entered the room from the only door. "*We* are to become better acquainted."

"And indeed, you shall," *Captain* George Patton interjected as he entered behind the Englishman. "Apologies, Major. Please continue."

"*My* name's Ian Talbott. I'm your primary machine gun instructor." Talbott had a quick eye and a somewhat haughty demeanor. "You and the *other ranks*[1] are to become machine gunners."

---

[1] Enlisted men, in British parlance.

"That's right, Major," Patton said. "If you gents will just come with *us*…"

"Sir," they answered, obediently following the two officers. They walked along a gravel path that ended at a pond where a picnic table and four chairs sat in the shade of a pair of large, old cedar trees—a cool spot on a hot day.

"Please take a seat, gentlemen," said Patton, gesturing to the chairs. "This assignment is very unusual, but you have been selected to be taught how to use machine guns in modern war so that you can teach *others*. Major Talbott here will give you your first instructions on your way to France…"

"*With* the Expeditionary Division, sir?" Buchalter asked.

Patton sat on the table and hunched over. "The Army renamed the Expeditionary Division the 1ˢᵗ Division. They have already *shipped* much of that unit. No…*you* will form a *very* special unit: a *motor machine gun unit*."

"A *what*?" Steele asked; the others blinked, glanced at each other.

"Never *heard* of such a thing," Brick declared.

"The Canadians have a *brigade* they *call* motorized, though they have had *bloody little* to do with those armored lorries of theirs," Talbott said. "You'll be getting the benefit of our experience in barrage firing, especially in *indirect* fire…"

"For *machine guns?*" Steele asked, incredulously.

"Oh, yes, indeed," Talbott declared. "And I have *just* obtained several crates of *these* from your War Department." He removed a small printed volume from a valise he carried: *Provisional Machine-Gun Firing Manual, 1917.* "*This* is what your War College produced after talking to *us* for the past two years." He made a face. "Machine guns are *not* what you *think*; not what *I* thought in 1914, not what *anyone* in America has thought except a few of your observers…and *these* chaps," waving the manual.

"And what *are* they, sir?" Steele asked.

"Think of machine guns as *light artillery* in the hands of the *infantry*, Lieutenant," Talbott said. "Light artillery that can fire for *hours* if need be. These manuals shall meet your ship tonight. Each of your men should *study* it. It will be a most important step in your training."

"You and your men will be on the *SS Euphrates* tonight, gentlemen," Patton said. "Take the *evening* to peruse this volume that I helped to *write*...."

"*You*, sir?" Grimes asked. "Might we have your name?"

"*George Patton*, Lieutenant," he said, in a way that suggested everyone should *know* who he was. "Now, as for *command*," Patton went on, "Lieutenant Steele is the senior officer in your group; he shall command the movement to France..."

"Ah, sir," Steele interrupted, "I *appreciate* the vote of confidence, but..."

"Now, now, Steele," Patton said. "You *are* a First Lieutenant after all. Now," he glanced at his wristwatch. "I'm sure you are all eager to gather your gear to be quayside by midnight. Your *orders*, Lieutenant." Patton handed Steele a stack of paper.

LIEUTENANT STEELE IS APPOINTED COMMANDER OF PERSONNEL (NAMED BELOW) ON SS EUPHRATES FOR MOVEMENT TO ASSIGNED DESTINATION....

"Yessir; *thank* you, sir."

"And now," Talbott nodded, glancing behind Steele, "your *tactical* instructor, *Commandant* Henri Dona, French Army."

They turned to see a diminutive man in an impeccable blue uniform with a pencil mustache. "Gentlemen," Dona smiled with a slight cock of his head. "Dona. I would be a *Major* in *your* army."

"I see," Steele said. "If Major Talbott's going to teach us about machine guns, what will *you*...?"

"Everything *else, mon* Lieutenant." Dona's English was clear, but accented. "I have been in *my* army since 1912, and became an officer along the *Voie Sacree* when they discovered I was the senior man in my company who was still *alive*. They sent me to *Quebec* last winter...."

"*Voie Sacree*," Brick mused. "Sacred Way...to...?"

"Verdun," Dona said. "The road between Bar-le-Duc and the front lines we called the *Voie Sacree. Parlez-vous Francais?*"

"*Mai oui*," Brick answered, followed by a string of French.

"*Thought* you were better at French than I was," Steele nodded. Though he was not *fluent*, like most Americans who went to school beyond grammar school/8th Grade[1] before the Great War, he had *some* French.

"Gentlemen," Patton said with finality, "we shall leave you to your studies. Quayside by midnight. Major; *Commandant…*"

And they left Steele and his officers alone.

***

"What do *you* think, Captain? *Commandant?*" Talbott asked in French as they boarded a touring car.

"I think Steele will do just fine," Patton said in his ungrammatical French. "He's got a reputation as a natural organizer; an instinctive leader. We'll see soon enough just *how* well those innate skills serve him in that *desert* of resources he's being sent to…"

"The other fellows," Dona mused in English. "They seem to accept his leadership."

"Lucky for us,*"* Patton declared. "Report on their training progress, *will* you, gents? There's some very important people want to be kept apprised of this experiment. And gentlemen: they are *not* to serve as *individuals* in British or French units, nor are they to be integrated into anything *resembling* a British, British *Empire* or French unit. Am I *clear?*"

"Perfectly, Captain," Talbott replied.

"So I am *told*, Captain," Dona answered, adding, "a waste of good men. In *French* units…"

"They will serve *only* in *American* units, *Commandant*," Patton snapped. "President Roosevelt has invested a *great deal* of money and political capital in getting those boys where they're going…"

"So I understand," Talbott said. "His volunteer divisions *can't* go, so he's paying for *these…?*[2]"

---

[1] *High school* and *Normal School* as known today were *alternatives* to college or university in the US. Colleges and normal schools granted *diplomas*; *universities* conferred *degrees*.

[2] In March 1917, with war fever on the rise in America, Congress authorized Theodore Roosevelt to raise four divisions of volunteers to send to Europe. Wilson, later, forbade Roosevelt's volunteers.

"Their equipment, supplies and passage to France, yes," Patton answered.

"How did he get *Regulars* into such a project?" Talbott asked.

"Understand how our War Department works, Major," Patton intoned. "Our bureaus are *so* disorganized and uncoordinated that anything that *looks* like a reasonable order gets published. Teddy just knows the right *people*."

"I see," Talbott said. "Sounds *deucedly* clever…"

"Almost sounds *French*," Dona muttered.

Patton grimaced. "Those poor boys are going to fall between *authorized* and merely *there*…at least for a *while*. Hell, their supply situation *alone* may be their undoing. I just hope that *Steele* fellow has what it takes to pull it off. Now," he said as the car stopped at a barracks building, "*I* have to catch *my* ship. Hope to see you in a few *months*…"

"Captain; Major," Dona said softly. "The future of *Europe* may be in their young and inexperienced hands. If we *remember* any prayers, perhaps we should *remember* them this evening."

August

1ˢᵗ August, SS Euphrates.

We walked up the gangplanks at midnight while the cranes loaded our equipment and supplies. I feel uneasy, that somehow this gangplank signals the end of many of us.

Our vessel is, I am told, the fastest of her type. She is a 3,500 ton, oil-fired liner with a crew of twenty that usually does a luxury trade. She is about 450 feet long and not quite 50 feet wide. I do not ask how we

---

Nonetheless, TR had collected *millions* from patriotic Americans to pay for the troops, and that money went *somewhere*…

got this kind of accommodation. Her Captain seems as baffled about our orders as I.

Our after hold is full of supplies, including food and equipment, but sans machine guns. The forward hold has three-tiered bunks for the men. The officers share three staterooms; Brick and I have one, Dona and Talbott have another, and Buchalter, Grimes and Ishim cram into a third with a rolling cot. NCOs share three larger rooms with both bunks and cots. As we cast off in the gathering dawn and watch the shore slip away behind us in the dark, I feel...I really don't know. But I know I have a job to do. There can be no "feelings" about that. So I set reveille for 6:00 ship time, then, alphabetically assigned Buchalter as Officer of the Day, Sergeant Adams as Charge of Quarters, and "fire watches" over our quarters right off the orders.

2nd August, SS Euphrates, Atlantic Ocean.

This is nothing like what I expected...McTee is the best NCO I could have asked for, a genuine treasure; knows as much about how the Army works as anyone in Washington...This Willis is quite the character...It is surprising how much can be done just by doing it.

Organizing started today...Now that I've written it down, it almost feels legitimate...don't know if I

"Gentlemen…we have a great deal of work to do," Steele told his officers, Dona, and Talbott in the 12-by-12 space the ship's Captain had set aside for an officer's mess and lounge.

"Whatever we *thought* machine guns are good for *isn't* how they've been used in France," Brick sighed, looking resigned.

"That's so," Grimes said, scratching his chin. "First paragraph of that manual *says* so:"

1. OBJECT OF INSTRUCTION—THE MACHINE GUN IS A WEAPON OF REMARKABLE POWERS AND LIMITATIONS. THE ULTIMATE PURPOSE OF MACHINE-GUN INSTRUCTION IS TO INSURE, BY MEANS OF THOROUGHLY TRAINED PERSONNEL, A MINIMIZING OF THE GUN'S LIMITATIONS AND A MAXIMUM EFFECTIVE UTILIZATION OF ITS FIREPOWER ON THE FIELD OF BATTLE.

"Stating the obvious," Brick said.

Steele shook his head. "We *hardly* knew it. Machine guns these days lay *barrages*; *patterns* of bullets called *beaten zones*. Two of 'em can lay beaten zones the size of this ship's deck. With practice, they shoot *over* hills, *into* trenches and shell craters. Some of them can reach out nearly *two miles* and hit targets they can't even *see*…."

"They *aren't* like rifles on the line anymore," Talbott added, pursing his lips. "A *section* of two machine guns can put out as much firepower as a company of infantry for as long as they have ammunition and the guns don't break down. A battalion—twenty-odd guns firing at the same target at once—as much as a *corps*."

"Huh," Grimes grunted. "Barrages? Beaten zones?" He shook his head. "Gotta *see* that kind of thing…"

"We *will*…*very* soon, but first," Steele said, "physical training for *everyone*. These weapons are heavy, and with the range finders, the ammunition, the spare barrels…"

"*Range finders*," Ishim looked startled. "These things *need*…?"

"When your target is a mile away, every *bad* guess you make about its distance gives the enemy's *artillery* range finders more time to find *you*," Talbott said with conviction. "These *barrages* are *planned; not* just a best guess."

"Yep," Steele added. "We need to make *range-estimating* and *height-estimating* training aids, and *weights* for strength training. The *Manual* tells us *most* of what we need. *And* we need to get the men *organized*…"

"They're doing close-order drill and manual of arms on the deck right now," Brick added. "McTee got the NCOs moving before chow."

"McTee…yes," Steele mused. "This stuff is *math*-intensive, too. All those tables and graphs…"

"There *are* tables, yes," Dona added, "but *they can* be, *malheureusement*,[1] wrong. They do not cover barrel wear correctly, I am told."

"Then *we'd* better," Steele said, scratching out a wire to Al that he had to send as soon as he landed.

> SEND ALL SLIDE RULES YOU CAN FIND STOP WE NEED
> THEM DESPERATELY END

***

"Sir," the knock on Steele's stateroom door was strong, assured. "You *sent* for me …?"

"*Yes*, Sarge," Steele answered, glancing at the open door. "C'mon in." The room Steele shared with Brick had two bunks, two desks, and two chairs, with empty floor space *almost* five paces by six. Two wall lockers accommodated their barracks bags.

"First, sir," McTee stuck out his hand. "Congratulations on your commissioning. I always *knew* I was going to work for you one day."

"Thanks, Sarge. Means a *lot* coming from you. Now…"

---

[1] Unfortunately…

"I've made up rosters for fire watch, CQ[1] and OOD[2], sir, but I'm concerned—the *other* NCOs are concerned—that we don't know what the *Hell's* going on," McTee grimaced. "First, we get orders for Camp Dix, *then* they move us to our own private little corner, and *finally,* they shove us into *this* tub, and we've got *no* notion of what we're *doing*. The men *need* to know. Without even a name to call what they're *in*…"

"We're all going to be machine gunners."

McTee blinked; his soft blue eyes puzzled. "*All* of us?"

"A machine gun *brigade*, if all goes well…" He'd been told *unit*, but *something* told him…

"Well, sir," McTee sighed, "the *rumor* goin' 'round…"

"What are they saying?"

"*They're* saying that they're being used as replacements for the British and French…"

"*No*; no way in *hell,*" Steele said decisively. "Definitely *not*. And you've *got* to tell the men we are *not* to be used as fillers for foreign units under *any* circumstances. That comes *straight* from General Pershing. Clear?"

"Yessir. Colonel Parker's[3] *with* General Pershing, I hear."

"*That's* more than *I* knew. Now…ever been a First Sergeant?"

"Occasionally; for short periods. Been doing the job since I got *on* this *spit-kit*…"

"Well, until we get *another* one, you're *ours*, OK?"

"All right, sir."

"Now, Top…I've got a *bunch* of things I need to address in a big hurry because there's an Englishman and a Frenchman who are going to start training us tomorrow…"

"Yessir."

---

[1] Charge of Quarters, an NCO assisting the Officer of the Day.

[2] Officer of the Day, an officer in charge of the unit while the commander sleeps.

[3] John Henry Parker commanded the Gatling Gun Detachment in Cuba, and was a leading proponent of machine guns in the attack. He ran an early AEF machine gun school in France, and later commanded infantry regiments.

"We need something to *call* ourselves…"

"Uh-huh…"

"We don't even have a unit designation. Hell, legally, I can't promote, demote or even *assign* people to the tasks they're already *doing*."

McTee shrugged. "I wouldn't worry about 'legal,' sir. It's been my experience that if you don't get anybody killed doing it, the Army don't much *care*…"

"Regardless, I need some *help,* some *organization*. What *can* I do?"

"You can create a *provisional* unit, sir," McTee said.

"Ever do that yourself?" Steele asked.

"Not *me,* sir," McTee shook his head. "*Seen* it done."

"What would happen if…if the Army doesn't *like*…?"

"*Well,* sir," McTee said expansively, leaning back in the time-honored manner of an old soldier[1] about to school a younger one, "General Crook once said if you do *something* that *works,* the Army will *make* it legal. If you do *something* that *doesn't,* they'll *protect* you…"

"*Yeah,* but…" Steele interrupted.

"*But…*"McTee continued, holding up his hand, "he *also* said that if you do *nothing* and people get *hurt,* the Army will *hang* you. Article 96 of the Articles of War states: 'Acts and conduct of a nature to bring discredit upon the military service.' Ain't nothing you *can't* find in there to punish everything and anything, *including* nothing." He looked resigned. "They can charge you with spitting on a sidewalk or walking out a door." He shrugged. "Dates from the Rebellion.[2] I've made out enough charge sheets. If the outfit you're in ain't the *best* you've ever been in, it's *your* fault. So, do what you gotta do…"

"You've always *said* that, Top."

His eyes narrowed. "Which *reminds* me, *Jack Willis* is here…"

"Who?"

---

[1] Not *aged,* but more imbued with wisdom, wiles and guile.

[2] A common term for the 1861-65 war.

"Jack Willis, a quartermaster. That *larcenist* can find water in a desert. Whatever we'll *need*, he'll *find*…and *then* some. Last *spring*, I *know* he was in the Iron Bar Barracks[1] at Fort Robinson…"

"What *for?*" Steele asked, suddenly concerned.

"Ah, *that* time, for fudging *too many* requisition forms *too well*," McTee said. "I hear tell he requisitioned more beef for the regiment than there were cooks to *cook* it or troops to eat it. I have to admit having a certain admiration for his, ah, *talents*. Never would have expected such from a *kid* leading a *pack string* out of Daiquiri."

"He was in Cuba?"

"Jack was a packer on the mule train who looked to be at least *twenty*, but turned out to be just a *kid* of *thirteen*…I *hear*. How he got *there* or in the *Army*, *I* never knew and I don't think anyone *else* does, *either*. And he's never *said*." McTee declared. "I swear he could have packed up that whole damn island on three mules. Never *saw* such a packer."

"He's been a Sergeant before?"

"*Twice* that *I* know of. *Always* convinces the brass that he's an invaluable asset, so they won't pitch him out, and they always believe him…because he *really is*. His superiors cover for him because he's the *best* scrounger in the Army, *bar none*. They don't need convincing, because they know *firsthand* how resourceful he is. When he gets *caught*, it's the *bigger* brass that gets peeved 'cause he can talk his way out of *most* pickles. I'll put it *this* way, sir," McTee declared, with an air of finality. "If Jack Willis is in *this* outfit, we'll never want for *anything*."

"Glad he's on *our* side."

"Yessir. Now, we'll start organizing. The *rosters*: we'd best figure out *how* to organize…."

***

"Sergeant; please, sit down." Steele pointed to his other chair and looked Willis over. He seemed *older* to Steele, older than *most* of his men, anyway. He was one of those guys whose age is hard

---

[1] Stockade.

to fix. With a weathered face and hair that seemed…clear, as if it had once been *some* color but was now bleached by the sun. "Willis, Sergeant McTee says you're good at getting things done."

"Sergeant McTee is too kind, sir." His voice was an odd tone, nearly bass but more tenor, that simultaneously commanded both attention and assurance.

"We need to make a unit, Sergeant. A machine gun company."

"Yessir."

"Nothing else?"

Willis shrugged. "Waiting for a direct question to answer, sir."

"Can you help me make a unit?"

Willis seemed to wait for a beat, thinking. "I will do as the Lieutenant asks."

"Fair enough. Can you find the materials and a clerk—preferably one with a bugle—to make it look like someone gave this mob more thought than just shoving a hundred men on a boat?"

Willis inhaled deeply. "*I* can make a Corporal's guard mount look like a regimental parade." He cleared his throat. "You, sir, have quite the reputation yourself."

"*Do* I?"

"Yessir. In Mexico, they called you 'Do-it Steele.' Said you could reorganize paint into its constituent components…sir."

It was all Steele could do to keep from…he wasn't *sure* what. "What else?"

"Well, some officers claimed you could lead anything, *do* everything, but your…*ahem…youth*, sir, held you back." He straightened his shoulders. "They, ah, I believe, were jealous."

"Of *me?*"

"The Army comprises a *lot* of egos, sir," Willis said simply. "Hurt feelings go a long way, especially in the *clubs*. Career officers *remember* those hurts for a long time. With the Army as *small* as it is…"

"Well, the new National Army[1] should take care of *that*…"

---

[1] Created to bolster the Regular Army and the then-mobilizing National Guard, which were harder to expand.

Steele started.

"But it'll be like the Volunteers during the Rebellion, sir," Willis interrupted. "It'll go away as soon as the war does."

"Willis, you and I both know that NCOs understand the Army better than most officers."

"Yessir."

"Can we make a unit together?"

"Yessir."

"Very well. Let's get you introduced to our officers…"

***

"Mike Brick; Gary Grimes; Dick Buchalter; Corey Ishim: meet John McTee, our Acting First Sergeant, and Jack Willis, our Acting Supply Sergeant."

"Pleased, Top," Brick extended his hand. "First Sergeant of *what?*"

"The 1st *Provisional* Machine-Gun Company," McTee chuckled.

"The…*what?*" Grimes asked, grinning.

"Yeah; why the *Hell* not?" Ishim nodded. "Nobody says we *can't*…"

"Nobody but the War Department," Brick declared, "not to mention Congress. But how about we do it up *brown* and call ourselves the 1st Provisional Machine-Gun *Instructor* Company, since we're *supposed* to *teach?*"

"It *would* be of a *very* temporary nature…" Buchalter agreed.

"*Sounds* as if we're making this up on the fly," Grimes declared.

"*Which*, indeed, we *are*," Steele said.

"*Yeah*, sure," Ishim said.

"I'm *in*," Grimes said, "hang *together* or hang *apart*."

"All *right*," Steele said, "at least I won't be alone in my court-martial. Now, we need to fill in Sergeants Nagurski, Kosten and Belling; tell 'em *where* to fall in this afternoon…"

***

"*All* right, *fall in* there. Just give me *three ranks* along the rail, there," McTee shouted at the men as they came out on the main deck after chow. "Just…*c'mon*, you chowderheads; you *ain't* no rookies; *none* of you…all right; *group, a*-ten-SHUN," McTee called. He gave the ranks a quick, critical once-over with the wizened expertise of a long-serving NCO used to taking charge. Satisfied, he did an about-face and saluted Steele. "*Comp*any formed and *ready, sir*."

"First Sergeant," Steele returned the salute. He lost his balance briefly as the ship heaved in a swell, but otherwise the weather cooperated with calm, if breezy, seas. "Men, you are now all members of the 1st Provisional Machine-Gun Instructor Company." He waited a moment for a reaction. "I'm Lieutenant *Steele*, your company commander. Lieutenant *Brick* is my executive officer; the First Sergeant is Master Sergeant *McTee*. Now: *First* Platoon is the *front* rank; *Second* Platoon is the middle rank; *Third* Platoon is the back rank. First Platoon's leader is Lieutenant *Grimes*; Platoon Sergeant is Sergeant First Class *Nagurski*. The Second Platoon's leader is Lieutenant *Ishim*; Platoon Sergeant is Sergeant First Class *Belling*." *Still* nothing… "Third Platoon leader is Lieutenant *Buchalter*; Platoon Sergeant *Kosten* is his Platoon Sergeant."

Again he waited…still nothing… "You'll organize squads this afternoon. Tomorrow morning, we start training as machine *gunners* on the foredeck." He pointed to the structure just a ladder above the main deck; no reactions. "The Army wants *us*— butchers, bakers, and candlestick-makers—to be machine-gunner *instructors* because they will need *lots* more machine-gunners before this war's over." A murmur arose. "Every day, *twice* a day, we will conduct physical training, come rain or come shine. As *most* of you already know, machine guns require a *lot* of hard physical work, so we need to build up our strength and stamina." Another pause… "If you have *any* questions, you can ask when we *both* have time, but that time is *not now*."

Still nothing.

"Now, then…this is a *new* unit. There will be a wave of *acting* promotions and a few *demotions* for those who *can't* do the job. I have only *one* requirement of anyone: *do the job*. If you *don't*, I'll replace you. If you *can't*, let me *know* and I'll *help* you; no one will hold incapacity against you *if* you seek help."

A louder murmur rolled over the formation. "Men, this is new to *all* of us, but I'm sure that as *Regulars* you'll adapt, as I'm sure *I* will. Now," Steele rolled his shoulders, "let's get this job done…First *Sergeant*…" Steele waited for McTee, who stepped in front of him and saluted. "Let's get to organize squads, Top."

"Yessir; *just* what I *had* in *mind*."

"*Carry* on." Steele moved off.

Then he heard, "*three cheers* for Lieutenant Steele! Hip, hip…*hurray…!!*"

"All *right*, boys; *save* it," McTee declared. "Platoon Sergeants; *form* your squads; you have an *hour* before you're to hand in your rosters. Physical training on the foredeck at 1500 ship time. *Platoon* Sergeants, *take* charge."

***

"Just *look* at this," Brick said, passing a sheaf of paper to Steele. "*Eight* carbons and *four* originals…" They met that evening in their little club/mess. Another, slightly larger adjacent space was their orderly room. Further forward was a space Willis *acquired* for *his* use.

"Who's the clerk?" Ishim wondered.

"Boy named Grissom," Grimes said. "McTee pulled him out…"

"Has he got a *bugle?*" Steele asked.

"He *does*, sir," McTee answered. "We'll begin bugle calls tomorrow morning."[1]

"Where'd they get the typewriter?" Ishim asked.

"Willis had it; swore up and down it *didn't* come from the *ship's* inventory."

Steele listened as he scanned the sheaf of orders that McTee and Grissom drew up. The header of the first order said it all:

> BY ORDER OF LIEUT EDMUND A. STEELE,
> COMMANDING TROOP MOVEMENT ABOARD SS

---

[1] Company clerks before the 1950s, musical or not, were also unit buglers.

EUPHRATES, THE 1ST PROVISIONAL MACHINE GUN
INSTRUCTOR COMPANY SHALL BE ORGANIZED IN
ACCORDANCE WITH ARMY REGULATION…

"Makes it all look *legal*," Steele murmured. "How would…?"

"They're *Regulars*," Grimes nodded. "They know how the Army bureaucracy *works*. McTee probably knows this stuff with no need to look it up. Look:"

LIEUT EDMUND A. STEELE ASSUMES THE ROLE OF
COMMANDER OF THE AFOREMENTIONED UNIT…

"Almost makes it look like we're supposed to be doing this," Brick grinned. "Got orders for the officers *and* the NCOs…"

***

"Sir," McTee knocked on Steele's door after retreat.[1] "You sent for me?"

"I *did*, Top. C'mon in," Steele said. "Have a seat." McTee sat gingerly. "Top, *what* happened this afternoon…?"

"Sir?"

"At formation, out on deck, those cheers…"

"Men *need* to be led, sir," McTee said, "but they need to know what they're being led *into*. And as you pointed out, these men are Regulars, used to being *told* what to do and when to do it, day in and day out. They came here a disorganized mob just waitin' for the next order, but you've organized 'em. They're *relieved*, sir," McTee declared, "and I believe, grateful. Now they have a sense of purpose; they know what they're doing and what's expected of them."

"I find that hard to believe, Top."

"Well, sir, you *may* have to get used to it. You know the officer's job in this man's Army is to *sign* for everything…"

"That's what we're *told*, yes. We're also to *lead*…"

"Yes, but you *know* leading a horse to water only works if an NCO *finds* the water and *says* it's safe to drink?"

"I'll grant you that."

---

[1] End of the duty day.

"NCOs *run* the Army, sir. Officers may *lead* it, and may do all the high-level *thinking*. But we *run* it."

"Granted."

"If I may be so bold, sir…why'd you *take* a commission?"

"You may: *briefly*, the Army *asked*; I *answered*."

"Need *more* than that. The higher you rise, the farther you can fall. Even *Corporals* know that."

"I thought I could make more of a contribution with a commission."

"*That's* better. So, you *want* to serve, to *lead*…"

"Yes."

"So do our men, sir; most of them want to serve. We don't have but one or two refugees[1] in *this* outfit." McTee looked thoughtful. "But we've got just enough of *this* and *that* to form a unit…"

"Think it was intentional?" Steele asked. "Our organization—or our compliment of *men*—I mean?"

"I've been *trying* to work that out. We've got three clerks, two supplymen, a couple mechanics, even some signalers and telephonists[2] among our infantrymen…*very* odd. And to answer your question, sir, it's too *good* a mix to be random dumb luck. It's like somebody got all these guys together to make an *independent* outfit; I just can't puzzle out *why*. Sir, you lead men and sign for stuff. *You* do that; *we'll* do the rest. One *more* thing…"

"Yes?"

"*Hope* and *respect* are the two parts of men's morale: *hope* for the future and *respect* for those they believe will *lead* them there. If you lead them the way you'd want to be led, give them *hope*, *respect* them as *men*, give 'em the tools to fight and they'll *perform* and *you'll* be a *superb* commander."

---

[1] Men who joined the military to get away from the outside world were often called "refugees" by the professionals. Many assimilated; some did not.

[2] In 1917, the *telephonists* were members of the Coast Artillery Corps. The *signalers* who used flags, pidgeons, and heliographs were members of the Signal Corps.

"*More* words of wisdom, Top," Steele grinned.

"Aside from that, sir," McTee smiled, "get stuff done *for* them and they'll *love* you for it. *You*, sir, *and* your officers, are *real* operators."

"Thanks, Top. You did a pretty fair job yourself getting all those orders cut *and* organizing the platoons. Now, If we had *cooks*…"

"We *do*, sir," McTee answered. "We have *four* of them." McTee shook his head. "And the cooks don't have any *inclination* to become machine-gunners. I'll detail them into the mess tomorrow, if *that* suits the Captain."

"I'll speak with him."

"*Thank* you, sir. Good *evening*."

***

Dear Charlie
You won't believe what I did today. Did you ever
make your own unit? Ever heard of it done? Washington
did it; militias do it all the time…but now…?

The knock on Steele's cabin door that night seemed unnatural: forceful, yet quiet. "Yes?"

"I brought *coffee*, sir," a voice answered.

"*What?*"

"*Coffee*, sir."

"All right; come in."

An older soldier opened the door carrying a tray. "Where would you *like* it, sir?" he asked softly.

"The chair there's fine," Steele, somewhat surprised, pointed to the other chair. The soldier set the tray down. On it was a pot, a mug, a small pitcher, and a sugar bowl. A spoon and napkin nestled comfortably next to the mug. Steele stared at the tray as if it were an apparition.

"Can I get you anything *else*, sir?"

Blinking out of his reverie, Steele asked, "what's your *name*, soldier?"

"Rodgers, sir," he answered. He might have been thirty or fifty; it was hard to tell.

"Who *told* you to...?"

"I'm a messman,[1] sir. I took the initiative and secured these from the galley."

"Uh-huh." Steele was...baffled is one *way* to put it. "Didn't know the Army *had* messmen."

"Well, sir, I was a gentleman's gentleman on civvy street," Rodgers answered smoothly. "When I enlisted, I told them I had been *in service* and they made me an aide to General Harris in Washington. I had no *other* Army jobs, so *they've* always called me a *messman*. When I wasn't doing *that*, I was General Harris's *private secretary*...."

"You *know* General Harris? He's been in the Adjutant General's Corps for a *dog's* age. He'll probably *get* the top job..."

"*Yes*, sir."

"Uh-huh." Steele waited a pace. "You *don't* sound..."

"My parents *were* English, sir; moved to New York with the Astors before I was born. Their English nannies and tutors taught me with *their* children." He was polite and patient.

"I see. Rodgers, Lieutenants don't *rate* personal servants. I find the idea of officer *privileges* to be un-American; certainly un-democratic. What do *you* say?"

"*I* say, sir, that the responsibility of command weighs heavy on an officer's head."

"I believe that Lieutenant Colonels and above rate enlisted aides," Steele mused. "But how did *you* end up *here?*"

"I received orders like everyone *else* here, sir; I *follow* orders. So, here I *am*."

"Ah, yes." Steele gazed at the tray. "So you're also a hand with Army paperwork? How about...first aid?"

"I have *some* facility with *minor* injuries, sir..."

"Ah." Steele waited a pace, working out what... "Rodgers: you shall be *a* Company Clerk who, when the need arises, will work with the cooks and bring refreshment to those in *need—particularly* at meetings—from the mess. *I* don't take milk or sugar, *but*...I know some of my *officers* do. You may *also* serve

---

[1] A mess servant in naval/maritime service.

the *sick* when needed. However, the only brass you will *polish* is your own. Do I make myself clear?"

"*Perfectly*, sir."

"Good. Now…" Steele sampled the coffee. "I find it hard to believe *this* came from an urn…"

"You have a *discriminating* palate, sir."

"*Thank* you, Rodgers. Now…tomorrow, find Corporal Grissom and give *him* a hand. Tell Sergeant McTee *I* sent you."

"*Yessir*."

3rd August, SS Euphrates, North Atlantic.

Introduced the meter system[1] to the men today; it's what they use in France so we'll use it, too. A different way to measure, but the mil[2] is going to be important to us. Organized a soccer match between platoons.

4th August, SS Euphrates, North Atlantic.

Cooks are more than willing, prepared…this man, Peng, will be valuable…

It was mid-morning when McTee tapped Steele on the shoulder in class. "Cooks, sir," he whispered.

In a corridor outside the steamy hold, Steele met a Sergeant and a Corporal. "Farrell, sir;" "Cohen, sir," they said.

"Ah," Steele nodded. "You're our ranking cooks?"

"Yessir," Farrell said. "Never *wanted* to be on the firing line. There're two more…"

"I *heard*. How long have *you* been a cook, Sergeant Farrell?"

-----

[1] Metric, or SI system. Its use in the US was uneven in 1917.

[2] Milliradian, or *mil*, equal to 1/6400th of a circle, or roughly one-twentieth of a degree.

"I just celebrated nineteen years in the Army, sir," Farrell answered. He was the older of the two, *certainly* old enough to be retired. "I *applied* for cook as soon as Congress authorized 'em in '99."

"You were one of the Army's *first* official cooks, then?"

"I *taught* in the *first* cook's school class in '06, sir," Farrell declared.

"And you would do *what* for recipes *if* we get equipment and supplies?"

"The *cook's manual,* sir," the Corporal answered. "We go nowhere *without* it."

"Ah, ha." Steele turned to the Corporal. "And you…Cohen, is it?"

"Yessir," Cohen nodded. "Cook and baker." He was dark, with a prominent nose and coarse hair.

"Well, can you work in the galley with the ship's cooks?"

"Well, sir," Cohen said uneasily, "we *would,* but…"

"What he *means* is, sir, *that* galley ain't fit to cook in, even if we *have* been eating out of it," Farrell interrupted. "Needs a *thorough* cleaning."

"All right. Can *you*…?"

"If we had another four *hands,* we could, sir, *but*…" Farrell sighed.

"Those cooks got a *union,* sir…" Cohen interrupted. "Won't let us do *anything*."

"Sir," came Rodgers' voice from somewhere behind Cohen. "If I may?"

The tone, the gentle reassurance of Rodger's voice kept Steele from being startled by it, but it rattled the cooks. "Rodgers," Steele asked, "you have something to add?"

"Sir, there are *two* galleys on this vessel. The *after* galley is in use; the smaller *forward* galley is not."

"If I may be so *bold*, Rodgers, how do you *know* this?" Steele asked.

"I've done some *exploring*, sir."

"Did you do some *testing* as well?"

"I did. It would appear as if the forward galley is perfectly functional, albeit *without* ice in the icebox, and has only two ovens. And it is *reasonably* clean, sir."

"Would anyone object if we used the forward galley?" Steele asked no one in particular.

Farrell and Cohen looked at each other. "I don't *know*, sir..." Farrell said finally.

"I don't think they *would*, sir," Rodgers answered. "At least she ship's steward dosen't *think* so."

"You've *spoken* to...?" Steele started.

"I *have*, sir. A very *coarse* but *pleasant* fellow. He explained that the union contract allows only union members to cook for the union *crew* and officers, sir. They feed *us* only with a bonus. I believe the steward will intercede with the Captain if needed."

Farrell grinned, nodded. "Their head cook *is* their *union* steward, sir."

"Then..." Steele and Farrell exchanged nods. "*Corporal* Rodgers can work it out with you and the steward?"

"*Yes*sir."

"Ah, one more thing, while I'm thinking about it," Steele said. "What about utensils?"

"Cooks have their *own* knives, sir," Farrell answered. "And we *all* have at *least* a mess kit cup and a #56 dipper[1] in our barracks bags, and I've got a hanging scale. The *other* things...we can improvise or borrow."

"Very well," Steele said. "Sergeant Farrell, I'm giving you *two rockers* and putting you in charge of the mess and sanitation section as a part of the company HQ. *Carry* on."

***

As Steele scribbled in his diary, a knock on the stateroom door roused Brick from his nap. "Drop *dead*," he growled. "We don't *need* any..."

"Sir," McTee said. "Someone you..."

---

[1] Measures of 1-1/2 pints and one quart, respectively. With these two, Army cooks made nearly everything.

"Who?" Steele asked.

"That *mechanic* you wanted to meet…"

"All right."

A small man, barely five feet six with slightly Asiatic features, stepped into the room. "Private Peng, sir," he said.

"I'm told you're a mechanical genius, Peng," Steele said.

"*I* wouldn't say *that*, sir."

"Where you *from*, Peng?"

"San Francisco, sir."

"Your name…?"

"My *grandfather's* name, sir. I'm a second generation American. Grandfather kept books for the Union Pacific; he had my father with an Italian/Irish prostitute he *married* the day before Dad was born. *My mother* is English and German."

"What's your father *do?*"

"Teaches mathematics at Berkley, sir…"

"What did *you* do *before* you joined up…?"

"I learned mechanics from my uncles, worked in their wagon and auto shop. My cousin experimented with machine guns and motorcycles in the Napa Valley, and I worked with *him* for a while. I enlisted in '15…"

"Other than motorcycles and machine guns, what…?"

"I'm a *scratch* hand at five-card draw, sir."

Steele grinned. "Do you have to defend your heritage very often, Peng?"

"Often enough that it no longer bothers me, sir."

"Do you know the Benet-Mercier?"

"Yessir, but I've *mostly* worked on Vickers and Colt guns."

"Can you *weld?*"

"Gas *and* electric, sir."

"What, ah…where *were* you before you got orders for here?"

"Ordnance Corps, sir."

"Very well, Peng." Steele sighed. "Thanks for coming by."

After Peng left, Brick noisily rolled off his bunk. "Seems to *me*," he said, tired, "that we have *at least* one each of everything we need in this outfit."

"Damn near," Steele sighed, "damn near."

5th August, SS Euphrates. Noticed a large Smith family crest on the wall just outside the Captain's quarters. What little I know of the Pattons is that the Smiths of Virginia are where most of their money comes from,[1] and Gen. Pershing *is* engaged to his sister.

Which makes me think it's no coincidence that Capt. Patton should have been at Ft. Dix.

1st Platoon won the soccer tournament by default when a 3rd Platoon player kicked our only ball overboard.

13th August, Boulogne-sur-Mer, France. Today we arrived in France…Never make the men do anything you don't, won't or haven't…Introduced to bubble and squeak…Genl. Lawrence is quite the character… I knew the British were tired; Talbott told us as much…Dona and Talbott are off to see their families…The men learn a new song…

"*All* right; *get* along there," McTee shouted at the men along the quayside. "*Fall in* along those tracks; company formation by platoons. *You*, there, just *hoist* your *bag* over your shoulder and…*get* moving, you *meatballs*…*fall* the *Hell* in!"

Steele walked down the gangway behind his men who, in ten short days, *seemed* to shape up into the semblance of a

---

[1] The illustrious Smiths of Virginia were Patton's mother's family.

company…even with a head count of just over a hundred.

"Sir," McTee saluted as Steele touched French soil, "formed as instructed."

"Very well; *thank* you, First Sergeant." Steele drew himself up in front of the four blocks of men; the Headquarters Section on his far left had never fallen in before. "Well, *here* we *are*…"

"Where's *here*, sir?" a voice asked.

"*This* is Boulogne-sur-Mer, which means Boulogne by the sea." Steele turned to see Talbott and Dona shaking hands with a British officer near a line of motor wagons. "As you can *smell*, they do a lot of *fishing* here…" There was a ripple of laughter. "We have a job to do that President Wilson *sent* us for, so we might as well get *on* with it…right?"

"*Yes, sir*," came the loud response.

"All right. Officers and platoon Sergeants report to me," he pointed to a shack near the quayside, "over *there*. The rest of you take a break in place."

A few minutes later, Steele explained: "That's our transport, I suppose," he pointed to the motor wagons.

Talbott, shaking his head with his hands on his hips, ambled towards them. "No *bloody* good, lads," he sighed. "I suppose hoping someone'd be waiting for us *was* too much to ask."

"Who're *they* for?" Steele asked.

"Another draft of replacements," Talbott said. "This is one of our principal ports of entry from Blighty."[1]

"Ah," Steele said. "So, *what's*…?"

"I shall *have* to wire the *camp*, I suppose," Talbott said. "*Bloody* nuisance. But…" he said, "*yours* will have to move to other accommodations. I can find *billets* for your officers…"

"We'll billet *with* the men," Steele declared.

"Yes, I keep forgetting; *sorry*, old chap." Talbott turned. "I can show you where you can stay the night." He smiled wanly. "I shall cadge a bedroll from somewhere and billet *with* you. Your *Yank* ways are rubbing off on me. I don't even have a *batman*…"[2]

---

[1] Great Britain, in the vernacular.

[2] Enlisted aide. Unlike in the US Army, *most* British officers had one.

"Stop *complaining*, Ian," Dona grunted in English, shouldering his bags. "Your *valets de chambre* make you lazy...."

The march up the road was brief—less than a mile—but after two weeks at sea, the men were stiff, despite their twice-daily run five times around the football field-size main deck. Steele, his officers, and his NCOs all carried their cylindrical barracks bags over their shoulders with their blanket rolls wrapped around them endwise, just like the men did. Steele's baseball bat jammed into his shoulder uncomfortably.

"Ugh," Steele grunted as soon as they arrived. The smell and traces of the previous occupants of the warehouse—horses— wafted out to meet him. "Let's get this place mucked out. Mike: find tools and someplace to put..."

"Who's in *charge* here?" a gruff voice asked.

"*Sir*," Steele answered, turning to find the source: a Brigadier General in a staff car. "Lieutenant Steele, sir."

"Ah, Steele; we were told to *expect* you. Talbott; is that *you* over there? You look *fagged*, man."

"Just got off the boat and *marched* here, sir," Talbott answered, saluting. "Trying to work out why these *Colonial* officers are always marching *with* the other ranks rather than *riding* like *gentlemen*."

"Of course, Talbott; that's why I *sent* you to the Colonies, being *half* an American yourself," the General declared, climbing out of the car. "See your family there?"

"I *did*; *thank* you, sir. Brigadier Lawrence: permit me to introduce *Commandant* Henri Dona, French Army, and Lieutenant Edmund Steele, United States Army. *Commandant*; Lieutenant; Brigadier Charles Lawrence, Machine Gun Corps, British Army."

"Sir," Steele and Dona saluted.

Lawrence returned the honor, stripped off his gauntlet, and extended his hand. "*Commandant*; Lieutenant, I am *so* glad to meet you," he said.

"Sir," Steele answered. "Pleasure's mine."

"*Monsieur le General*," Dona grinned.

"They've put you up in *this* barn," Lawrence clucked his tongue. "Shouldn't treat our *friends* this shabbily."

"Since our transport *wasn't* here, sir, they had to find *somewhere* for us," Steele answered.

"Yes, I would suppose. Still…Talbott," Lawrence walked away; Talbott followed, gesturing to Steele to wait. After a few moments, Talbott turned and waved Steele towards him.

"Lieutenant," Lawrence said, "Major Talbott tells me you are one of the *best* machine-gun officers in the American Army. Your army has tasked you and the others with creating a *motorized machine gun company…?*"

"Yessir," Steele answered. "Machine-gunners, we shall *be*, sir."

"Very good, Lieutenant. We shall have *some* of the required equipment ready at your next stop. We will embark you on trains in the morning. Now there's *dinner* available for you and your officers, if you *wish.*"

"We mess with our men, sir," Steele said.

Lawrence smiled slightly and nodded. "Of course, Lieutenant." He thought briefly, motioned to a Sergeant in the staff car. "Sergeant Putnam; we mess *here* tonight."

***

"*Marvelous* bubble and squeak," Lawrence said after downing his chow with alarming alacrity.

"Is *that* what you call this fried potatoes and cabbage, sir?" Steele asked. It was filling and, he believed, both cheap and quick.

"It is, *indeed*, Steele," Talbott answered. "*Just* like me old *Mother* used to make. *Bloody* good common tucker for *common* people. *Some* add whatever *meat* they've got in their larders."

"*We* call it *pomme et chou*," Dona added, mopping his plate with bread. "Needs *garlic* or *oignons….*"

"It's kept Ireland *alive* for *centuries*," Lawrence declared. "So, Lieutenant Steele," he set his tin plate aside. "I understand you've been in the Army for some years…"

"Since 1914, sir," Steele answered.

"And all of your *officers* as well?"

"Yessir/nosir," came the chorus of replies. Only Ishim had been in longer than Steele.

"Well," Lawrence said, "your coming to France has been a *considerable* relief."

"How's *that*, sir?" Buchalter asked.

"Because we're *quite* at the end of our tether, old chap." Lawrence briefly looked lost. "We can *hold* our position, but we cannot advance. The *Germans*, God *rot* their *livers*, can hold out in Flanders forever if they wish. *Passchendaele* will break us like *Verdun* broke the French." Dona nodded sadly.

"We *heard* of French mutinies, sir," Brick said.

"Not *quite* that, my lad, but...*nearly* that. I'd call them more *work stoppages*, like our sailors did with *their* mutiny in Nelson's day. They said they'd fight if the French came out, and they *did*. But they by *God* would *not* attack unless Parliament addressed their pay and their *God-awful* food.[1] And those poor French *poilus* wouldn't waste their lives in attacks they knew wouldn't go *anywhere* last month."

"So...what role are we Americans expected to fulfill, sir?" Ishim asked.

"I shall *tell* you, Lieutenant, and I'll have you *drawn and quartered* if you say it came from me." He hunched over, rubbing his hands together. "My friends, many of my fellow Englishmen and my French comrades want you to just fill in our ranks, but *I* say that would be a waste. No," his voice dropped an octave. "*I* say your President Wilson has the right idea: you Americans are our *reinforcements*, not our *replacements*. *I* say that in *time*— soon, perhaps—your General Pershing will command a mightier host than *anything* Europe has ever *seen*. If I don't miss my guess, America will mobilize an army of one or even *two* million men; perhaps *more*. If not *next* year, then by 1919 Britain and France will surely *gleefully* follow them when they fight their way into Germany."

"An *American* army of *two million*," Brick mumbled quietly. "Over *here?* Not in *my* lifetime."

---

[1] In 1797, when the series of actions called the Great Mutiny began, British sailors hadn't had a pay increase in over a century and a half. Some food casks issued that year had been put up during the American Revolution and earlier.

***

"I shall take my leave of you, Lieutenant Steele," Dona said, extending his hand.

"Off home, *Commandant?*" Steele asked. The company was bedding down in the barns and sheds they had for shelter.

"*Mai oui.* I have not seen my wife or children for nearly a year. When I return, we shall begin *our* training in earnest."

"Where in France *is* your family?"

"A small town near the Spanish border, Orloron-Sainte-Marie. Do you *know* it?"

"Never *heard* of it, sir."

"It will only take me two or three days to get there by train. I only hope to see Maurice before he has to report to the depot...."

"Your son, sir?"

"My oldest; he is *now*," Dona searched for the word, "*dix-sept?*"

"Seventeen?" Steele asked. "They take boys *that*...?"

"Yes. So do the *Boche* and the English. I have two sons and two daughters. I *pray* this war does not consume them all."

***

Mademoiselle from Armenteers,
Parley-vous!
Mademoiselle from Armenteers,
Parley-vous!
Mademoiselle from Armenteers,
She hasn't been kissed for forty years,
Rinky-dinky parley-vous!

"Any idea what *that* is, Top?" Steele listened to the lyrics—there were several, many bawdy—with bemusement.

"A popular song with the British, sir," McTee answered. "Not sure *where* they *got* it from, but there it *is*."

"Don't suppose they're *hurting* anything," Steele murmured.

"No...catchy, though, sir..."

"That it *is*, Top."

"All *right*: everybody *off*," McTee shouted from the ground, opening boxcar doors as he did. "Everybody, fall *in*, facing *me*…c'mon, you guys; hurry it up. *Move, move, move!*"

Steele swung down from the last car, stared at the sign on the boxcar; *40 Hommes; 8 Chevaux.* "Anybody know what that forty and eight means?"

"Forty men or eight horses," Brick answered. "Carrying capacity for the cars."

"No *wonder* they smell like horseshit," Ishim grumbled.

"All right, men," McTee called. "*Form* up. *C'mon*, boys; let's show our *hosts* what we…hey, you *meatballs! Fall in! Dress* and *cover!*"

With *alarming* alacrity, the company fell into its large platoon formations, squad leaders watching down the ranks, checking the dress while the platoon sergeants checked how each man in the rear squads stood *exactly* behind those in front.

"Company *formed* and *ready*, sir," McTee declared.

Steele looked around the place where they unloaded, expecting to see buildings…or a tent city…or *some*thing…but…

They were in the middle of a recently cleared wood. Woodcutters had stacked fresh-cut logs around the two-hundred yard-square clearing. Piles of brush burned nearby, where more woodcutters expanded the clearing on both sides of the tracks. A handful of erected tents and several mountains of canvas, wooden poles and stakes awaited Steele's men.

"We weren't able to accommodate your people well, old boy," Talbott said lightly. "This new *expansion* camp…well, it needs some *muscle,* as *you* like to say. The Corps shall leave you *to* it for a fortnight while they sort out more *trainers* for you. And I'm off to see my family…"

"Uh-huh," Steele sighed. "See you in a couple of weeks, then?"

"Aye, you shall," Talbott waved.

"Some *muscle,*" Steele sighed, then shouted, "all *right!* First, *land* clearing for the tents. Lieutenant *Grimes*: lay out three platoon streets; *fifty* yards long. Lieutenant *Ishim*: organize *three squads* to sort through this canvas…"

"*Tools,* sir?" Brick asked.

"Over *there,* I *think,*" Steele pointed to a small stack of crates. "Find what there *is* there, else use our *own* shovels. Lieutenant *Buchalter*; find water, firewood, and rocks for the mess. Lieutenant *Brick*; HQ Section can get the *supplies* off the *cars…*"

"Sir," the officers answered.

"Sergeant *Willis,*" Steele called. "Report to me," he looked around, "over *there.*"

Willis joined Steele at a cleared spot near a road that paralleled the railroad tracks. "Sir?"

"Willis, we're going to need *some* of *everything.* I'm uncertain just what we're *supposed* to have…" Steele began.

"We want to *start* with mess facilities," Willis nodded. "We *have* a couple of scalding pots, and *some other* cookware. Then we need *milled lumber*; *tools*; *lime* for the *latrines…*"

"Yes, that's *right,*" Steele said. "But I don't…"

"*I* do, sir," Willis said. "I'll get *started,*" he declared, and…*seemed* to *vanish.*

Steele started searching among the crates and strange-looking equipment he *thought* he recognized from the manual, *but…*

McTee appeared. "Sir, *cooks* here with some questions."

"*Water,* sir," Farrell said.

"Yes," Steele said, "what *about…?*"

"There's a water point half-a-mile back up the line, sir," Farrell said. "And we have two water *casks.* We need to detail men to *fill* them and fetch them here."

"All right, Sergeant; take men from HQ when the cars are…"

"*Latrines*, sir," Cohen said.

"I found a *low* spot for the latrine sinks, sir," Cohen added. "Down the hill there just a few yards, there's a *flat*…"

"Very well, Corporal. Take two men and start…"

"Sir," Peng came up behind Steele. "I've got material to build at *least* one wheelbarrow…"

"Get started…"

"Sir," Rodgers declared. "I'll put an aid station over by the mess sinks…"

"Very *well*…"

"Sir, *four men* for a *supply* tent…"

"Go *ahead*…"

"Sir, we have five hammers, two saws and a keg of big spike nails…"

"Build platforms for the supply, mess and aid tents…"

* * *

McTee entered the HQ wall tent, setting his lantern down on a crate, sitting on a cot. "Grumbling about the Maconochie[1] that Farrell made *edible* in a scalding pot with some wild garlic he dug up," he sighed, sitting on the other end of the crate and beginning to unwrap his puttees.

"Willis is addressing the food situation," Steele said casually, scanning another roster. "At least he *said* he would be when I last saw him…this morning…Top…?"

"Sir?"

"Seems to me there's a lot of very, ah…"

"*Smart* people here, yes, sir; I've noticed that. Including yourself. Good night, sir."

"Night, Top."

---

[1] British canned ration of sliced turnips, carrots, potatoes, onions, haricot beans and beef in a thin broth—edible but detested.

"Ned," Brick stuck his head inside the tent that morning, "you'll need to *see* this."

"OK; I'll come." Steele put his diary down, closing his pen inside.

A small locomotive pulling several flat cars rolled down the tracks. While not unusual for this spur—they'd seen others—this one *slowly* rolled to a stop. A small man with an old-fashioned American officer's cap, Sam Browne belt, empty epaulets,[1] and quartermaster collar tabs jumped down from the cab. "Looking for a Captain… *Steele*…" he said.

"*What* have you *got* there?" Brick asked, gazing at the flat cars covered in canvas.

"*Four* mess wagons, *three* cool storage cans, *four* cooks' utensil sets, *twelve* gallons of fuel oil, and *nine tons* of *food*," the officer read from a stack of paper clamped to a board. "All for a…ah…1ˢᵗ Provisional Machine Gun…"

"That's *us*," Brick acknowledged.

"Then I need Captain Steele's *signature*…"

"*Lieutenant* Steele," Brick said. "You *mean*…?"

"Nope; says here, *Captain*," the officer said. "Maybe I've got the *wrong*…"

"*No, this* is the *right* place, sir," Rodgers, appearing behind Steele, was suddenly fussing with Steele's epaulets. "*Captain* Steele's right *here*. Just got his *new* insignia…"

"Then *here*, sir," the officer said, holding out the board.

Steele casually—he hoped—scanned the top inventory page

---

[1] Army 2ⁿᵈ Lieutenants had no insignia until 1922.

like a man making sure it lists everything he ordered, giving the flatcar an occasional critical glance. Blinking furiously, he called: "Lieutenant Brick, please make sure the fuel tanks are *with* the mess wagons *this time*."

"Ah, *yessir*," Brick said, motioning to McTee and Peng. "Top, Peng, we need to have a *look* before we *unload* the...."

"They're *there*," the officer insisted. "Lieutenant Willis already inspected them."

"Have a look, *any*way," Steele repeated. "Make sure we don't get caught in another *shell game*..."

"*Sir*," the indignant officer protested, "I *assure* you that Lieutenant Willis himself inspected this train. It was bound for Gondecourt before he stopped it and..."

"Lieutenant," Steele said patiently, "I *believe* you, but these things *have* happened to us *before*..."

"Under*stood*, sir," the officer replied, then fell silent as Peng and McTee lifted the tarps on the new field kitchen carts, ice chests, cans of fuel, and crates and barrels of foodstuffs. Steele, trying not to *look* surprised, gazed at the bounty as the men gathered around the train.

Peng and McTee, acting as if this were routine, completed their inspection, and McTee called. "*Looks* like it's all here, sir."

"Very well," Steele sighed...and signed the forms in triplicate. "Let's get it offloaded and..."

That was *all* he had to say...,

***

From two mess wagons, the delicious smell of *fresh* food rose as the men fell in; from another arose the welcoming aroma of baking-powder biscuits. Cauldrons of steaming hot water for cleaning mess kits sat on a low fire.

Steele fell into line like any Private, as did his officers in different places in the queue. The Corporals ahead of him fell quiet; the Privates behind just *stayed* quiet. They shuffled ahead quietly, unlike those elsewhere in the mess line.

Turning around, Steele asked, "what's *your* name, Private?"

"Dent, sir," the Private answered.

"Where are you *from?*"

"Cincinnati, sir."

"You're a *rifleman?*"

"Ah…yessir."

"*Now* you're a *machine-gunner…*"

"If you *say* so, sir…"

"Well, the Army says we *both* are…for the moment."

"That could change, sir?"

"As *fast* as you can *roll* your *puttees*, Dent."

That raised a chuckle from the men nearby. "I think machine-guns might be safer than being in a rifle trench."

"We'll have to *see*, won't we?"

Dent looked puzzled. "You don't *know*, sir?"

"Not firsthand, I don't. Never fired a machine gun at a *living soul*; just some scorpions and paper targets, like everyone *else* in the Army."

"I took some shots at some of them bandits on the border, sir," a Corporal ahead in the line sniffed.

"I *remember* seeing you. What's *your* name, again?"

"Miller, sir."

"Miller, what's *your* trade in this man's Army?"

"I *was* a rifleman, sir. Then I was in the Machine-Gun Section in Mexico with you. *Now*…? Been digging latrines all day…"

"I *thought* you looked familiar. You know, machine gunners need to keep their infantry skills sharp. Can you *teach* those?"

"Ah…*yessir*," Miller said.

"Then you'll be doing *that*, too. Come by the orderly room after chow and we can make you a Sergeant."

That little chat—plus getting fed a decent meal—created positive rumbles of anticipation all along the chow line.

Steele rinsed his mess kit in a boiling cauldron, then took the bubbles and squeak—*this* time with *some* kind of meat—biscuits and coffee to a stump to eat. Two Privates, a Corporal, and a Sergeant joined him on adjacent stumps.

"Sir," the Sergeant said, nodding.

"Sir," the Privates added, watching the Sergeant.

"When will we *see* a machine gun, sir?" the Sergeant ventured.

"After we've built a decent camp," Steele answered.

"Hard to do *that*…here, sir," one Private said sourly. "Lots of stumps; can't line up the tents well…"

"We'll do as best we *can* with what we *have*," Steele said, sipping coffee. "This place ain't *ideal*, and we've got a job of *work* to do, *but* this is what we've *got* and *this* is what we're *told* to do."

The men looked…appreciative. Not happy, but at least not rebellious. "Where are you men from?" Steele asked.

"Stevensville, Oklahoma," "Atlas, Texas," "Nashville, Tennessee," "Flatbush," came the answers.

"Enjoying France so far?"

"Looks a lot like *home*," "Ain't seen much *of* it," "It's OK," "Lots more *trees* than I thought would be in France…"

"How's the chow?"

"It *ain't* like *Momma* used to make," "I've had *worse*," "Considering what the cooks have to *work* with," "Better than that *canned shit* we've *been* eating."

After more similar exchanges, Steele and his men washed their mess kits in the cauldrons, then scrubbed them in a box filled with sand that the cooks had seined through a flour sifter before a final rinse.

That done, Steele went in search of Farrell. He found the mess steward picking through the crates and barrels that made up their larder/pantry while a detail erected two tents end-to-end nearby. "Yessir," Farrell said on seeing Steele. "Was there something you *didn't* like…?"

"Not at all, Sergeant. Just wanted to *compliment* you and your crew on a job well done."

"*Thank* you, sir…"

"Sort of like a fish and loaves story, eh?"

"Well, sir, we used a hundred fifty pounds of fatty meat, *nearly* as much flour, thirty pounds of lard, fifty pounds of cabbages, and fifty of potatoes to feed one hundred three men this evening. Now, I got us on a food and fuel allocation with the British commissary up there…"

"You *did*…?"

"*Yessir*. Part of *my* job as mess steward, sir."

"Good job, Sergeant. Carry on."

17th August, Camiers.

Never question the ways of the supplyman; you might run out of something someday and he won't get it…Just hope this one doesn't land me in jail…This outfit can run itself without officers. NCO's do the important work…Now if only the machine guns would run themselves…

The line of *camions*[1] rolling up the railway embankment, loaded with lumber and crates, gunned their engines before coming to a halt opposite the HQ tent. The rider in the first *camion*—a Captain with "Canada" shoulder bars—swung down, his boots raising dust.

Steele and McTee approached the vista with some haste, hoping the vehicles and their cargo were not mirages that would vanish the closer they got. "Lumber, Top," Steele mumbled. "We can build *better* platforms…"

"We can build proper latrines, sir," McTee said. "And *buildings*…"

The Canadian looked around the camp, stretching his legs and pulling off his gauntlets. Wearing his Captain's bars from yesterday, Steele extended a hand. "Ned Steele, Captain," he said.

"Francis Parterres," the Canadian answered, gripping Steele's hand. The hand was rough and very strong, but Steele could tell that he *tried not* to squeeze. "Number 17 Forestry Company. We *have* your *lumber* and *other* material; Major Willis said it was *urgent*…"

"And he was *right*," Steele agreed. "As you can *see*, we need

---

[1] French for truck, but the French versions were so visually distinctive, both the Americans and British persisted in using that term for *them*.

every *stick* we can lay our *hands* on…"

"Well, no *sticks* here," Parterres said, "just 125,000 board feet of *green* dimensional lumber and a few thousand *duck* boards. That *and* a dozen rolls of tar paper…"

"We'll use all you've got," McTee replied. "And…?"

"*That's* what we thought *queer*," Parterres said. "He *also* said you desperately needed *tools* and *nails?* Sent you over here with nothing at *all*, eh?"

"That's *right*," Steele agreed. "Whereabouts in Canada are you from? *I* hail from Detroit…"

"Indeed? I'm from *Kingston*, just across the river. We have *several* Ontario lads in the company. Small world, eh? Major Willis said he was from Iron Mountain, too?"

"Ah…*yes*, I *believe* you're *right*," Steele agreed. "But we *have* to get…"

"Of course, Captain. If your men can *just*…"

"Yessir," McTee said, turning around. "*Fifty* men, on the double! *C'mon*, you guys…"

Like an army of ants, the 1st Provisional swarmed over the *camions*.

18th August, Camiers.

Some real bigwigs came around this morning. That I

am still in charge sometimes feels like a miracle. Or

maybe I just haven't stepped too far out of line…

"*Brass*, Ned," Brick called to Steele, who had been in a woodpile looking for appropriately sized branches for making machine gun dummies. "Orderly room."

"Who *are* they? Steele asked.

"Patton and some full Colonel. They just rolled up in a Cadillac and started asking questions, like 'who's in charge here,' and 'who authorized all this.' Didn't *sound* all that friendly."

"OK, Mike," Steele said, wiping his hands on his puttees and putting his Sam Browne belt back on. "Let's face some music." Straightening his hat, Steele picked his way through the rough, sparse grass that had been forest floor only a week before. They passed men moving logs and branches, lashing branches into tripods, building platforms from tree trunks and cut lumber, and erecting a flagpole in front of the HQ—two wall tents end-to-end on a rough log platform. The prevailing sounds were hammering and sawing. The frames of several structures had already risen.

Outside, Patton, hands on hips, gazed around him, blank-faced. On seeing Steele, he called out, "*you're* responsible for all this." It was *not* a question.

"*Well*, sir," Steele started, approaching warily, "*You* told me the Army wanted to turn my men into machine-gunners. The Brits put us on the cars[1] and sent us here because they lacked other facilities, so we're building a *camp*…"

Patton cleared his throat and stared at Steele. "Lieutenant…I have *expected* to see many things in my time in the Army, but…" he swept his arm around, " before I saw anything like *this*, I would have expected to see a *cat* nursing *piglets*."

"Does the Captain desire an answer to his direct question?"

Patton broke into a grin. "*No*…" he glanced at Steele's epaulets with a grin, "*Captain*, the Captain does *not* require an answer. Let's…" he gazed around, "*what* do you call this unit?"

"1st Provisional Machine-Gun Instructor Company, sir," Steele said.

"*Just* so," Patton nodded. "The *first* item of business," he went on, pulling a paper out of a gauntlet, "will be to return this *Morning Report*. Though it is a near-facsimile, the adjutant *can't* accept this *hand-drawn* form…"

"Didn't *have* anything else, sir," Steele said. "We created it from memory …"

"Yes, *Captain*," Patton answered patiently. "Considering everything *else*…"

Inside the HQ, a bemused Colonel chatted animatedly with McTee. "Captain Patton," the Colonel said as they approached, "I was *right*. As soon as I saw his name on that morning report, I knew that *somebody* who knew *something* had done *this*." He turned to Steele and stuck out his hand. "Captain, I'm Johnson

---

[1] A common soldier term for being loaded on a train, dating to the Civil War.

Rorshack, Assistant Adjutant General of the AEF." Rorshack was a big man with the overall pleasant demeanor of an innkeeper. "McTee would *not* put his name on something that would bring discredit to the Army."

"*No*, sir," McTee said modestly. "The Colonel knows me too well."

"Sir," Patton said expansively, "*Captain* Steele has organized this company adequately. But..."

"There's *nothing* on the books about it," Rorshack declared. "And what books we *have* made *Steele* out to be a *Lieutenant?*"

"An *error* of *necessity*, sir," McTee declared, suddenly standing *rigidly* at attention.

"One of *those*, McTee?" Rorshack asked with a malicious grin.

"*Yessir*," McTee answered, without flinching. "The *British* made the error in their paperwork and insisted that *Captain* Steele..."

"I could *believe* this," Rorshack nodded. "Took the British Army a hundred years to raise soldier pay by a shilling a day. Hell, they *still* use the lunar quarter[1] to pay their troops. All right," he declared expansively, "Steele, you've shown sufficient efficiency to be in command, and you'll be commanding a *battalion* before too long," Rorshack sighed. "First, *everyone's* getting advanced. *Captain*, do you *have* enough officers?"

"I *believe* so, sir, for *three* platoons." Steele answered. "I have *platoon sergeants* and squad leaders. The book says an infantry company needs *four* platoons, but we don't have the *men* yet. I want to create a few..."

"Yes, yes," Rorshack sighed. "The National Army has an unlimited acceptance for promotions for the moment. I must say, though, Captain, that you have done an admirable job here, making a silk purse from a sow's ear..."

"*Thank* you, sir," Steele said.

"Right," Patton added. "But they need to get *some* connection with AEF?"

"If they want to get *paid*, they do," Rorshack agreed, glancing

---

[1] An irregular three-month long period ending at the end of March, June, September and December.

at Steele. "We will send a detail from AEF up here to straighten your paperwork out to create your *company* properly."

"*Thank* you, sir."

Rorshack inclined his head to Patton, who nodded. "Let's take a walk, Steele." He and Patton walked out of the tent silently, maneuvering around stumps for ten yards, then twenty. They strolled towards the wood line, near where the latrines and showers were being built. "Your name's *Edmund?*" Patton asked. "You go by *Ed?*"

"Ned..."

"Ned; call me George..." Patton noticed a man building a barrel, watching him shave duck boards with a hatchet for several minutes. "He's a lot like you, Ned; resourceful, skilled. Nobody probably asked him."

"They *asked* me, George..."

Patton stopped, turned around, watched Rorshack in a more casual conversation with McTee just outside the tent. "Not *officially*. AEF only *officially* noticed your *unit* when the British said you were *here* and were drawing rations on them..." He stopped. "Pershing *approves* of the unit you, ah, *organized* from *nothing*, but no one but *him* and *me* thought you could *do* it." He looked around. "Congratulations."

"Thank you, sir...George," Steele mumbled. "I, ah, noticed the Smith family crest on our ship, George..."

"*Very* observant, Ned. Did you tell anyone?"

"Only my diary, sir."

"*Thank* you. Another *error of necessity*, I'm afraid. If anyone knew of my family's connection with this *wild* scheme..."

"I understand. This, ah, detail from AEF...?"

"A couple of clerks and an officer." Patton looked at him and grinned. "Your father is a big noise in Michigan politics, I hear; staunchly Republican Michigan is something President Wilson wants on *his* side..."

"I would *think* so..."

"Enough of politics," Patton declared as they stopped at the treeline. "I don't know *how* your motorized machine gun outfit will work, but I believe it will be a good addition to a *tank* formation...better than the footsloggers they've got working with them up at Passchendaele right now…" Patton looked dreamy, as if he imagined himself somewhere else.

"I've never *seen* one of those things…" Steele admitted.

"You will, soon enough," Patton mumbled. "I believe *they* are the *future* of land warfare, not slogging in the mud of trenches."

Just then they heard a sound, a dull booming followed by soft rattling, then more booming…then silence. "What's…?" Steele started.

"*That's* the front," Patton said, staring, blank-faced, eastward. "That's our *future*."

19th August, Camiers.

The most astonishing thing to me is this camp appearing out of nowhere. How many builders working with green lumber could build so many structures so fast?

It never occurred to me before that the sounds we heard at night were artillery and machine guns, carried on the wind from the front all the way to the sea…haunting…how could it be so loud as that? I spent the rest of the morning with an ever-increasing line of men with personal needs that I had to address…

"Yes," Steele, at his new British-made field desk in his office/bunk/orderly room, set his pen down. The room had the unmistakable aroma of fresh-sawn wood. It also had a new, *handmade*, three-panel door that smelled of beeswax, plus an installed as-if-by-magic *glass* window.

"Coffee, sir?" Rodgers offered, bearing the inevitable tray and coffee setup into his office.

"Rodgers," Steele answered patiently, "just *where* did you find a serving tray? And a napkin…?"

"I found sources in Camiers, sir," Rodgers answered.

"And you brought *me* coffee...?"

"I brought refreshment for everyone in the orderly room..."

"What does McTee have you *doing*, Rodgers?"

"I divide my time between the aid station, mess administration, and the personnel rosters, sir. Lately I've been inventorying lumber with Lieutenant Grimes."

"You have *time* for all that?"

"I *make* time, sir." Rodgers cleared his throat. "Just as *you* do, sir; just as *all* the officers and NCOs *should* make time for the men's *concerns*, sir."

"Are you trying to *tell* me something, Rodgers?"

"I believe *so*, sir."

This spurred Steele to check his new window; two Privates, two Corporals waited outside. "Very well," Steele sighed. "Send the first man in."

The Corporal snatched off his hat and entered Steele's office, a tiny space with room for his field desk, his cot, two chairs and not much more. "It's what I've got for now," Steele said. "What can I do for...?"

"Sir, I may as well..." he started.

"What's your name, Corporal?"

"Cooper, sir," the Corporal answered, paused, then took a breath and blurted, "I may as well just *fess* up to it: I *cain't* read."

Steele, caught off-guard, blinked. "Huh?"

"This stuff they want me to read off them charts...I cain't make *heads* or *tails* of it..."

"All right," Steele started....

"So you can do with me what you will, sir," Cooper said loudly, "but I suppose I cain't *be* a machine gunner if I cain't *read*."

"How did you get to be a Corporal without being able to *read*, Cooper?"

That surprised him. "Well, sir, I can read numbers and I can read my name, but..."

"How long have you been in the Army, Cooper?"

"I joined in '05, sir. I reckoned it was a good place to put my feet under the table. Been good to me, too. They made me a Corporal 'cause I *am* good at shootin' *rifles*, but..."

"All right, Cooper," Steele said. "Do you *want* to learn to read?"

Cooper blinked, cleared his throat. "I ain't *had* much schooling, sir..."

"How are you at arithmetic?"

"I can do sums..."

"Again, do you *want* to learn to read?"

"I, ah, wouldn't *mind*, I suppose, sir."

"Then we'll *teach* you. Send in the next man."

"Attleboro, sir," the small Corporal said.

"What can I do for...?"

"Sir, it strikes me that this is a very math-intensive line of work..."

"You're right," Steele answered.

"*Most* of the men can barely *read*..."

"True..."

"Is there any value, sir, to having someone do some, ah...?"

"Attleboro, can you *teach* math?"

"I did *some* formal teaching, sir, before I joined the Army in '11. Been doing it off and on since."

"Can you teach reading?"

"What language, sir? I studied Greek and Latin at university, can do well enough with German and French..."

"English..."

"*Yes*sir..."

"Report back here to me in an hour. Send in the next man."

"Sir: Private Thompson," the Private said.

"What *is* it, Thompson?"

"Sir, the Private wishes to report that the latrines are in danger of flowing into a swamp."

"How do you know this?"

"I've been to the swamp, looking for cattails for a toothache…"[1]

"Did you tell the cooks?"

"No, sir. I…I didn't know I *could*. The Captain…just seemed more…*friendly*…"

"Ah, hah. Very well. *We'll* inform the cooks. Send in the *next* man."

A skinny Private shuffled in. "Sir, request permission to desert…"

"That's *not* something most would-be deserters would ask, ah…what's your name?"

"Sir, the less you know…"

"*Yes*, but…first tell me why…?"

"Sir, I have not *heard* from my folks in nearly a year, and…"

"Didn't you get *leave* before they shipped you here?"

"*No*, sir…"

"I'll get a wire off to the authorities. *Where*…?"

***

"Gentlemen," Steele told his collected officers and NCOs that evening, "we need to tell the men that they can come to *you* for help."

"*That* would be…" Grimes started.

"The way *we* are *going* to handle problems, sir," McTee intoned. "The company commander spent most of his morning dealing with the men's problems; some of them *you* could have handled just as well…"

"Top," Steele chided, gently. "I can defend myself. There's only so many hours in a day, fellows," he added, "and some of the men's concerns could be serious. A Private *has* to be able to report an imminent sanitation issue to the cooks…"

"That swamp *wasn't there* until it rained last night," Farrell said. "Cutting down the trees changed the water flow."

"All right," Steele said. "Make it known that they can and

---

[1] Cattails have been used for many medicinal purposes.

should come to you *first*. If *you* can't address it, buck it up to me."

And *that* was the way, contrary to the Army tradition of top-down management, *Steele's* outfit worked.

20ᵗʰ August, Camiers.

The prodigal returneth. His story is as convincing as a patent medicine drummer selling a miracle cure. I suppose anything they could catch him doing...

"Sergeant *Willis*," Steele said as soon as he saw his supplyman swing off the *camion* that morning. "*What* have you brought us *today?*" The company was noisily running around the camp on a round of physical training. While spending their days hammering together storage buildings, a mess hall, and other structures based on rough plans created by Grimes, who apprenticed as a carpenter, they also did physical training twice a day.

"Driving from Amiens, sir," Willis declared. "Got a few, ah, *toys* in the back, here..." He beckoned Steele and McTee to follow him, lifted the tarpaulin, and..."*Lewis* guns, sir."

Steele blinked, gazing at the stack of crates. "*Lewis* guns..."

"Not much *ammunition*, I'm afraid, sir, but..."

"Willis," McTee sighed, "just *how* in the *name* of *bleeding Jesus* did you get a truckload of Lewis guns, *and* a *camion* to carry 'em? Them *damn* things gotta to be *accounted* for, ya know."

"*Well* aware of that, Top," Willis answered cheerfully, producing a sheaf of paper out of a satchel he wore around his shoulder. "All *perfectly...*"

"Willis, I *know* you were in the stockade at Fort Robinson," McTee said.

"Oh, *that* was a misunderstanding, Top," Willis said with a straight face. "Got it all straightened out, and they released me..."

"After eighteen months," McTee went on.

"And *cleared* my *record*, Sarge," Willis declared. "Write *Washington* and *see* if..."

"Very well, Sergeant," Steele interrupted, with a dismissive wave, "we'll save *that* for later. Right now, I'm more concerned about reports of you impersonating an officer...*several* officers, in fact. Any *truth* to...?"

"*Well*, sir," Willis declared, not missing a beat, "I have *seven brothers;* I ran into *two* of them here in France. *Fine* men, they turned out to be, too. Why, Charlie's a *Major* and Harold's a *Lieutenant*. I hadn't seen them for a dog's age and here they were in the Army, same as me. I *may* have mentioned our supply situation and they *might* have..."

"Sent material and supplies *here* just *because*...?" Steele asked, then..."all right, Sergeant. Let's see about this *camion*..."

"It's a *pool camion*, sir," Willis answered. "Got it *signed* for here..." he rooted around in his satchel. "Just let me find...*here*."

Steele read the form, as well as his grammar-school French would allow, signed *Staff Sergeant Willis*. "Willis, can you find some paint and paper for making signs...?"

"And *field gear*," McTee added. "We're short on cartridge belts, *helmets*, and office equipment like *field* desks and *filing* cabinets..."

"*All* in *hand*, Top," Willis said solemnly. "Should have American field gear in the next week..."

"And another typewriter," Steele said. "And we have *damn* few forms or even copies of the regulations..."

"*Add* them to the list, sir," Willis said, fetching a small pad from a pocket. "*Type*writers...*field* desks...*filing* cabinets..." He stopped, thoughtful. "Forms. *They* might be harder to come by, sir. But...regulations..."

"Start with a manual for courts-martial," McTee growled.

"Top," Willis said, acting hurt. "Are you suggesting...?"

"No, Willis," Steele added, "he's saying it *out loud*. If you get caught doing what we think you're doing, we'd better be familiar with what our *trials* will look like."

21ˢᵗ August, Camiers.

Willis will make us all liable for his larcenies. We

have machine guns at last, though almost certainly not

the kind we're going to be using once we go into

"Fall in!"

On the railway embankment platform, McTee waited patiently. Satisfied, he nodded to Steele, who got on the platform and called, *"post!"* As his platoon leaders moved to the front of their units, the platoon sergeants moved to the back in the time-honored fashion.

"Men," Steele began, "I know we've been through a *trial* lately, but it'll only get worse. Now…our *real training* will begin this morning…"

There followed some excitement in the ranks; even the officers hadn't been told. "I know, yeah. Surprised *me*, too. But as of this afternoon, *this* outfit will no *longer* be *provisional*…"

"Hey," someone shouted, "does that mean our mail will catch up to us?"

"It *does*," Steele answered. "*And* our pay." That started a minor cheer. "And *now*, gentlemen, that *estimable* Limey you've *all* come to know *and* hate…*Major Talbott* is here to introduce you to the mysteries of the Lewis gun…"

***

"Congratulations, sir," Steele extended his hand to Able Lucas, now a Major. "I *knew* you were meant for bigger things."

"Thanks, *Captain* Steele," Lucas answered. "Congratulations to you, too, and *not* just on your commissioning. Building a company *and* a camp from scratch; *quite* the feat."

"Not as hard as it looks if you've got a top kick like Sergeant McTee. I just hope we can *keep* him…"

"Yes; certainly," Lucas answered; McTee nodded but said nothing. "Now, here's a *plan* from AEF…" He laid out a large roll of brown paper on a big table Steele and Grimes built, surrounded by all of Steele's officers and senior NCOs. "Commander; executive officer; admin section and four platoons. Now, *here's* a departure: a *training section*, with a training officer, training NCO and two clerks."

"Why a separate section?" Brick asked.

"Ranges, equipment, and ammunition take a great deal to organize and build," Lucas answered. "Training section coordinates all those, *first* for the instructors; *then* for the people they train."

"Yeah," Buchalter said, "but do we need *another* officer for…?"

Lucas nodded. "Yes, *we* do: me."

Silence. Everyone looked at Steele. "You'd *outrank* me, sir…" he mumbled.

"Yes, *but*…" Lucas smiled, "I wouldn't *command* the unit. I'd just be in charge of the *training*. Once you become a *battalion*, they will abolish *my* role…."

"A *battalion*…?" Ishim asked, surprised.

"Eventually, yes," Lucas said. "They didn't *tell* you?"

"We were told *company*," Ishim answered, looking at Steele.

"At first, yes," Lucas said, "but *eventually*…"

"But we're *instructors*," Grimes chimed in, "ain't we?"

"For *now*," Lucas said; Steele shrugged, nodded. "Yes, we will contribute instructors to other units once we have *enough*. But," he smiled, "as we all know, not everyone *can* teach. Once we train everyone to be gunners, we will choose the most suitable as instructors and detach them as needed. Now…" Lucas sighed. "All the MGCs[1] are *supposed* to be motorized, but…" he shrugged. "When we'll *get* vehicles and mechanics, I cannot say. But as of *today*, this unit is no longer *provisional*, but the *instructor* part…"

"Me and my bright ideas," Steele sighed.

"Yes," Lucas said. "Took *me* out of the 1st MGB[2] to take this job here…and, *oh*, yes…*here*." He handed out silver bars to all the Lieutenants. "Congratulations; you are now *First* Lieutenants in the National Army. In two days, we march to the sea…."

"For…what, sir?" Steele asked.

---

[1] Machine Gun Companies.

[2] Machine Gun Battalion.

"A demonstration…"

22nd August, On the road to the sea.

Long march, good for the soul but not the feet or anything else. The stiff straps of our unbroken-in rucksacks dig into our shoulders. If we had the means to move the mess wagons and carts for the supplies, we would, but I won't have the men hitched up like animals for the seventeen miles to the sea. So we must make do with canned rations again.

23rd August, Sainte Cecile Plage.

How calm; how peaceful the sea is…They showed us what we do not know, graphically and loudly…what could live through that…all our mathematics makes sense now…

The men sat on benches five hundred yards from the placid sea, on a bluff overlooking the wide, smooth mud flat of a beach. The beach itself was featureless except for four anchored buoys marking the corners of a rough square about two hundred yards to a side.

"Gentlemen," Talbott declared, his hands clasped behind the small of his back, "*you* are *going* to be machine gunners, but you do not know what *that means*…"

"We've been *training* on Lewis guns…" "What have we been *doing* for a month…?" "*Most* of us were in the Machine-Gun Section on the border…" came several answers.

"Aye, you *have* been training, and some of that was in your Machine-Gun Section. But *that*, me lads, was *then*, in Mexico, where you didn't know *what* you were about, and those *Mexican* blokes surely as *Hell* didn't either. It *did not* include what you're about to see. This is *France*, boys. The Huns and us have been doing this for *three years* now. Permit me to *show* you what *we've* learned to do, and what we *just* did at Messines."[1]

Talbott loaded a Very pistol,[2] aimed it up over the sea, and fired a green star cluster…

Suddenly, a machine gun chattered from the bluff above and behind them….

Many men *instinctively* went face-down into the sand or wherever they *could*….

"*Up*, lads," Talbott called calmly, standing in front of them. "*Up* and watch the *show*…"

So they got up…and gazed out at the once-smooth, flat stretch of sand as the machine gun's bullets struck inside the buoy's square…

Then, another machine gun off to their right added its voice, soon joined by *another* to the left, and *another* behind *them*, and *another* farther behind *them*…and *another*…

The sand within the buoys became turbulent with bullet strikes—four hundred square yards of mud turned into splashy chaos, minute after minute, before Talbott fired a yellow flare…

As if by magic, the chaos shifted to smaller areas *around* the square…

After several minutes, Talbott fired a white flare, and the chaos swept over and around the square…

This went on for ten, twenty, thirty minutes of shifting back and forth, the pattern changing with successive green, white, and yellow flares. Occasionally, it *sounded* like one gun would go silent, then start up again. If not for the *relentless* gunfire, the show *might* have been boring.

Finally, Talbott fired a red flare, and the firing stopped…and silence descended; *blessed* silence. "*That*, me lads, is a wee bit of what we've *just* done at Messines. That first bit was a *standing barrage no one* can get through. The second was a *rolling barrage* that moves in front of advancing troops. The last was a *sweeping barrage* that *shifts* as the *Hun* moves around."

He paused, pointed to his target area. "And *barrages* like *that*

---

[1] The battle of Messines Ridge, 7-14 June 1917, was the first time…

[2] A large bore pistol for firing flares.

are what the brass expects *us* to fire at least *four times a day*, *every day* of a front line tour…in a *quiet* time."

"Quite the show, sir," Steele ventured. "Very…"

"Me lad, you've seen *nothing* yet," Talbott declared. "The lads on these guns were just back from Blighty. They've been to the front a half dozen times and more. They consider *this* little job a holiday, showing *you* lot what they *can* do. You *see*," Talbott grinned, "*they* didn't have to *move*. But on the line, no machine gunner *dares* stay in one place for over five minutes; the *other* fellow's artillery and mortars and machine gunners will pot[1] them in *less*."

"Sounds rugged…" Grimes mused.

"Aye, *rugged*, as you call it. It's a *bloody nightmare*." Talbott looked around at Steele's men. "But we fired *these* barrages indirectly; over your heads. That's *new* to war, and that's *most* of what we will concentrate on. Now, *you* lads have known me for upwards of a month now; you *know* I won't lie. So, truth be told, for every shift in the trenches, *one* of *two* of you *will* get hurt. *And,* me hearties, *one* in *five* of you will *not get home alive*."

"Should you be frightening the men…?" Steele started.

"I'm *doing* what I'm *told*, just as *you* are, Captain," Talbott snapped. "We will teach you how to gauge target height, how best to account for barrel wear, how to strip out a feed box in the dark wearing a smoke hood[2] while under artillery fire, how to select a new machine gun site *before* you've set up the one you're in. But I will not lie to you *or* your men about how long you will be *able* to do what we *teach* you to do."

"*That*, me lads, was three sections—six Vickers guns. Three sections for *us* are *half* a machine gun company. I'm told *your* divisions will have a machine gun company for each *regiment*, a machine gun battalion for each *brigade*, and another machine gun battalion for each *division*." He shrugged. "That's a bloody great number of machine gunners to train. Now, *next*…"

"We learned a great deal about mathematics and ballistic physics already, sir," Steele said. "We need to learn *more?*"

"That and *much* more, my boy; *much* more. Captain Steele,

---

[1] In *this* sense, targetted.

[2] An early gas mask.

take your men to the *next* range…"

***

"Lads, *this* is your *most important* lesson." Captain Lash was not what Steele had expected. Though he wore the pips of a Captain, Lash was more casual, exhibiting little of Talbott's stiff-upper-lip demeanor.

"Listen," Lash grinned, cocking his head, then said, "one…two…*three…four…FIVE…SIX…SEVEN!*" He stopped. "*That's* how long a firing machine-gunner's *got* on the line before a *Hun sniper* finds him: *seven seconds.*" He paused and looked around. "Surprised? So were *we* the first time we noted our gunners were being potted. But that's *one* reason we're *here*, lads: so you can learn from our hard experience." He looked around at the ninety-odd faces, listening *intently*.

"You thought *artillery* was your worst enemy…and indeed it was—with properly masked[1] observers—until *very* recently. Last winter, the Hun discovered we could *un*mask his observers and blind them with our machine guns, and so changed his tactics. He now sends snipers forward with his attacking waves…only those snipers don't *want* to reach our trenches. No, indeed. *They* just go out to pot our gunners—pick them off, as *you* might say—firing through our loopholes…view ports or gun ports, *you* might call them. *That's* why," he shifted his podium to reveal a rusty metal plate with a square hole in the center and dents around the hole's edges, "we had *these* made up. Gives us *plenty* of room for the muzzle so we can still fire our missions…"

"That's *all*?" Steele asked. "What about overhead protection?"

"Well, Captain," Lash grinned, "now *that's* up to you. You need to *protect* the guns, me buckos, protect them as you would your *children*. One machine gun is worth an infantry *company* on the line."

"Aye, but that's not the *biggest* of *your* worries," Lash went on. "Nay; the *biggest* of *your* worries will be, *masked* or *not*, the Hun will *always find* your position on the line. The *most important thing* for Hun gunners to *find* is *your* position. So their snipers, their Maxim gunners—they *invented* the beaten zone, ya know—

---

[1] Hidden *from*, in the vernacular.

and their double-seven[1] gunners will *hunt* for you on the line or behind it. That's why you need to work in pairs at least; threes or fours when you *can*. That, and, you *need* alternate positions you can *move* to and *fast*. *Two* at least; *three* if you can manage the trick. Then you do your calculations and get firing again before they find your *mates*…and *they will find lone guns*…because they rely on *sound*. So the more *noise* you make…"

***

"*Defilade*, lads," the burly British Corporal named Hayes said. "The most important word in your vocabulary from here on out. *Defilade* in *direct* fire means you don't shoot *straight at* your targets in line, because *that* makes it easier for snipers to find you, and besides, you can't *hit* a *bloody* thing after your first burst. I'm going to show you patterns of *direct* fire with the Lewis gun, and we'll show how *defilade* works in direct *and* indirect fire."

The training site included several dozen logs buried end-on in the ground, rank on rank, some five hundred yards from the bleachers. "*This* is how the *dead* lay machine guns for direct fire." Hayes held a Lewis gun to his shoulder and squeezed the trigger. Bark and wood chips flew from one or two columns of logs. "That's *enfilade* fire, me lads. *Straight on*, you'll get a *few* that way. *And* it's how you'll get *killed. Now*…" Hayes mounted the gun diagonally on a handcar on railroad tracks in front of the viewing stand. "Now *watch*, me lads. These targets *can't* move, so the gun *will, simulatin'* them comin' on." As a Private pumped the handcar, Hayes lay behind the gun and squeezed the trigger…and hit every log as they passed, with chips and bark flying every which way.

The company sat mute. Some grinned; some looked stunned; others looked curious.

Hayes got off the handcar and addressed the company once more. "You *see*, me lads, in *defilade*, they can't *see* you 'cept from the *side* of 'em, and they ain't *lookin'* anywhere but *straight ahead* of 'em when they're coming over the top, '*specially* if they're wearin' *smoke hoods*. Understand?"

"*Yes*, Corporal," the class answered.

---

[1] The German 77 mm howitzer, a small and quick shell-firing gun.

"All *right*, then," the Corporal declared. "*Now* we're gonna talk about *findin'* these defilade positions on the *line*. *First* thing you have to do is *forget* about *straight ahead and* think *angles…*"

∗∗∗

"*My* name is *Monk*; Colonel Cornelius Monthon *Monk*. I believe I was the first to realize that the marriage made in Hell— the combination of barbed wire and machine guns that has turned Flanders and much of France into a graveyard—can best be overcome by using *more* machine guns more *wisely* than that *other fellow*."

Monk—a slightly stooped, portly man—stood in front of Steele's men in an auditorium, and behind him were three maps made using aerial photographs. His delivery was clear and concise. "I was a professor of mathematics at King's College before the Territorials were called up in '14. Now, I am the foremost tactical machine gun planner in the BEF."[1]

"I am told that *all* of you—officers *and* other ranks—are to be machine gun instructors. I find *that* peculiar, but like you, I follow *orders. Therefore,* I shall introduce *all* of you to planning machine gun barrages." Monk turned to the left-hand map and slapped it with his pointer. "*This* is the Messines Ridge." He moved to the center map. "*These,*" he carefully traced several blotches, "are where we put our standing barrages during the first attacks on that *other fellow's* line." He moved to the third map. "*These* are the rolling barrages we put down *during* the attacks. Now," he returned to the first map. "Our sweeping barrages were more, ah, hasty, and were based on where that *other fellow* moved…"

"Who's that *other fellow?*" Brick loudly asked. "It ain't the *Irish…*"

"*Worse* than that; my *in-laws*," Monk answered without hesitation or change in his facial expression as Steele's men snickered and guffawed. "My wife's *father* was born in Prussia. She has several *cousins* and *uncles* in *their* army. *One* of those cousins was her best pal in her school days. Now, the *main* thing about planning sweeping barrages is *guessing* where your target *needs* to be, *knowing* where he *is*, and putting bullets by the

---

[1] British Expeditionary Forces.

hundreds in between. We use *these* maps or maps *like* them…"

"What's that do for that *marriage*, then?" Grimes asked.

Undisturbed, Monk calmly replied. "*Creeping* barrages allow our infantry to get past that devil's rope and into their trenches. *Sweeping* barrages let the heavy guns' work on the wire actually do some *good* by keeping those *other fellow's* machine gunners back from their line as we approach. *Standing* barrages keep *those fellows* from counterattacking as swiftly and as effectively as they always *insist* upon doing by blocking their approaches to our troops. Now," Monk stopped, tapped his pointer against his boot. "Planning all of this may *appear* to take a great deal of patience and a great number of hours studying both maps and those *other fellow's* positions. It's not a *mean* thing, yet not that difficult and, once learned, *can* be very swift. It's just a matter of geometry and physics. First: the sweeping barrage, which is the *hardest*…"

"Why's that?" Steele asked.

"Be*cause*, my good man, they are controlled *after* planning. You see, *we* say we want to barrage *here*." Monk pointed to a spot on the center map. "Splendid. Now…that *other fellow* has a machine gun *here*." He pointed to a spot just below the first. "Now we have to move *this* barrage…but…in between there are *also* targets you wish to affect. So…*now* the Machine-Gun Officer calls for a shift *off* this barrage to *this* point in a *sweep*…calls for the gunners to recalculate to targets *not* on their range cards they perhaps haven't even *ranged* on…"

He stopped. "I understand all of you Yanks are to be machine gunners, but, honestly…yes, *you*, Captain, will be a Machine-Gun Officer one day. And you Lieutenants will probably be, too. And it's just *possible* you Sergeants may be. But…I believe only you *Americans* think your Corporals and Privates may *work* a *sweeping* barrage on their own…"

"Sir," Steele smiled, "I have in my company a Corporal who once taught *Einstein* arithmetic. Corporal *Attenborough*, Please…"

"Sir." Attenborough stood up.

"*Tell* the Major your experience."

"I was in Switzerland on an exchange in '07 and I encountered Mr. Einstein when he was getting his *Physik* article on acceleration ready for publication. I helped him with some of his calculus.[1] It was *nothing*, sir…"

"It was *enough*, Corporal; *thank* you. Major," Steele went on. "I believe my men are capable enough for your course of instruction. *Please* continue."

"Yes. Then, the *creeping* barrage shall be *next*…"

September

Labor Day 1917, Camiers.

Back at camp. The men have a day off after six

fourteen-hour days of physical training, manual

training on the guns and their equipment, mathematics,

physics, ballistics, differential calculations, and more

physical training. I'm wearing myself out just writing

about it.

Officers still have work to…and more bounty…A

football game this afternoon….

"Everybody up! Fall *in*, Goddammit! Fall *in*!" McTee stalked through the camp, shouted and kicking down tents, pounding on doors. "*Up! UP! UP!* Uniform or *not*, everybody *up!*"

"What's…what's going on, Top?" Steele asked, emerging from his room.

"A *train*, sir, full of supplies and equipment."

"On *Labor Day*…?"

"The Brits and the Army don't *know* from Labor Day, sir."

"Well, can't it *wait*…?"

"The conductor says we either unload it in three hours or they take it back where it came from…"

"Sounds like we're being *Willised*, Top."

---

[1] Albert Einstein was a notoriously poor mathemetician but a brilliant theorist.

"Sounds *about* right, sir."

Grudgingly, tiredly, the men fell in...yet, the company formation was *not* as long as the train...

Willis, sheaf of papers in hand, spoke to the train conductor, seemingly in disagreement about *something* while the company stood in awe of the fifty boxcars and twenty flat cars covered with canvas.

"Post!" Steele called; the officers moved forward, and the NCOs moved back.

Willis stepped up to Steele, motioning for Brick and McTee. "Everything we need and a *good* deal more..." Willis said. "It...I'm not sure *how* we got..."

"What?" Steele asked.

"Well, sir, there's three *more* kitchen wagons, and there's mule harnesses for 'em, and there's..." a loud braying emitted from a boxcar. "Fifty *mules*, and there's lorries—what the Brits call..."

"Motor wagons...*trucks*," Steele finished.

"Yessir. And there's machine guns and machine gun *carts* and belt loading machines and pistols and uniforms and web gear and forms and helmets and telephones and batteries and a pigeon loft..."

"Just about everything..." Steele said. "Just about everything..." Steele turned to Willis. "Want a *commission*?"

"*Hell*, no, sir," Willis declared. "Can't do *my* job as an officer...And there's..."

"Chow?"

"Yessir; *boxcars* of it..."

"Willis, did you *know* this stuff was coming?"

"Did I *know* it was coming, sir? Well...I knew it was all needed; I know it was *all*..."

"You just didn't know *when*?"

"Just didn't realize we were going to *get* it all at the *same time*..."

"Well," Steele sighed, "nothing for it but to get it unloaded...what's *this*?" He saw a small group of men jumping off a flatcar at the back of the train.

"Wasn't expecting *them* until *tomorrow…*" Lucas, striding up to Steele and still in his union suit, said.

"Them…*who…sir?*" Steele asked loudly.

"Machine gunners," Lucas answered. "*Fifty* Americans from the French Foreign Legion. Here to *help* us…"

"And you were going to tell your company commander…*when, sir?*"

"*Tonight….*"

"Well, with their *help*, three hours is reasonable. Get 'em started…"

"When it *rains*, it *pours*," Brick sighed.

***

"What's *your* name, soldier?" Steele addressed one man, still in French blue, guiding a mule down a ramp.

"Camilion, *mon Capitaine*," he answered, stopping to salute. Just then, the mule bucked its head, braying *loudly* in Camilion's face.

"*C'est ton nom de guerre?*"[1] Dona asked, returning the salute.

"Ah, *oui*, sorry. Converse, sir," he answered, ignoring the mule.

"Did discharge you?" McTee asked.

"They *did*, Sergeant," Converse answered, reaching into a pocket and producing a paper. "We got out of Marseilles *prison militaire* last week. Told us we had a choice between going back to Algeria or joining *you* guys. *We* picked…"

"Yeah." Steele said. "What were you *in* for?"

"*I* was in for chronic drink, sir. The *others* for *that* or *minor* black marketing and the like."

"Do you want to serve your *own* country?" Steele asked.

"Wouldn't be here if we *didn't*, sir."

"Then Major Lucas will swear you all in…" Steele looked around, "*before* the football game."

---

[1] Legionnaires rarely used their own names; *nom de guerre* is literally "war name."

"Most of these trucks would be in a junk yard if *we* didn't need them," Willis shrugged. They were surveying their fifty-three motor vehicles, including thirty Ford Model T trucks.

"Marked with *crosses*," Brick observed, rubbing his shoulder he dislocated in the football game.

"Many of *them* came from the American Field Service," Willis said. "Some of 'em probably worked the *Belgian* evacuation in '14.'"

"*Could* be," Steele nodded. "I know who paid for *some* of 'em…"

"Sir?" Willis asked.

"Never mind. How many drivers do we have among us, Top?"

"Ah, I hadn't *completed* that list, sir," McTee answered. "Last count was fifty-two."

"Of a hundred and ten men…"

"Hundred and *sixty* men now, sir," McTee interrupted.

"And…I believe *all* the officers have some experience driving automobiles?" Steele said.

"Lieutenant Buchalter has *very* little," McTee answered.

"Everyone will *have* to, Top," Steele pronounced. "We need a driving instructor team and we need to start with the basics…"

"We need more mechanics…" Brick said. "One enlisted and one officer ain't enough, even with *your* skills. The others at least need to know how to change a tire…"

"The telephonists, sir," McTee said. "They say the batteries *have* acid, should be enough to wire all our guard posts and platoon HQs. *Should* we?"

"Yes, Top, then string wire…" Steele pointed across the tracks, "over there for telephone training. *Everyone* will need to know…."

"And we need more mule-drivers," Willis said.

"We need to train *everyone* in *everything…now,*" Steele finished.

"*Everything*, sir?" McTee looked surprised.

"You say it *yourself*, Top, every other week," Steele said. "Your *most important job* is…"

"*Training* your *replacement*," McTee nodded.

"And *everyone* is *everyone else's* replacement here," Steele said.

"*Cooks*, sir?" Willis asked incredulously.

"They can *drive*, they can learn *infantry skills*, they can skin mules and perform *first aid*," Steele declared. "No man in *this* unit will *not* contribute to our fighting power."

And thus began the cross-training whereby everyone in the 1st Machine Gun Instructor Company of the United States Army learned to be all things to all soldiers.

5th September, Camiers.

Today, Dona began training us on barbed wire. The nasty stuff is called the devil's rope for a reason. We have been training drivers and today we received two motorcycles. Only three men know how to ride them, and I am not one of them. My foot will hurt for a while.

Not one man in five in this unit has ever handled a telephone. That will change.

6th September, Camiers.

Dona continued our barbed wire schooling while Peng repaired the bike I banged up yesterday. We shall learn about scores of different machine guns. The need for this variety is a mystery to our instructors, but AEF apparently gave the orders and is adamant. We shall learn the Hotchkiss and the Chauchat from the French, the Lewis and the Vickers and German Maxims from the British, and Bergmanns from a Belgian ordnance Sergeant who worked at the factory in Germany. This was all planned by Major Lucas.

We have one man who has used pigeons. We have equipment but no birds.

9th September, Camiers.

A visit by a Canadian chaplain. Our Catholic members are grateful to have someone to hear their confessions and bless their communion. The chaplain instructed two men in leading the Mass, said the spirit of communion is as important as a blessed host. We have a chaplain's manual now that dates from before the war with Spain, so they can do everything but hear confessions. And the Corporal's Club has a point...

"Have a seat, Corporal Fitch…How many men are *out* there?"

"Quite a few, sir," Fitch answered, sitting gingerly. "I didn't count them."

"OK. What can I do for you?"

"Sir, I'm here on behalf of the Corporals' Club. The men need to get *out* of this camp, and soon."

"I was in the Corporals' Club," Steele said. "Matters that concern discipline and morale. *Corporal's* business."

"That's right, sir. Sir, *khaki fever*[1] is coming…"

"We're going to do something about it within the next few days. Anything *else?*"

"*No*, sir."

"Very well. Send in the next man."

10th September, Camiers.

I have to instruct the men to avoid the whores without

a sheath….

"And so, when we hand out passes for town on *Saturday*," Steele announced, to a cheering formation, "There is a *house* in town that you will *not* visit *unless* you have some protection…"[2]

"We *got* 'em, sir?" a voice asked.

"We have *some*," Steele said. "But hear *this*, boys: I will have *no one in this unit* with the *clap.*"

As the company fell out, McTee and two Sergeants approached Steele. "Sir," McTee said. "Sergeants Markey and Williamson have acted as MPs in the past."

"Sergeants," Steele said. "I *ask* if you would wish this duty again."

A glance passed between them; then Williamson spoke. "It's no fun having to put one of your own people in a headlock because they got drunk and belligerent after a few *months* in camp."

---

[1] Caused by isolation from society.

[2] Condoms.

"I know what to *do*," Markey added, "done it *before*, but we think MPs need real training, be in separate outfits."

"I'm inclined to *agree* with you, Sarge," Steele said, "but until *that* time comes,[1] I need MPs to help keep the peace. Your squads can take an extra *day* on pass."

The two NCOs exchanged glances. "All *right*, sir," Markey said. "We'll *do* it. Bob—Sergeant Williamson—and I should have a look around the town, sir?"

"I'll write you a pass…"

12ᵗʰ September, Camiers.

A most unusual inventor…

"Well, sir," Nagurski said, having set up his device, "it came to me that needing both a rangefinder *and* an elevation finder just added *weight*…"

"True," Steele agreed, gazing at the tripod and Nagurski's simple *attachment* under rangefinder.

"Just *raise* this…and *lock it* once you've got the object's *height*, then dial in the *range*," Nagurski said.

"And read the *angle* on the *side*…" Steele mused.

"Then just do the geometry," Nagurski said. "Don't *need* that extra ten pounds of elevation finder deadweight." An elevating platform with a protractor segment between the rangefinder and the tripod showed the *angle* of elevation…

"Not to mention lugging around an extra piece of gear, *plus* having to swap it out for every setup, and the extra time needed to change one device for another on a tripod," Steele nodded. "What's it take to fabricate?"

"I made *this* one from some sheet brass I scrounged," Peng answered. "I used one of our school protractors for the angle; made the hinge pin and locking parts from brass rod and a knob I found.…"

"How long did it take to make?" Steele asked.

"About half an hour," Peng answered.

---

[1] The US Army formed a military police corps in 1942.

Dona and Talbott both stared at the device, speechless.

"Make *more*," Steele grinned at both Peng and Nagurski.

"Make one for *me*," Talbott mused, "*I'll* have 'em rolling off a production line in a month."

"*I* can have it in *two weeks*," Dona said. "Just give *me* one…"

15th September, Camiers.

Today the men began their two-day liberty… their passes don't allow them over three miles from camp, and Camiers is two miles off and barely a half mile square… had to appoint MPs for the occasion …imagine turning 245 strange men loose on any American small town…I have to admit that getting out of camp for a day and an evening has been liberating…

"Simple and not too expensive," Steele said, cutting into a cheese. This *Estaminet,*[1] run by a woman and two daughters, sported only ten tables and a tiny bar.

"It's both," Brick agreed. "Dinner for both of us is about six bits,[2] if I got the exchange rate right."

"Um…yeah, I think you're…aw, *nuts*…" Steele grimaced as Williamson marched into the dining room. "Sergeant; what's up already?"

"Just a *small* matter, sir," Williamson said. "The local *gendarmerie* would have a word when you can spare the time."

"I should have coordinated with them?"

"*They* would appreciate seeing *you*, sir. So would the Tommy MPs. Just go down to the police station at your convenience, sir. No *rush*, they said." He looked uncomfortable for a moment. "It

---

[1] A small café that served liquor and light meals.

[2] $0.75.

was the first thing Roy—Corporal Markey—and I did that other day."

"Sergeant," Brick sighed, "*We* have been derelict...."

"I wouldn't say *that*, sir," Williamson said. "You just didn't *know* no better."

"Very *well*, Sergeant; *thank* you," Steele said. "Have you seen any trouble?"

"Nothing to *concern* you, sir," Williamson said mildly. "Couple of boys got into a *scuffle* over a *mademoiselle* we had to break up; a misunderstanding over the price of a couple of sticks of bread they call *baguettes*. A drunk got sick in an *Estaminet* the Brits put off-limits; the *gendarmes* put *them* straight. Nothing *much*."

"Did they *find the house?*" Steele asked.

"In the first few minutes, sir," Williamson sighed. "The *Tommies* have a pair watching it, making sure they have sheaths; we'll relieve 'em later tonight." He cleared his throat. "If there's nothing *else*, sir?"

"Yes, Sergeant," Steele said. "*Thank* you. *Carry* on."

***

"So," Brick said, ambling along the road with Steele near midnight, their coats shedding misty rain, "feel any better after a meal and a drink that doesn't stink of khaki and wet wool?"

"I do, indeed," Steele answered. "Get used to *that* routine and all that it entails and you'll go khaki-happy in no time."

"First time we could take two days off without getting our instructors mad at us," Brick mumbled. "Having to coordinate *their* schedules with *ours*..."

"Yeah." Steele walked silently for several yards. "That police chief *seemed* like a friendly fellow."

"Probably glad he ain't at Verdun," Brick answered.

"*That's* probably true...but I hear that every family in France has someone in uniform."

"*I* hear that every family in France has suffered at least one casualty."

"*That*...many?" Steele grimaced. "Hard to believe."

"Better *believe* it."

"Sergeant Cohen," Steele nodded. "*Fine* bakery, you've got going." Cohen had come to Steele's office during another Open Door hour Steele had about every other day...there *was* that much need.

"Thank you, sir," Cohen said. "I, ah, have a, uh, *question*, sir."

"OK..."

Cohen brought a small menorah out of his blouse. "Do you have any objections to having *this* in the kitchen from today until the 27th?"

"No. Why the 27th?"

"Today is Rosh Hashana, sir, the Jewish New Year *this* Gentile year. The 27th is the end of Yom Kippur, the *end* of the season."

"If the mess section dosen't mind, *I* can't...are you the only Hebrew here?"

"There are *two* others, sir. May we hold a seder tonight?"

"That's a ceremonial meal of some kind?"

"Yessir." Cohen waited a pace. "I will invite any *others*..."

"What *time?*"

***

"Did you have *any* idea, Top?"

"Just by the *names* and, well, Cohen *looks* Jewish."

"By *that* standard, so do *most* of the men in the company."

"I'll grant you *that*, sir."

"Wasn't what I expected, though."

"Just a few prayers in a language we can't understand and some carrots in honey because they couldn't find apples."

"Yeah. Can't *hurt* anything, I suppose..."

"So," Talbott began, brandishing a cigar case; Steele took one; "your company is doing well. I hear rumors of *action* soon."

"More than *I* hear," Steele said, accepting a light from the mess orderly who hovered behind them. "I just get ten more men every week, *more* ammunition to fire up, and more *promotions* to award."

"Ah yes; promotions," Talbott sighed. "I hear from Windsor that *I* may be up for one."

"Windsor...?" Steele asked. "As in Windsor *Castle* and the *king...?*"

"The *Horse Guards*,[1] old boy," Talbott answered. "There shall be no royal bread-knife for *me...*"

"A *what?*"

"*Knighthood*, lad. The Horse Guards *forward* the promotions, or they *used* to. *Your* promotions, what are *they* for?"

"Mostly NCOs, and since I have enough men now for *six* platoons, I need more Lieutenants..."

"That's how *I* was promoted; expansion," Talbott said. "Was

---

[1] Before the mid-19th Century, British Army promotions were *confirmed* or *gazetted* by the Horse Guards.

a Sergeant at Aldershot in '14, training on the new pattern Vickers gun. My company commander called me into his office, handed me my first pips, said, 'Talbott, you're now a machine-gun section leader. Go get your uniforms.'"

"*That* simple?" Steele wondered.

"Indeed. I was off to Bristol for a two-week course in handling a swagger stick and mounting a horse—and I've done *neither* since." He chuckled lightly. "Then I was off to Flanders and my first command. I barely knew my lad's names before we met our first Huns near Ypres[1] that October." He took a drag on his cigar, a slug of brandy. "By the end of the year, *half* of those Territorials were dead. Most of the rest either hurt or promoted to other sections. They made me a First Lieutenant and gave me a *platoon*."

"Still in Flanders?" Steele asked.

"I *was*. Got my first leave at the end of May, went home to see the wife and children. My boy was trying to enlist, but he was only 10 then and they wouldn't *take* him…yet. My oldest girl volunteers with the Red Cross, and my youngest girl hands out white feathers at train stations…"

"What's *that*?"

"Ah, an attempt to *shame* men of military age who aren't in uniform. *They* think it's patriotic, but it's *deucedly* misguided and inconsiderate. And some lads out of uniform because they're on leave or been discharged get *mighty* wound up[2] when they *get* one of those *blasted* things, trying to shame *them* as cowards."

"You set her straight?"

"I *tried*, but *you* know young *women*; they hardly take advice from their fathers."

"Young women *are* hard to *know*…"

"*Some* are. Is someone waiting for you back in Detroit?"

"I *like* to think so." Steele frowned. "I just can't figure her out…"

"*My* advice: don't *try*," Talbott finished his brandy, motioned for more. "My *flighty* fiancee left me when I was in Training

---

[1] Pronouced "Eeeps" in Flemish. British soldiers called it "Wipers."

[2] In this sense, bitter or angry.

Regiment." He shrugged. "I went back to the counting house where Pater worked himself to death, hired on, met and married my wife in five weeks with no fuss at all. If you *can't* figure *that* one out, *don't*. Find another you *can*."

"*Sounds* like good advice. In *our* Army, Congress approves Major promotions. Yours?"

"It goes up the chain a *bit*, yes, but when the Machine Gun Corps began in '15, *that* became *their* bailiwick—*not* the Horse Guards' and *not* Parliament's. I was a Captain by the time *that* happened and I transferred into a Major's position as trainer in January '16."

"Out of the trenches, then?"

"*Not* on your *life*, lad," Talbott sighed. "No; was just an instructor learning the new ways we could kill the Hun in Flanders while *they* killed *us*. I got *my* Blighty[1] that September, spent four months in hospital and another four on leave. I was in Canada training over *there* and seeing my mother and *her* family in New York when your Congress declared war."

"*That's* when you came by *us*…"

"Correct. *Now*," Talbott leaned forward on his elbows, "Tell me about *your* Army career. You enlisted?"

Steele gave a capsule rendition of his meteoric career, finishing with, "I've been in just over three years, which is probably a *fraction* of *your* service…"

"A *big* fraction," Talbott said. "I joined the Territorials in '01 when Pater passed and Mother went back home; was a Corporal in Natal before I was *twenty*, which everyone thought was a bloody *miracle*. Posted as a Sergeant in 1913 and…well, *Bob's* your *uncle*."[2]

"Well," Steele raised his brandy glass, "*here's* to our careers."

"Here's to *having* one when *this bloody war's* over."

22ⁿᵈ September, Camiers.

Today, ammunition maintenance. Bullets need

---

[1] A wound bad enough to require evacuation to England.

[2] *There* you are…

looking after, too. Turn the bullets in the canvas belts every other day; keep them dry; turn the crates over every day. Thinking about an ammunition NCO in the platoons.

24th September, Camiers.
External ballistics, the effects of weather and humidity at long ranges, indirect fire physics. A lesson on what anyone knows about counter-battery calculations against machine guns. And rain all [expletive] day.

26th September, Camiers.
Dona has built a very respectable trench for us to practice in. Our vehicle driver training continues during the day, but gas is scarce. Dona says he knows where he can get white cross bombs.[1] Everyone having a turn on the telephone, stringing wire. Got a dozen pigeons and three French fanciers to train them.

29th September, Camiers.
The arts of camouflage. Truly art. We have men who can build a new MG position in less than an hour in the dark now. The boys are making bets on pigeon races between the sides of the camp.

---

[1] Tear gas grenades.

October

1st October, Camiers

We train every day but Sunday, but we still do calisthenics before church call, games after. McTee is our best pitcher, bar none. Range-finding, height-finding, visualizing target distances, math drills, and scores of formulas and tables which we need to know how to use. Men do homework before and after duty. Now, every man is a mule skinner or a vehicle driver or he is both, including the officers. Officers are training on the guns as well. Our training is nowhere near complete, according to our teachers, because we have so many weapons to train on. Just what the [expletive] is AEF's idea?

8th October, Camiers.

The British are performing most of our training, but it's the Americans who are deciding where to concentrate their efforts. Thus far, we haven't fired an [expletive] shot in anger.

10th October, Camiers.

Dona teaches us about the German's determination to hold on to their Stellungen—defensive lines. Their trenches, Dona says, are much better built than ours.

Steele read Georgia's letter with some interest and confusion:

> *Neddie, dear;*
> *Your family is well. I see them in church every Sunday. I got three new dresses for fall and winter; so glad I can still get hats in Paris fashion. Danced with Herbie Morse at the summer cotillion; he's been called, wants to enlist in the Cavalry. Still haven't heard from Stan, and Father and Mother are getting concerned. Have you heard anything about him? Please let us know by wire if you can.*
> *I close with a prayer for your safety,*
> *Affectionately,*
> *Your Georgia.*

Uncertain how to find a soldier in the rapidly growing Army, he called for Willis. "Is there any *easy* way to find a new National Army soldier?"

"I confess I can't say, sir," Willis admitted. "The Army's expanding so fast I don't even know the *dimensions* any longer. Why, I just saw that *another* division's been formed, and *half* of it is Marines…"

"*United States* Marines?" Steele asked. "How the *Hell* would *that* work?"

"As I understand it, one brigade in this *second* division will have two Marine regiments."

"Well, I hope someone knows what they're about. But if you *can*, see if you can locate this fellow, will you?" Steele handed him a slip of paper.

"I shall *try*, sir, but I can give no assurances." After studying the paper for an instant, Willis asked, "um…if I may be so *bold*, what's your *interest?* It may *help*…"

"He's the brother of a correspondent, Willis. That's all *you* need to know."

"*That* should be *enough*, sir." He sat, fiddling with his coat sleeve. "It's…"

"A *lady* correspondent, if you *must* know." Steele furrowed his brow. "Do *you* have a next-of-kin somewhere that we might notify? You know we're going to get into the shooting sooner than later."

Willis normally wore a slightly clownish demeanor, but suddenly he was serious. "I *have* seven brothers, but I have seen none of them in some time; don't know if *any* of them…our parents are gone; *long* gone. We *had* an uncle and aunt in South Dakota when I went to Cuba; have heard *nothing* from…." He sighed. "I've a wife and daughter living with *her* family in Arkansas. I get letters from her and I send her money. *Her* address is in my leather secretary,[1] in my barracks bag. If *anything*…I'd *appreciate* it, sir."

"All right, Jack," Steele said quietly. "See if you can *find*…"

"*Yes*sir."

15ᵗʰ October, Camiers.

As of today, we have 201 men assigned. At a rate of

ten men every three days, we will be about a thousand

next July…

"Sergeant Kapelski," Steele began, "you have *some* college, I understand."

"Yessir," the big man answered, visibly tense. "Two years…"

---

[1] A folder for letters, stationary, and small documents.

"I'm offering you a commission and a command:4th Platoon."

"Declining isn't an option, sir?"

"It is not. Pick a Platoon Sergeant."

"Corporal Orleans, sir."

"He was one of the Legionnaires, wasn't he?"

"Yessir. Good man, sir. Was in the Legion for three years. Got reduced on account of drink. Sober now, though."

"Very well. We'll take fifteen men from each of the other three oversized platoons and form *your* platoon. Go get a uniform from…why the *Hell* isn't Willis an officer?"

"*That* would be a long tale in the *telling*, sir."

"You *know* Sergeant Willis?"

"I've been in this man's Army for *fifteen years*, sir. Hard not to know Jack Willis from *some*where or other…"

"On your way, then…"

> 28th October, Camiers.
>
> All came through with the slide rules, but many types and sizes. Getting them all the same was too much to hope for. I teach welding, but I spend much of my time on mundane.
>
> But I cannot simply ~~leave~~ ignore G; I have to find some way to put her off…
>
> A surprise visitor…and the diversity of MG training now makes sense…

"Sir," the Corporal knocked on Steele's door. Continuing his daily diary habit, he scratched out his thoughts freely. He once thought about organizing his thoughts *first*, writing them down elsewhere before making his entries, then discarded the thought as too much work.

"*Yes*, Corporal," Steele answered, not looking up; unwilling to lose his chain of thought…

"Sir, you'd *better* come out here."

He set his pen down and got up.

"*Sir*," Steele saluted Pershing. "We weren't *expecting*…"

"Indeed *not*, Captain," Pershing agreed. "Come with me."

"*Certainly*, sir."

They strolled quietly toward the tree line, Pershing apparently lost in thought. "Steele…" He sounded frustrated. "I've been missing my wife and daughters lately, thinking about the Presidio." They walked on, off the beaten trails onto the grass, walking in silence.

"Steele, when I think of *that*," Pershing finally said, "I cannot help but think of how someone with *your* drive and organizational skills might have averted that tragedy." He stopped, his mustache working furiously. "If I might ask, where did you gain your *splendid* skills?"

"Well, sir," Steele said, "I'm the *middle* of nine kids: *five* boys and *four* girls. I learned to get things done, to get people going in the right direction, and helping our dad with his inventions…"

"Ah," Pershing answered. "Acquired honestly enough." They walked on, slowly. The platoons were in weight training, hoisting logs at the end of poles. "You've organized the men well, I'm told, Steele. Nothing but excellent reports. Major Lucas is *very* pleased with your work."

"*Thank* you, sir."

"Have you wondered why *you're* here, Steele?"

Steele cleared his throat. "Permission to speak *plainly*, sir?"

"Go *on*."

"Sir, it has *baffled* me ever since I got orders to report to Dix," Steele said quickly. "I was never a Second Lieutenant and suddenly became a Captain by *accident*. Then I'm told by senior officers to organize a company from scratch—a company of *teachers*, no less. I have *little practical* experience in formal teaching despite my Normal School training. I know machine guns and machinery but—"

"Captain, have you ever *seen* what machine guns can do to a human body?"

"*No*, sir.…"

"*I* have." Pershing fell quiet, his voice barely a whisper. "I saw the Japanese charge Russian trenches…*tore* men apart as if they met *tigers* in a *pit*." He turned away from Steele. "*That's* the consequence of positional warfare, because the Russians eventually lost at *tremendous* human cost to the Japanese."

Steele was quiet, remembering the demonstration the British put on. He blurted, "Why *me*, sir?"

"Because we need to know a great deal more about fighting with machine guns while I persuade those *mutton-heads* in Congress and in the War Department that we need *oceans* of easily portable machine guns like the Lewis gun. We need them because the bayonet and the bomb aren't *enough* in open warfare. *We need machine guns we can attack with.* Mister Browning has a box magazine shoulder machine gun—or *automatic rifle*—chambered for 30.06, our standard rifle caliber. There will be the usual production delays, I suppose, but…" He stopped. "*God*, I *want* those *weapons* in the hands of…." He sighed. "But if the *Germans* got one, they might *copy* it to our *peril*." He turned back to Steele. "When I think of *that*, I think back to *you* on the Mexican border. If anyone can *sense* and *organize* my *breakthrough* effort, *you* can. Colonel Parker is *competent,* but I feel he lacks imagination and your organizing ability. That is why I wanted *you* for *this* job. So I selected a group of men to form the nucleus of an *attack* machine *battalion—your* battalion—led by a man who could *organize* them: *you*."

Steele murmured, "I don't know if I should be honored or frightened, sir."

Pershing chuckled lightly. "I'd say *both* would be prudent." He cleared his throat. "The *company* wasn't *my* idea but President Roosevelt's, and it was *his* influence and money that *got* you here…"

"And Captain Patton's *ship*…"

"His *family's*, yes; you put *that* together. And you intuited the instructor part yourself, as I'd hoped. In the meantime, *you* will train your people on *everything automatic*…"

"We *have* been, sir," Steele interrupted.

"Excellent," Pershing said. "You will be able to use whatever weapons you pick up, then."

"Yessir."

"You will get *Stokes mortars* as well. And rifle grenades, and 1-pounders. Whatever an *infantry* unit has, *you* will use."

"Like the Canadian Motor Machine Gun Brigade..." Steele said quietly.

"*Very* much," Pershing agreed. "Though I'm told that *they* don't use their fancy vehicles very often. Perhaps *you* will *when you* get them. But *that* could be awhile yet."

"We'll *train* with what we..." Steele started.

Pershing interrupted. "You've *also* trained in trench warfare techniques and tactics: gas drill and discipline, stringing barbed wire...all of that?"

"Yessir," Steele offered.

"The time *has* come I *must* send you to fight in the British sector." Pershing looked pained. "But—and I *can't* stress this enough—you must resist, even *fight*, to prevent amalgamation into their army. We are *reinforcing* as *co-belligerents*—America is an *associated* power, *not* allied. We will be *attackers* when we are strong enough, not just *defenders*."

"*Yes*sir," Steele answered.

"I threw you into the water because I knew you could *swim*, Steele," Pershing sighed. "I gave you the *very cream* of our enlisted men and four of the best young and unassigned officers I could lay my *hands* on. You've exceeded *everyone's* expectations, including mine. You've shown that you can organize *matches* in a *box*." He stopped, seemed to straighten up even taller. "We've *been* organizing machine gun battalions, but not like *yours* shall be, Steele..."

"*Yes*sir."

"Yours will be a *very* large, *very independent* machine gun company *before* you become a battalion. The other machine gun battalions will be brigade and divisional units, but yours...*yours* will belong to the AEF..."

"Yes, *sir?*"

"You're going to Flanders next month, Steele. Test your mettle and help the British out for a few days. What are your questions?"

"I will command this large company as a *Captain*, sir?"

"In due course, you shall be a Major in the National Army." He waited. "Anything *else?*"

"Sir, more *ammunition*…"

"I'll see to it, Steele. You'll get, ah…*enough*…" Pershing stopped and stared. Steele turned to look…Rodgers saluted Pershing, who returned the courtesy. "How's *Rodgers* working out for you, Steele?"

"Fine, sir; he's a Sergeant now. Are you *acquainted* with…?"

"I *am*, yes. He accompanied me and his employer—a British officer—to Manchuria in '05. Good man, I thought; *very* resourceful."

"He is, *that*, sir."

29ᵗʰ October, Camiers

The men still have personal matters needing my attention…they seem very nervous, perhaps sensing that the idyll of their training days is coming to an end…they seem too distracted to play football, but play they do…

"*Next* man," Steele called.

A Private named Greene shuffled in, dragging his left foot. "Greene, yes? Something wrong with your foot?"

"*I'm* not one to complain, sir," Greene started, "but the Sarge says I should come see *you*…"

"It's OK, Greene. What is it?"

"My bunions, sir; these brogans hurt 'em something *fierce*. I can't hardly walk in a straight line; always falling behind on our run. And bunions don't *shave* like corns, sir."

"Sick call?"

"Them Brit docs take one look and call it malingering, sir."

"Well, we'll be getting an American doctor here tomorrow. Go see *him*." Steele scribbled a note. "Give *this* to your squad leader and go on sick call tomorrow."

"*Thank* you, sir," Greene said, shuffling out.

As he left, Sergeant Harrington entered. "Sir," Harrington said quietly. "It's a *personal* matter…"

"All right."

"I don't *want* to sound… the *thing* is, sir, I got a letter from home. My Ma's got awfully sick, and Paw's got *his* Ma and my sisters and brother to care for. Ma *can't* work, and…"

"Where are they?" Steele asked.

"Denver, sir," Harrington said, twisting his overseas cap in his hands.

"What's your Paw do?"

"Blacksmith, sir, only 'smithing ain't what it *used* to be…"

"*My* Paw says the *same*….and you can't *send* enough money home…?"

"No sir. I could send *all* my $37 a month home and it ain't enough. I could make more *digging ditches…*"

"Have you tried the Red Cross? *They* offer home relief…"

"They *do?*"

"Yes. We need to do a better job of getting *that* word around. Take *this*…" Steele scratched out a note, "…to your platoon. And *this*," Steele scribbled another note, "to the First Sergeant for a pass to go to the Red Cross office in town. Just be back *before* lights out…"

Harrington stared at the notes, then at Steele, then back to the notes. "Sir, I…"

"Just be back before lights-out. Send in the *next* man."

November

1ˢᵗ November, Camiers.

Writing G is hard—what do I say to her? The men

learned another song…

Staring at the blank piece of stationery, Steele twisted his pen in his fingers for several minutes, waiting for inspiration as his lantern hissed. Then he realized…if *Georgia* writes about *her* life…

> *…From time to time, the wind shifts and we can hear the machine guns and cannons on the front; we are*

about a hundred miles behind it. Sometimes we get a whiff of the fresh-cut hay smell of green cross gas[1] and don our smoke hoods quickly...we shoot up ammunition faster than we can replenish it, but we never seem to run out of Mills bombs. We had bayonet drill yesterday; pranged my thumb on the back of the bolt of my rifle. I am looking for your brother through the agency of a supplyman who seems to know more about the Army than the Army does. He can find water in a desert (ha-ha) so he should be able to find Stan. Looking forward to your next letter. My best to your family and let mine know you heard from me, if you will.

> *Your friend,*
> *Ned*

He sealed up the self-mailing stationery with its patriotic flags around the margins, scribbled in her address, and put it in the postbox.

***

> *When this Goddamn war is over,*
> *Oh, how happy I will be!*
> *When I get my civvy clothes on,*
> *No more soldiering for me.*
> *No more church parades on Sunday,*
> *No more begging for a pass,*
> *I will tell the old First Sergeant*
> *To stick his passes up his ass*

"Another one, Top?" Steele asked McTee. "Is there no end to them?"

"Soldiers and their songs, sir," McTee answered.

"Yeah," Steele sighed. "*This* one was *clean* until that last verse."

"Men without women, sir," McTee said. "They tend towards the ribald."

"Or morbid," Steele said. "That 'Bells of Hell' song…"

"What they wish for and what they see, sir," McTee said.

---

[1] Phosgene.

"Myron Miller," the middle-aged Captain with a limp said, offering his hand. "Just call me Murph. I'm your Medical Officer."

"Pleased to meet you, Murph. I'm Ned Steele. Did you come alone?"

"No; I brought five enlisted aid men, a Red Cross man, and two YWCA volunteers with me."

"Ah," Steele smiled. "I imagine *that's* why they're lining up for sick call even now."

"Like horses to a trough in summer," Miller sighed. "Soon as those YWCA ladies *got* here, the rumor spread all over camp they were *nurses*…"

"They are here *for*…?"

"Recreational purposes, Ned, and of course, not *that* kind. They'll introduce themselves and their programs today." Miller grinned. "They're old enough to be most of your men's *mothers*."

"Ah…I had a man go into town to see the Red Cross…"

"Oh, yes; he called in yesterday. Tragic story…"

"Well, I got *part* of it yesterday," Steele began.

"…And the Red Cross will verify it in Denver," Miller said. "Sent the wire out last night. Now, the YWCA ladies will *billet* in town, but they need a little space for their programs *here*…"

"And *a little* equals what?"

"About a trunk's worth of space to store their game materials. They'll put up posters and the like on your bulletin boards…"

"Um…*no* bulletin boards…we use the sides of buildings. I'll have someone show the ladies where. And I can have the trunk stored in supply."

"That should suit. *Tough* little things those ladies are. Now, I'll get to sick call…"

***

"So Greene needs surgery…" Steele sighed, scanning the sick call list.

"Or he'll have a gimp all his life," Miller nodded. "He might, *any*way. I never *saw* a bunion that big before, even in the picture books."

"*You* can't fix it…?"

"He needs an orthopedist, and even *then*, he'll need at *least* a month to recover, if he *ever* does."

"Huh…so, a rupture, several scabies, unknown rashes. We've had *some* cooties[1]…." Steele surveyed the list with interest. "Um… Dent: an eye cyst?"

"Yes. It needs hot compresses twice daily."

"Dangerous?"

"Not usually. But in camp conditions…?" Miller shrugged. "He tells me he sleeps on a wooden platform in an unheated building. He *should* go into a clinic for at *least* a few days, if possible."

"If *possible*," Steele mused. "You're *not* a military doctor, are you?"

"Not hardly, Ned; I volunteered. I have a practice in Hammond, Indiana, where I left my wife and children. Hope to get back there in one piece. They gave me this rank because while still in medical school, I volunteered in '98[2]—got as far as Tampa—and I have *fifteen years* in the practice of general medicine."

"Ah," Steele said. "So you know your stuff. How long will…Durell be out with his rupture?"

"Like Greene, at *least* a month."

Steele finished with the list and handed it back to Miller. "One more thing, Murph: *your* gimp? What about that?"

"It does not interfere with my duties, Ned. Just a bad hip. The Army's so desperate for doctors they'll take nearly *anyone*. I can

---

[1] Lice.

[2] Spanish-American War.

run to save my life, but probably not much more. I've noticed that this unit is mostly Regulars with a few former Legionnaires and some new National Army men. Is that…?"

"We train who they send us," Steele answered.

5th November, Camiers.

Here and now our war is serious…

They walked in silence for a mile from town, avoiding the deep ruts where vehicle wheels had churned the mud into bottomless pools. As they approached the camp, they saw very little movement; nearly everyone was on a pass. Someone lingered outside Steele's door wearing a leather helmet, long slicker and gloves; a messenger. "Captain Steele?" he asked.

"Yes…?"

"For you; sign for it inside?"

"Yes…"

The sealed envelope contained only a simple warning order:

> 1ST MACHINE GUN INSTRUCTOR COMPANY TO PREPARE FOR MOVEMENT TO FORWARD ZONE NO LATER THAN 19 NOVEMBER 17. ALL REQUISITIONS SUPPORTING SUCH MOVEMENT TO BE FILLED BY 18 NOVEMBER 17.

15th November, Camiers.

Rodgers has a brilliant idea…

"Sergeant Rodgers, sir," McTee said to a dripping wet Steele, who just came into the orderly room.

"*Yes*, Sergeant," Steele said, shaking off his poncho.

"Sir, it has occurred to me that the cooks need to be better deployed…"

"Traditionally, they're stretcher-bearers, aren't they?"

"Yes, sir," Rodgers agreed. "But, during a gas attack…well, they can't *cook*…"

"True." Steele looked at McTee, who shrugged. "What do you suggest?"

"Well, sir, if they can't *cook*, they *can* boil water for decontamination; help the aid stations with *that*...."

"*Yes*," Steele said. "For mustard we wash-rinse-wash-rinse; for phosgene we strip and boil..."

"*Yes*, sir," Rodgers agreed. "The aidmen will be busy with the wounded."

"Excellent idea, Rodgers," Steele declared. "Have you spoken to Sergeant Farrell about this?"

"We worked it out together, sir," Rodgers said.

"Then *you* shall be the company's decontamination NCO."

"*Thank* you, sir."

"Got your way into a combat zone, Rodgers."

"Yes, sir," Rodgers declared. "I just want to do what they *sent* me here for."

"Sergeant, you said you enlisted. *Why...?*"

"I frankly wanted more, ah, *freedom*, sir."

"Have you found it?"

"I have *certainly* found more variety."

"General Pershing says you were with him in Manchuria. Not enough variety?"

"It *was*, sir, but...I *frankly* loved *that* kind of, ah, *adventure*, rather than..."

"Yes; I see."

20th November, Amiens, France.

Leaving Maj. Lucas and 90 men behind. We have moved here by train, loading our vehicles and equipment on flatcars, bringing our mules, too.

Talbott tells me we need a scouting group to guide us into the trenches. They say a Sergeant named Thorsten is an excellent scout. I will try him first.

We will support a Canuck battalion on Hill 90 that has been in British hands since 1915. The locals call it Colline Mortelle, which Brick says is Deadly Hill...

"You're Thorsten?" Steele asked the youngish blonde man, who probably had at least two years on him.

"Yessir," Thorsten answered.

"Any experience in the wilderness, lad?" Talbott asked.

"I traveled with my father, sir," Thorsten answered, "with him on his surveys for the railroads and the mines. We lived rough. A cabin was a luxury. We got store-bought food only on holidays. Learned to shoot and track before I ever kissed a girl."

"You know surveying?" Steele asked.

"Yessir," Thorsten answered. "I learned mathematics plotting Dad's data."

"Ah," Steele said. "And you joined the *Army* because…?"

"Can't raise a *family* like *that*, sir."

"Family?"

"My wife's living with her parents in Wyoming. Got a baby now."

"Well," Steele said. "Grab your gear and let's go see the elephant…"

"The *what??*" Talbott asked, genuinely puzzled.

"Get shot at," Steele grimaced.

"You'll get *that*…" Talbot nodded, leaping onto the side of the touring car as it bumped up the road…towards that rattling, roaring…

21st November, Iroquois Line, Flanders.

A continuous racket like a factory that smells like

gunpowder and fresh-cut hay even a mile behind the

"front line."

Met Brigadier Butcher commanding the brigade in

"*So*, Captain Steele," Butcher said, tamping his pipe. "I *hope* you can understand our *needs* up here." Butcher was a tall, lean man who interrupted everyone he didn't outrank.

"I *do*, sir," Steele sighed. "Your Canadian and British machine gun companies are exhausted, and replenishing their ranks will take longer than expected. We…"

Butcher nodded and grimaced. "Normally, Captain Steele, you would be relieved from the front area in four days…but…" Butcher intoned, "you must be available for *more* because we don't *have* units to replace you. You're filling in for *three* MG companies…"

"Sir," Steele asked, "does AEF know this?"

Butcher inhaled deeply and rolled his shoulders. "Yes. They…you shall have *complete* discretion, of course…but," he set his pipe down on the table between them. "If you withdraw before we can replace you, we shall be in very, *very* dire straits."

Talbott and Dona appeared sheepish or embarrassed; Steele couldn't discern which. "*Yes*sir," he said.

They found battalion headquarters in a barn held up with sandbags and mine pit props near the base of the hill. Burly, chain-smoking McFadden had a nasty scar resembling a second mouth. His greeting spoke volumes. "Talbott, ya nasty *bugger*," he cried, "got over your *little scratch*, then? And *what* hae ya brought me for a *gunner*, then?"

"I've *recovered*, sir, and this is an American named Steele," Talbott pointed to Steele. "Angus McFadden of the

Newfoundland Black Watch, meet Ned Steele of the American First Machine Gun Instructor Company. Steele's brought a *big* Hotchkiss machine gun company."

"A *Yank* with them *Frog* things," McFadden sniffed, regarding Steele as if he were a day-old fish. "So you'll be telling me *where* will ya get ammunition, then?"

"He's *brought* enough for his *shift*, sir," Talbott said. "We'll arrange for some *Vickers* guns so he'll be *sure* to have…"

"And *why* am I gettin' *Yanks*, then, Talbott? Tell me *that?*"

"If I *might*, sir," Steele interrupted, "an American *invented* the Hotchkiss,[1] and at least *some* of *your* men are Americans…"

"Aye, and a lazy, *shiftless* lot of ne'er-do-wells they *are*, too," McFadden spat. "Can't barely dig a *funk-hole*, let alone a *trench*…"

"If you *want*," Steele interrupted, "I'll take them off your *hands*…"

The big man broke into a wide grin, extending his hand to Steele. "Talbott, you've brought me *just* the man I need on this *bloody dung-heap*. Have a look around and we'll swap ideas on how to keep the Huns *off* it."

23rd November, Colline Mortelle..

I have seen the Inferno from the edge of

Purgatory…mud, wire, holes, water, and the remains

of man, beast, and civilization. There is no sadder

sight than a ruined town…No training can get anyone

ready for this [expletive] *shit.*

I could never have imagined what a howitzer shell

landing so close could have felt like…. machine-gun

bullets hum like giant bees or kazoos in the air and

sound like meat hooks hitting a side of [expletive] *beef*

---

[1] Built under licence in France.

when they hit...Sgt. Thorsten and I went down to the

"front line" ...like [expletive] *animals in unbelievable*

filth and indescribable stink...in the forward posts, we

endured a small bombing raid[1]...Don't think I've

ever been so [expletive] *humiliated in my life....*

"*This* is your PC[2] as the battalion machine-gun officer," Talbott said as they negotiated an up-and-down maze of gas steps,[3] and sandbags into a sandbag, soil and log entrance. "Helps keep the rain and the gas out. This roof can withstand everything short of a direct whiz-bang[4] hit," he added. Loopholes, built through three feet of sandbags and protected by iron plates, gave views to the sides, front and back. "Have a look at the *front*, there, through this periscope."

Steele put his eye to it…

The outpost lines—the closest lines to No-man's-land—*jumped* into view: a chain of holes, ditches, old ruined trenches and wreckage, joined by ditches and other holes, not *proper* "trenches" at all.

"Turn *this* handle," Talbott instructed, turning the right-hand grip. "Changes the elevation."

Steele was at once taken by the starkness, the utter *devastation* of the scene accompanied by the continuous rattle of machine guns near and far, and the occasional artillery burst. Barbed wire and mud, wrecks of wagons and carts, bodies of mules and horses and wreckage of equipment combined into a ghastly tableau. The misshapen stands of shattered trees and masonry walls, dripping in the chilly rain, added to the pall of devastation cast over the landscape but made the scene no more horrid than did the *scattering* of bits and pieces of human beings that *dotted* the

---

[1] Hand grenades thrown simultaniously by several men.

[2] Post of Command.

[3] Posion gases are heavier than air. Gas steps protected bunker occupants from high concentrations.

[4] A large, heavy artillery shell or mortar bomb, so called for the sound it made: a buzzing followed by an explosion.

landscape.

"A little *higher*," Talbott said.

Suddenly, Steele was looking *above* the *ghastly* horrors of No-man's-land. "You should see the German outpost line now."

"Is *that* what that is? That line of dirt above the wire?"

"It *is*. Now turn the scope to your left."

He did. He saw a ribbon of soil past two ruined walls, an old-fashioned water well, parts of more walls, a remarkably intact arbor, a smashed piano, and what had been a henhouse and a small barn. The devastation seemed so *random*. "That was a…farm?" Steele asked.

"Once," Talbott answered, "With all the gas and shell fragments in the soil, it'll *never* be a farm again, even if the farmer's still about. Now…elevate again."

He saw heaps of shattered masonry holding up what were once walls, a sign reading *Brasserie[1]* standing almost upright, a church steeple's crooked cross, the steeple so perforated it was a wonder it hadn't fallen apart. "Sad," Steele whispered. "*Terribly* sad; it was a town. How far back *is* it?"

"Line up your reticles on a field wire post[2]—three meters high, usually—and *you* tell *me*."

Steele lined up the range reticles etched into the glass on a post. "Just over a mile from the front of their outpost line."

"Yes; *very* good. *That* was Vienville, once," Talbott muttered. "Over two thousand souls lived there before the war. Now, there in the ruins, it's a Hun aid station, mess, and supply dump."

"If we know what it *is*," Thorsten asked, "why *don't* we…?"

"Because of *how* we know, lad," Talbott answered. "The Huns want us to believe it's abandoned, but we know because of our prisoners, our patrols, listening on their wires, and…well, *other* means."

Thorsten looked curious. "You have patrols going *across* the enemy lines?"

"From time to time," Talbott answered, then asked, "Why?"

---

[1] A more casual place to eat and drink than a *Restaurant*.

[2] A pole made of steel rod with a screw base.

"Just…might be thrilling to *be on* such missions…"

"Indeed. Back *there*," Talbott gestured toward the back of the bunker, "behind *us* two miles is the ruin of St. Beth, or St. Betharius, that *we* use for the same things. Now, I'd wager that the Huns know just as much about St. Beth as we do about Vienville, and they've come to know it by the same means. One day we'll destroy what's left of Vienville or they'll destroy what's left of St. Beth, or both. But *not* today, and *probably* not…*DOWN!*"

A *riotous* burst of noise, dust, and yellow smoke filled the air as a great weight seemed to *crush*…and just as suddenly, *lift*… inside the bunker.

"Looks like they've got our range," Steele declared loudly, a few moments later.

"*Had* it for *years*, lad," Talbott said, just as loud, brushing the dust off his coat. "*That* was a double-seven. The camo lads will check the tree for damage…"

"Camo lads?" Thorsten asked. "Tree?"

"*Camouflage* section, pal," Talbott answered. "We hid the periscope within a hollowed tree on top of this PC."

"You know this position well, sir?" Steele asked.

"Well *enough*," Talbott answered. "Got my *Blighty* here. Now…forward." They exited the same way they came in. "We can plug up the loopholes and barricade the back entrance if we have to, to keep *Huns* out." He stopped, peered around a sheet-iron-built corner into a communications sap. "If they ever get *this* far, lad, *blow the place up*."

"I shall," Steele said. "Ian," he asked, "did you *know* how long…?"

"I *suspected*; Henri did, too." Talbott grimaced. "I'm a little surprised *your* Army didn't tell you it was *possible* you'd have to replace *three* MG companies…."

"So am *I*…Happen often?"

"Only seen it *once before* myself, lad. During the Somme *fracas* last year. But it *won't* be more than a *week*."

* * *

"Daytime is for *resting*," Talbott told them as they picked their way through the trenches. "Nighttime is for *working*. You'll move in tomorrow night. You have…*how* many?"

"Eighteen Hotchkiss and eighteen Lewis guns in service," Steele said. "I have *other* guns, but not much ammunition for them…"

"Your Hotchkiss guns can reach into Fritz's *reserve* trenches from behind the hill; five hundred yards farther than our Vickers or Lewis. *That* might surprise them." Talbott squinted in thought. "You have new barrels, so wear isn't a problem…"

***

"*Little* detour, lads," Talbott said, inching back from *another* turn in the communications sap. "Cave-in ahead."

They went back, moved north a hundred yards, then back east until…

"Just ahead, lads," Talbott declared. "Another fifty yards…" They crawled through mud and water that in places sank them to their bellies, but they kept moving. Steele repeatedly saw rats so big he thought they were muskrats.

The vile stench suddenly filled Steele's sinuses when his hand sank into what was once a human being, and he made to… "Ah…*ah*…" Talbott shoved Steele's face into the mud of the side of the sap… "*CHOO!*"

"A sneeze is a sound you *dare not* make up here, lads," Talbott declared. "*Nor* cough. They're not natural to nature *or* warfare…"

"Nothing natural *up* here," Thorsten said softly.

Talbott pointed, chuckling. "Right *there*, pal. Just a *bit* farther, now…"

"*That's* the proper No-man's-land, lads," Talbott whispered, pointing over the edge of a hole a hundred yards on. Two men in the crater looked on curiously. "This is a *ramp now?*" Talbott asked.

"*Night* ramp," a third man answered; he blended into the hole perfectly, invisible. "Just over *here*."

"A ramp's a way *into* the wire," Talbott explained. "We use *this* one only at night because it's under observation."

A burst of machine gun fire buzzed over their heads, more persistent than the howitzer.

"Think they know we're *here?*" Steele asked, still picking mud out of his ears.

"Hun listening post a couple hundred yards *that* way," a fourth invisible man said, his arm pointing northeast. "They heard you coming through that last sap in the stillness…"

"Stillness?" Steele asked.

"*Quiet* day today," one said. "Usually a *lot* louder." He shifted, raised a crude periscope. "Someone in the *wire…*"

"Someone…?" Thorsten asked, daring to edge up to the side of the…

"*Movement…DOWN!*" It was the *second* time they had heard that, that day, and Steele didn't know where to duck. He dove to the bottom of the hole, running into Thorsten. The next thing he knew, bombs went off around the hole.

"*Bombs*, lads," Talbott shouted, taking several from the hole occupants. A Lewis gun appeared as if by magic; Talbott slapped a grenade into Steele's hand. Thorsten leaned his rifle over the hole's edge and squeezed off a shot, then another. Three of the residents of the hole cocked their arms with grenades; Talbott and Steele did the same. "…Two…*three…now*," one of them yelled, and all hurled their grenades. The Lewis gunner propped his weapon on the edge of the hole and fired a full drum as the grenades went off and the gunner retreated…

And *silence*…more stark than any Steele had ever known. Even with his ringing ears, *that* silence was…eerie, bordering on terrifying…but soon broken by the rattling of a machine gun to the east…and a Canadian mumbling, "I counted *four*, Jock…"

"Me too, Brian. Who's got their *rings?*"

"*I* do;" "here's *mine;*" "mine's *here;*" "here's mine;" came the replies.

Steele looked in his hand…seeing nothing. "Oops," he mumbled.

"Eh, yer just a *colt*," Brian grunted. "*You'll* get the hang of it."

"*Hope* he does before the Huns throw *that* one *back*," Jock sighed.

"That happens a lot?" Steele asked. "They throw 'em *back?*"

"Been *known* to," one of them mumbled. "We do the *same* when we *can.*"

As they departed, Steele could hear soft singing:

Glorious! Glorious!
One shell hole between four of us.
Soon there will be no more of us
Only the bloody old hole.

A similar melody in German wafted across the wire…

24th November, Hill 90 (shorter than that other name), Flanders.

I have brought 190 men this far and hope to take ninety Per. Cent. of them back. Rain as we moved in….

Our HQ and vehicles are miles behind the hill, but they say we are on the 'front.' That word means very little here.

It is an odd thing, this horizontal fortress…this little [expletive] hill is an insignificant mound on a long ridge blasted barren by artillery and transformed into a bastion of dugouts, trenches, and bunkers. Tunnels below us…They haul the spoil out at night to avoid detection by the Hun balloons and aeroplanes.

We moved into the positions in complete darkness and cold, soaking rain, taking the range cards and positions of a battery of the 1st CMMBB[1] as if we knew what the [expletive] we were doing. I got a briefing from the outgoing 'battery' commander, a little

---

[1] Canadian Motorized Machine Gun Brigade.

fellow with a rambling speech who looks haunted.

To our left, on Hill 84 four miles to the north, another CMMGB battery backs up another Canuck battalion; to our right, another CMMGB battery backs up the battalion on Hill 85. The CMMGB is less a brigade than it is a five-company (that they call batteries) battalion with odd-looking Armored Autocars (that they use very little), plus mortars, motorcycles, and bicycles. I know the Autocar firm makes good ~~motor wag~~ trucks. I hope to get close enough to inspect one. These positions have been here for a little over a year, moving only a few yards of the front at a time, mostly of barbed wire entanglements in 'no-man's-land'. We are best thought of as an annoyance to the Huns on Hill 92 that the Huns hold just three and a half miles southeast of us.

Steele went over the defensive fire plans with McFadden: the barrages that covered the German forward positions, the known avenues through the wire in No-man's-land, the *Canadian* positions…all the places his guns *had* to hit should the Hun be so bold as to attempt what everyone *expected* them to do…

And there was the Final Defense Barrage—or SOS—that the AEF *Manual* did *not* cover. "Right here on our reserve trenches and approaches," McFadden explained. "They get *that* far and we're in *trouble*, laddie."

"So, we fire on *your* trenches once the Huns *take* them," Steele tried to clarify…

"Nay; *while* they're *trying* to take them," McFadden declared, as if to a child.

"And *your* people…?"

"Will *have* to *duck*…" McFadden said with resignation, lighting another cigarette; his fourth in ten minutes. "*Best way,* laddie. And, we have a gang of Chinee if you should need 'em…"

"We *shouldn't,*" Steele said. "We'll be OK, but thanks for the offer. I have an idea for *directed* fire…"

"How's that?" McFadden asked.

"Constant contact with my platoons to provide a *centrally directed* fire plan…" Steele explained, pointing on the map.

"*How…?*" McFadden asked again.

"We just keep the phone wires *connected* or we use flares and runners if we *have* to…"

"*And* ye move guns every three hours…?" McFadden asked.

"*And* we brief the runners every three hours," Steele explained patiently. "We sweep fire from fixed points and these barrages…"

He outlined his idea for several minutes before McFadden finally nodded. "*Like* Messines only for the defense. *Might* work, lad. *Try* it if ye *can.*"

25th November, Hill 90.

Rain. Tried to [Illegible].

Men work much of the night building, repairing.

Talbott and Dona in the rear.

We should simply pull this shift as if the duration is of

no consequence because it isn't a matter of [expletive]

choice. I must learn to sleep during the day.

Gen. Pershing thinks too highly of me…

"Sir," McTee shook his foot. "*Sir…*"

"Make it *import…*" Steele glanced at his watch: all of twenty minutes of sleep.

"Dispatch from AEF, sir. You need to sign for it yourself."

Shaking the cobwebs from his mind, Steele swung his feet

down from his pallet in the HQ dugout. A bare candle glowed on a table near the entrance. "Where's the rider?"

"Down the hill, sir," McTee said. They had spent all the previous night and most of the day inspecting gun positions and directing trench repairs, while dodging the occasional artillery and machine gun barrage while Steele's gunners fired back, then moved. "Something hot, sir." McTee handed Steele a steaming cup of liquid.

"Thanks, Top." Steele took his smoke hood bag off its nail, slinging it around his neck before he took the cup, sniffing it; the aroma was unfamiliar. "What's *in*...?"

"Better you don't *ask* what's *in* slum gully,[1] sir."

As Steele followed McTee out of the dugout and into a communications sap downhill, he swallowed the mysterious yet not-*bad* concoction before the rain chilled the contents. After half an hour of climbing, descending and turning, they came to where the vehicles were laagered[2] and guarded by HQ Section men.

The motorcycle dispatch rider looked familiar. "I *know* you," Steele said.

"Three weeks ago, sir," the rider answered. "I knew the way up here, so they sent me. Sign *here*..."

Steele signed and took the portfolio from the rider. "I can offer you a cot for the night..."

"No, sir," the rider answered. "I'm to carry your response to HQ immediately."

"I'll have a look in that guard shack..." He glanced at the rider. "Dry out in that tent. Grab what you can for food or coffee."

"*That* I *can* do, sir." The 1st had already run thin on the fresh provisions they had brought with them; Farrell and Willis were scrounging for anything edible. Even the Canadians had limited access to *fresh* food; signs of scurvy had appeared among *them*.

Steele and McTee stepped into the chicken coop-cum-guard shack. In the bare light of a shaded lantern, they saw several pages of organization tables, all with the title "432nd Machine Gun Battalion, AEF." On top of all the papers was a hand-written note:

---

[1] A thick soup made of whatever is at hand.

[2] Afrikaans for *camp*. A defensive position formed of vehicles.

> *Capt. Steele,*
>
> *Col. Conner worked this up based on the Canadian's brigade that you might have a look at. It will have, we believe, enough firepower and mobility to suit the purposes that we have spoken of before. Your views on this matter would be invaluable.*
>
> *Pershing*

"We should *live* so long," McTee mumbled, scanning the organization tables. "*Five* companies," he whistled softly. "It strikes me that *everyone* should have some sappers[1] attached."

"Some pom-poms,"[2] Steele said, reading other sheets. "A maintenance outfit for all those vehicles, to do it up *brown*…"

"A *good-sized* medical platoon," McTee added.

"And *infantry*…"

"And *artillery, while* we're indulging ourselves in *pipe* dreams…"

"Add *cavalry* and we'd be a *real* outfit…*Right*." Steele, using a pencil stub, wrote his reply on the back page.

> *Sir,*
>
> *I appreciate that you have confidence in me, and I hope it is not ultimately misplaced. My staff advises me they prefer to attach engineers, maintenance men, pom-poms, a substantial infantry attachment, and medical staff instead of the fourth and fifth companies that you propose. You also suggested Stokes mortars or light artillery; these would be essential for offensive action through the Hun lines. Pom-poms for handy firepower and anti-aeroplane protection would also be ideal.*
>
> *Yours sincerely,*
>
> *Steele*
>
> *P.S. This answer is necessarily hasty, as I have other duties requiring my attention, and the dispatch rider says he cannot rest here. EAS.*

Steele thought to add something about their indefinite shift, but thought better of it. He folded the note into fours, creasing each

---

[1] Combat engineers, a name derived from an old French word for *spade*.

[2] Automatic small-caliber cannons.

edge with his revolver barrel.

"Get *this* to the boy," he sighed.

26ᵗʰ November, Hill 90, Flanders.

Have to admire Prussian consistency...Night plus

minor trench raid, gas and shelling adds up to a major

attack...but the rain has stopped for now...

"Bombing party had a run-in with a Hun patrol, sir." The runner, spattered with mud, shook water off his poncho as he stepped into Steele's PC. Though a machine-gun unit didn't normally go *out* on bombing missions, Steele insisted—to the bemusement of the Canadians *and* Dona and Talbott—on sending out his *own* bombing party.

"There's *flares* all along the line, Ned," Ishim's voice penetrated Steele's exhaustion as he entered the PC moments later. "Looks like *something's* up; phone line's down."

"OK." Forward gunners on both sides of the line fired at *any* noise or movement, especially at night.

Tactically, machine gun companies were to *support* the infantry on the line or in the attack, even though they *were* infantrymen themselves...*sort* of. But the Army armed their machine gunners only with pistols. Steele had Willis "acquire" as many rifles as he could to supplement the rifles *most* of the initial company members brought with them to France.[1]

"Just some small action," Dona said. "Nothing more than an affair of patrols."

"Says *you*," Ishim growled.

"1ˢᵗ Platoon, sir," Sergeant March, the company's communications NCO, handed Steele a phone.

"Steele," he answered. "What's...?"

"Our bombing party was halfway in, halfway out, Ned," Grimes said. "Suddenly we were getting *showered* by *Hun* bombs.

---

[1] Machine guns are crew-served weapons, not personal weapons. Their operators are only *issued* sidearms. In 1917, this was either a M1911 pistol or a M1917 revolver, both firing .45 ACP cartridges.

I lit a flare, and my guns opened up. A few seconds later we've got Huns in the trenches and we're fighting 'em off with clubs and shovels."[1]

"How are you holding now, Gary?"

"Lost a gun position for a few moments, but we took it back. *Canucks* got a couple of them gray devils trapped in a sap."

"*Let* 'em…Steele," he said into a second phone March handed him, dropping the first.

"Butcher: Report."

"Huns followed our bombing party in, sir," Steele said. "Got 'em contained." Dona frowned in the dimming flare light; they were not supposed to say *sir* or mention rank on the wire in case the Germans were listening. "It'll quiet down in a few moments."

"Very well. Out."

Steele handed the phone back to March; Dona nodded. "*Better*, Captain," Dona said. "Keep all calls brief and to the point. Say only what *needs* saying."

"Brief; yes," Steele sighed. "Can they *really*…?"

"It is surprising how much the *Boche* can glean from a single conversation—even a single word—Captain," Dona said. "You *Amis* have so *much* to say about so *little*…"

"*Merci, Commandant*," Steele sighed. Dona was right; he was *always* right; he was very *persistent* about being right. There was so much to learn and *un*learn, casual, unconscious habits to be broken; so many ways a man could get killed, even by doing nothing. Even a Mills bomb in a pouch drew scrutiny: the ring on the pin could rattle unless they were in the pouch upside down, and they had to be in the pouch *just* the *right* way or they would be difficult to pull in a hurry. There were literally hundreds of such minor *tricks* the Americans had to learn that Dona, Talbott and their Canadian hosts were teaching them every waking hour. "How did we ever fight a war *before*…?"

"You didn't fight the *Boche* in this war, Captain," Dona said. "Ours is a *different* way of war. I have been fighting since 1914, before we began to act like so many *moles*…"

---

[1] Preferred to the bayonet for close-quarters fighting.

Then the *metal clanged…"GAS!"*[1]

Everyone ripped off their helmets, pulled their smoke hoods over their heads, quickly adjusted the chin and head straps, recovered and donned their helmets…and waited for the *screaming* seven-sevens with their distinctive yellow smoke that usually followed the heavier gun's gas shelling…and *that* came in as if on a *schedule*…

Somewhere on the left, a machine gun rattled, followed by the minor explosions of grenades. "Everyone on your toes," Steele said.

A flare burst into the darkness on the left; first one, then another, until once again the entire line was lit up by streaks of magnesium fire.

But the machine guns fell silent…*no* movement in No-man's-land…

Silence…

27th November, Hill 90.

Gas attack last night. Could feel myself breathe in the smoke hood…We ran and stumbled up the hill…Trenches at night are disorienting, especially during an attack… Twenty-eight casualties, including Grimes. Not that bad for an evening in a [expletive] charnel house…

"Major Dona," Steele asked, his voice muffled by his smoke hood. "*What* are we…?"

"Perhaps the *Boche* just want you *Amis* to know that they are aware of your presence, Captain," Dona said. "A special *Bonjour* for you."

"This is *common*?"

"It is *not* unusual. We do something *like* it when the Prussian

---

[1] The gas alarm was simply any metal striking metal.

Guards move into the trenches."

"Well, *that's* a relief," McTee grunted.

In the darkness, a line of flickering lights, like candles, followed by the dull *BOOM* of artillery. "*VERS LE BAS,*"[1] Dona shouted, throwing himself on the bottom of the dugout.

The night exploded into a kaleidoscope of flashes of explosions…mud and trench props flying amid shrapnel and bodies…

And again…silence…except for a chattering machine gun in the distance…and muffled explosions.

"*Mon Ami,*" Dona said, "we should move back to your *main* post of command…"

As they picked up their weapons and gear, the battle picked up….

His chest aching, Steele watched the scene before him as soon as he reached his PC, twisting the handle of his periscope to lower the viewing angle until he could see *most* of No-man's-land, and the outpost line on both sides as a flare lit the landscape….

Steele watched a panorama of flashing lights and moving shadows, of ghostly lumps moving in the glare of flares, of dark fountains of earth and debris lit by internal fires while the machine guns rattled and roared and blasted in the inky night, their muzzle flashes barely visible….

As suddenly as it started…it stopped, followed by the eerie silence.

Steele picked up the phone. "Give me 1st Platoon…"

"*No* answer…"

"Try 3rd Platoon…"

"Ishim."

"What's your status?"

"Counting noses now. Out."

"Dona," Steele yelled, "grab your rifle and come with me." They filed through the dark trenches, feeling their way through the muck and debris, checking the occasional body for signs of life as the aidmen and litter bearers hustled past, machine guns firing

---

[1] *DOWN!*

scheduled missions all the while. Ammunition parties added to the confusion while others cleared damaged trenches.

It was some time before Steele found Grimes' dugout. A pair of German grenades had simultaneously found its opening, blowing out the door canvas and killing a man inside. Grimes *was* inside, but *behind* two men.

"You all right," Steele asked.

"Eh?" Grimes answered loudly. "Ears ringing." He pointed to a man badly gouged by shrapnel. "He's *bleeding*, at least."

"So are you," Steele shouted. "Your *ears*…"

"I'm *just* about to look around," Grimes said, getting to his feet unsteadily, almost shouting, shaking his head. "Ah, on *second* thought…where's Sergeant Nagurski?"

"Ammo bunker, sir," a voice replied.

"Send a runner for him," Steele said.

"*I'll* go, sir," the voice answered.

"Wait a minute," Steele said. "Who *are* you?"

"Private DeHaan, sir."

"Be back with Nagurski in ten minutes and I'll make you a Corporal."

"Sir."

"Your phone's knocked out," Steele yelled at Grimes. "Switchboard can't get through to you."

"Explains why I can't call out," Grimes shouted.

Steele watched the aidmen working, machine gun crews carrying guns and gear, ammunition crates hauled, and telephone wire strung. He dimly wondered if he'd *trained* this kind of drive into them…

"Sir," a voice shook him from his reverie, "Nagurski."

Steele couldn't see the big NCO's face in the dark, but remembered a dark-skinned man with a thin mustache. "All right…DeHaan, find some stripes."

"Sir," came the voice.

"Sergeant, it's *your* platoon, now. Let's have a look around." Steele followed Nagurski, groping in the dark and dodging bustling men.

Nagurski rattled off a summary as they went. "Three live and six backup and dummy positions in forward trenches; five live and twelve backup and dummies in the support positions."

"Gun status?" Steele asked.

"We *lost* one gun that I *know* of so far this evening."

"Repairable?"

"*Probably*; else it will be spare parts."

"Let's have a look at your ammo supply." The pair picked their way to the ammo dugout, a cavernous hole stacked high with ammunition crates and divided by thick wooden partitions. "How's your supply?" Steele asked a Corporal.

"*Fair*, sir," the man answered. "Twelve boxes and forty-eight Mills bombs per gun on hand."

"You're *sure* of that?" Steele asked.

"Only one way *in* and one way *out*, sir," the man declared. "Two boxes for each carrying party; we had twenty-five carrying parties this evening; still…"

"*How* can you be…?" Steele started.

"Sergeant Nagurski's idea, sir," the man said. "Each box contains *two hundred* rounds on strips and *four* Mills bombs. *This* way we can…"

"Distribute and count both at the same time," Steele finished. "*Smart*, Sergeant."

"*Thank* you, sir," Nagurski said.

"We'll implement this system company wide," Steele said. "We *need* that kind of thinking."

"Yessir," Nagurski said. "Now, sir, if I can get back to…"

"Yes, of course. I'll take Lieutenant Grimes to the forward dressing station. Sergeant *Nagurski*, take charge."

***

Under hooded lanterns and canvas, a medico moved from litter to litter, from soldier to soldier. "What's the *count* and who's in charge?" Steele addressed the entire dugout.

The delicate-looking senior aidman had an odd crease across his forehead. "Corporal Beringer, sir," a voice said. "*We* have nine *litter*; twelve *walking* wounded…"

"*Gone west*…?"[1]

"We've seen *seven*, sir; three of *ours*."

"Take charge of Lieutenant Grimes, here…"

"*Yessir*…"

28ᵗʰ November, Hill 90.

Quiet night. No more [Blotches of ink] *bn. from Prince Edward Island relieved the Newfoundlanders. Met senior Capt. as Col. and Maj. are casualties. He has 567 men in a bn. that should have 900.* [Expletive] *Passchendaele has used them up.*

Tomorrow would be Thanksgiving. We won't get any [expletive] *turkey up here; even Willis isn't that good. Canucks mounted heads on sandbags, left them on a parapet as bait for a Hun they've been trying to get for days. I resist calling this place a Golgotha, but it certainly is a place of suffering and skulls.*

29ᵗʰ November [No entry; pen date]

30ᵗʰ November. Hill 90. [Pencil entry and date]
Pen became a casualty…absolutely still…the Canucks call it Toilet Time…My only reaction was oh, [expletive]…*There was no time to lose… hundreds of*

---

[1] Killed.

Click-click-click..."Steele." Even though they'd been on Hill 90 for only seven days, it was hard for Steele to recall a time when he wasn't in a stinking, rat-and-lice-infested trench, bunker or dugout. During that time, his machine guns had supported *many* Canadian patrols, bombing raids, and wire parties, responding to fire missions from all over the hill, shooting planned *and* unplanned missions at all hours.

He'd lost track of the German raids and full-blown attacks.

"Get *ready*..." the soft telephone voice said. "It's only *this* quiet before..."

The eastern horizon was lit by explosions, and suddenly the night stillness was ever-so-gently broken by the rumbling of heavy guns, followed by the *crack* of light howitzers...then, the *shush-shush-shush* of shells passing overhead...then, the ground seemed to *explode* ...

The German Maxims opened fire, the *bzzz-bzzz-bzzz* of the bullets ending abruptly in a muddy torrential blizzard of *thut-thut-thut* as they hit the reverse of the hill...

Half of Steele's guns were where *most* of the bullets were falling...

All of this happened within a few moments while Steele dumbly held the telephone receiver, watching and listening to this awful spectacle, as if he were someone *else,* some*where* else. The telephone crackled again, and Steele... "*Steele!*"

"On our left and right," the voice said. "Missions 6 and 9."

"*Out,*" Steele answered, grabbing his company phone and Missions List. "1st Platoon fire Mission 6, *standing*; 2nd Platoon Mission 9, *standing*..."

Behind him, Steele heard the Canadian and British artillery open fire, followed by trench mortars to his left and right. "All right," he told his runners and telephone operators. "*Forward* post *now!*"

As they decamped for the forward command post dugout at the crest of the hill, Steele heard his machine guns opening fire...

"Get to 3rd Platoon," Steele told McTee…

Steele had a hard time figuring out just *what* he was seeing through his binoculars. The ghostly lumps in front of the outpost zone kept moving, stopped, and occasionally started lighting up in the glare of their muzzle flashes. In the dull glare of the flares, he could see clouds of dust and mud thrown up as if in a motion picture….

By the time he reached his forward post, March had already got there and handed him the telephone. "Fire Mission 5, *sweep left to right*…"

"Sir," March handed him *another* telephone…

"Steele."

"B Boy Company: my flank is open. Give me your Mission 12, and a *lot of it*."

"*Out*." To the operator, he said, "1st Platoon."

"*Here*."

"Fire Mission 12, *standing*."

"*I'm* on…"

"*Split fire*."

"*Out*."

A cloud of…*something*…descended in front of the outpost line.

"Sir," March tapped Steele's shoulder.

"Steele…"

"B Boy again. Shift east two hundred; you're too bloody close…"

"*Out*. 1st Platoon…*sweep left* two hundred…"

"*Out*…"

And the flares burned out, pitching the scene into darkness…

"3rd Platoon: Mission 9, *standing*…" Steele's guns kept firing…he kept adjusting…"2nd Platoon: Mission 7, *standing bump left*…"[1]

---

[1] A "bump" adjusted the weapon by striking the reciever with a fist. A bump could shift the impact area up to fifty yards at a thousand yard's range.

December

1ˢᵗ December, Hill 90. [Pencil date only]

2ⁿᵈ December, Hill 90.

[Illegible; unknown stain]*...we were in a standing barrage that cut and hit everything... and then we heard the iron ringing...And here they were...How glorious the sunrise...thin like every other on this God-damned hill...That "minor attack" cost five dead and thirty hurt...Hot food will restore the soul better than a million* [expletive] *sermons...fed a hot meal to everyone who showed up...Newfoundlanders back in last night... You would think they could wait another day to get on this* [expletive] *rock.*

"*Gas,*" Steele shouted, grabbing for his smoke hood as he pitched his steel helmet off. "*Keep firing,*" he shouted again, muffled by his smoke hood.

The German artillery became heavier...*thunderous, deafening* high explosive and *screaming* shrapnel...mortar bombs fell all around Steele's bunker, joining the artillery by reaching into the very depths of the trenches, spewing their deadly cargoes within those confined spaces...

But Steele's fire didn't slacken...

"3ʳᵈ Platoon..."

"*Yo...*"

"*Sweep down* one hundred...*bump* left and right..."

The artillery *thundered*...Steele's guns *chattered*...machine-gun bullets *bzzz-bzzz-bzzz* like a million hornets before they *thut-thut-thut* into the earth...and *men*...

"Sir," March tapped Steele on the shoulder... "1ˢᵗ Platoon..."

"Steele..."

"1ˢᵗ Platoon...place," he heard...*thut-thut-thut-thut-thut-thut*...

"Hello? Hello?" He looked around the bunker. "Runner: get to 1ˢᵗ Platoon; tell me what they just said."

A shell landed nearby...*thut-thut-thut-thut-thut-thut*...

"*Check* the *wires*," Steele yelled at another runner. The boy switched wires on the telephone, cranked, switched again, then scrambled out of the bunker, wire reeling off the rig on his back...*thut-thut-thut-thut-thut-thut*...

"They're *in* the outpost line on the right," a panting runner shouted into Steele's ear.

"*Get to 4ᵗʰ Platoon*," Steele shouted at another runner. "Tell them *SOS Right Immediate*."

"*Sir*," the boy said, and dashed away...*thut-thut-thut-thut-thut-thut*...

"*Here they come*," someone said; Steele grabbed for his Enfield; March shouldered a Lewis gun and went out of the bunker...

The *bzzz-bzzz-bzzz* and *thut-thut-thut stopped,* but Steele's guns still chattered...

Shapes appeared out of the darkness as if they were wraiths, their rifles and shovels dark, their grenades pitching forward, their gas masks making them look like unworldly blobs. Steele shouldered his rifle as he looked up to see a specter raise its bayonet as if to stab down. He fired; the specter fell. March's Lewis gun kept blasting into the darkness; some blobs fell. Other shadows grew larger; more menacing. A grenade came towards Steele; he ducked down as it *swished* over his head, bouncing away before going off.

The battalion telephone in the bunker rattled and rang...

"*Sir*," a runner called to Steele...

"*Steele*..."

"Huns in *front* of the *main...right*..." Ishim yelled.

"*Out*...react *right*..."

"*Out*," Brick answered. Vaguely, Steele could imagine Brick and his men—cooks and clerks and supply men, Dona and Talbott and McTee and Rogers—armed with two Lewis guns, four

Hotchkiss guns, rifles and grenades somewhere behind him….

More shadows appeared near the front of the trench. Steele fired at them; March's Lewis gun blasted away. The shadows stopped, one fell. More grenades *swished* over Steele's head, exploding behind him….

Steele's guns kept firing…

More shadows in front. Steele and March fired; the shadows vanished.

Steele's guns kept firing…

***

Sunrise….

"*This* is getting monotonous," McTee grumbled, stretching his long frame outside Steele's PC. March, inside, struggled to rewire the switchboard…again.

"Let's get to work, Top," Steele sighed, standing beside him, twisting his shoulders. "We'll have to use 4th *Platoon* to make up our losses," Steele said.

"Yessir," McTee agreed. 4th Platoon, the ammunition and service platoon, was *larger* than the other three. It had its own four guns to provide emergency support fire, including the reaction force. Now they needed to feed the insatiable needs for ammunition and spare parts in the firing platoons. "We're already down to three sections per…"

"I know, Top, but unless you've got a better idea…"

"I *don't*," McTee said.

They knew just how *minor* this attack had been. Their 1st Platoon, covering the 2nd Company on the left of the hill, had lost two entire five-man gun crews and one gun damaged. 3rd Platoon, covering the 3rd Company on the right of the hill mass, lost parts of three crews. The attack *overran* Steele's 2nd Platoon in the middle of the hill, but had miraculously *lost* not a man, but *wounded* nearly all of them.

"This unit is now officially at half effective strength," Steele sighed. "Our *tenth* day."

"We *could* get some wounded back today, sir," McTee offered.

"We could *not*, too, Top," Steele said.

"Let's organize some Chinee; get the men some rest from moving ammo," McTee suggested.

"*Good* idea," Steele said. "*Forgot* about them. Have Willis see to it while I…re-figure the barrages."

***

"The cooks say they've got *fresh chow…*" McTee said, sticking his head in the PC.

Suddenly Steele felt hungry. "I'm *famished.*" Together, they made their way to the chow bunker. McTee sniffed the air. "The cooks have *something…huh.*"

Steele sniffed, the aroma of warm food rousing him. "Smells like *something,* but *not…*familiar. And *biscuits.*" Moments later, Steele gazed at his dinner—whatever it was—and two biscuits. "It's *not* beef," he declared, tasting it.

"After *Maconochie* for the past…*how long?*"

"Can't remember…"

"Me neither."

"Didn't *Willis…*last night?" Steele pulled a scribbled note out of a pocket:

Mule corral hit; total loss. Cooks cleaning up.

"What's *Jack* got to say?" McTee asked…then said, "*this* is *long-ear stew…*with *potatoes* and *onions* and *cabbage…*"

"Yep…never *had* it before."

"Keeps you from starving. They're feeding everyone today: Canucks, Chinee…*everyone…*"

"Good." Steele thought for a moment. "Have 'em take a pot to St. Beth, too. Biscuits if they've got any left."

"*Yes*sir." He smiled, chuckled lightly. "Just thinking about that *other* song," he started:

The bells of Hell go ting-a-ling-a-ling
For you, but not for me!
For me, the angels sing-a-ling-a-ling
In three-part harmony!
Oh death, where is thy sting-a-ling-a-ling,
Oh grave, thy victory?

They finished their food, licking their pans clean after sponging the last juices up with their biscuits. They rinsed out their mess kits in the cistern reserved for gas relief.

And made their way back up the hill…

***

"How are those laborers working out?" Steele asked.

"They can haul their weight in ammo, I swear," McTee declared. "Can't speak a *lick* of American, but they can do what they're told in *French*.[1] Lieutenant Brick's got them organized."

"Good," Steele said. "Machine gun units *expect* 50% casualties every tour at the front.…"

"In *ten days*," McTee said. "We've averaged…let's see…a little *less* than five percent a day…?"

"Yeah," Steele said. "Let's hope the Huns don't try anything before they find us some relief…" Steele blinked, stretching out. "Now, if the *war* doesn't mind, I'm sacking out."

3rd December, Hill 90.

[Unidentified stain covers the rest of the page.]

Watching the bodies in the zone like the song:

If you want to find the old battalion,

I know where they are,

They're hanging on the old barbed wire

I've seen 'em. I've seen 'em,

Hanging on the old barbed wire,

---

[1] France imported thousands of Vietnamese and Chinese laborers during the war, among them a *camion* driver who would later go by the name Ho Chi Minh.

I've seen 'em,

Hanging on the old barbed wire.

4th December, Hill 90.

Silence is strange here, even in the morning. And so is the sunrise, peaceful and warm through the smoke and gas...yet, here we still are...I cannot imagine how these medicos do it, up to their elbows in blood and gore, day in and day out. We have suffered nine dead and twenty-two wounded last night. [Illegible]

"Bells of Hell," Top.

The Huns killed five gunners and two others; one with a bullet; the rest with shrapnel. One killed by gas; not a mark on him, but his mouth was foamy. Talbott, Buchalter and Ishim are among the hurt, to be evacuated. Thirty-one in all. I should write letters... We are being relieved this evening...McTee's replacement has very big shoes to fill...My Canuck counterpart is a fragile-looking man with a ragged mustache who obviously knows his business. Never knew anyone could hang that many Mills bombs on himself...

We leave Hill 90 with no regrets, having learned more in eleven days than in the previous eleven weeks...and we have lost a most helpful trainer...

Sometime during the night, the artillery fire had fallen off;

Steele didn't have a sense of time any longer; he couldn't tell if that was hours or minutes or days before. His lungs ached from having to breathe wearing his smoke hood all night, *and fight* in it, *and yell* in it...

McFadden appeared in Steele's PC. "All clear, lad," he said. "Take it off and come on *out*."

"Thanks, sir." Steele pulled off his gas hood and grabbed a lungful of air as he stepped out, still smelling vaguely of hay.

"Anytime," McFadden answered. "Smoke," he passed Steele a cigar.

"Sir." He put the cigar to the proffered match.

"You've done *well*, Steele," McFadden said, leaning on the trench wall opposite Steele. "Held 'em *off* again."

Steele nodded, his ears still ringing.

"That'll pass, by the way," McFadden mumbled.

"*What* will?"

"Battle shock," McFadden said. "Your first shift up here is the worst. Survive *that* and every one *after's* easy."

Steele looked at McFadden sideways. "You believe that?"

"Nay, but I say that to *everyone*."

"Does it help?"

"It *seems* to." McFadden lit a cigar himself. "Have your people regroup; they got somewhat *scattered* last night."

"Yessir. I need to *check* on them," Steele said. "Casualties and..."

"Your *replacement's* just drawing up in the rear now..."

* * *

"Ned," Miller nodded. "Here for service or just snooping?" Steele stood outside Miller's main aid station just as the morning twilight glowed on the horizon.

"Just snooping," Steele said. "Seeing what this evening brought you." Miller's aid station was a busy place, dealing with casualties from the entire hill.

"It brought me another thirty-one casualties," Miller declared, glancing at a bandaged arm. "And *nine* went west ..."

***

He put his diary down, took up his company notebook and checked off the names of the dead. He read silently until he read…"Dent," he said aloud.

"Sir," the clerk, a boy he didn't know, asked as he jerked his head up.

"*Dent* got killed."

"Didn't know him, sir. You…?"

"Met in the chow line…Bachmann?" Steele wondered.

"A machine gunner; 3rd Platoon."

Steele stared at the boy, unable to pull the clerk's *name* out of his memory. "I should know *your* name…"

"Chinn, sir."

"*Oh*, yes; sorry…*Baker*," he mused. "Who's Baker?"

"Third Squad, 2nd Platoon, sir," Chinn said. "Ammo bearer."

Steele tried to visualize the man. "Small; from Tennessee…"

"*Yessir*. Had a four-foot tapeworm the doctors pulled out of him before we came over."

"You *know* him," Steele asked.

"From my hometown, sir," Chinn sighed. "Murfreesboro, Tennessee. Served with him in Mexico. Gave up the *cavalry* to come here."

"Ah…"

"Was *sweet* on my *sister*…"

"Oh…"

"She got *hitched* last May. Got a baby on the way…"

"Who's the senior Sergeant in the company now?"

"Nagurski, sir."

"I've gotta go see him."

***

"At *ease*," someone called as Steele entered the 1st Platoon dugout.

"Carry on," Steele said quickly. "Sergeant Nagurski."

"Sir," the dark Sergeant stood near a board table.

"Sarge," Steele said, "*got* a moment? Outside?"

"Sir," Nagurski nodded, following Steele.

They stepped aside as an ammo party passed. "If you haven't *heard*, Sergeant McTee…last night." He paused, letting it set in…

Nagurski didn't flinch. "We *heard*, sir," he said.

"As the senior NCO in the company, now…"

"*Yes*sir," he said simply. "Let me pack, turn my *rosters* over to…ah, Chris Bellows."

"Go ahead, Sergeant. Come by Company HQ before dark, if you can. Ask Sergeant Bellows to join me here."

"Yessir." Nagurski nodded and ducked into the dugout.

"Sir," a small, wiry man with dark eyes approached Steele a few minutes later. "Sergeant Bellows…"

"Sergeant, the 1st Platoon is yours now…"

"Yessir," Bellows answered. "*Stan* told me…"

"Stan…Sergeant Nagurski?"

"Yessir."

"All right," Steele said. "Get your range cards in order, and your signal book. The relief team should be here in a few hours…"

***

"We'll pull ye *off* this *rock* now," McFadden said breezily; it was just dusk. "You did what they *sent* ye here ta do…"

"Which was?"

"Help us hold on to this *worthless dung heap* we call Hill 90 and the Belgians call Deadly Hill."

"That *and…*"

"Aye, I reckon…and *that*."

"*Much* more *that* than…"

"*Above* me *station*, lad, and *yours*, too. Such matters as providing battle experience for our Yank friends are far above *our* meagre purses. I can only say that we're *most* grateful for the assistance ye provided."

"And…*Commandant* Dona? His family's somewhere near the

Spanish border. Can *you…?*"

"I'll make *sure* the word gets home."

5ᵗʰ December, Amiens

I find myself too weary to write now.

7ᵗʰ December, en route west of Camiers.

I am informed that we are to get a new camp.

"Captain Steele," the dispatch rider, now a familiar figure, held out his envelope for Steele. He had just met the train at a water stop.

Steele regarded the wiry lad quickly. "What's *your* name, now that *you* know *mine?*"

"Erskine, sir."

"How'd you get *this* job, Erskine?"

"I speak French, Dutch, Walloon, and German, sir. I know—or *knew* before the war—the roads, and I could ride and repair motorcycles before I joined."

"*How* did you…?"

"My father was in the motorcycle business, sir; we spent most of my first fifteen years here, doing research and development with Peugeot and Triumph, and with some Belgian and Dutch firms." He shrugged. "I just picked up the local languages."

"Ah. Are you to *wait* for…?"

"Yessir."

Steele fished two letters out of the envelope, and read the first…

> *Capt. Steele*
> *Your trains are being diverted to Boulogne-sur-Mer and a new camp to facilitate your training of US Army machine gunners in the British zone. This assignment will not detract from your imminent expansion. The rest of your unit will meet you at your new destination, Camp Steele.*
> *Fox Conner, ACoS G3, AEF*

"Huh," Steele shrugged. Then he read the second letter…

> *Steele,*
> *Your changes have met with some skepticism but are accepted after consultation with wiser heads.*
> *Yours,*
> *Pershing*

"Huh. *Got* what we asked for?" Steele stared at the note. "Dad always said, be careful what you wish for; you *might* get it."

"I've always heard 'ask,' sir, but it's wise, either way," Erskine said, adding, "do you have a reply?"

"I do." Steele took his pencil out of his diary, ripped out a blank page, and wrote:

> *Sir,*
> *Appreciate your confidence in me. We will do our very best to both train new gunners and reorganize.*
> *Steele*
> *P.S.: What do I have to do to get Erskine assigned to me?*

"Want to work for me, Erskine?"

"I go where I'm *sent*, sir," he replied.

7ʰ December, Camp Steele, Etaples, France. [Second

entry with the same date; different location]

Bedding them down takes more than I thought I

had in me… Whose is that face in my mirror…?

The train rolled to a halt at a genuine railroad station with ramps and a sign that read *Etaples.*

"Huh," Steele declared, stepping down to the platform from his boxcar. "Our new home's *near* here, I'm told."

"We gonna have to build it?" Brick asked, stretching his back. "If we've gotta train new gunners right away, *and…*"

"Find out when we *get* there," Steele declared. "Let's unload the vehicles and…"

"Looking for Captain Steele," a loud voice on the platform called. "Is Captain…?"

"Steele *here*," he answered.

"I'm Griffin, your guide, sir," a slight British Lieutenant answered. "I'm to show you to your new camp."

"Well, that's a better reception than we got the *last* time," Brick growled.

"No *doubt*," Griffin nodded. "Sir, my *car* is waiting."

"Very well," Steele said, waving to Nagurski. "Sergent Nagurski, come with me to our new billet. Lieutenant Brick, supervise the unloading."

Steele followed Griffin to a big town car with a hard roof, a make Steele didn't recognize. "*What* kind of auto is this…?"

"Vauxhall, sir," Griffin said as they got in. "Apologize for the smell, but the heater's lit and it's warm…"

"*Quite* all right, Lieutenant," Steele declared. "Been *cold* for two *weeks*." They splashed down a rutted track, riding it well. "*Good* suspension," Steele observed.

"Indeed," Griffin said, unsurprised. "Not quite a Rolls Royce, but it'll do. Handles this track *quite* well. Your camp is just ahead."

They approached a gate with a small guard shack manned by an American soldier braving the misty snow. The driver stopped; the guard peered in the driver's window, then at the back seat. "You belong here?" he asked rudely.

"I believe so," Steele answered. "I'm Captain Steele."

"Captain…*oh*, sir, I didn't…I just *joined* the outfit."

"It's all right, Private. I believe I am expected."

"You *are*, sir," the guard said. "I'll raise the gate."

They drove through on a hard dirt road, passing several wooden buildings before stopping at a two-story brick structure with a sign that read: HQ, 432nd Machine Gun Battalion (Provisional), AEF.

Willis stood just inside the open front door. "If I didn't *know* better," Nagurski grunted, "I'd say Jack *conjured* this camp out of thin air."

"*Some*one did," Steele declared, looking around. "He's still *conjuring* it. Construction all over."

All along the road further down from the brick structure,

frames of buildings rose. Scores of wagons and carts carrying lumber, ladders, and stacks of materials joined a handful of trucks and autos parked along the road. A few muddy steps brought Steele to the building where he met Willis at the entrance. "Willis, I take it *you* are responsible for this?"

"Well, not *exactly*, sir, *no*. But I *suggested* that our accommodations over *there* were rather *primitive* for…"

"Sir," Griffin interrupted, "we started this camp for a cavalry battalion that got sent to Egypt, anyhow. General Haig *gifted* it to you Americans while you are *here*."

"Uh-huh," Steele said, glancing around. "Well, gentlemen, let's have a look at our new camp."

***

Steele could only take stock of his own small room behind the orderly room in the big brick building after it was dark. It was no bigger than any room he had shared with a brother, but it held a canvas cot, a side table, two chairs, his field desk, and a standing iron locker. A single electric light hung from the ceiling. A coal stove, hastily lit, notched in the wall shared by the orderly room, provided welcome heat.

But his little room connected to a bathroom with a shower bath. Griffin took pains to point out the *electric* water heater on the wall.

Stripping off everything that had stuck to him for two weeks, Steele didn't much *care* where the hot water came from as he rubbed his hands under the faucet for several minutes, splashing his face. Then, with his last new razor blade loaded in his Gillette's razor, he worked up a *good* lather and…

Steele beheld an unbelievable, if wet, distortion of who he remembered the last time he saw himself. He stared at the face in his mirror, seeing minor cuts and scrapes on his chin and jaw. A bigger scrape from a flying bit of *something* he barely remembered scabbed on his nose. His brown hair was greasy, with streaks of an ashy color. His eyes were deeply sunken holes.

He was not quite twenty-two and he could not recognize his own reflection.

"I wonder when Dad turned gray?" he asked himself, too tired to think much about it.

Methodically, he soaped and shaved before he dunked his

razor under the tap without looking into his eyes in the mirror.

After a swift shower with warmish water, there came a knock on his door. "Sir," Rodgers' voice came through Steele's fog.

"What *is* it?" Steele asked, toweling off.

"Would you care for an apéritif?" Silence. "Sir? Dr. Miller thought you might need something *medicinal*."

"All right."

Rodgers set a tray, a small glass, and a bottle of brandy on the field desk. He stepped back towards the door. "Will there be anything *else*, sir?"

Steele stared at the bottle. "Can you find Canthrox[1] powder?"

"I *think* I can, sir, but I *have* a recipe if I can't."

"Can you *cut* hair?"

"If you mean *barber*, sir, I *can*. I can *shave*, as well." He still waited. "Dr. Miller wants me to *ensure*…"

"Yes." Steele poured the *liquer* into the glass and sipped. "*Better* brandy than…"

"From the doctor's *personal* stores, sir…If that will be all?"

"Yes; *thank* you. Goodnight, Sergeant."

"I'll set aside time for a haircut at your convenience, sir?"

"*Thank* you."

Steele finished his brandy, poured another, then lay down on his cot…and dreamed of a young woman on a train amid the buzzing of Maxim bullets and the stink of gas and excrement and blood and cordite…

10th December, Camp Steele, Etaples, France

Odd how that looks, now that I write it…we finally

have the whole of the company present, but with only

164 of the 255 we had just three weeks ago…G will

never know what her brother might go through…I got

---

[1] Canthrox was the only commercial shampoo available in 1917.

"Fall...*IN!*" Nagurski eyed the formation critically for several moments. "*Cover,* damnit!" It always amazed Steele how old Sergeants knew *instinctively* when a formation wasn't perfect from *any* angle. Finally satisfied, Nagurski faced about and waited for Steele to march up. "Sir, *company* is *formed.*"

"Thank you, Sergeant," Steele saluted; Nagurski moved off. "Post!" Steele shouted; the officers (those present) moved forward, replacing the Sergeants in front of the formations. "At *ease,* men," Steele ordered. The men all gazed at him in anticipation. "Men, we've suffered our first combat losses, and we shall miss them all. But we have a few replacements, *and* the men we left behind, and I'm told we're going to be getting more. Now..." he waited for the murmurs to die down. "Easy, men. We'll be forming," he pointed to the sign on the HQ, "a *battalion* while we're training new gunners; new *American* gunners coming over here in larger numbers; more Americans are arriving every day." More murmurs. "Yes, we took some *knocks* up on Deadly Hill, but *we,* by *God, gave* as good as we *got!*" More murmurs, plus a few shouts of "here, here." "Now, as you well know, we've taken on *Vickers* guns that...*I* know, *I* know; ain't got the *range* and the water system's are trouble. But it's what we're *told* to use, to *train* on, and so we *shall.* Along with our good old Hotchkiss, I'm told these *newer* Vickers guns are simpler and far more reliable than what we've used in the past. Now, let's get back to work. Comp-*NAY! At*-ten-SHUN! Platoon leaders, *take* charge."

"*Hooray* for *Captain Steele!*" someone shouted, followed by a loud roar.

Steele couldn't help but shiver as he moved off....

***

Looking at the small pile of mail he received when it finally caught up to them, Steele tried to figure out which he might read first. He resolved the conundrum by starting with the oldest postmark: Georgia's letter sent a week after the last one...which meant she hadn't got his *first* answer yet.

My Dearest Ned,

The more I think of our brief association, the more I believe I am losing my heart. I cannot imagine my life without you....

I went to the late-summer cotillion with your brother George, who was a perfect young gentleman but was not you, *my dear. Your father was most gracious in allowing such a young man to escort me. I wore a pink lace and crinoline dress with my white shoes and a funny little pink hat...*

There is a Red Cross function your sister Betty wants me to take part in; dancing for tickets. I find such a thing crass, crude and demeaning for all concerned...

Write to me as soon as you can, dear heart.

Your loving,

Georgia

Reading her letter over and again, the utter *tragedy* of her sheltered life struck Steele. She could not appreciate that her brother might go to one of those *crude and demeaning* functions just to talk to someone *not* in uniform for a while. And did she not realize how absolutely *trivial* the color of her shoes was to either of them? He decided…not, and composed a reply in his head:

Just got back from the front, lost a little more than a hundred men killed and hurt and found out what vomit, gunpowder, blood, rotting corpses, rat droppings and green cross all at once smell like...

He opened the thicker envelope from home.

Dear Ned:

All is well here and hope you are, too...Your mother is fine, sends her love along with the enclosed notes. The children are well; I got a letter from Charlie last week, is well and now has a commission, too...

The factory has more orders than it can fill, may have to contract out the assembly work...

Red Cross and Field Service people, YMCA and the like are everywhere collecting money and volunteers for their work...

Al has finished his Four-Minute Man training and has become a spectacular orator (don't tell him I said that). He makes mention that he might run for Congress. I will

*forward any of your news to Charlie and Betty (she shall
be at Camp Custer with the Red Cross in a week) and
hope you can stay safe.*
    Yours Sincerely,
    Dad.

There was also a note from his mother.

Neddie, Dear
    *We are all quite well. Francine is starting her
internship in January; Helen and Irving are rolling
bandages in your honor. I wanted once again to implore
you to please take care of yourself. We are all well here
and it is not your job to worry about us. Make sure you
change your stockings whenever you can.*
    Love,
    Mama

Another from Diane:

Ned,
    *...Georgia, I believe, is seeing things in <u>your</u> absent
eyes I did not see when you were <u>here</u>. Beware of the
siren song of lonely hearts, buddy. We're all well here
and I'm working at the factory again, keeping the books.*
    Miss you,
    Di

And from George:

Ned,
    *All's well here and I am getting straight A's at the
Normal School, and I feel confident I will pass my
examinations. I went to a cotillion with Georgia and she
could not stop talking about you. Real confidence boost
to walk out with a gal and she only talks about some
other guy, even if it is your brother. Don't worry about
us, just keep your head down.*
    George.

Steele folded and tucked them all away for answering
sometime later, when he had both the energy *and* something more
positive to say other than, yes, he was *still alive.*

"…And it is with *great* pleasure that the Secretary of War confers upon Edmund A. Steele the rank of Major in the National Army, effective on the first day of October, 1917…" Rorshack read the orders in the dry fashion that adjutants read all such orders as Pershing pinned the gold oak leaves on his epaulets.

"Congratulations, *Major*," Pershing smiled as he shook his hand. "I *knew* I saw something in you when we met on the border."

"*Thank* you, sir," Steele answered. "I just hope I can fulfill your vision."

"I'm *sure* you *will*, Major. We'll talk *later*, when I have more *time* to *palaver*."

"*Yes*sir."

"*Three cheers* for *Major* Steele!" someone in the formation shouted…and cheer they did.

But Rorshack wasn't done…

"…The Secretary, having confidence in the leadership and fidelity of Major Edmund A. Steele, assigns him to the command of the 432nd Machine Gun Battalion, that shall be formed at Camp Steele, Etaples, France, under the command of the American Expeditionary Force, effective this 15th day of November, 1917."

The hand-shakes came later and were many….

***

Dear Georgia
…Hope you do not mind my pencil as my pen became
a casualty of war. I find myself at a loss of for anything
to write about, as much of what I do with my time is dull
routine and the other? You don't want to read about it.
I wish you would not find Red Cross dances to be at
all demeaning. The Red Cross helps many, including me,

my men and your brother. It is a great morale boost to
talk to someone who isn't in the Army for a little while.
    I achieved a promotion to Major and am now
commanding a machine gun battalion. The camp here is
nicer than any we have had since we arrived in France.
My room is in a brick building with an electric light. I
took my first shower bath in nearly a month...
    Your friend,
    Ned

Steele folded the letter carefully, thinking, wondering if she would catch the irony of his primitive conditions, exemplified by his pencil...and he needed a pen; even *Willis* had trouble finding those...

    Al,
    A quick letter in pencil, begging for a pen, as Dad's
graduation gift broke down, not from overuse but
combat. I need nothing fancy; a Parker or Sheaffer, not
a Waterman. Tell everyone I am promoted to Major and
now command a battalion. Not much else to report other
than water pressure here is very weak. My best to all.
    Ned

With a grin—water pressure in Dearborn was notoriously strong—Steele folded the letter and put it in the postbox, knowing the new censors would have to open it, anyway. He made a note to have Willis get a stock of field postcards.

***

"Ned," Lucas offered his hand, "time I took my leave of you." They met in Steele's office. Noise from all over the building meant it was a beehive of activity.

"Sir, um...Able," Steele shook his hand. "We learned so *very* much from you..."

"And now you get to pass it on as your own, Ned," Lucas said. "And add the wisdom and experience you gained up there in Flanders. How *did* that central fire control idea of yours work, by the way?"

"Seemed to work just fine; no complaints from the Canadians. Haven't *heard* what the *Germans* think..."

"Well, if you pass that wisdom on, perhaps we will."

"What have they got for you now? They asked me to report on your—"

"I'm to report to Chaumont," Lucas interrupted. "Whatever you reported, Ned, is what you reported."

"Nothing but *good* things, Able."

> *12ᵗʰ December, Camp Steele.*
>
> *Nothing more but cleaning up and* [illegible rest of entry.]
>
> *13ᵗʰ December, Camp Steele, Étaples*
>
> [Date and location only]
>
> *14ᵗʰ December, Camp Steele, Étaples.*
> *Wish I had more to say and the strength to say them. Now is the time I miss McTee's wisdom.*
>
> *15ᵗʰ December, Camp Steele.*
> *I am invited to a soiree of some kind, hosted by the Canucks we supported on Hill 90. They do not invite my officers...Never saw so clean a tablecloth...They called the champaign* [sic] *a fair vintage, but I've never had enough to know. But the whiskey was good; that I <u>could</u> tell...the Huns risk their lives for bully beef and potted pork now...*
> *Toasting McTee and Dona, I could not help but <u>try</u> to cry, but I cannot...*

"I'm invited to *what?*" Steele blinked at a young Canadian Lieutenant named Ball in a too-clean uniform with woefully mud-spattered boots standing in the orderly room.

"*Dinner*, sir, at the Division Mess. Brigadier Butcher has *asked* for Captain Steele."

"*Has* he, indeed?" Willis sighed, watching. "Does the Brigadier wish the *Major* to *dress* for dinner?"

"I've got a clean pair of puttees, Ned," Brick grinned. "My *best* Sam Browne's with my *dinner jacket* in our *penthouse suite…*"

"My *instructions*, sir," Ball ignored the mockery, "are to tell Captain—*Major*—Steele, that you may come as you *are*." He cleared his throat. "I would *advise* a *fresh shave*, sir, and *perhaps* those clean puttees that your *subordinate* has so *politely* offered."

"Very well, Lieutenant," Steele smiled. "*When…?*"

"You're to *accompany* me, sir, as *soon* as *you* are *ready*." Ball gazed placidly at Willis and Brick, who grinned back. "The Canadian Army isn't *quite* as *formal* as our British cousins, nor as *boorish* as our American *neighbors*." He nodded to Steele. "I shall wait out by the *road*, sir…"

"I'll be along *directly*, Lieutenant…" Steele thought carefully. "Willis, why *aren't* you an officer?"

"Sir, we've *discussed* that…"

"Discussion over. I'm making you a Lieutenant."

"Sir, *please*, I…" Willis protested.

"Jack, you change your rank more often than I can change *socks*. Change it back when you *have* to, but I need a supply officer, and *Captain* Brick will soon be a *battalion* exec.…"

"I *will?*" Brick gulped.

"Yes…now, about those puttees, Mike?"

***

Steele and Ball entered the hotel through the front door guarded by two soldiers with *too*-clean uniforms. Compared to the gathering dusk outside, the glare of the hotel lights—miles behind the front lines—was startling.

"Captain, er, Major *Steele*, I trust," a red-nosed General grinned, extending his hand as soon as he entered a large room crowded with officers.

"*Yes*sir," Steele sighed, shaking it. "*Thanks* for the invita—"

"*Major* Steele," a mustachioed General beamed, "*welcome* to the Canadian Corps Mess. I *hope* Lieutenant Ball wasn't too abrupt in *fetching* you here. He *can* be…"

"*Steele*," McFadden exclaimed, waving from across the room. "Here's the *very man* I was *telling* ye of, Bertie: Captain—oh, *so* sorry—*Major* Steele. Positive *genius* with a machine gun battery…"

For the next several minutes, the entire roomful of senior officers, including *five* Generals, greeted Steele as if he were a genuine hero—aside from Lieutenant Ball, the only *other* junior officer was McFadden's battalion Major.

"*This* might interest ye, Steele." McFadden beckoned to Steele to join him and several other officers at a table. "Have a look."

Steele studied a small map for a few moments, noticing a circled area labeled *Der Amboss* that, if Steele wasn't mistaken, was that stretch of the long ridge that included Hill 90. "My German's a bit *thin*. What's *der Amboss* mean, again?" Steele asked.

"The *Anvil*, Major," the Corps Commander beamed; McFadden nodded. "This Hun corps committed major attacks in that area *three times* in the *eleven days* you and your people were up there, and they never *got past* our fire trenches."[1] The Corps Commander smiled widely as the other officers gathered around. "*Our* war is won and Germany is *doomed* if the rest of you Americans fight like *your* command."

"They're after *food*, Major," another General declared. "They haven't seen *decent* tucker in over a year; that is what most of their raids are *for* now."

Steele stared and blinked at the map….

***

"*Dinner* is *served*, gentlemen," a Corporal announced. They seated Steele to the right of the Corps Commander, naturally at the head of the table. To Steele's right was McFadden; opposite him at the table, Butcher.

After the last course—a lemon cheesecake with a cherry on top—and *several* wines, the Corps Commander rang his glass for

---

[1] Second level. Outpost (first level) and Support were the other two.

attention. "Gentlemen," he began, nodding, "Lieutenant Ball: I believe *you* have the *honor…*"[1]

"Sir," Ball stood. "If our *American* guest will permit, gentlemen, I give you *the king!* Long *may* he *reign!*"

As one man, the guests—including Steele—stood. "*The King! And confusion to his enemies!*"

While they still stood, the Corps Commander declared, "gentlemen, I give you *President Wilson!*"

"*President Wilson!*"

The Corps Commander raised his glass once more as the rest sat. "We are here this evening to honor a *most* distinguished guest, our southern neighbor—even though *his* home is *north* of Canada…"[2]

"Here, here," several voices called.

"*But*…but…he has answered the call of his country and has come to France to help us…*bail out the French…*"

"Here, *here,*" *more* voices called, louder.

"And for *eleven days*, it seems, he bailed *us* out…"

"*Here, here!*"

"So *stand to* your glasses, gentlemen, and be upstanding to raise a toast to *Major Edmund Steele!*"

"Major Edmund Steele!"

"Speech! Speech!"

Steele blinked, unsure…but stood, anyway. "Well, *thank you,* gents. I had to *borrow* clean puttees to *come* here…" Great merriment met this admission. "But, you set a *fine* table…"

"*Here, here…*"

"Ah…if I were to admit to you that…a *year* ago I was a Corporal in a machine gun detachment in Mexico, I don't know if *that* would change your…"

"Certainly *not*, old boy," Butcher grinned. "What *matters* is

---

[1] The first/loyalty toast of any evening is given by the youngest or lowest-ranking officer.

[2] The Detroit River flows northeast-to-southwest, putting the east side and much of downtown Detroit *north* of Windsor, Ontario.

that *shift*…"

"*Here, here!*"

"My company never *fired* a *shot* in anger *before* we got up to Hill 90…"

"*Bully*," McFadden called; the room applauded.

"We took our first casualties there: *sixty percent* of our company, a *third* of them *went west.*" Silence; motionless. "They included our First Sergeant—you'd call him *Color* Sergeant, I believe, and one of our trainers, *Commandant* Dona. But John McTee and Henri Dona were *instrumental* in *building* our company, helped to make it what it was on Hill 90, and we shall *miss* them. So, if you *would*, gents: raise your glasses for *Commandant* Henri Dona and First Sergeant John McTee: May they *rest* in *peace*…"

As one, the room raised their glasses and solemnly intoned, "*Commandant* Dona and First Sergeant McTee…"

"Behold, their brave men weeping," the Corps Commander whispered as Steele turned away….

16ᵗʰ December, Camp Steele, Étaples.

I find it extraordinary that we keep taking on men.

Since we arrived at Camp Steele we have received over two hundred. We fill barracks as fast as we build them….

18ᵗʰ December, Camp Steele, Étaples.

I am summoned to see The Boss in Paris…

Steele stood at the front of the room, pointing to the map on the easel. "Then, lay out the range fans,[1] making sure that the barrel wear fans are *shorter before* you plan your barrages and reference points…"

Just then, Erskine approached Steele, handing him an envelope

------

[1] A map of a position's arc of fire.

that contained a hand-written letter:

> *Major Steele*
> *Please report to AEF Headquarters, Paris, tomorrow morning. There are important matters to discuss. Bring ~~Lieutenant~~ Captain Brick. I will reserve rooms for you at the Hotel Sacher.*
> *Pershing*

"Gentlemen," Steele sighed, "Captain Brick and I have to catch a train."

19th December, Hotel Sacher, Paris, France.

I was thinking Paris was more impressive...big city, busy, wide streets. Nearly every man in uniform and about every woman and girl draped in black...We met with General Rorshack...another promotion with less fanfare...told him about our replacement problems; he's addressing them. I find it hard to believe what the Army thinks of me...New top Sergeant, Massie...

"You ever been here?" Steele asked Brick after their breakfast. AEF Headquarters was within walking distance of the small hotel where Pershing booked their rooms.

"Sure," Brick answered, glancing around. "It was summer, though. And a lot more...*colorful*, as I recall." In a few blocks, they saw a sign that read "AEF HQ PARIS," posted outside a wholly unremarkable, singularly unimposing office building. Although Pershing made his headquarters at Chaumont, many administrative functions were better done close to the communications hub of France. *This* was that office. "Huh," Brick sighed, "just a building."

"I brought you because I was *told* to," Steele sighed, "*not* to criticize the decisions of our *betters*. Besides, it's mostly for the quartermasters and the like."

"*Far* be it from *me* to be critical," Brick agreed.

"When do you *stop*?" Steele asked.

"Not before you *fire* me," Brick answered. "Any idea where we're supposed to go?"

"None," Steele answered. "Let's just go in and find somebody who knows more than *we* do."

"*That* won't be hard."

Just inside the guarded main entrance, Steele gave his and Brick's name to a Staff Sergeant who looked on a list. "One floor up to General Rorshack's office, sir," he said.

***

Steele knocked on the door labeled "BG Rorshack." A Private opened the door. "Major Steele for…"

"Yessir," the Private said. "*This* way." The Private led them through a long room that had been a lounge—sofas and chairs stacked along a far wall—to another door.

"Come on in, Ned," Rorshack called from his desk. "*Thanks*, Private." Rorshack's office, also a bedroom, wasn't large, but it was well-lit…and clearly temporary. A bank of windows let the thin sunlight in from outside.

"*This* is Captain Mike Brick, my Executive Officer…" Steele gestured to Brick.

Rorshack extended a hand. "We've *met*, I believe. Have a *seat*," he gestured to two chairs.

"Sir," Steele sat on a small wooden chair lightly, uncertain how strong it might be.

"You'd think the Assistant Adjutant General of the American Expeditionary Forces *should* have a bigger office, wouldn't you, even if this one's one of *three* I have?"

"I'd imagine, sir," Steele answered.

"Just call me Jack like everyone else does. You're *Mike* or a pretentious *Michael?*"

"Mike…Jack," Brick answered.

Rorshack blinked, blew out his cheeks. "McTee was with *you* when *he*…?" he asked quietly.

"*I* was," Brick coughed lightly. "He *didn't* suffer."

"He was my Sergeant in the 89th," Steele offered, "and in the Machine-Gun Section in the Provisional Division…"

"*I* was with McTee for ten years, give or take," Rorshack mumbled. "But *this* was always in front of us, even when we were just chasing Indians."

"Yeah…*always* a possibility…" Steele added. Even in peacetime, there were many ways soldiers could get killed, from accidents to disease to drunken brawls.

Rorshack nodded sagely. "The War Department will inform his brother…"

"Can *I*…?" Steele started.

"I'll get an address for you. The news, I hear, *moved* the General. McTee was *also* with *him* for several years…"

"You're well acquainted with the General?" Brick asked.

"I was his secretary," Rorshack answered. "And Major Dona…"

"*Commandant* Dona," Brick corrected. "*He* went down at the same time as McTee."

"Congratulations on *your* promotion, Jack," Steele said.

"Thanks. We've heard nothing but positive reports about you and your unit. I know *little* of machine guns, so I couldn't *possibly* comment on your people's performance, but your trainers and the Canadians submitted glowing reports."

"Thanks," Steele and Brick both said.

"The British say that your performance has improved their outlook on the conflict and made them confident of the future value of the American Army."

"Uh-huh…"

"You're forming an independent machine gun battalion."

"Yes…"

Rorshack raised an eyebrow. "What's your progress?"

"Slow but sure."

"*Some* have suggested that we should just keep your people as instructors…"

"Yeah…?"

"*But* General Pershing believes that would deprive the Army of valuable fighters." Rorshack made to straighten some already orderly papers. "I don't *have* a vote in this matter. Ned, have you recovered from your, ah, experience?”

“*I* have,” Steel said, and added, “The *unit?* We can’t *get* the replacements we *need*. All we’ve been getting are supply and engineers and staff people to fill the *company* ranks.”

“*That’s* what we’ve been *sending* you…”

“Why?” Brick asked.

“It’s what *we’re* getting here as replacements, mostly to build up the Services of Supply to keep up with the divisions as they arrive.”

“We understand,” Steele said, “but we lost more than half our strength, killed and wounded. *Some* will come back, but I’m short of NCOs—talented gunners—who will be *impossible* to replace. We trained for *three months* on damn near every machine gun in Europe; Hell, in the *world…*” Steele stopped; Rorshack looked tiredly grim. “We’ll *work it out.*”

“I know, Ned; *WE* know. General Pershing *chose* you for your *silk-purse* skills—your ability to make something out of nothing. Brace yourself to be outnumbered in a few weeks. The British and Canadians are sending many of *their* American-born machine gunners to *you.* Near as anyone can *tell*, there’s about *four hundred* of them.”

“*That’ll* fill us up,” Steele nodded. “Bring us to battalion strength…”

“And our vehicles?” Brick asked. “Mules? Other…?”

“Your *special* trucks are on the cars now; should *reach* you in a week. We’ll send you the other vehicles, animals and equipment as it becomes available. In two weeks, you’ll be seeing machine gun troops from the First and the Second Division for *advanced* training.” He stared at Steele. “Are you prepared for *that?*”

“With what *guns*, sir?”

“The Hotchkiss.”

“We *can*,” Steele declared.

“*And* we’ll have some *American* divisions training in the British zone, as well. You can train *them* in the Vickers?”

“We *can.*”

“We have a senior NCO for you: Sergeant Major Emil Massie. *Know* him?”

Steele and Brick exchanged glances. "*No*, sorry."

"He'll report within the week. Not a lot of *time* for *this*, Ned," Rorshack handed him a small sheaf of papers. "You have been a Lieutenant Colonel in the National Army since the first of December; just got the orders yesterday…"

"Ah…?"

"Can't stand on *ceremony*, Ned. Good luck, *Colonel* Steele." Rorshack stood up and offered his hand.

"*Thank* you, Jack," Steele said, somewhat numb, shaking the proffered hand.

"Congratulations, Ned," Brick offered his hand. "And…"

"Uh, *Mike*," Rorshack thumbed through more papers, "here's your *Major's* orders." He handed Brick another sheaf of paper. "And please take *these* promotions to your battalion; save *us* the trouble…"

"Ah, Jack," Steele asked, "do you know where we might get some new uniforms? I never *had* a full suite and *ours* are…"

"Yes, of course," Rorshack said, "there's a uniform store on the third floor. And, *Colonel* Steele," he handed Steele a note, "for *you*. He sends his regrets. Good *day*, gentlemen. And congratulations again."

The note from Pershing was short…

> *Col. Steele*
> *Called to England for a meeting with the British and*
> *French Prime Ministers. Sorry I cannot meet with you,*
> *but some gentlemen will take my place tomorrow. I am*
> *sure your quarters in the Hotel Sacher will be*
> *comfortable; they are on me.*
> *Pershing*

"I suppose the Prime Ministers of England and France are more important than *we* are," Steele sighed.

"For *now*, anyway," Brick sighed.

20th December, Hotel Sacher. Paris.

Half-decent chow…a summons to a chateau, where

"Colonel Steele?" a tall Sergeant asked, approaching their table at breakfast.

"*Yes*," Steele answered, somewhat surprised. Even though the quartermasters at the clothing store had called him *Colonel*, it still *sounded* odd.

"I'm to deliver *this*." The Sergeant handed Steele an envelope, withdrawing out of earshot while Steele read:

> *Colonel Steele*
> *We require the pleasure of your company at the Chateau de Fontainebleau for a conference. Please bring Major Brick with you. Be prepared to stay overnight.*
> *Charles Dawes*

"We're being *summoned* again, Mike," Steele said.

"Where?"

"Chateau Fontainebleau…?"

"No shit? Lemme see…" Brick scanned the note, staring at the signature. "Charlie Dawes…huh."

"You *know* this guy?"

"I know *of* him. *Genius* with money. Didn't know he was over *here*, though."

"Huh…Sergeant," Steele called, beckoning the Sergeant back to their table. "What are your instructions?"

"I'm to *bring* you, sir," the Sergeant answered firmly.

"I see," Steele said. "When?"

"My instructions are to have you at the Chateau by twelve-thirty, sir."

"Then…*luncheon* at the *Chateau, Major* Brick."

"Looks *like, Colonel* Steele."

"Do we have time to get into our new dress uniforms and *pack*, Sergeant?"

"*Un*dress is acceptable, sir. We need about two hours to *get* there. I'm to bring you back tomorrow afternoon, and to tell you your rooms are paid through Friday night if you want to take in the sights of Paris." He cleared his throat. "I have a *way* to get tickets for the *Folies Bergère*, sir."

Steele and Brick looked at each other. "*Maybe.*"

***

"You'll be writing in that thing when they bury you," Brick said, shivering. The drive from Paris was practically silent.

"Probably," Steele sighed, putting his new Shaeffer pen in the loop of his diary cover; he was running out of pages in this book, having torn many out for want of note and *other* paper. "This is a Silver Ghost," he said, loudly enough for everyone to hear.

"Yessir," the Sergeant answered. "Prewar Rolls Royce with electric lights and four-speed transmission…"

"And the bigger engine," Steele said. "453 cubic inch, I remember. Big engine for a passenger sedan."

"Yessir," the Sergeant answered. "You *know* automobiles, sir?"

"Grew *up* among them," Steele said. "Ever have a ride in a Rolls Royce, Mike?" he asked.

"Can't say I have," Brick answered, looking around the countryside. "Hardly know there was a war on…Sergeant, is this *all* you do?"

"I *drive* when I'm not working on airplanes, sir."

Steele stared hard into the mirror. "*You're* Fast Eddie Rickenbacker." It was a statement, not a question.

"Yessir," Rickenbacker answered. "*This* is a favor for a friend." He glanced in the mirror. "You follow auto *racing*, sir?"

"I saw your picture in the newspapers winning races."

"Ah…" Rickenbacker said.

"I'll be glad when they put good *heat* in these things," Steele muttered.

"Me, too…*icy* back here," Brick complained, "even with the windows closed. Those hot water bottles didn't last long."

"Sir," Rickenbacker handed back a stone jug wrapped in wool. "Warm yourself for a while; it's still got heat. General Pershing ordered the heaters *out* of all the AEF motor vehicles. I spent a *week* doing it…"

"Why?" Steele asked.

"Fire hazard, he said," Rickenbacker answered. "Frankly, *I* think he didn't just like the smell of the fuel burning. And they *are* dangerous."

"*That's* so. I put out more than one fire in a car…what?" Steele caught Brick staring at him.

"I just…never knew there was so *much* to motorcars before I *had* to learn to drive one, *and fix* a *flat*, in *your* outfit…"

"That's because *you* had a chauffer…"

"*And* a mechanic, you *slave-driver*…"

***

As they approached, it surprised Steele to see so much traffic going in and out of the…*compound* was the best description he could think of. From its beginnings in the 1300s as a single crenelated tower, Fontainebleau had expanded into more than a score of connected and non-connected buildings. The complex had served variously as a defensive castle, a *royal* residence, a hospital, an *imperial* residence, a royal *and* imperial guest house, and a school.

"Holy *shit*," Brick said, gazing at the outer walls. "What's this used for *now*, Sergeant?"

"The French use it for training signal officers," Rickenbacker said. "They also have an aerial photography interpretation and map-making center here. There's a gas medicine clinic, a hospital for senior officers, and a few *other* things. They let *us* use it for conferences and specialized offices." The car stopped at a guardhouse, where Rickenbacker flashed his identification. "Gents; the man wants to see your identity cards."

Brick and Steele fished the flimsy cardboard squares out of their wallets. "First time anyone's ever asked to see it," Steele groused.

"*Merci, mon Colonel*," the guard touched the lip of his helmet before waving his hand. "*Passer, Sergeant.*"

The car followed a horse-drawn dray into a fenced area in a courtyard, where signs pointed in several directions and barbed wire coils divided the space. "It's as big as the Indianapolis brickyard," Rickenbacker declared, "and paved the same way."

The car rolled silently past several rows of parked cars, carriages, and wagons before coming to a massive portico. "Just go right in, gentlemen. *They* are expecting you."

Steele and Brick walked toward the huge main doors—each twenty feet high and eight wide, with smaller doors cut into them—as men passed in and out. "How's this supposed to work?" Brick asked.

"*You're* asking *me*?" Steele replied, adding, "if we're expected, I don't think we *have* to ask."

Just then, a French *Commandant* stepped outside and asked, "Colonel Steele and Major Brick, I presume?" in English.

"Uh, yeah," Steele said. "We're supposed to meet a Colonel Dawes…"

"Yes. Come with *me*, please."

Brick and Steele followed the officer, puzzled. Inside, the officer removed a glove, then turned. "In America I'm Jack Haliburton, but here I'm *Commandant* Jacques Haller, *Legion Estranger*."

"Ah," Brick said. "Foreign Legion!"

"Yes," Haller/Halliburton declared, "They brought *us* here in '15." He beckoned down a long hall. "Come."

Haller led them down a wide corridor lined with tables and desks, most of them unoccupied on Sunday. "So, how come you're in the Foreign Legion?" Brick asked.

"I *disagreed* with my commander in Mindanao; a disagreement that would have landed me in the stockade," Haller said, leading them up a broad, winding, well-worn stone staircase. "I jumped on a ship that took me to Cochin China and I joined the Legion there." On the next floor, another corridor, just as wide and just as crowded with furniture, were signs in English. "The State Department and the Army tell me that if I live through *this*, I can come back to the 'States 'cause that Captain kicked off *years* ago."

"You *expect* to live through this…?" Steele asked.

"*Frankly*…no," Haller answered, coldly matter-of-fact. "Down this way."

Walking down the corridor, Steele and Brick read the signs that sounded *odd*. Currency Exchange Control (France); Finance Liaison Officer (Britain); Purchasing Control Office (Britain); Food Accounting Office (Belgium)…

At the end of the corridor, an American Corporal sitting at a desk, reading a month-old newspaper, watched them and stood up slowly as they approached. "Help you, sirs?" he asked.

"We're meeting with Colonel Dawes," Haller said.

"And *you* are…?"

"Colonel Steele, *Commandant* Haller, and Major Brick."

"Right in here." The Corporal showed them a nearby anteroom; a small Colonel awaited. "Come in, gentleman," he said as he rose to shake their hands. "Colonel Steele and Major Brick, I trust? I'm Charlie Dawes. *Commandant, thanks* for bringing our guests."

"My pleasure, sir," Haller replied, removing his kepi.

"Colonel," Steele offered, shaking Dawes' hand, "a *pleasure*."

"Pleased to meet you, sir," Brick said, shaking Dawes' hand. "Are you the Charles Dawes who wrote 'Melody in A Major?'"

"I am," Dawes agreed. "Do you *know* it?"

"I *do*. My *future* wife loves the tune; made me learn to play it for her on the piano."

"Well, at *least*…" Dawes started.

"Trouble is, I can't carry a tune in a gunny sack," Brick admitted. "But she's going to marry me, anyway."

"Does *she* know that?" Steele asked.

"She *will*…" Brick answered.

"Well, best of luck to you," Dawes grinned. "*Come*, gentlemen.*"

They strolled down another long corridor, light patches on its bare walls revealing the former presence of works of art. In a large room edged with tables, chairs and map boards were two officers; one was Talbott, his left arm in a sling. "Gentlemen," Talbott nodded. "Congratulations, *Colonel* Steele."

"Thank you, *Colonel* Talbott," Steele grinned, extending his hand. "You're out of the hospital and the Horse Guards smiled upon you?"

"Just a *scratch, Colonel* Ned, and the *Horse Guards* can *go to blazes*," Talbott declared, shaking Steele's. "And *Major* Brick: *well* deserved, *both* of you."

"Colonel," Brick said, shaking Talbott's hand, "they made the *same* mistake with *me*, as we have *all* risen *above* our levels of competence..."

"Gentlemen," an austere Lieutenant Colonel called. "We need to speak of important matters." He gestured to a table in the middle of the room, holding an *enormous* relief map, tilted slightly upwards. "Gentlemen," he said, using a pointer. "*This* is our best contour model of the *Kriemhild Stellung*, the defensive complex guarding Germany."

Steele and Brick studied the model. Steele guessed the scale by the distance from Paris to the German border. "I make it about three miles deep," Steele said, "and perhaps three hundred long?"

"*Close*, Colonel," the Lieutenant Colonel said. "At its deepest, we believe it to be over *six* deep; at its *shallowest*, three."

"A fortress wall six miles thick," Talbott exclaimed. "That thin part is in the *French* sector. The *thickest*," he pointed with a stick, "will be *General Pershing's*."

"Because you *don't* like us," Brick said ruefully.

"Because we *do*, old man," Talbott declared.

"How do you figure that?" Steele blurted. "They don't think we can...?"

"On the contrary," Dawes said softly. "Because the army we're building will be bigger than *all* the other armies on the Western Front *combined*."

"The Allies know we're going to have the most troops to *lose*," the Lieutenant Colonel said. "So they are giving *us* the hardest nuts to crack."

"That's where *you* come in, Ned," Talbott said. "The part you and your battalion are to play will be as a model for your *mobile* operations."

"You've *seen* the front, Steele," Dawes said. "You *know,* for a *fact,* it's not *quite* the wasteland that the dime novels make it out to be."

"That's...*true, sort* of," Steele said, still staring at the map. "But we're to be a *machine gun battalion*. We..."

"You will be a *machine gun* battalion in name only, Steele," Dawes declared. "Your organization..." He handed Steele a broadsheet with a familiar indented breakdown.

At the top, in bold letters, 432nd Machine Gun Battalion.

Steele quickly went over the assigned strength he and McTee had seen...each machine gun company with *four* platoons... sixteen machine guns to the platoon...but... "*four* MG companies...?"

"Yes; plus one *infantry* company and one HQ *and* one *support* company," Talbott said. "The support company will have pom-poms, mortars and *howitzers* ..."

"And engineers and a medical platoon in the HQ, as *you* suggested," the Lieutenant Colonel said.

"*You* will have the mobile firepower to tear *bloody great holes* in the Hun lines, Steele," Talbott declared.

"Paired with an artillery brigade," the Lieutenant Colonel said, "you can create a hole in the German lines that we can drive an *army* through."

"And *my men* and I shall be there with you, Colonel," Haller said. "We are to be attached to you; the *French* contribution..."

"Who's *we?*" Brick asked.

"A *large* Legion company," Haller answered. "At *least* 200 Legionnaires."

"Might not be that *simple*...this *hole*..." Brick sighed.

"Look, Steele," Talbott said. "Up in Flanders last fall, we *might* have pushed our lads harder if we'd had *enough* of those *deuced* tanks of Churchill's..."

"*That* theory is excellent," the Lieutenant Colonel added, "but the *tank* has too many teething problems. But heavy trucks? Now, *those* we can make go without as many problems. *And* we believe the Germans are training large numbers of troops in their infiltration tactics."

"The Russians have talked about an *armistice*," Dawes said quietly.

"And their revolution is tearing them apart," Talbott agreed. "If they make peace with Germany and Austria, they could free a *million men* to fight us. And *if*, as we believe they *might*, the Germans begin a major offensive with their troops from Russia *trained* in those tactics…"

"Those devils could do considerable damage to our worn-out troops. The Huns *are* effective, after all that," Talbott said. "They've shortened their lines to make even *more* veterans available for attacks. But," he added with a slight smile, "they're running *out* of men."

"They have seventeen-year-olds in the trenches now," Dawes said. "Next year they will *have* to put sixteen-year-old boys on the line."

"They're running out of *fight*, Steele," Talbott said. "We need to punch them *hard* and *fast*."

"I see," Steele said. "Mine is *one battalion*, gentlemen. Can we make *that* big a difference?"

"We need the right *opportunity*, Colonel," the Lieutenant Colonel said. "When you *succeed*…"

"*If* we succeed," Steele corrected.

"You *will*," the Lieutenant Colonel grinned.

"*Machine Gun Steele*," Dawes smiled lightly. "That's what Patton called you not that long ago. And we have *this* for you, Steele," he said, handing Steele a letter.

> *You are to train your battalion to make breakthroughs, not unlike the Canadians. Once we get our men out of the trenches, we can use your unit and those like it to pursue the Hun straight into Germany. This trench warfare will only wear our men down. I have always advocated open warfare, as you know; your chariots will help to get us there. Take two months to train your unit.*
>
> *I had a feeling about you down on the border. Each time I've tasked you with something, you have achieved it splendidly. If this <u>can</u> be done, you are the man who can do it.*
>
> *Pershing*

"We have our *eye* on you, Colonel Steele. You seem to have a, ah, peculiar effect on the General," the Lieutenant Colonel said.

"I've known John Pershing for nearly thirty years," Dawes said, "and I've never had the *practical* influence on him you seem to."

"That *Frenchwoman*," the Lieutenant Colonel spat.

"Miss Resco[1] is probably the best thing *for* him, George," Dawes said.

"Just…be ready for the opportunity when it arises, old boy," Talbott suggested.

"Gentlemen," Steele said softly, "do you have *any* good idea how many casualties we took at Hill 90?"

"We have the figures, Colonel," the Lieutenant Colonel said lightly. "They are within the ranges expected of MG units…"

"I lost *sixty percent* of my men in *eleven days*," Steele interrupted. "It took nearly *three months* to train them to do their jobs. We lost *all that*…"

"*Any* infantryman takes that long," Dawes declared…but looked concerned.

"Machine gunners are *not just any infantrymen*, Colonel," Steele said loudly. "They're smarter, quicker, and more physically fit than any *three* infantrymen because the guns demand those qualities. Colonel, *how's* your range estimation?"

"Fair as *any*…" the Lieutenant Colonel started.

"At *night?*" Brick added.

"Not as…say, Colonel, do you *want* your battalion broken up?" the Lieutenant Colonel asked loudly. "There *are* those who…"

"I do *not*," Steele said, adding, "but I *do* want them to have a fair chance at surviving this…so-called *plan* of yours."

"Steady on, Ned," Talbott soothed. "You're among *friends* here."

"What do you *mean*, Steele?" the Lieutenant Colonel asked, suddenly in a conciliatory tone.

"I mean…the Hotchkiss machine gun can be accurate out to 4,500 yards on a good day and down-slope with a new barrel. That weapon has to be clamped down tight, and the fire sheaf is only *so* big…."

"The Huns can get *around* it," Brick continued. "And their

------

[1] Micheline Resco was a French/Romanian artist who became
  Pershing's mistress in 1917. They would marry in 1946.

artillery and snipers spot them. That's why they have to *move*, and often."

"The gun alone weighs just over fifty pounds," Steele said. "The tripod is *another* sixty; two boxes of ammunition, *another* hundred…"

"And there's the range/height finder," Brick went on, "and the tools and spare barrels…"

"Moving just one gun needs *five* men hauling over a hundred pounds of deadweight *each* over uneven ground to what you *hope* is a suitable spot," Steele said, "where they can fire the mission and not get *killed* in the next few minutes…"

"Because that's *all* they've *got*," Brick said. "*Maybe* five minutes in one spot before a Hun sniper gets the gunner, and the *assistant* takes over…"

"And the barrel needs to be changed every two or three hundred rounds, new calculations made, the whole gun adjusted," Steele nodded. "Know what all *that* means?"

"I'd *hate* to guess," the Lieutenant Colonel smiled ruefully.

"*That* means that our replacements need the *mind* of Aristotle and the *strength* of Hercules," Steele declared. "Give me a *thousand* average men and I *might* make *four hundred* OK machine gunners out of them in *three months*. These men are *not* expendable warm bodies; just so much cannon fodder to overwhelm an enemy *en masse* with bullets."

"If we're *lucky*," Brick added, perusing the broadsheet. "This organization calls for…256 gunners? And another *thousand* men carrying everything else they need?"

"Yes…" the Lieutenant Colonel said guardedly.

"Fifty percent casualties among the machine gunners alone," Steele said. "Means for every shift in the front lines, I'd need two hundred replacements to stay at full strength. That's a *lot* of gunners…"

"We'd need a company in the rear doing nothing but training *gunners*," Brick said.

"While true," the Lieutenant Colonel declared, "you will *not* be in the front lines like any *other* battalion."

"Here's the *rum* in your *tea*, Ned," Talbott smiled.

"No?" Steele asked.

"No," the Lieutenant Colonel answered.

"Colonel, may I have *your* name?" Steele asked.

"Marshall; George Catlett Marshall."

"I've *heard* of you," Steele said, grinning. "You're supposed to *go* places…"

"So are *you*, Colonel; so are *you*."

"What would be more manageable," Brick mused, "would be *three* MG companies of *three* firing platoons and a support platoon, *and* your support company. A triangular maneuver organization is easier to handle…"

"Very well," Marshall said, nodding. "Try it *your* way, gentlemen; but *try* it."

21st December, Chateau Fontainebleau.

A most extraordinary meal, congenial company and a good night's sleep on a feather bed.

22nd December, Hotel Sacher, Paris.

Saw the Eiffel Tower, the Arc du Triomphe. Quite the city, Paris. The Folies Bergère are everything they say they are, but those ~~girls~~ women looked cold in those scanty costumes. Those in the tableaus who were <u>completely</u> starkers were breathtaking <u>and</u> blue with cold. We save the Moulin Rouge for another day. Today we return to Etaples.

23rd December, Camp Steele, Etaples, France.

We left too many good men on Hill 90. We will miss them in the new organization… got half a mind to get Peng what he needs just to see him put it together…Rodgers is finally doing what he's always done.

I have one more page in this diary and must start another; one I bought in St. Louis just last April.

Has it been that long?

An empty warehouse that still smelled of wet canvas and paint housed Steele, his officers, and senior NCOs. Steele gazed around and took a deep breath. "Men, we have a job of work to do and not a great deal of time to do it in. I'm organizing the staff like AEF does, so…OK, Gary," he said to the recently returned Grimes, "will *you* be chief of staff? I need someone who knows how stuff *runs*…"

"Have you lost your *mind*, Ned?" Grimes asked. "What do *I* know about…?"

"Probably as much as anyone *else* here…"

"*I* can help, sir," Massie declared. Massie, like many senior NCOs, was of an unclear age but *probably* between 40 and 50. He'd arrived just that morning.

"Then…*yessir*," Grimes answered.

"Mike: *Battalion* exec?"

"What *else* I got to do, Ned?"

"That's the spirit. Jack: Supply? Called the $S4$[1] these days. You'd work *for* Gary…"

"Just what the Hell *else* would I *do*, sir?"

"Jack…"

"I mean, *yes*sir; of *course*, sir."

"I'm going to make you a *Major*, Jack…."

Willis looked as if he would wilt. "You *wound* me with *honor*, sir," Willis said, bowing his head slightly.

"Very well." Steele looked around the small sea of unfamiliar faces, officers and senior NCOs he really *needed* to know, but… "Gents, *most* of you don't *know* me. Many of you NCOs do, but

---

[1] Fourth assistant to the Chief of Staff. The others were S1, personnel; S2, intelligence; and S3, operations, based on the French system.

that doesn't help the officers. Now…these *insubordinate* officers," he waved an arm at his old classmates and Willis, "have been with me for…five months? Yeah, all of that. Came over to France together. Just because they *sound* familiar…well, they *are*, damnit. Some day, perhaps soon, you, too, will be as familiar and insubordinate as *they* are." *That* raised a chuckle. "Trust me when I tell you that this outfit will be unique in this Army, at least for a while. We've been told that *this* machine gun battalion will *fight* as a *mobile battalion*, as a kind of battering ram through the lines."

"*Who* said this…?" Grimes asked.

"Blackjack himself," Brick said.

Steele and Brick explained, as best they understood, what they'd been tasked—and authorized—to do by Dawes and Marshall. "So, following the Canadian example, we will form HQ and support companies, three MG companies, and an infantry company."

Ishim blinked. "Somebody *thought* about this…"

"We *did*. So," Steele went on, "Captain Buchalter?" Buchalter, older than all the other officers present save Willis and one other, had returned to the unit while Steele was in Paris.

"Sir?"

"You know something about surveying, I understand?"

"Yessir; got a surveying service in Washington…"

"Since you're senior among my officers—your National Guard commission's over *three years old*—think you can take command of Headquarters Company?"

"I *can*, sir."

"Thorsten has a similar surveying experience and is a real outdoorsman. On Hill 90, he found the *best* positions *first*…"

"I can work with him, sir," Buchalter smiled, a pleasing look on a boyish face.

"Good. Now…Lieutenant McCall…"

"Sir?" McCall asked. Frank McCall was a lanky Texan with a decided drawl who reported just the night before.

"The Army has certain traditions and, as you are *next* in seniority, would you like to command A Company as a Captain?"

"*Yessir*."

"Good. Lieutenant *Benson*..."

"Yes...sir." Thomas Benson had sloe brown eyes and an oddly paced speech pattern, as if he were fighting a stutter. He'd come in with McCall.

"B Company?"

"As a...Captain, sir?"

"Yes."

"Yes...sir."

"OK. Lieutenant Magruder..."

"Yessir," Philip Magruder answered. Much older than most of Steele's officers, Magruder had been a schoolteacher. He had yet to unpack his bags, having arrived just that morning.

"You'll wish you were back in your classroom, Lieutenant, but I have orders for you to be a Captain and command Company C."

"You may be *right*, sir, but I accept."

"Exellent." Steele gazed at Ishim. "Corey...the best for last. You may be senior in rank to *all* these guys but Dick Buchalter, but our D Company needs *your* kind of leadership because it will have our *artillery*. Accept?"

"You got Captain's orders in that stack, Ned?"

"Yep."

"I'll *take* 'em. But, ah, *Ned?* Don't we expect to be operating as *companies*? Even as individual guns?"

"That's what the *other* battalions expect," Steele mused. "We'll form the companies based on the machine-gun *section*— two guns make up a section of ten men," Steele continued. "Four firing sections to the company, and an ammo and service platoon. We'll equip A and C Companies with Vickers guns; B Company will keep the Hotchkiss guns because of their *range*. D Company will have two pom-pom sections of two guns each, two Stokes mortar sections of two tubes each, and a howitzer section of two guns. They will also have a fuel platoon, a *mobile* maintenance platoon, and an ammunition platoon."

"*Big* company," Ishim mused.

"Pom-poms," Grimes mused. "You're *dreaming*..."

"Not...*dreaming*," Willis mused. "I *know* a fellow..."

"Just go *find* them, Jack," Brick grinned mischievously.

"Your *wish* is my *command*, Mike," Willis nodded.

"Now, Headquarters will have all the usual clerks, but we'll have a communications platoon, a scout/survey platoon with motorcycles, a medical *platoon*..." he nodded at Miller, "and a sapper platoon."

"How about bicycles for couriers?" Buchalter nodded.

"And Peng said he could use a milling machine or even just a drill press," Ishim said. "He's a wonder with a file and hand drill, but..."

"*How* would he *power* it?" Steele asked. "Those things don't run on *air*...and we're supposed to be *mobile*..."

"Ask *him*," Ishim shook his head. "*He's* our one-man ordnance shop."

"I *will*. Now..." Steele looked around, nodded to Massie. "First Sergeants are hard to come by, but we'll just...Sergeant *Nagurski*: A Company?"

"*Yes*sir."

"Sergeant Belling: B Company?"

"My *pleasure*, sir."

"Sergeant Kosten: C Company?"

"*Yes*, sir."

"Sergeant McCloskey, you're new to us. How'd you *get* here?"

"By boat and, *well*, sir..."

"I *sent* for him, sir," Massie said. "He knows *mules*, and he knows *men*. We came over on the transport together..."

"And Ted McCloskey can drink *anyone* under the table, too," Kosten said.

"Got *that* right," Belling added.

"OK, then: D Company first shirt?"

"I can *do* that, sir."

"Sergeant Dugan, you just came in with that last bunch. What magic do *you* have to convince me that there's not another Sergeant in this battalion worthy of being HQ Company's top kick?"

"If it's *magic* the Colonel's wanting, then Seamus Dugan *has*

none, sir," the diminutive Dugan drawled. "But if it's *fightin'
Irishmen* from South Boston yer wanting, then *I'm* yer man."

"And a fighting fool he *is*, too," Willis declared. "Dugan,
how'd you get out of the stockade again?"

"Why, Jack, they started a *war*, and they recognized me *fine
qualities…*"

"Top boxer in every regiment he was ever *in*," Kosten said.
"And he's a welterweight…"

"*Lightweight*, I'll be thanking you, Harry, ya damn *bridger*."[1]

"Then will *you* be First Shirt in HQ Company?" Steele asked.

"Of *course*, sir," Dugan answered.

"Very well, gentlemen and Sergeants," Steele grinned. "Let's
get to work."

***

"You *sent* for me, sir?" Peng said after Massie ushered him in.

"I *did*, Corporal," Steele said, gesturing to his other chair.
"Captain Ishim says you want your own machine shop. That so?"

"It would make my repair work a good deal easier, sir," Peng
explained. "Both for weapons *and* vehicles."

"Well, we're supposed to be able to *move…*"

"Yessir," Peng said. "I'd mount the shop on a large truck and
trailer."

"It would be hard to get a truck and trailer across No-man's-
land."

"It would only go *closer* to the front, sir, never *into* it."

"How would you *power* such a thing?"

"Electric power, sir, driven by the truck's engine. I found a
dynamo.…"

Steele fell silent, staring at the young man…younger, perhaps,
than Steele, but not by much. "You have this all worked out?"

"I *have* plans, sir."

"If you had to choose just *one* tool…?"

---

[1] In South Boston patois, a *bridger* is from *North* Boston.

"Vertical mill, sir," Peng answered quickly. "It can do everything a drill press can, *and* can act as a vertical grinder in a pinch."

"*Tapered* spindle or…?"

"*Tapered* might be hard to find or make *tools* for, sir, so… threaded?"

"I'll see what Willis can find, Peng." Steele stared at him. "Want a commission?"

"I could use the *money*, sir."

"Do you need anything *else, Lieutenant?*"

"A ticket back to San Francisco, sir…?"

"*I'll* take one to *Detroit*…do you know Sergeant Rodgers?"

***

"You *sent* for me, sir," Rodgers asked as he reported to Steele's office a half-hour later.

"I *did*, Sergeant," Steele answered. "As you can *see…*" he pointed at his tunic hanging by the window, "they promoted me to Lieutenant Colonel…"

"*Congratulations*, sir," Rodgers smiled slightly.

"Thank you." Steele pointed to his other chair. "Have a seat. What does the unit have you doing these days?"

"Well, sir," Rodgers began, sitting as if on a hot stove, "I've been a unit and mess clerk, helping with the victualing. I *also* act as an auto driving instructor."

"Well, as we *talked* about back in…was it *July?*"

"Hard to *believe* it's been only that long, sir."

"Yes. I now *rate* enlisted aides…and I believe I may *need* them because…"

"Heavy is the burden of command, sir."

"*Yes*. And the paperwork. We'll be a battalion sooner than later, Sergeant. The Colonel needs help. Want a job as clerk and driver?"

"And decontamination, sir?"

"Train someone *else* in the mess, then you'll head the HQ aid station decon team."

"*Yes,* sir," Rodgers answered quietly.

"*And* you'll be a *Staff Sergeant.*"

"*Yes, sir,*" Rodgers answered louder, with his small smile.

"It's what the Army sent you *here* for, Sergeant."

"*Yes,* sir. Indeed *fortuitous,* sir."

"Find some stripes, Sergeant…"

"*Yes,* sir…"

25th December, Camp Steele, Etaples, France. Another Christmas away from home; was in Mexico last year. The boys found a tree, decorated it with shell casings and ammo strips. They scrounged a piano from somewhere. Someone had a squeezebox; another a fiddle; another a guitar; others played the spoons and harmonicas. The YWCA and Red Cross gals joined us for the party, sang hymns and carols and dance hall tunes all night. The cooks prepared goose, found cranberries and made stuffing with some sort of sausage.

I couldn't have had a better Christmas anywhere. They had a new verse to "Mademoiselle from Armentières."

"You might forget the gas and shell
But you'll never forget the Mademoiselle!
Rinky-dinky parley-vous!

I only hope we won't still be doing <u>this</u> next Christmas.

Volume XIIA
1918

N April 1997, WE SOLD A MAGAZINE ARTICLE ENTITLED "ELEVEN DAYS in Purgatory: A Diary" to a British magazine that appeared just in time for the 80th anniversary of Ned's shift on the hill.

Ned bought three journal books of prewar British manufacture in St. Louis before he left the United States. Volume XIIA and the next two volumes are in these journals. He sacrificed at least fifty torn-out sheets for other uses at the end of Volume XII. Some entries crawl up the margins at the end of Volume XII, making them cramped and hard to read. Ned obtained a well broken-in pen in December 1917 to replace the one broken on Hill 90.

A split volume is unusual for any diarist. However, Ned did it before in Volume XA. Somehow, his orderly mind didn't allow him to just start a *complete* new volume in the last quarter of *his* diary year.

Volume XIIA covers only three months and a week, but it was a *momentous* three months and a week. Not as momentous as some later volumes, perhaps, but...

January

"Have another drink, Ned," Brick passed the stone jug to Steele in the little room they called the Officer's Club.

"Mike," Steele took it and downed a swallow of *something* strong.

"Funny how quiet *this* New Year's Eve is, eh?"

"Yeah," Steele agreed. Training troops at Etaples—many of them already half-trained on the Hotchkiss gun—would have been elementary if not for the *retraining* to break bad habits, and *un*-training just plain wrong things. A good number of "instructors" from other units were learning from Steele's veterans. "They know the *basics*, at least…"

"And we teach them your central fire control…" Brick started.

"*Not* in the *books*, *that's* for sure. I just look at the map; decide *which* barrage we need; assign a gun section and adjust. All there is to it."

"Yeah; *all*," Brick answered, taking another swig. "My students look at me like I had two heads. 'You *plan* this in

---

[1] Ned had been skipping days, weeks and even months for some time, entering only dates and sometimes locations. He continued doing so intermittently, making this entry puzzing. If he *tried* to clean up his language, he failed for some time.

advance, then *move it around* by telephone or messenger?' When I say 'yeah', they *laugh*. 'How would you plan *this* fire on the attack?' they ask. 'Maps,' I tell 'em. Then, they're mystified. They can't *imagine* machine guns can do what we *have* 'em do."

"*And damned few* are familiar with the aerial photo maps we're using. They'll just have to *learn*."

"Yeah," Brick sighed, standing up. "Let's *finish* this…this… *whatever* the Hell this *is…and…*"

"*One* for the *ditch*, Mike."

***

Steele awoke in his bunk, his tunic open, puttees off, blanket draped over him like a shroud. Both his shoes were off…and he couldn't remember how he *got* there. The last he remembered he was in the…Officer's Club?

Gathering what he could of his wits, he got up and shrugged his tunic off…before he draped it over his shoulders against the cold…and the *stove* was *cold.*

Though it *should* have been a duty day (Tuesday), Steele had given the boys a day off…but there *should* have been someone in the orderly room on telephone watch *and* lighting his *stove…*

He stuck his head out the door; the orderly room was empty. Growing irritated, he pulled on his greatcoat and opened the outside door…to see a baseball game. "*Hey*," he shouted, wincing at the sound of his own voice. "*Who's* on *duty* here?"

The game stopped, the pitcher staring at him. "Sir?"

"I said, *who's on duty?* There should be *someone….*" Steele winced, thinking the sun was *much* too bright.

"*Me*, sir," the batter answered. "I'm listening for the telephone…"

"And the stove has *gone cold* in the meantime," Steele snapped, *aching* with the strain. "Aren't you *supposed* to…?"

"Ain't *that* cold, sir," the batter said. "Was warm enough to…"

"Cold enough for your commander to want the *stove lit! What's* your name?"

"Polen, sir," the boy answered.

"Who's the officer of the day?"

"Lieutenant Griswold, sir."

"Well, *where*...?"

"Perimeter inspection, sir," Polen said.

"Well, *get your ass in there* and *start* that *damn stove*, Polen."
Steele pointed to the pitcher. "*You*: go find *Lieutenant* Griswold
and tell him to report here, *now*, because his *commander* is about
to make him a *Sergeant*."

Polen lit the stove up a few minutes later; Griswold was
pounding up the steps moments after *that*. "Sir," the Lieutenant
panted. "I was..."

"So Polen told me," Steele snapped, his head ringing. "You
know the stove is to be lit at *all times*..."

"Well, sir," Griswold answered, "Other than *you* in *your room*,
there was no one *in* the orderly room, and SOP says the stoves are
only to be lit when someone is *awake* and in the room to *monitor*
it."

Steele...stopped, chagrined. "Lieutenant: you're *right*. Guess I
was just surprised by...where's your runner?"

"*Here*, sir," Polen said from behind Griswold.

"Boys," Steele sighed, rubbing his hands on the stove as it
warmed up, "waking up with a *hangover* in a cold room is a
sonofabitch, ain it?"

"It is *indeed*, sir," Griswold agreed.

"That's why I don't *drink* no more, sir," Polen declared. "Far
too many nights with Who-Shot-John[1] got the best of me on
Montana mornings. Only warm *there* in mid-July."

"I'm sorry, men," Steele said, trying just a hint of contrition
through his hangover. "Shouldn't have taken my headache out on
you..."

"It's all *right*, sir," "Water under the *bridge*, sir," were the
answers.

"Anybody got any coffee?" Steele asked.

"Mess hall, sir," Polen said.

"Yeah," Steele mused. "I should *get* some...Can you find

---

[1] Any kind of alcoholic drink.

Sergeant Rodgers for me?"

***

"You *sent* for me, sir?" Rodgers knocked softly on Steele's door.

"I *did*, Sergeant," Steele answered. "Do *you* know how I got here last night?"

"I *helped* you from the Officer's Club, sir. Major Brick summoned me when you, ah, became *disabled* by drink."

"Uh, huh. Did you *also* take my shoes and puttees off?"

"I thought I'd make you more *comfortable*, sir."

"Uh, huh. You're *not* a body servant, Sergeant."

"No, sir. I *am* your driver and personal clerk. *And* a human being, sir."

"You are *that*, Sergeant. Thank you."

"*My* pleasure, sir."

2nd January, Camp Steele, Etaples, France.

We'll never get to full strength, but by God, we'll have

the organization for it and keep them busy...got Peng's

workshop...

"Huh," Steele grunted. "Dodge chassis...Insley body...what do they call *this* one, Jack?" Steele had his hand on the smaller of two vehicles Willis had just delivered at the railhead.

"Light repair truck, Ned," Willis replied. "We are authorized *two* of them and this is the *first*..."

"The *other*, Jack?" Steele pointed to a larger vehicle on the same gondola.

"That *was* German; the French *captured* it and I..."

"*Yes*, Jack; you *acquired* it." Steele gazed at the vehicle, seeing a lion logo on the radiator. "Not familiar with the Büssing firm. Let's look inside." He climbed onto the gondola and figured out the latches for the folding split sides. Inside were a lathe and a milling machine connected to the truck's driveshaft by belts.

Bolted to a lower door/platform was a heavy vice. "Think *this* will be enough for Peng?"

"If it ain't," Willis sighed, "*nothing* is."

3ʳᵈ January. Camp Steele, Etaples, France.

More men pouring into camp every day. This morning, they <u>marched</u>...Now we have more than a company of British-trained Americans...Attleboro would be useful anywhere...we <u>badly</u> lost a soccer game to our British hosts, to no one's surprise. We played <u>that</u> because we could not agree on football rules, as they are more familiar with rugby and we are not.

"Parade...*halt!*" The block of marching men in British uniforms stopped on the road at their Captain's command. "Left...*turn!*" The men faced to the left. Steele, unprepared for these *visitors*, straightened his jacket and his Sam Browne belt and lowered the chin strap on his helmet.

"Sir, Captain Cunningham with two hundred and fifty-six of *your* countrymen desiring to serve under their *own* colors," the Captain reported with a stiff open-hand salute. "Trained machine-gunners they all *are*, sir..."

"I *see*," Steele said, returning the salute and gazing at the formation. "Yes, well...Captain, are *you*...?"

"*No*, sir, I am *not*. I'm English *born* and under the Union Jack I shall *perish*."

"Uh-huh." Steele heaved a sigh. "Very well. Sergeant Major Massie will get them organized..."

***

"Six hundred and nine, now, sir," Massie sighed, checking his roster in Steele's office. "A *real* battalion."

"Yeah," Steele agreed. "How's the billet situation?"

"Well, we have *shelter* and blankets for everyone, though some are sleeping on floors," Massie answered. "We're working on bunks or pallets…"

"Only saving grace is that we don't have to train them as machine gunners…" Steele said.

"Just *soldiers*," Brick declared. "They're trained as *English* soldiers, not American. We've got to bring them around to American drill, procedures and ceremonies. Hell, we even gotta teach 'em how to *march*."

"*That* won't take long," Massie said. "I can detail Dugan to teach them to march…"

"The *problem* is food," Willis interrupted. "We used part of our breakfast to give them lunch, and now everyone's on Maconochie stew until I can increase our allocations, *and* get it delivered…"

"And they *don't* know the Hotchkiss," Steele said. "But…*Hell*, we can *train* them…"

***

"Corporal Attleboro, sir," Massie nodded, leading the slender man into Steele's office.

"Sir," Attleboro saluted.

"At ease, Corporal," Steele sighed. "Have a seat. How's our literacy program going?"

"Slow, sir," Attleboro sighed. "Without textbooks, I have to teach reading and arithmetic out of Army manuals meant for 5th Graders and officers."

"I can see where that would be hard," Steele said. "Are you making progress with math?"

"More than I expected, sir," Attleboro declared. "Some take to the calculus like they were made for it. Some don't get it at all. A lot of men are eager to read; some don't care for it."

"Corporal," Steele said, "since you apparently speak German well, I'm assigning you to Lieutenant Burkhard's S2 section as a Staff Sergeant. Dosen't change your tutoring, but Burkhard needs help."

"*Yessir.*"

"We understand you know soccer…" Massie said. "Can we get a team together to play the British?"

"A *team*, yes," Attleboro said. "Win? Probably *not*. The Brits are quite avid at *their* football."

And he was right. The score after 30 minutes of play was 6-0 Britain, and play was suspended.

4th January, Camp Steele, Etaples, France.

Company officers are harder to identify, but every few hours another Lieutenant stumbles in the gate. I'd promote the former British NCOs, but not sure yet if that's wise.

Began regular 24-hour passes to Etaples. First time they came back with more songs:

"When this bloody war is over,

Oh, how happy I will be!

When I get my civvy clothes on,

No more soldiering for me.

I'll sound my own reveille,

I'll make my own retreat:

No more NCOs to curse me,

No more Goddamn army stew."

5th January, Camp Steele, Etaples, France.

Now, former Canucks…

"Major *Willis*," Steele yelled into the big supply building; "*Jack*, where *are*…?"

"*Yo*," came a reply from under a stack of crates. "Just a moment."

Steele gazed around the musty domain of sacks and crates, of boxes and bags, wondering how anyone could keep track of it all. But Willis, his deputy, and his *one* clerk seemed to do it well enough…

"Ned, how may I help you?" Willis asked, suddenly appearing from behind the crates.

"You're aware of another hundred and some men who joined the company this afternoon, yes?"

"Certainly, Ned," Willis answered. "Got uniforms and gear on the way now; be here *Tuesday*…"

"We need to feed the men something other than Maconochie stew in the morning or—"

"We shall have a shipment of supplemental chow in…" Willis glanced at a pocket watch, "*two hours*. Afraid I couldn't do *better* than beef hocks[1] for Sunday supper, but…"

"*How* did you…? They only just *got* here four *hours* ago…?"

"Well, I got this, ah…" Willis handed Steele a paper, "*schedule*, the Brits call it; *I* call it a packing list. Anyway, they were sending us *this*," he patted the stack of crates, "on Friday; a supply of *boots* for an additional four hundred ten *other* ranks we were gaining on-strength in the next fortnight. *I* just figured…"

"You figured what?"

"I figured *you* knew all about it, Ned."

"A perfectly reasonable surmise, Jack, but in this case, quite wrong. I had no *idea* we were getting another…what did you say? *Four hundred?*"

"Four hundred ten men. 'Other ranks' is what *they* call the enlisted."

"I'm *aware* of that, Jack. Four hundred and ten? We're aware of…Jack, how long have you been in supply?"

"All my career."

"Uh-huh. How do you get so…*aware*…of…?"

"Just a matter of getting to know the right *people*, Ned."

"Uh-huh. In the *future, Major*, when you get such *news* through *your* sources, I'd appreciate it if you would also make *me*

---

[1] Shanks.

aware as *soon* as possible."

"*Yes*sir; I'll do that."

6ᵗʰ January, Camp Steele, Etaples, France.

Not sure just how to get this collection of men into a

unit...

"Mike," Steele nodded to Brick. He was accustomed to sitting outside at night, recording his thoughts. The men were used to seeing it.

"Ned," Brick sighed, sitting on a step next to Steele.

"How in the *Hell* am I supposed to build a *battalion* with what I've got? Barely one officer for every sixty men, and barely one *American* Army NCO for every twenty?" Steele asked.

"What were they saying about British-American and Canadian-American officers?"

"They said that *transferring* a King's Commission to a country outside the reach of Crown courts is not possible." Steele shook his head in the dim porch light. "*Possible*, I suppose, but it sounds like an excuse..."

"An excuse for the British to *not* release them," Brick said. "They can't resign without *permission* or *cause*, they say."

"Yeah. And those men we've *got*..."

"Hard cases," Brick finished. "Drunks, womanizers, gamblers, malingerers. They shed their deadwood on us."

"But machine gunners," Steele added, "although our people think *little* of their skills..."

"We're training 'em different, Ned," Brick interrupted. "*Our* gunners have to *think* more..."

"Well, they're *our* problems now," Steele grunted, standing up. "I'm for bed. You're on duty?"

"Yep. Night."

"Night."

Just as Steele was about to go inside, out of the shadows of the night, Nagurski, McCloskey, Dugan and Thorsten approached. "Sir," Nagurski said.

"Men...."

"We've been *talking*, sir," McCloskey said. "We, ah, believe we have some solutions to the integration problem."

"I'm all ears, Sarge."

"*Most* of these guys have been in the *trenches* too long," Nagurski said.

"Yeah?"

"It's the British idea of disciplining miscreants, sir," Nagurski added. "They screw up, they get sent *back*..."

"Hold on a minute," Steele interrupted, holding up a hand. "Let's ask ourselves why these guys joined up in the *first* place. Anybody ask 'em that?"

The NCOs looked at each other, surprised. "If I had to guess..." Thorsten said.

"We should not *guess*, friend," Dugan declared.

"Let's find *out*," Steele said. "If they just wanted *out* of *life*, there's lots of ways to do *that*. They served like *soldiers* on the front or they wouldn't still be *alive*."

"Well, some of 'em are walking posts right now," McCloskey mused. "Let's just ask 'em. Nagurski: you've buddied up to one..."

"Yeah, *I* had a chat with a boozer," Nagurski said. "He's probably awake yet..."

"I trained a *few* of 'em on the Hotchkiss," Thorsten said. "They seem bright and willing enough; they know the *Vickers* gun inside and out. Can use 'em *there*, but *our* kind of *planning*..."

"I think they're *technically* competent gunners, *but*..." Nagurski added.

A long silence followed.

"At least *some* of 'em are *mortally certain* they're gonna end up back in *British* units," Dugan said. "Hell, they joined *us* to get *away* from them *damned British*..."

"We need to get them to *want* to serve *here*...with *us*," Steele began, "and we need to *convince* them they will *not* revert to British command, *ever*."

"*How* we gonna...?" Thorsten asked.

"Tomorrow we swear 'em all in," Steele finished. "We'll see what they think of *that*."

> *7ᵗʰ January, Camp Steele, Étaples, France.*
>
> *Mass swearing-in…I believe I face an impossible situation, as I have nowhere near enough officers or NCOs to organize the battalion properly…I shared McTee's wisdom on leading, don't think they'd heard it before…These guys have been with the British long enough to sound like them. They resent the attitudes of the British officers…*

"That I will bear true faith and allegiance to the same…" Steele read from the book.

"That I will bear true faith and allegiance to the same…" the crowd intoned.

Steele finished the reading; the crowd followed along to the end. "Very well; congratulations, you are now members of the United States Army. Sergeant *Major!* Let's *get* 'em to *work*."

"*Yessir*," Massie said, calling, "All Sergeants and Corporals, fall out and fall in by the orderly room over there. The *rest* of you, Sergeants Nagurski and Dugan have *plans* for you."

"All right; *close ranks*, ya lazy *gobs*," Dugan yelled. "close it *up*, then." He perused the ranks with an expert eye as Nagurski watched. "Left…*face*. That's *left turn*, ya…Forward…*march* …*left*; your *left*; your *left*…pay *attention*, ya…we *don't* swing our arms like *damned Englishmen* here, ya gobs…and *slow* it *down*, here, lads; *we* march at 120 paces, *not* 140…" as they marched away.

Steele, with McCloskey and Thorsten, looked over the sixty-odd former British and Canadian Army NCOs standing uneasily in the chilly wind; only a handful had greatcoats.

Steele, with his new "trench coat" over his greatcoat,[1] felt out-

---

[1] Trenchcoats in WWI were raincoats worn over the uniform.

of-place because he was warm-ish. "Men," Steele began, "you have the leadership experience that we need. I hope *most* of you will wear stripes in this battalion, and Sergeants McCloskey and Thorsten will decide *who* will keep their stripes. If you can *lead*, if you can *soldier*, and most important, if you *know* your *role*, you can have stripes that reflect that."

"Our...*role*, sir?" a Sergeant asked.

"As NCOs, Sergeant," Steele grinned. "*I* was a Corporal not *that* long ago. I *knew* what I was supposed to *do*..."

"What was *that*, sir?" came the question.

"Our *first* job is to train our replacements," McCloskey declared.

"If you *disagree*," Thorsten snapped, "*take off* those stripes and fall out *now*."

No one disagreed.

"Sergeants McCloskey and Thorsten," Steele said, "get them *inside*; figure out who's going to keep their stripes."

***

"Think it was a good idea to have the NCOs...?" Brick started. They were in the mess hall at noon chow. With the shortages of meat, they relied heavily on Maconochie. Despite the limitations, Farrell—recently promoted to Warrant Officer and battalion mess steward—and his cooks could scrounge enough "extras" to turn the barely edible tinned stew into something palatable. They served fresh biscuits—flour, lard, baking powder—at every meal, which never seemed to run out.

"Figure out who should wear the stripes?" Steele grinned. "Who better?" Open spaces informally divided the long tables and benches into NCOs' and officers' country.

"But they need to be *vetted* by officers," Grimes declared. "We can't have just *any*..."

"Why not?" Ishim chimed in. "*Their* role is..."

"*Everyone's* most important job," Steele said softly, "is to *train our replacements*. I believe *other* NCOs are the best judges of that."

"Huh," Grimes grunted. "Can't agree..."

"*You* were an NCO," Steele chided. "What's changed?"

"I realized that not everyone can *be* an NCO," Grimes declared. "Yes, they have *that* role, but it is *subordinate* to…"

"*Nothing*," Steele said. "All of us have that same important job: train our replacements. And if we don't know *our* jobs well enough to *train* it, the rank is meaningless. That makes *you*," he pointed at Brick, "a potential battalion commander. Hell," he looked around, "*all* of you are."

"Scary prospect…" Ishim shook his head. "*I* could command *this* outfit?"

"That's *right*," Steele declared. "Everyone's *got* to be prepared to step up if they *have* to. And if *you* don't *like* something about the outfit, *change* it or *get* it changed. *This* is the *best* outfit you've *ever* been in. If it *ain't*, it's *your* fault, *and* it's *mine*."

"Words to live by, Ned," Brick said, getting up. "In that vein, your executive officer has to organize the motor pool, since the supply officer…"

"Be *right* there, Mike," Willis declared, getting up himself.

***

"So, they're *all* good NCOs?" Steele asked, presented with the list McCloskey and Thorsten worked from. They were in Steele's office just after the sunset gun.[1]

"The British are pretty careful about non-com promotions, sir," Thorsten said. "Some of 'em I'd say would make good *officers*."

"We indicated *that* there, sir," McCloskey added. "The O's."

"Ah, yes," Steele said. "*This* eases our leadership problems…"

"Just let 'em keep their stripes, sir," Thorsten said.

"OK." Steele eyed the two NCOs, standing nonchalantly before their commander, who had the power to promote or demote them for any reason, or no reason at all. "*Smoke* what you've *got*. You talk to these guys; find out what's making 'em tick?"

Thorsten produced a tobacco bag; McCloskey a half-smoked cigar. "*Well*, sir," Thorsten said casually as he rolled a cigarette,

---

[1] Part of the flag-lowering ceremony signifiying the end of the duty day.

licking the paper, "I *still* think *some* of them suspect that this outfit's little more than a break from the trenches, that after a while, we'll just send 'em back."

"There's *some* like that," McCloskey agreed, offering a new cigar to Steele; he took it. "*But…*" he struck a match for Steele before he puffed his own butt into life again, "most of 'em really want to serve in an American Army, but they *ain't* sure this outfit won't use them like the *Brits* did."

"I see," Steele sighed, half-inhaling. "I don't know how *best* to disabuse them of that idea."

"*Talk* to 'em, sir," Thorsten shrugged. "You're good at convincing people…"

"That's right, sir," McCloskey agreed. "*You* could convince a *whore* to join a *church*."

"I'm not *that* good, McCloskey," Steele grinned, standing up, "but let's see *how* good I am. Just…hang back while I walk around, just in case somebody makes trouble."

***

"Gentlemen," Steele said softly as he approached three figures deep in discussion near the front gate.

"Yeah," one of them said. "Who's a bleeding *gent*, then?" The day's blustery wind had died down, leaving another layer of frost that crunched underfoot.

"Name's Ned. What's yours?"

"Ned *who?*" one asked.

"Does it *matter?*"

"It *might*, mate," another answered. "Calling us *gents* like we're toffs."

"Nobody's accusing you of that," Steele answered. "Just passing the time while I walk around. You haven't got a *swig* of something, *do* ya, then?"

"Sure," the third answered, holding out a bottle. "Makes you want to *holler*, this stuff does."

"See for myself." Steele sipped the contents; an *awful* gin. "*Woah*," Steele exclaimed. "Put *hair* on your chest or strip *paint*."

"It would *that*, mate," the first said. "Who *are* you, anyway?"

"Just a mate you offered a drink to," Steele answered. "I'll be on my way…"

"*Hold* on," one of them said. "We've been trying to work out who's really in *charge* in this place. You *know* the officers here?"

"I *know* 'em," Steele answered. "What do you want to know?"

"We know *our* business," one said. "Know it well. *I've* been on the Vickers since '15. Will *these* bastards put us in front and wait for us to get *killed* off while…?"

"No," Steele said, loudly. "*This* outfit's in *training:* still building, and *you* guys can help, *share* what you know. We're a *way* from being on the line…if we *ever* are. We're trainers, *too*…"

"How *long* a way," one said warily. "At the rate they're using the blighters in Flanders, it *can't* be…"

"No; General Pershing won't *allow* Americans to be used as replacements in British units: *you* guys are immune now you've taken the oath…"

"And how would *you* know, pal?" one of them sneered.

"Because those are the orders they gave *me*."

Silence…

"You're an officer," one of them said.

"Colonel Steele, yes."

"Sir," the three shapes came to attention.

"As you *were*," Steele cleared his throat and produced his cigar stub. "Anyone got a light?" *Two* struck matches. "Thanks. Where are you guys from?"

"Upstate New York;" "Sacramento;" "Pittsburgh," came the answers.

"Why in the *Hell* did you join the *British* Army?"

"Out of *work*," one said. "*Looked* like it would be a lark." "The Heinies sank my ship and I landed in Bristol with no job," another answered. "*Had* to get off the farm," the third said. "Crossed into Canada and…"

"Nothing to do with bashing the Hun?"

"No, sir;" "Not at first;" "Didn't *occur* to me *then*," they said.

"So what happened? Why did the British come to *not* want you in *their* army any more?"

Silence again…

"Ypres happened, sir," one answered.

"For *me*, Albert, sir."

"Gassed a *second* time; *that* was enough," the third declared. "*Thiepval Ridge…*"

"What, exactly…?"

"They threw us up against the Huns and they didn't care what *happened* to us as long as we kept *fighting*, sir. Didn't see any Generals getting a smoke hood on, *did* we, boys?"

"Nope;" "not hardly," came the answers.

"OK, boys, tell ya what. *I* won't let you do anything I don't, won't, or haven't done. What's more, I'll *always* tell you *what* you're doing, *why* you're doing it, and *what* we'll accomplish when we're *done*. If I *don't*, you have my permission to beat the *bejesus* out of me. How's *that* sound?"

"Like bold talk in the dark, sir," one said.

"Then just listen up real close at morning formation."

8ᵗʰ January, Camp Steele, Étaples.

To get them to trust us, I have to convince them we won't send them back to the Brits…We are training intensively now, running in the snow and all. We need these former British and Canadian gunners to fit in as well now as did their once-Legion predecessors, so long ago I almost forget them. I wonder how many of them are left…

"Men," Steele began, "some of you have been dealt a bad hand in other units. Some of you feel the higher-ups sacrificed your messmates for no good reasons. And while that may be so, *I* can't change that. *But…*" he paused as subtle murmurs rippled through the formation, "*but*," he continued more loudly, "what I *can* do is guarantee that *will not happen here*. In *this* outfit, you will *always* know *what* you're doing and *why* you're doing it."

Mild rumbling swept through the ranks. "You new men, you who served so gallantly under other flags against our common enemy: *talk* to the old hands. They'll tell you that the officers in this unit do what the men do…*we* just do it in *Sam Browne* belts…" *That* raised a laugh. "*We'll* learn what *you* need to learn; what *most* of you already know…with different *machine guns*, perhaps, *but*…" A genuine laugh. "Now, the most important thing for you new men who are coming back to your native colors…"

"Not Alaska," someone said; "not Hawaii," another said.

"*Close* enough for the government," Steele answered.

"Not if I'm an *Indian*," said one.

"So I'll *adopt* ya," Steele called back; *that* started some grins. "Hell, *Willis* drove a wagon for Geronimo; maybe *he'll* adopt ya." *That* brought an outburst of laughter, which soon subsided. As it did, Steele raised his arms for quiet. "But whatever happens, come hell or high water, I *will not* sacrifice you for no reason, not if I can help it. *That's* a promise. And we will *not* parcel you out to French or British units, either; *that* promise is from *Black Jack Pershing* himself." *That* garnered a rousing cheer and applause.

"You'll always know *why*, boys. If you don't, *ask*. My ear's *always* ready to listen…when I'm *awake* and *sober*." *Everyone* laughed at that. "So let's get to work, men. There's details to be formed, classes, and we need *more* officers and NCOs, so let's get *to* it. *Comp*-any; *a*-ten—*shun!* Sergeant *Major*…"

"Perfect, sir," Massie said beneath his breath.

Moments later, Brick extended his hand to Steele. "I couldn't have said it better, Ned," he said earnestly. "Let's just hope they don't resent us when their pay starts."

"Any idea how little the British Army pays?" Steele asked.

"That bad?"

"*Half* what *we* pay."

"Reason enough to want to come back, I suppose."

9th January, Camp Steele, Etaples.

Today we started organizing in earnest, since

truckloads of equipment and more men are arriving

"Gentlemen," Steele began his address to the newcomers, "and I use the term *loosely...*" That caused a ripple of laughter. "*Many* of you, I'm told, have trained as machine gunners. *That* will change. We will *all* train as machine gunners. Are we clear?"

"Yes, sir," came the reply.

Steele saw three men shivering in civilian clothes. "*You* three," Steele called, "*what* are...?"

"Enlisted in *England*, sir," one voice said. "Joined up here in *France*, sir," said another. "Haven't signed papers anywhere at *all*, brother; just came along with some of these *other* fellows..." the third declared.

"All right; the three of *you* fall out," Steele sighed.

Suddenly Massie was at his elbow. "*I'll* take care of *them*, sir," he mumbled. "Find something for them at headquarters."

"Very well," Steele said. "One of them has to actually *enlist*, apparently."

"Yessir; I gathered that last *night...*"

"Of *course* you did, Top."

***

"Sir," came the knock on his door. "Something you've *gotta* see..."

Steele grabbed his greatcoat and went out into the frosty evening. It was snowing lightly, which muffled the sounds of the marching men coming up the road. Steele immediately noticed the slow marching pace of the men...almost a lope. "Well, have you *ever* seen the like?" Steele asked no one in particular.

"*La Legion*," a Sergeant nearby declared. "Only *they* march *that* slow."[1]

---

[1] The French Foreign Legion's marching pace is 88 paces per minute, said to have been the pace of the Legion's ancestor, the Hohenlohe Regiment.

They watched the formation of four files of about fifty men each, with full field packs on their backs and barracks bags balanced on them, on what seemed like a leisurely, albeit in-step, stroll up the road.

As the head of the column reached the gate, a commanding voice called, "*Compagnie…halte!*" As one, the files stopped and came to a noisy halt. "*À droit tour…nez!*" was the next command, and the files snapped to face to the right. "*Capitaine Lomax,*" the voice called; the voice was relieved with a swift and snappy salute.

The commander strode to the guard shack, saluted smartly, and handed the Officer of the Day a piece of paper. Steele, already on his way to the gate, met the Lieutenant halfway. By the light of the Lieutenant's lantern, Steele read:

> 9TH COMPANY, 1ST MARCHING REGIMENT OF THE FRENCH FOREIGN LEGION IS ATTACHED TO 432ND MACHINE GUN BATTALION, BY ORDER OF COL F. CONNER, CHIEF OF OPERATIONS, AEF.

"Short and sweet," Steele sighed. "This is our infantry company."

"Their commander speaks English, sir," the Lieutenant offered. "*And* he seems sure of himself."

"I know who he is," Steele said, walking towards the gate. "*Commandant* Haller," he called. "Cold night for a road march."

"Don't *I* know it?" Haller answered, walking towards him. "*Good* to see you, Colonel. Maybe *half* are Americans, British, Irish, and Canadians mixed with the Spaniards, Dutch, Norwegians, Indochinese, Mexicans, Cubans, Italians, Greeks, Senegalese, and Indians. The *usual* mix."

"How many Germans?" Steele asked.

"*None,*" Haller declared. "They weeded *them* out in Algiers. *And* the Turks, Austrians, Russians, Hungarians and *other* Balkan types."

"Can the French *spare* you?" Steele asked.

"The Marching Regiments of Africa are being disbanded, sending the men back to Algieria." Haller declared. "Didn't want to *waste* the shipping on *these*."

"These…what?"

"*Les porteurs du nœud coulant,*" Haller said quietly. "*Wearers* of the *noose*. They're *excellent* soldiers, most of 'em, but they did something they *shouldn't* have and are charged with, but not *convicted* of, crimes warranting a death sentence."

"Like what?"

"Mostly striking an officer or NCO. Some *others*, for *not* following *idiotic* orders."

"And *you* ended up with them?"

"Ah…yeah, My commander took exception to my *refusal* to order my men to slaughter prisoners. Legion standards dictate that my officers be *similarly* dishonored for similar so-called offences. But France *needs* us too much, so they didn't shoot *us* like those poor bastards last April."

"We *heard* about that," Steele mused.

"Yeah, well, *some* deserved it; some *didn't*. Don't *ask* me any more, OK, pal? Now, where can I bed 'em down?"

10th January, Camp Steele, Etaples, France.

They didn't tell me how I was supposed to integrate a large infantry company into a machine gun battalion. Willis got fuel trucks and more repair trucks and heavy trucks from firms I've never heard of. Barely had enough drivers to roll them off the flatcars.

11th January, Camp Steele, Etaples, France.

Getting the Legion to cooperate with the movements of three inexperienced companies is interesting. But, remarkably, they absolutely love baseball.

18th January, Camp Steele.

A battering week of marching and driving through blizzards.

Some entertainers made a detour for us. Song and

dance revue from a burlesque troop lightened the
spirits. I've seen _burlesque_ girls before, but _these_ look
like the Folies Bergère, get arrested in America.
And a new version of Auld Lang Syne:
"We're here because,
"We're here because..."
Repeat ad infinitum...

20th January, Camp Steele, Etaples, France.
Religious services with real priests this morning. A
Monsignor came out from Etaples, gave a Mass.
Nearly half the unit took part. Two more priests came
out with enough English to hear confessions.

28th January, Camp Steele, Etaples, France.
[Smudged paragraph]
HQ Co will practice a road march with vehicles this
week. We will see how Willis' fuel planning works.

February

1st February, Camp Steele, Etaples, France.
Willis' fuel planning OK; road march was a disaster
otherwise. Icy roads made for many accidents
because of driver inexperience. We now have half our
HQ vehicles damaged; some beyond repair. But our
Autocars and the big Berliet trucks are as rugged as
bulls. Two smashed together without damage; one

destroyed a Model T truck after a collision.
Casualties among the drivers, luckily, are minimal.
Need more training before the line companies should
try road marches.

7th February, Camp Steele, Etaples, France.
1st Division machine gunners have learned much, but
have far to go. McCall & Benson suggest two
training "tracks," one for gunners and one for future
gunner instructors. I suggest a third for gunnery
control officers and NCOs. We proceed with the first
two for now. We recreated our old Training Dept.
in HQ Co., put Brick in it to start. Detached five
NCOs and three officers to 2nd Div.

9th February, Camp Steele, Etaples, France.
A typhus outbreak, almost unheard of here in France
but common in Russia, Doc Miller says. Looking
for the source. Delousing everything we can, boiling
everything possible. Personal inspections by Miller
and his crew.

10th February, Camp Steele, Etaples.
Our first typhus deaths, two Legionnaires.

15th February, Camp Steele.
A French medical team is here to help. Three French

He put his pen down. "We gotta figure out…maybe *this* one's too big a bite," Steele sighed, dejected. "What's our headcount now, Mike?" Steele asked.

"Can't leave it *be*, can ya?"

"How *many*?"

Brick consulted a file. "This morning…836 answering the role. Fifty-one absent; mostly sick."

"Can't get the uniforms boiled fast enough," Steele said. "Let's get the cooks involved."

"Yeah," Brick nodded. They both looked up as Erskine entered the room. "Yes?"

"Sir; *Colonel*, sir; for *you*, marked *urgent*." He handed Steele an envelope.

> *Congratulations on a job well done. I will see that they promote you to Captain in the Regular Army. Your battalion is a credit to your ingenuity and resourcefulness.*
> *Pershing.*

"The battalion is a credit to my ingenuity and resourcefulness," Steele sighed. "I'm gonna be a Captain in the Regulars."

"Congrats," Brick nodded. "We need a *welding* truck to fix the bodies…"

"What do *you* know about automobiles?" Steele grinned. "You grew up in an orange grove."

"I grew up on Long Island, *Colonel*," Brick answered snidely. "I spent a few weeks *some* summers in Florida, on my uncle's farm. You've *made* me learn about motor cars, you slave-driver."

"Your *chauffer* should have taught you…" Steele said.

"Our chauffer had other things to do," Brick sighed. "Dad

wanted me to follow in the family business…"

"Which was?"

"The law. I *started* school, but I went to Plattsburg camps in '15 and '16 and…"

"*Here* you *are*."

"And *here* I *am*. Dad still wants me to *have* a chauffeur, not to *be* one…"

"But we need to get control of this typhus," Steele mumbled. "I'm going to inspect the hospital…"

28ᵗʰ February, AEF Testing Grounds, Reims, France.

The Pioneer Section[1] works better than I had imagined… what are they keeping us for if we're not going to fight? Maybe they want to break us up…wish this fever of mine would just go away…

As Steele watched, the Pioneer Section made quick work of shell craters on the artillery range—including sloping the sides—using anything at hand to fill and make the holes at least passable. Peng's *platoon* of mechanics and a fuel platoon improved the battalion's mobility and independence…which had *yet* to fight as a unit.

And that rankled Steele.

They had performed demonstrations, done machine-gun training for American units, attached instructors to other units, even acted as "aggressors" in war games…but they had not yet fought as a battalion.

"When are we gonna get a chance to fight, sir?" Thorsten asked about every other day.

"Are we just a fancy display unit?" Ishim often chimed in.

"I don't *know*," Steele would tell them. "If they didn't *want* us, they'd cut off our petrol," he'd add.

---

[1] A unit with the skills and tools for building roads and bridges.

And so, they continued to train…and practice…and move around…

March

1ˢᵗ March, Étaples.

So ill today. Can't concentrate. Hope it isn't the

typhus.

3ʳᵈ March [no location; date struck through]

Wrong date.

Steele blinked his eyes open. The light was dim; only a small window on an unfamiliar plaster wall. He felt as if someone had beaten him, twisting and cramping his guts.

"Hello," he croaked weakly. "Anyone *out* there? How did I…?"

"Sir," Rodgers appeared.

"*Where…?*" Steele managed.

"The American Hospital in Paris, sir. I fetched you here two days ago."

"*Why…?*"

"You were *delirious*, sir. Dr. Miller diagnosed typhus and dispatched me here with you."

He could barely move any limb, let alone his head. He felt cold, shivering violently despite several blankets. And he was horribly thirsty.

"Water…"

"Just a sip, sir," Rodgers held a straw to Steele's lips; he sipped greedily….and…nothing.

He fluttered his eyes open.

"Hello, Colonel," a pleasant, dimly familiar voice cut through the fog in Steele's mind.

"Miss," Steele whispered, not looking. The rain pattered on the window; beads of water ran down the walls in the light of the solitary electric bulb dangling from the ceiling.

"To answer your question, you've been here for *four days*."

"Huh," Steele sighed. "Feels like *weeks*…"

"That's common for trench fever and typhus patients," she said.

"Miss," Steele sighed, turning his head…"*Gibson?!*"

"Colonel," she smiled.

"Miss Gibson, sorry, but you have no idea how *happy* I am to see *you*…"

She reached out to touch his hand. "Don't apologize, Colonel, I've dealt with worse. Besides, I was *so* surprised and *alarmed* to see your name on the roster that I volunteered for an extra shift."

"Would I be too forward if I were to ask for some water?"

"No, indeed, Colonel, you would *not*." She poured two tin cups half-full from an earthenware pitcher on a small wooden bedside table. "Drink *this* first, then swallow *these*," she held out a cup and two tablets.

"What's *this*…?"

"Aspirin," she said, "The only treatment we *have* for either trench fever *or* typhus is palliative. Then *drink* this." She held out the second cup.

"Controls the body aches and shivers," Steele said, taking the pills.

"Yes." She waited a beat. "How do you feel?"

---

[1] Entry probably made when Ned was too ill to be lucid.

"*Gawdawful*," he grunted sincerely. "Like I've been *rode hard* and *put up wet*, if you'll pardon my *crude* expression."

"Oh, I've heard *far* worse, Colonel."

"I'll wager you have," he grunted.

"I've heard words I never *thought*…"

"Surely your training got you…"

"My training has *become* more comprehensive," she said. "I now attend a crash nursing course at the Sorbonne five nights a week. If only *Mother* had allowed me to…" She stopped. "My whole life's story."

"Perhaps I'd like to hear it sometime."

She regarded him curiously. "Perhaps."

"Pardon me," he said, struggling to stay awake. "If I can *ask*…I *need to*…"

"*Finally*, you can *go* with no need to clean you *up*. I'll *take* you…"

"*Thank* you." He sat in the wheelchair quietly, using his feet from time to time to fend off errant furniture between his room and the bathroom.

Mercifully, Miss Gibson did not have to take him *into* the toilet…

Staggering slightly, Steele came back to his wheelchair, clutching his robe about him. "Makes me feel cold."

"Relieving yourself lowers your body temperature," she said.

He reached up to his head to scratch an itch…and he had no hair… *anywhere*. "What…what *happened* to…?"

"Sergeant Rodgers shaved your head *and* everything else. We needed to find your, ah, *critters*."

"Did you find them?"

"Yes. I'm surprised Sergeant Rodgers hasn't been here today."

"Oh?"

"He hasn't left your side since you got here. Been cleaning you up for *days* of fever delirium." They rolled back to his room. As they entered the small room, she sighed, "sorry, Colonel, but I *have* to…um, *examine*…"

"You *needn't* apologize; you've got a job to do." He suffered the indignity of having a pretty young woman examine his backside for…"What, exactly, *are* you looking *for?*"

"Sores; swelling of the glands…bleeding…*sorry*, Colonel, but…"

"I understand, Miss…" When she finished her examination, Steele laid down again. "Miss," he sighed, "I *need* to…"

"Yes, of course, Colonel," she said. "You need rest. I'll be back this evening."

"*Thank* you, Miss Gibson."

***

"Colonel," she murmured as his eyes fluttered open.

"Miss," he answered. "Time is it?"

"Just before noon. How do you *feel?*"

"Better. *Tired*, but better, Miss…"

"*Please* call me Angela. I think we've moved beyond 'miss,' don't you? At least when no one *else* is around…"

"In which case, I'm Ned," Steele answered. "*Pleased* to meet you."

"Ned, we didn't have time on the train…*where* in Michigan are you from?"

"I was born in Crawfordville, but we moved to Dearborn when I was six."

"Where's Crawfordville? Never *heard* of it…"

"It *was* close to Houghton in the UP.[1] Population was about fifty; village that died when my family and its only blacksmith left. *Where* in Michigan are *you*…?"

"Lansing, of course. Father started there in the state legislature. That's where we're *supposed* to call home." She looked at him curiously. "Ever been to Grand Haven?"

"Some lovely homes there."

"We have a cottage on the Grand River near there…" She stopped; looked away. "My life has always seemed so *artificial*. I volunteered to go overseas *just* to…"

---

[1] Upper Peninusla of Michigan.

"Just to help us poor doughboys…" Steele sighed.

"That, as well. Mother *cried* so when I told them I was going to France; Father…he seemed more…resigned." She reached for his hand. "Tell me about Ned Steele. And why 'Ned' and not…"

"Not much to tell, Angie," he started.

"I haven't heard *that* name since I was in pinafores and pigtails."

"I *hope* you don't mind. Why do you think they stopped?"

"I'm not *sure*. At a certain age, I just became 'Angela.' It was Mother's *mother's* name." She gripped his hand tightly. "I *like* it from *you*, though. What were *you* called as a child?"

"Depended on *who* was doing the *calling*," he said lightly. "*Most* of the time I was 'Ned' or 'Neddie;' if I was in *trouble*, I was 'Edmund;' *some*times I was 'Number Five…'"

"*Number Five…?*"

"I was the fifth of nine kids," he sighed.

"Oh, *my*," she said, with a look of surprise. "Your *poor* mother."

"Mama only had *five* of us," he answered. "Dad's *first* wife had the *first* four."

"Oh, dear…" she giggled. "I only have an older brother and sister…you shall have to tell me *all about* your family sometime."

"How long do they expect to keep me here?"

"About three weeks," she sighed. "They're half-conscious for the first few days, then they get stronger for about a week, *then* they become irritating as they start to feel well enough to leave…"

"*Well* enough…?"

"If you left in your current state, you would be prone to pneumonia because you're so weak and malnourished." She smiled slightly. "To *that* end, I'll tell the orderlies you're well enough to eat semi-solid food."

"You can do…?"

"The fever wing has *three* doctors, *nine* nurses, *fifteen* of us nurse's aides and student nurses, and *twelve* orderlies for *three hundred patients*, more or less. If each patient gets to see *one* of us four times a day, that would be a lot. The average is about *two*. We each have a *great* deal of autonomy…"

"Well, the AEF will get bigger; *much* bigger. *What* are you going to do when…?"

"This student nurse/nurse's aide is not privy to *those* grand plans, Ned." She looked thoughtful. "How much of France have you *seen?*"

"Paris, some; Fontainebleau, but not a *great* deal more, except to fight in it. We were in *Flanders* for a couple of weeks. I haven't been *out* of uniform since…since before I left America."

"How is your French?"

"Grammar school French; enough to get in trouble. Picking up some here and there…"

"Would you like to learn?"

"I *would,* but…"

"Then I will *tutor* you."

"Well…"

"We shall start now: you are lying on *Le bati*—a bed."

"*Le bati,*" Steele repeated.

"You are wearing *une chemise De nuit*…a nightshirt."

"*Une chemise De nuit*…French nouns have different articles…"

"Indeed; you remember *that* much. You are in a room; *une chambre*…"

"*Une chambre*…"

"*La Chambre* is in *une hôpital*…"

"*Une hôpital*…"

5ᵗʰ March [Second entry with same date]*, American Hospital, Paris, France.*

Mike brought my diary. I have got typhus; had it for at least five days before I got here 2ⁿᵈ March.[1]

I have encountered Miss AG here. She is

---

[1] Ned's dating is confused for days. Since no other record can be found of his illness, it shall be forever thus.

enchanting; teaching me French. I haven't heard back from G, but G may not be interested in what I have to say; She is interested. We still observe the proprieties. She is wiring her parents about me. Wish I knew what was going on in her head. But I know what's in my heart…

Steele woke up, not knowing where he was for a moment…that odd, dreamlike state of unknowing. The first thing he saw was his little window, where a bright ray of sunshine shone through. For the first time in days, his belly didn't hurt, nor much of anything else.

And there, in a chair next to his bed, sat Mike Brick, studying his fingernails…

"Mike," Steele grunted. "Who's minding the store?"

"Gary's got it in hand," Brick said, pushing the black-bound diary to Steele. "Thought you'd be lonely without *this*."

"Thanks…"

"You were vibrating like a *tuning fork* in your bunk when you didn't get up for reveille. Rodgers brought you down here in your auto; wouldn't *leave*. He's around here somewhere." He stopped. "You look *funny* with no hair at all."

"Thanks."

"Doc Miller called it a 'typical presentation of mild typhus.'"

"That's what *these* doctors said."

"How do you feel?"

"Like I went three rounds with a heavyweight."

"*This* is a busy place…"

"Yeah. Fever ward's pretty…"

"No; whole hospital. Seems the 28th Division ran into some…*hello*…"

Angela walked into the room, bag looped over her arm. "Hello, Major; Colonel," she smiled.

"Morning, or *bonjour, mademoiselle*," Steele said. "May I

introduce Major Mike Brick of New York? Mike: Miss Angela Gibson of Washington and Michigan.”

“Major,” she offered her hand.

“*Enchante, Mademoiselle* Gibson,” Brick replied as he stood, taking her hand, followed by a flurry of French between them.

Steele stared at them. “You two *know* each other?”

“Only from the society pages and the Social Register,” Angie said. “I asked if the Bricks of Long Island knew they are the *first* of the Four Hundred[1] to send their scion off to the war.”

“And *I* said, much to Father’s chagrin and Grandfather’s pride, I *assure* you, Miss Gibson. Then I asked if the senator’s *younger* daughter knew how *charming* she is…”

“And *I* answered, ‘Oh, *Major*, you *flatter* me,’” she smiled. “But *can* the *charm* and let me check on the patient, Major.” She turned to Steele, taking his pulse. “*Bonjour, monsieur*,” she said. “*Comment allez vous?*”

“Um…how do you say ‘not bad’ in French?” Steele asked.

“Ah…*pal mal*…”

“That’s *one* way,” Brick sniffed. “There are others…”

“That’s *quite* enough, Mike,” Steele sighed. “Miss Gibson…I *need* to…”

“Can you get up on your own?”

“Yes.” He planted his hands on his knees and stood, his feet bare on the floor.

“*I’ve* got to get back to camp,” Brick declared, going out the door. “Back in a few days…”

***

When they returned to his room, *he* sat in his chair; the first time since he’d been in the hospital…and gestured to his bed.

“What *would Mother* say,” she chuckled, taking a seat and smoothing her skirt, “or *Matron, if* they *knew*?”

“I dunno; what?”

---

[1] The cream of New York society members, an affectation invented by Lady Astor in the late 19th Century.

"*Sitting* on a *man's bed!*"…affecting a haughty falsetto: "How *utterly shameless!*" She smiled. "Just being here without a chaperone would have been *bad enough* six months ago, unless we strapped you down. When we got so *many* patients…"

"Don't you have *other* patients…?"

"Today's my day off. *One* day every *other* week."

"Um…they'll be bringing my breakfast around…"

She looked at her watch. "I can go *get* it *now. And* I'll find another chair."

***

"Not much of a breakfast. I could eat a horse…"

"Thin but nutritious, Ned," she said, setting her spoon down.

"Yes," he answered…then gathered his courage and blurted, "Angela Gibson, you are an ex*ception*ally handsome woman. I would *very much* like to get to *know* you better."

"Edmund Steele, *you* are an ex*ception*ally handsome man, with or without hair. *I* would very much like to get to know you *very* well." She reached across the tiny table, touching his shoulder. "And right about *now*, if we were in *normal* times, you would ask Father if you can *walk out* with me; discuss your *prospects* and your *intentions*."

"Yes. Except that our families are on the other side of an ocean, and times *have* changed."

"They *have*, but I believe *that* will do for the preliminaries," she nodded. "I'll cable Father and Mother that I have *met* a young man. Oh, they'll be upset for a fortnight, like they were about my coming here, but they'll come around."

"So…what *now?* I've never been…never *had* a girl…not that I didn't know for years…with *one* exception…"

"Well," she said easily. "I was engaged once until the *cad* showed his true colors. I can lead you through all the steps of courtship…if that's what *you*…"

"It *is*. Miss Gibson, are *you* taking *advantage* of my weakened health to…I have a little money of my *own*…"

"It's not your *money* I'm *after*, Colonel."

"Then…?"

"I want your *friendship* to start. How *many* women *are* you acquainted *with* at this time? And who *was* this exception?"

And they talked, lightly, for hours and hours until Ned needed another nap…

***

He awoke; it was dusk, or nearly. Rodgers sat in the chair by the door. "Sergeant," he mumbled.

Rodgers stood quickly. "Sir? May *I*…?"

"Just…sit down, please."

"Water, sir?" he asked as he sat back down.

"*Not* just yet. I owe you my thanks…"

"Nothing *of* it, sir."

"And you're still *here?*"

"Y*essir*."

"Once *again*, you're *not* my body servant, Sergeant. Nor my bodyguard."

"I am under your *command*, sir. And…"

"So are several hundred others, Sergeant; officers and enlisted men. You are no *longer* a gentleman's gentleman."

Rodgers blinked, quiet. "Do I *displease* you, sir?"

"*No*, but you…I'm not *about* to…"

After a long moment, while Steele collected his thoughts, Rodgers sat stock-still…before he looked away. "My fiancee was on *Titanic* with my employer. I still think of her. I was supposed to be *on* the ship but…" He looked at Steele. "When I *enlisted*, I took refuge in the Army, thought I could forget her. When I was ordered to your unit, I…I relished the *chance* to be a *real* soldier, but I find my *talents* are…" He smiled slightly. "I see something of *her* in you, sir. Some of her *fire*." He looked away again. "But I *have* neglected my *other* duties."

"You should return to the battalion, Sergeant." Steele wrote a quick note on a page of his diary and tore it out. "Here; a *pass*."

"Yessir." He looked curious. "I shall take my leave of Nurse Gibson and depart. Is there *anything* I…"

"I believe Miss Gibson would be flattered to be *called* a nurse."

"She shall *be* one soon enough, sir. In another two months…"

"You know more about *that* than *I*…."

"*Yes,* sir."

"*Thank* you, Sergeant."

"My *pleasure,* sir."

10th March, American Hospital, Paris.

A nurse I do not know looked in on me this morning with [smudged] the doctor called her sister; I believe she is Canuck.

A Canuck chaplain called around noon, offered a prayer, and invited me to a service tomorrow, being Sunday.

She came in the evening and we held hands, with the chairs side by side.

If I lose my heart to her, I shall not miss it.

11th March, American Hospital.

I think about her more and more, day and night, waking and sleeping. I am overwhelmed… confronted with death so much I have trouble with being shocked or saddened when it happens close to home…

"Morning, Ned," Grimes said, bursting through the door. "My turn to visit the boss, get some decent booze in Paris…"

"Gary," Steele said, setting his pen down. "How goes the war?"

"Well, our sick rate's way down now after our last delousing and uniform-burning. Doc Miller wants to talk to you about that; he came with me."

"Ah," Steele grunted. "Can't leave a sick man to recover on his own…?"

"Brick told us about that nurse…"

"*Not* a nurse; a nurse's aide…"

"She's of the *female* persuasion, *beautiful* and *here*. She could be a *lumberjack* for all *Brick* cares…"

"Didn't think he was a ladies' man…"

"He's *not*, not really. He writes to that gal of his every day…"

"*You* got hitched before you shipped, didn't you?"

"I did indeed; *wonderful* Sandra." He looked down. "Baby girl was born premature in January."

"Sorry, Gary."

"Thanks, Ned." Grimes looked up. "Despite the abeyance of *typhus and trench*, we now have an epidemic of *knock-me-down* fever.[1] About ten percent of the unit is on the sick list from *that*."

"Keep 'em working, Gary," Steele mused. "Flu only lasts a week or so…"

***

"Doc," Steele greeted Miller, limping in an hour after Grimes left.

"Sir," Miller answered, offering his hand. "Are you on the mend?"

"I am," Steele answered, shaking Miller's hand. "Please, sit."

"Sir," Miller said, sitting across from Steele at the table. "I'm here for the latest medical gossip."

"How *else* is the unit? Heard there's a flu outbreak."

"Yes; a *minor* outbreak." Miller rapped his knuckles on the table. "You were one of our last *fever* cases."

"I *feel* better. Have we lost any men to it?"

"*Five* went west of it, but in *most* cases, *I* believe there was something underlying." Miller made to stand. "I came to beg most humbly for another surgeon and *three* more aid men. I told them who I was with and I'm leaving with *two* surgeons, *two* ambulances, *two* male nurses, two *female* nurses, and *four* aid

---

[1] Influenza.

men. Your *name* seems to carry a bit of weight hereabouts. I doubt Willis could have done as well as *I* have by using *your* moniker." He made a face. "They're *also* getting more Red Cross and YMCA volunteers in France."

"Finally…"

"Yes. We can thank *Mrs.* Grimes for that."

"How's that?"

"She wired Major Grimes via the AEF about *their* tragedy. Chaumont wasn't sure what to *do* with the wire, but knew Grimes deserved better than a letter a month or more after the fact…since they *read* the wire. AEF contacted the Red Cross; *they* knew nothing, but verified it." Miller shook his head. "The Red Cross has an emergency notification service now. Did *you* know that?"

"I hadn't *heard*…" Steele said.

"Neither had I. But they *do*,[1] and now Red Cross is sending another volunteer to us to tell us about it officially." Miller extended his hand. "Your chart says you'll be back with us within a fortnight, but *I* must be off."

> *12th March. American Hospital, Paris.*
>
> *Been telling her about my family; she's been talking about hers…heard from her parents…I said my dear; she said my sweet…and more…*

"So…your oldest brother is *Alan*; your oldest sister is *Betty*…" Angela picked off Steele's brothers' and sisters' names on her fingers as she recited them.

"That's *right*," Steele said when she reached Irving.

"Alphabetical order," she smiled, "because your *father*, also *Alan*, has an over-organized mind…"

"*He* says it's just coincidence because Alan, Betty and Charlie were the *first* three and he stuck with it for the *rest*."

"If he *planned* that big a family…"

---

[1] Family notification services via the American Red Cross started in 1918.

"I never asked him, but..." Steele shrugged.

"What do they all *do?*"

"Al's an engineer like Dad. Only Al went to *school*; he's getting married in June. Betty is in Battle Creek with the Red Cross; she *has* a sweetheart in the Army she's waiting for. Charlie's in the Army in the Philippines; an officer, too, now. Diane just divorced her husband. Francine's training to be a doctor. George has an appointment to the Naval Academy. Helen and Irving are still at home—Irv's eleven and Helen's thirteen."

"What happened to your father's first wife?"

"Corinne died soon after Diane was born. She never quite recovered, they say."

"That's sad," she said, touching his hand as she shifted in her chair. "Now, mine."

"Your brother Edgar's a lawyer in Maryland, a hopeless bachelor. Your sister Margaret has two boys in Virginia."

"Right. Nowhere *near* as impressive an achievement as *your* family. Feel strong enough to walk around outside some?"

"Sure."

The weather had dried up, and they had broomed the duckboards clean of their coating of mud. Other patients made their way around the hospital, enjoying the sunshine. "Brighter than it's been," she sighed, holding his arm.

"Yep. How long are they going to keep me?"

"If you're tired of my company, just *tell* me..."

"Not *that*, Angie. I just want to know. I came here to do a *job*..."

"You came here so we could *meet*..."

"A most pleasant outcome from a most unpleasant event, my sweet, but still..."

"Pleasant indeed, my dear." They walked on. "I *think* about another fourteen days." They walked. "I shall *miss* you."

"Did you hear from your parents?"

"I got a telegram."

"And...?"

"Father said you come from an excellent family of good

Republican stock, influential in military affairs in Lansing *and* in Washington." She sighed, gripped his arm. "*Dad's* interested in the *votes* he can garner."

"It *is* his profession…"

"And *you* are my *heart*…"

***

23rd March, American Hospital, Paris.

I hear artillery…something's going wrong….

More dull rumbling in the distance woke him as someone entered his room. He remained motionless as the footfalls neared his bed. Night visitations weren't unusual…but then came a *swish* of…*fabric?* Then…the soft touch of *her* hand on his shoulder…

"*Mon coeur*," she whispered. "Move *over*…*shh*, my love…" She lifted his blanket; he felt *bare skin* against his legs. "You're being discharged this morning…"

"OK," he managed, as her hand slipped down his chest, raising his nightshirt.

"They have moved your battalion to St. Quentin…" She kissed his chest languorously.

"You *know*…?"

"The Germans have broken through the British lines. A wire came asking for your emergency discharge…" She kissed his chin, then his lips.

"I'll…*miss*…*oh*…" Her hand *touched*…*caressed*….

"*Yes*, my love; *yes*," she drew her breath sharply as she *slid* atop him. "*Shh*…I won't *see* you again…" She *rocked slowly…gently…so gently*…

"I'll find…*you*…*oh*…"

"I'll find *you, mon destin*…"

"What's…?"

"My *destiny*…"

24th March. ~~Am. Hospital, Paris~~ Traveling north? I can still smell her...feel...I dash out these lines, not knowing exactly where I am, only that I am headed for Flanders in a camion with Brits, Canucks, and two Americans. The rumble and rattle of battle grows ever nearer.

She has become so important to me I cannot conceive of my life with her not in it, next to me, holding me, atop me, surrounding me. Is this what love feels like?

25th March, Somewhere West of Peronne, France. Great confusion at British HQ...found some reinforcements...

"*All* you lot, *OUT*," a muddy Corporal called into the back of the *camion*.

Steele had jumped into this *camion because* it was bound for Flanders. The occupants treated Steele, the only officer aboard, with great deference and curiosity, allowing him to sit close to their only lantern as they drove northeast. "*You*, there! Stand...oh, didn't see your *rank*, sir," the Corporal said to Steele. "Traveling *rough*, sir?"

"Just *traveling*, Corporal," Steele answered as he dismounted from the truck, a steady rain soaking everything and everyone. "Who's in charge here?"

"Well, sir, General *Haig*, of course, but *Corps* HQ is down *there*."

"Thank you, Corporal. I'll be taking the Americans off your hands. Can you tell us where the 432nd Machine Gun Battalion is?"

"*No*, sir; *sorry*, sir," the corporal said before turning his attention back to the others and shouting, "All right, you lot: over to that *fly* over there..."

"*Americans*: come with me." Steele led the two American privates, equipped only with puttees, helmets, and smoke hoods, towards where the Corporal had pointed.

He found a sign that read VI CORPS HQ in neat letters with two wet and miserable sentinels outside. "I *can't* let you in, mate," one of them said when Steele walked up. "*Security*, you know."

"*I'm* Colonel Steele. Who do I talk to about the 432nd Machine Gun Battalion lending you a *hand?*"

"Lending a…ah, *yessir*…Sergeant *Major!?*"

"What *is* it, Justin?" a small man appeared at the door.

"Sergeant Major, the *Colonel* and his machine gun battalion want to lend a hand."

The Sergeant Major blinked several times, looking Steele up and down. "If you would come *in*, sir," he asked.

"My *men*, here," Steele answered, gesturing to the two privates.

"Yes, certainly. Come *in*, the three of you." The Sergeant Major led them into a busy outer room, where telephones rattled and rang and messengers scurried back and forth…and *officers*…

In his months in Europe, he'd known British officers to be irritated, or haughty, or drunk, or helpful, or sad, or just plain *British*.

But he'd never seen *so* many, *so rattled* at once.

From what he could overhear, the German push had ruined divisions, pushing the line back several miles.

Waiting and listening, Steele turned to his men. "What are your names?"

"Magorski, sir." "Rayburn, sir."

"Whatever your *former* jobs were, boys, you've *just* joined the machine guns.…"

After a few minutes, a weary Major edged over to them. "Colonel…?"

"*Steele*, Major,"

"Colonel Steele…*Steele*…" Suddenly recognition crossed his face. "Colonel *Steele*: it is an *honor*, sir. *My* name's Pownall; I'm a gunner by trade…"

"I need to *find* my battalion," Steele answered. Pownall wasn't as *uppity* as most British officers Steele had encountered. "The 432nd Machine Gun Battalion…"

"Yes…don't suppose you know any *Portugee, do* you?"

"*Yessir*, a *little*," Rayburn volunteered.

"Well, *that's* more than most of *us* have," Pownall declared. "There's sixteen Portugee soldiers in a barn up the road a bit; their Major wants to *employ* them somehow. *Most* of the Portugee buggers are *dead* or *run off* now, so…"[1] Pownall shrugged.

"*I* can find employment for them," Steele said, he *hoped*, reassuringly. "Do you know *where* my battalion is?"

"Indeed I *do*, sir," Pownall said, producing a map and holding a lantern. "We're…*here.* Up the road *there*, about a-mile-and-a-half west of *this* junction, is this low ridge…just north and east of *this* road junction. Your battalion's been arriving on the road between the junctions all night."

"All *I* have to do is get *up* there," Steele mused. "Twenty miles?"

"*Yes*, sir. Around the *back*…" Pownall jerked his thumb. "I can give you a *camion,* a driver and a Lewis gun crew…"

"What's…who're *you?*" a British General stepped up. "*What* the *devil* are *you*…?"

"Steele, sir…" Steele began.

"Commanding the American motor machine gun brigade gathering up near Junction A412, sir," Pownall added.

"Oh, yes; Steele. *Heard* of you," the General sniffed. "Pownall, if you're *quite* done…"

"Yes, sir; just a moment." Pownall turned back to Steele as the General stalked off. "*We'd* feel a great deal more easy if we had something to *stall* the Huns at that *ridge–Hornful* it's called 'cause there's a *spring* at the base—by tonight. We *believe*…" He stopped. "Colonel, I'm going to be straight with you: we here at HQ don't have any bleeding *idea where* the front line is, and only a *bare* idea where our 5th Artillery Brigade has got." He traced his finger along the three roads that led through a line of hills,

---

[1] The two Portuguese divisions on the Western Front were destroyed in the first few hours of the March 1918 offensive.

villages, woods, and low ridges. "Hornful Ridge is fifty feet *higher* than any of the ground around it for five miles. If the *Huns* get to it…"

"*Yes*," Steele said, putting his helmet on. "I'll…"

"Steady *on*, Colonel," Pownall said. "Now, we don't expect a *great* deal from a mere MG battalion, but if you could *hold* Junction A412—where these three roads meet—overnight, and Hornful Ridge as a *bonus*…"

Steele stared at the map. The area was just over three miles square. "Where do you *think* your gunners *may* be?"

"Ah," Pownall frowned before he pointed, "*here*." His finger rested on a spot another ten miles east of Hornful Ridge.

"*Yes*," Steele answered, "I'll get started…"

Watching him go back out into the rain, Pownall and the Sergeant Major shook their heads in wonder. "Think *all* Americans are like that?" the Sergeant Major asked.

"No *bloody* idea," Pownall growled, "but I certainly *hope* so."

***

"I'm Colonel Steele," he began, lifting the *camion's* canvas flap. Three British soldiers sat in the back, a lantern lighting the space. "*We're* going to hold the Huns so your artillery can get away."

"*Col*, sir," one of the Englishmen answered. "*How* in the…?"

"We'll get to *that* soon enough," Steele said. "How are you armed?"

"Rifle, pistol…" the frightened boy stammered. "Lewis gun, sir," another said. "Ten drums for the Lewis gun, sir, *and* me rifle," the third added.

"All right," Steele said. "Food: *have* you any?"

"Um…a case of Maconochie tins, another of bully beef and one of plum pudding," the driver declared. "Had a *mind* to…"

"All right," Steele said. "We're going to be joined by a Portuguese section. Now…driver, what's your name?"

"Alpert, sir," he said.

"Then, Alpert, let's get this *camion* moving up the road. You gunners, front seat. Magorski, get in back. Rayburn, you're with me."

Steele and Rayburn walked while the *camion* followed.

***

"Hello," Steele declared, walking into the barn bearing tins of bully beef and plum pudding. The roof was more *symbolic* than functional; driblets of rain splashed everywhere.

"*Olá*," one man said, staring at the tins. Portuguese uniforms looked like a cross between a British high-collar pattern and the French in light-blue, topped with corrugated soup-bowl helmets.

"For you," Steele said, holding the tins higher. Rayburn said *something* that sounded a *little* like Spanish.

A man walked forward, staring at Steele; Steele nodded. He took the tins. "*Obrigado*," he said, handing the tins to another, mumbling something Steele couldn't make out.

"*Thank* you," Rayburn declared. "Spread them…no, *pass* them out." The men opened the tins quickly and passed them around.

"You're welcome," Steele said; Rayburn translated. "My name is Steele; *Coronel* Steele." Rayburn translated.

The man who took the tins nodded. "*Coronel*," he repeated. Then, pointing to himself, "*Mayor* Salavas."

"We have a mission…a *battle*," Steele said.

Rayburn said something, then added, "my Portuguese ain't *that* good, sir."

Salavas stared at Steele for a long moment, then Rayburn, then nodded. "*Batalha onde?*" He glanced at Rayburn, nodding and smiling.

"*Donde?*" Rayburn asked, squinting.

"*Sim: onde em Portuguese.*"

"Battle *where? Where's* the battle?" Rayburn said, nodding. "*Learning* as much Portuguese as I am *translating…*"

"Where we're *going,*" Steele said; Rayburn translated, then Steele added, "…and *you're* joining the French Foreign Legion; *Legion Estranger…*"

Rayburn said *something*; Salavas blinked, grinned, and nodded. "*Sim…*"

The truck splashed through the muddy track. Sounds of battle grew louder around every turn, on the other side of every hill, between every copse. Steele noticed that hardly *any* of the scores of trudging refugees streaming west even bothered to look up.

A parked Autocar appeared out of the gloomy rain, with three men behind it. "D Company," Steele called as he walked forward. "Is that *D* Company?"

"It...*Colonel*?" a voice asked. "*Hell*, sir, we'd given *you* up for..."

"I ain't dead yet," Steele yelled. "*Answer* the *question*: Is this *D* Company?"

"*Yessir*," another voice answered. "Just getting the mortars in position for..."

"Carry *on*. Where's Headquarters Company?"

"Up ahead, about three hundred yards, sir," the voice said. "We got *new*...?"

"We *do*. Now, do you have a messenger here?"

"*Yes*, sir," the voice said. "May I say we are glad to see—"

"Just get *ready for a fight*, whoever you are," Steele said, turning to look behind his *camion*. As he did, another *camion* pulled up behind them, with Willis at the wheel.

"Sir; *glad* to see you," Willis said as he stepped down Englishmen with Lewis guns, panniers of ammunition and crates poured out of the *camion*. "Got some *more…*"

"*Yes*," Steele said, pointing to Salavas, walking next to him. "This is Major Salavas of the Portuguese Army. He and his men are going to *help…*"

"*Yes*, sir," Willis said, turning to Salavas. "*Soy el Mayor Willis…*"

"You speak Portuguese, Jack?" Steele interrupted.

"Enough to trade for their *wine*, sir," Willis answered.

"Of *course*. Get them to E Company, can you?" Turning, Steele asked, "Alpert, do you have *any* idea *what…*?"

"Yessir," Alpert declared. "Mons[1] all over again. Wasn't *there* meself, sir; I were still in *school*. But me *officer* was; he'll be on the other end of *that* road *if* he's still *alive*. Ah, *sir*," Alpert asked shyly. "If I may be so *bold…* how many fights have you *been* in?"

"Just a few," Steele answered, then, "Alpert, *you* and *all* your mates there will join the 432nd Machine Gun Battalion of the United States Army for the next few days. Pass the word."

"*Aye*, sir. We'll hold on *here*, sir."

"That's right." Steele went to the back of the *camion*, listening to Willis direct the Portuguese and some Vietnamese in the unloading of an *unnatural* volume of material. "Willis," Steele said, "I need to…"

"Yessir," Willis answered. "Just as *soon* as the *next…*"

"The *next…*?"

"Just down the road there, sir." Willis hitched his thumb over his shoulder. "Got chow and ammo and two more Vickers guns. Couldn't *get* more men; just *this* mob I *happened* to…"

"You just *happened* to…?"

---

[1] The battle of Mons in August 1914 was the British Army's baptism of fire in World War One. Outnumbered three-to-one, the BEF held up the German advance for two days before withdrawing, losing half their strength in that time.

"Yessir; while I was arranging the supplies, I met an old quartermaster buddy who knew of a little depot where the…"

"Very well…Carry on." Steele stared at the refugees shambling through the mud and the rain along the road. Steele heard battle to the east; machine guns, but little artillery…just some *booms* in the distance. "Jack, where's the *mess?*"

"There's D Company's mess up the road a piece…"

"Get them *cooking*. If all they *have* is Maconochie stew to heat, then they can heat *that* up. Otherwise, have them cook whatever they have on hand, even if they have to slaughter mules, but make it *hot*."

"Um, Ned," Willis frowned, "ain't *that* a bit, um…?"

He watched limbered guns headed west, their bedraggled gunners seeing nothing. "Jack: look around you. There's a *company* of men passing us every *ten minutes* who I'll bet *dollars* to *dumplings* will fight for whoever feeds them *hot chow*…"

"*Right* you are, Ned," Willis said. "I'll get *right* on it."

***

"Sir." The bicycle messenger handed him a dispatch folder. "*A* Company."

"*Thank* you, Corporal. Get some coffee by the mess wagon." Steele flipped the case open, grabbing a hasty message.

IN CONTACT. HOLDING.

"That's *it*," Steele declared. "We shall *counterattack*. Sergeant Major, get all the company and platoon commanders you can get *here* in *twenty* minutes."

"Begging the Colonel's pardon, but…*have* you *lost all* your *marbles*…with *all* due respect?" Massie asked, handing him a tin can of coffee.

"Maybe I *have*, Top," Steele admitted, "but, just *get 'em up here*."

***

"Say that *again*, Ned?" Ishim asked loudly.

"We're going to *attack down the A21*," Steele repeated. "The Brit's artillery park is…"

"*Ten miles* through the lines," Brick said. "*How* do you...?"

"There *are* no *lines*," Steele said firmly. "That's the *point*. There's *depths of penetration*, but no *lines* as in *trench lines*."

"*Yessir*," Ishim declared. "When all else fails, do what your opponent does *not* expect." The other twelve officers stared at the dark Captain; he stared back. "The German lines are *paper-thin*..."

"That's *right*," Benson said. "Their mop-ups are stalled in the towns and dumps, looting. All we'll encounter is *thin* lines of their assault troops..."

"Their, ah, *Stoss*, right?" Buchalter asked. "*Read* about them in one of those intel summaries..."

"Exactly that," Steele said. "All right," Steele declared, pointing at the map spread on the ground. "Here's a plan. D Company and a platoon of E Company will *lead* down the A21 with the pom-poms; their mortars will fire and shift forward as they go; the howitzers will stay *at* the ridge. At *this* junction, C Company will branch off and attack south by east to edge *that* flank; one mortar section will go *with* them. *All* the machine guns we can carry will be aboard one vehicle or another. We need as many Mills bombs as we can *haul*. *Commandant*, load another platoon of *your* men up with B Company and follow D Company...A Company, since they're in position on the ridge already, will stay in place for an anchor. The rest of E Company will stay on the ridge as a reserve."

"*When* do we plan to do this, sir?" Ishim asked.

"We start..." Steele glanced at his watch, "in *exactly ten minutes*."

***

"You *see* anything?" Steele asked the Sergeant manning the Lewis gun next to him. The big touring car sported a Lewis gun out each side and a Vickers on the back seat. In an hour, they had fired at scattered German troops, not knowing exactly to what effect.

"Not in a *while*, sir," he answered.

Rolling slowly east, they had reached the branch where the B19 went south by east; C Company was halfway through the intersection when Steele's car reached it. Other than the two mortars firing smoke down the road, there was no other fighting except where D Company led the way, and that was only intermittent. A platoon and a half of British refugees, Willis' British gunners, and a section of Legionnaires (under Salavas, who spoke *enough* French) reinforced A Company. A hundred-some British stragglers and two howitzers that Company D's mess section fed an *enormous* mess of slim gully and stray mutton augmented the battalion. Another *two hundred* or more British soldiers with ten machine guns, two trench mortars and another howitzer section protected HQ Company's mess wagons (that were still serving food to whoever came, capturing more than a dozen *hungry* Germans) and strung themselves out behind Steele to protect his escape route.

Scribbling a message, Steele said, "get *this* to Major Brick," to Massie, who held onto the door, riding on the running board. The message read:

IF NO RESISTANCE, HALT AT DARK OR WHEN YOU REACH NEXT JUNCTION. IF RESISTANCE, WE WILL COME TO YOU. REPORT CONTACTS FRIENDS OR FOES.

***

"*My* name's Standhaven," the British General declared. "*You* are…?"

"Steele, sir," Steele answered, shaking the offered hand, still watching the string of vehicles and guns roll by his car. "*Your* outfit's…?"

"Fifth Artillery Brigade, Colonel," Standhaven said, treating Steele's hand as if it were a water pump handle. "*Cut off* and *desperate* until *you lot shot* their way here. How the *Devil* did you *manage* it, old boy?"

"Well, we just did what the Huns *didn't* expect, sir," Steele lied. Yet, he didn't…*exactly* lie…but did, *kinda*. The runner never reached Brick, and Brick's force kept rolling and skirmishing until they reached the British guns and troops laagered just off the road. A brief but furious firefight that preceded that discovery was, to be fair, a bloodbath of *mostly* German blood.

"Well, *deuced* good that you did *that*, my good man," Standhaven grinned, finally releasing Steele's hand. "This is *most* of Fifth Army's artillery and a good portion of the survivors of two divisions. Your con*found*edly well-timed counterattack could *not* have aimed better!"

"Just doing what that staff officer of yours said he wanted…" Steele said.

"And you're a *machine gun battalion?*" Standhaven asked, waving at a vehicle driving by loaded with men and gear. "A mere *machine gun battalion…*"

"We're really motorized infantry, sir," Steele answered. "General Pershing wants us to…"

"Pershing," Standhaven said softly. "*Pershing* said to motorize an *infantry battalion…?*"

"Yessir, in a manner of speaking," Steele answered, shrugging in the growing dark. "He said that once we break out of the trenches, *this* kind of outfit…"

"By *Jove*, Steele, that's the most…by *Jove…!*" Standhaven shook his head. "If my *stallion* were to throw *lambs*, I would *not* be more *stunned…*"

"Sir," Steele asked, surprised. "You *know* General Pershing?"

"We've had *talks*, Steele; *serious* talks. If we had *our* way, you would be under the command of an *English* officer. *But,*" he shook his head, patting Steele's car, "I cannot *imagine* a British officer these days coming up with a *counterattack* under *these* conditions." He shook his head wistfully. "Eh, perhaps Pershing's *right*; perhaps you operate better on your own hook. Perhaps we *do* suffer from a trench mentality…"

"Trench mind, sir," Steele said, not *thinking…*

"Just so, Steele; just so." Standhaven turned, nodded to another officer. "One *moment*, sir. But I *must* be off, Steele. *Thank* you again, Steele, for the rescue." Standhaven climbed into his own car, then turned. "*Trench mind…*I shall *remember* that."

27th March, Flanders.

I find it hard to [Rest of the page obscured by stains].

30th March, Amiens, France.

Mon Destin…she called me her destiny……What am

Dimly, in the dark reaches of his mind, he heard her voice—soft, melodious, calm. He *felt* her body against his, *smelled* her, *felt*...

"In *here*," he heard a voice say. "Colonel Steele's in here."

"*Yo*," Steele called, swimming up from *oblivion*...

"Steele," another voice called...Pownall. "Steele, are you *well?*"

"Ah, yeah," Steele answered. "Must have dozed off."

"Dozed *off*, the man says," Pownall declared. "Stay *there*, lad...."

Shaking his head, Steele tried to make sense of...what? A dream about a woman he'd never see again? Before he could answer any of those questions, Brick stepped into his tiny room bearing a water bottle. "Ned, drink this," he said, pressing it to his lips. "Just *water*, just what you need right now."

Steele drank greedily, letting the water splash down his chin. "What...?" he managed before Brick cut him off.

"Just you *relax*, now, Ned," Brick soothed. "Grimes and I have everything in hand...."

"Grimes...?" Steele asked. "This is..."

"If you'll *recall*, Ned," Brick said, sitting in a chair at his bedside, "You left us in command when we reached the ridge again because...well, you weren't *yourself*."

---

[1] Sent to the Classification Camp at Blois, France. Any unfortunate officer sent there was said to have 'gone blooey' and would be sent home, career over.

"I *wasn't?*"

"The orders you were giving stopped making *sense*."

"They *did?*"

"You told us to find McCall and get A Company back on the road west. McCall was *dead*; you'd already *gotten* that word."

"He *was?* I *did?*"

"Then you ordered Magruder to cover B Company's withdrawal. *He's* dead, too, Ned." Brick cleared his throat. "You hadn't slept in nearly two days, Ned. Just out of the hospital…You pushed yourself *too* hard, too *fast*."

"You're right," Steele said, swinging his legs…he was in his union suit and nothing else. "Who…?"

"*Rodgers* took your uniform off, Ned…"

"How long have I…?"

"We carried you in here twenty hours ago."

"Is there a uniform somewhere…?"

***

"*Sah*, ya *done* yer job *most* admirably," a small man with a Red Cross armband and a decided accent said. "Your MO sent *me* ta *hae* a *look* at *ye*…"

Still weary, Steele let the aidman examine him perfunctorily. "Could *do* wit some *nourishment*, sah," the man said. "I'd advise soup; just down the way a *wee* bit in our *mess, sah*."

"Thank you," Steele said, standing up. "Just might do that." He looked around. "Major Brick…?"

"*Other* duties, *sah*," the aidman declared. "Major Pownall would hae a *word* with ye, *sah*…"

"All right." Steele followed the aidman out of the small sleeping room and into a much larger room, where a hearth blazed away with a welcoming fire. Pownall, now resplendent in a clean uniform and over-shined, knee-high boots, stood as Steele entered, though Steele felt underdressed…

"Colonel," Pownall extended his hand as he crossed the room. "*Damned* glad to see you well…"

"Damned glad to *be* well, Major," Steele smiled, grasping

Pownall's hand. "But you wanted a word…?"

"I did, indeed, Steele," Pownall said. "I wanted to make certain you knew, ah, that we have *mentioned* you *and* your battalion in our *dispatches*, particularly because, well, the Prince of Wales was *visiting* the front when…*you* know…he was *with* the *Fifth*…"

"Um…"

"It's a *great* honor, my good fellow," Pownall beamed. "You don't have such things in America. 'Mentioned in dispatches' gets a fellow noticed at court *and* in the press. Sure way to promotion in the King's forces, get your unit more recognition, especially when there's *royalty* involved. Only those who do something as important as *you* did with your carbuncle…"

"My…*what*, Major?"

"That's what the Huns were calling your *foray*, old man: *das Geschwür*—the *carbuncle* that *burst* out of nowhere. They couldn't use that road as long as you and your rag-tag band of refugees were there. Threw an entire *brigade* at you to clear it again, but you *held on* and saved…." Pownall looked proud. "You accomplished far, *far* more than *we* believed you *could*, Colonel. And rescuing our next *King*, well…"

"If you don't *mind*, Major, I have to see to my unit, but *thank* you for the honor you have bestowed upon us…"

***

"Who all's *left*?" Steele asked dully.

"Benson, B Company; Ishim, D Company," Grimes pronounced. "Lost five officers and just short of two hundred men killed and wounded."

"Vehicles?" Steele remembered Buchalter's face, a dark man with a blonde mustache and bright eyes. He had trouble remembering McCall, *or* Magruder.

"Five vans and seven carts lost," Brick answered. "A pom-pom truck broke an axle; we're dragging it around with a service truck. Two ambulances had to be abandoned, but we got the casualties out."

"Guns?"

"We captured *three* Maxims and *four* Bergmanns in our attack. We lost *one* Vickers, *two* Hotchkiss, and *three* Lewis guns in their counterattack." Brick said.

"We'll keep the captured guns in reserve," Steele said. "They *sound* different…"

"Beg pardon, sir," Thorsten interrupted. "My *scouts* captured those Bergmanns. They're light enough to use when we're *deep*…"

"Just how deep did you *get*, Lieutenant?" Steele asked.

"They led the *way*, Ned," Ishim interjected. "Broke through to that laager and kept moving…"

"About *another* twenty miles, *maybe* more," Thorsten added. "When our lead bike ran into a machine gun on the road, we turned around."

Steele stared… "OK," he mumbled. "Just *how* did you…?"

"Just *went*, sir," Thorsten said. "Once we got past their resistance, we just high-balled it east until we got to the Brits, then rode past *them* until…we didn't *take* a *lot* of fire on the way there; didn't see many Fritzes for *most* of the way; just a few civilians near the road. I think we woke 'em up, sir, so we had to *shoot* our way back. If we hadn't run into that Maxim that made us out as Americans in the morning light…"

"You did this at *night*?"

"Yeah; complete dark. Come sunrise, they figured us out."

Steele blinked, looked around at his other officers. "Captain Lorenzo," he said to the sandy-haired officer, "do we have a qualified Captain to take A Company?"

"Ah…" Lorenzo thought for a moment, "there's Moss; good man…"

"Good. Move him up to A Company." Steele looked at Thorsten with interest. "Can you write up a report on your…advance?"

"Yessir," Thorsten said, grinning.

Steele thought dimly of the message he'd got from AEF a couple hours before:

> BRILLIANT OPERATION. COULD NOT HAVE EXPECTED
> MORE. MOVE YOUR COMMAND BACK TO HOME BASE AS
> SOON AS PRACTICABLE.
> CONNER.

Volume XIII
1918

OUR ARTICLE GOT US NOTICED. ONE CRITIC CALLED US "UP-AND-coming Great War scholars." A book publisher noticed the Hill 90 article and expressed interest in prublishing *more* of his diaries.

It took me and Maria nearly a year to transcribe and verify Volumes XII and XIIA; his handwriting sometimes deteriorated into illegibility. While we did that, I did as much research on his unit and activities as I could manage between my other duties.

Ned's extensive family left traces. His father's inventions were notable, and some of his siblings made significant marks on history as well. There were many bread crumbs we could follow.

I neglected Ned for a while, then came back to him with a renewed sense of direction. I hoped to have all of Ned's WWI diaries transcribed by the centennial of American entry into the war, but I had my proper work as a department head....

Transcribing Volume XIII, we saw he was *really* going into battle with the AEF...

April 1918

"If I didn't *know* better, Ned, I'd say you look about...*35*," Brick declared.

"Thanks a *heap*, Mike," Steele sighed, downing the *better* wine the staff had *procured* for his birthday. "If *I* didn't know better, I'd say you were...*50*."

"*Far* more appropriate for a man of my *great* wisdom than my *actual* age of four and twenty," Brick answered. "I *shall* go back to law school when *this* mess is over and I shall be..."

"Married, I understand," Steele interrupted.

"Of *course*, that," Brick agreed, "But I shall be an elder statesman among those mere *children*."

"If we live that long."

***

"You *sent* for me, sir," Rodgers said in his usual flat-yet-warm tone.

"I did," Steele said. "Can I entrust you with a *personal* matter when you take the daily[1] down to Paris on Monday?"

"*My* turn for that isn't until *Wednesday*, sir."

"It can wait. Can I trust your...ah...?"

"*Discretion*, sir?"

"Yes."

"You *can*, sir."

---

[1] Units routinely dispatched mail, reports and other documents to their higher HQs, which for the 432ⁿᵈ was AEF Paris, returning the next day. The detail that carried them got an evening in Paris.

Steele pushed a bundle across his desk. "Can you deliver this *only* to Miss Gibson at the American Hospital with *this* note?"

> *Angie*
> *Can you please safeguard these and, if needed, see that*
> *they get to my family? If you feel compelled to read*
> *them, please remember that they are my private*
> *thoughts.*
> *Love,*
> *Ned.*

"I *can*, sir." Rodgers waited a pace. "Should I await a reply?"

"If she *asks* you to, yes."

"*Very* well, sir," Rodgers bowed his head *slightly* and made to leave. "Ah, sir," he hesitated. "What shall I tell the *rest* of the detail should they ask, sir?"[1]

"It *looks*…like…" Steele started.

"It *does*, sir," Rodgers said softly. "And you often speak out against such…."

Steele thought for a moment, regretting the entire idea…until Rodgers gathered up the bundle *and* the note, saying, "I can think of *something*, sir," and left.

10ᵗʰ April, Étaples.

Miracles (named Pershing and Edward) that we're

still together as a battalion…

The message bundle labeled "Commander, 432ⁿᵈ MG Bn." contained, among other things, three dispatches. The first, dated 5 April, read:

> G1 HQ AEF BELIEVES 432ⁿᵈ MG BN. TO BE A BURDEN
> ON PERSONNEL AND ADVISE REDISPOSITION OF
> PERSONNEL.
> CONNER

And, dated 8 April, was *this*:

---

[1] The daily detail included three to five officers and men.

CG AEF WILL MAINTAIN 432ND MG B_N AS AN
INSTRUCTOR AND STRIKING FORCE.
PERSHING

Followed by, also dated 8 April…

PRINCE OF WALES' OWN AMERICANS STREAMER TO BE
PRESENTED AT EARLIEST OPPORTUNITY.
ROBERTSON, CIGS[1]

12th April, Etaples, France.

Read a most inspiring message to the men this

afternoon…got a most inspiring message from her…

"Bat-*tal*-ION…*at*-ten-*shun*," Massie shouted; the 751 men snapped smartly to attention.

Steele marched to the center of the U-formation and shouted "*post*." The company commanders took their places in front of their companies.

"Men; I have this message to read to you. I will post it on your bulletin boards right after this formation."

THE PRINCE OF WALES WISHES TO EXPRESS OUR DEEP
GRATITUDE TO THE COURAGEOUS MEN OF THE
AMERICAN ARMY'S 432ND MACHINE GUN BATTALION
FOR THEIR GALLANT ACTIONS IN FLANDERS IN MARCH
LAST. WE HOPE AND PRAY THAT OUR CONTINUED
FRIENDSHIP WITH AMERICA AND OUR UNITED ACTIONS
IN THIS WAR WILL BRING THE CONFLICT TO A RAPID AND
SUCCESSFUL CONCLUSION. EDWARD, POW.

"*Prince Edward* of *England*, boys; thanks *us* personally." There was a ripple of approval through the ranks, especially from the *Legionnaires*. "There's *more:*"

GENERAL PERSHING AND THE ENTIRE AMERICAN
EXPEDITIONARY FORCES ARE PROUD OF THE 432ND
MGB, AND WANT TO CONVEY THE THANKS OF THE
ENTIRE NATION. WELL DONE MACHINE GUNNERS!

---

[1] Chief of (British) Imperial General Staff.

That got a great cheer from the ranks.

***

"Sir," Rodgers said, standing in front of Steele's desk. "For *you*." He held out a tightly folded note.

Steele took it with a hint of trepidation, but he didn't know *why*.

> *Ned,*
> *You honor me with your trust. I shall, of course, do as you ask. If curiosity gets the better of me, rest assured I am the soul of discretion.*
> *All my love,*
> *Angie.*

"*Thank* you, Sergeant," Steele sighed. "What did you tell the *rest* of the detail?"

"I said I had a personal errand."

"And they…?"

"They know I was once *in service*, sir, and that Paris is familiar to me."

"Ah." Steele reached into a cubby on his desk. "I have here an application for a medal for you." He pushed it across his desk.

> SGT. CEDRIC RODGERS, ON HILL 90 IN FLANDERS ON THE 29TH OF NOVEMBER 1917, ACTED WITHOUT REGARD TO HIS PERSONAL SAFETY AND WITH COURAGE ABOVE AND BEYOND THE CALL OF DUTY. DURING A REACTION FORCE COUNTERATTACK, SGT. RODGERS LED FIVE MEN IN A CHARGE ACROSS HAZARDOUS TERRAIN WITHOUT REGARD TO HIS OWN SAFETY….

"Supporting statements from Major Brick and Warrant Officer Farrell cite your 'unrelenting energy and courage.' Colonel McFadden has endorsed this citation, adding, 'never have I heard of such a display of faithful courage from a former butler.' Another statement cites your use of a *shotgun*." He gazed at Rodgers. "This is going in as a Medal of Honor application, but the *shotgun* is…where'd *it* come from?"[1]

---

[1] The use of shotguns in combat was controversial in WWI.

"My former employer, sir," Rodgers answered, acting as if this were all quite routine. "I learned to shoot as a lad."

"Ah. *Pump* or…?"

"A *Remington* pump, sir. *Slugs* penetrate Hun armor pads at close range; bullets and buckshot *don't*."[1]

"How would *McFadden* know you had been in service?"

"I can't *say*, sir."

"Well," Steele sighed, "thanks again, Sergeant. I can't say what the result of our request for an award will be, but…"

"I shall carry on as before, sir," Rodgers nodded.

May

"Colonel Steele," Colonel Fox Conner intoned, opening the door. "We're ready for you." Pershing and the AEF Chief of Operations had come up to Etaples for a personal inspection.

Looking up from a large table, Pershing smiled slightly as Steele approached. "Steele; *good* of you to see me alone. I trust you've recovered from that business in Flanders?"

"We're *getting* there, sir. Training all our machine gunners…"

"Of *course*, Colonel," Pershing declared. "We're *all* anxious about training. We cannot train men unless they are properly equipped, and this *rush-rush* to get infantry and machine-gunners over from America because of this Hun *push*…"

"Sir," Steele nodded. "Getting more *gunners* than I *am*…"

"Are you getting *enough*?"

"We'll make *do*, sir," Steele declared.

"Good; excellent," Pershing smiled. "I read your reports on

---

[1] Some German soldiers wore upper-body armor greatly resembling modern football shoulder pads.

Hill 90 and that *Flanders* business, Colonel, and have some questions that need answers."

"If I *can*, sir."

"Did it convince you as to the futility of trench warfare?"

"Sir, I was pretty convinced before *that*."

"Good; excellent. Was not *my* idea, Steele," Pershing said tightly. "Washington informed me I was to loan *your unit* to General Haig for a 'demonstration of ability' or lose shipping."[1]

"Yessir."

Pershing paused, glanced at Conner. "Your counterattack in Flanders: *your* idea?"

"Thought *that* was what we were training for, sir."

"Indeed, it *is*, Colonel." He cleared his throat. "The Germans are using something different..."

"*Auftragstaktik*, sir," Steele said,

"You've *heard* of the German methods?"

"I *have*, sir. Mission-oriented orders. Tried to *implement* that philosophy. I just give my people instructions about what *their* part of the battle is, what the objectives are, leave it to *them* to figure out how to do what they're supposed to do."

"And that *works?*"

"Yessir."

"Have you *trained* your people in...?"

"No sir, there's been no need. They're *Americans*, machine gunners. They *have* enough initiative on their own."

"I hear the Germans *do*..."

"The German soldiers, sir, are used to the trenches. *That's* why they *need* training in Hutier's tactics."

"Everyone *else* has been using the trench raid since '15," Conner added. "These new *storm* tactics are just those on a larger scale..."

"But the German application means *not* to retire at daybreak,

---

[1] Ship space, always at a premium for the Americans, was often used as a bargaining tool by the British to get the Americans to comply with their wishes. It sometimes worked.

sir. *That's* a difference. And *they're* better equipped. And *fed*. But their *follow-on* troops *aren't…*"

"We need you to go down to Lorraine," Pershing said.

"Something up, sir?" Steele asked.

"We *want* there to *be* something up, Colonel," Conner said. "We're planning the first American attack in this war…other than *yours*, of course."

"You know, sir, that this Hun push, as you call it, is going to be the *very last* they can do?" Steele asked. "They have *boys* and *old men* in the trenches now. They're simply running out of men to fight. The Huns no longer have anything to attack *with*."

Conner and Pershing exchanged glances. "*Very* astute, Colonel," Conner nodded. "The British know that, too. The French…they'd rather *not* know it, they're so beat up. But the British have their Canadian and Australian troops to lead the way. *We'll* be leading the way for the French."

"Um," Steele mused, "That's not *strictly* true, sir. The French still have the Legion, and they have the Moroccans."

"Moroccans?" Conner asked.

"I've *heard* good things about them," Steele said.

"We shall see," Pershing declared. "Prepare to move your battalion to Lorraine. I'll conduct a *brief* inspection here before we go."

"On to *England*, sir," Conner interrupted.

"Yes," Pershing sighed, "one *more* meeting with the British brass."

11ᵗʰ May, Étaples.

I got a letter from her…

"Here's a *letter*, Ned," Brick said, handing him a small envelope…with a grin. "If *that's* a *sister*, *I'm* in the wrong kind of *family…*"

The envelope was elegant, with a pleasant scent; handwriting neat, feminine…*hers*. The return address…*A. C. Gibson, AP New York*… "Remember that nurse's aide in the hospital?"

"Yeah? Huh." Brick sighed, opening a letter of his own.

"Better news than *mine…she's* been hinting at divorce."

"Didn't think you were *married* yet."

"Not, but she might end our understanding if she…no…*second* thoughts…eh…"

Carefully popping the seal away from the envelope, Steele took out the one-sheet note, catching a *stronger* whiff of perfume.

> *Mon Coeur*
> *Hope this note finds you well, for all is well here.*
> *At the end of the month, I shall sit for my final examinations for my nursing licence. No one here knows what value it will have in America, but it gives certain privileges here in France. It has been a very trying six months to get this far, and I am very proud of myself.*
> *I find I can think of no one else but you any longer. Every moment I spend alone, I want to be with you. Our reunion cannot come soon enough. No, dear heart, I am not with child.*
> *Love,*
> *Angie*
> *P.S. I have not felt tempted to read your diaries. AG.*

He stared at the note for some moments, breathing the *smell* of her, recalling the *feel* of her, the *sound* of her….

"Ned," Brick said loudly. "Ned! *Officer's* call in ten minutes. Should *I*…?"

"No…I'll be there."

"Looks like…*good* news?…*That* good?"

"*That* good. Ain't *asked* her yet, either…not that I'd *have* to…I don't think…"

"Oh, man, Ned: she's *just*…?"

"Yeah. How about yours?"

"Maybe *you'd* better ask her. *Hell*, maybe *I'd* better… mine's got a young man—some *shirker*—sniffing around in her *father's* firm…but she's *resisting* his, what she calls 'dubious charms and intentions.'"

"She *might* be a keeper, Mike. Just *ask* her and see what she says."

"Hey, Ned," Grimes called out as he knocked on the small HQ cottage door. "We've just contacted our, ah, allies…"

"Good," Steele said, setting his pen down, thinking. "Do we have enough French-speaking…?"

"Plenty," Grimes said. "Between the Legion and our many volunteers from Canada…"

"Good…Gary…there's a young lady I met. She's in Paris…"

"Ah." Grimes sat down. "That *nurse?*"

"Yeah."

"Serious?"

"Yeah. I've never *been so…*"

"Does *she* feel the same way?"

"She *says* she does. Says my family is *acceptable* to hers."

"Ah-*hah.*" Grimes paused. "What's Dear Old Dad *do?*"

"He's a senator from my home state, Michigan."

"One of the *elected*[1] ones?"

"Yes; the voters sent him *back* in '15."

"Means he comes from money himself." Grimes looked

---

[1] Prior to the ratification of Amendment XVII to the Constitution (1913), US senators were elected by their state legislatures, not by popular vote.

uncomfortable. "Is your *family…?*"

"My father is a big noise with the state militia. As a major contractor with the auto companies, he's got enough juice to get my brother an early appointment to Annapolis…and we're well *enough* off…"

"That answers *that*." Grimes pretended to examine his nails. "Now, what's the *real* question, Ned?"

"I…I don't know if I should answer *her* or write *my family*…but my family *hasn't*…"

"Protestant or Catholic?"

"Ya know, I never *asked*, but *my* family baptized *me* in a Lutheran church. Haven't *been* to *services* regularly since I enlisted…"

"That *may* not *matter*…but…*is* she…?" Grimes hung his head and smiled slightly. "*Can* she be *in trouble?*"

"She *could*…" Steele stopped, embarrassed. "She *says* she's *not*."

"No need of urgency, then. If it were *me*, I'd let the lady know that you either agree or *not*. Then tell *your* family the same thing." Grimes shrugged. "Paris will get your answer before your *family* will, but if it's the same answer, it won't matter." He cocked his head. "I take it you *agree?*"

"I do."

"Then write to both."

"Sooner than later," Steele sighed. "Pass the word for officer's call in an *hour*. And…*thank* you, Gary."

"Anytime, Ned…."

> *My dearest Angie*
> *I am in complete agreement with your sentiments*
> *and look forward to our next…[1]*

Steele set *that* one aside.

> *Angie*
> *Of course, my dear. Tell your father that I fully*

---

[1] Found on the back of a list of unknown persons.

intend to ask his permission before...[1]

And *that* one...

> *Darling,*
> *I can count the hours since we parted. My heart*
> *beats for you alone. I can still feel your...*

There was more of *this* one—that he *sent*—which we shall *not* share *here*...

***

"What's the vehicle status, Major Willis?" Officer's call—a *staff meeting* by any other name—was when everyone got to know everything about everything else, at least in theory. Steele always insisted on one at least every *other* day, as duty requirements made it *possible*. He believed it was the key to keeping the battalion in top shape...the *fewer* surprises, the better.

"We have...*thirteen* vans and *nine* motorcycles under repair; another thirty *vans*, four *cars* and seventeen *bicycles need* service but are still operating. Two armored trucks are undergoing routine service. *Those* things are like locomotives: can't *stop* 'em. Two mess wagons need new wheels; one has a hole in the firebox and is only good for cold service. As requested by the commander, we still have forty-five mules that *can* work, and three on the sick list."

"*Why* do we still have mules?" Grimes asked. "They take up more..."

"Because they are meat on the hoof if we *need* it," Willis said lightly.

"Right," Steele said. "Speaking of *sick* list, Doctor..."

"Twenty-five in hospital; nine on bedrest. Our latest influenza wave has passed."

"Very well. Available personnel, Captain Everly?"

Cobb Everly was a recent addition, the S1 (personnel) officer. "Seven hundred five on strength, twenty-one on detachment, thirty-four on sick list."

"Gentlemen," Steele said, taking in the reports, "we may be on

---

[1] Found on the back of a laundry list.

the job again, and *very* soon. General Pershing thinks we should show our capabilities to more than just the British." He looked around. "Yes," he grinned. "We're going to be supporting an *American* offensive…"

"Yeah," Grimes added, "supported by those crazy *mountain men* over there…"

"French African colonials," Stevens Macon, the new S2 (counterintelligence) officer, agreed. "*I* want to see *them* in action."

"Their operations section at least speaks enough English so we can agree on boundaries," Matt Holbrook, the S3 (operations) officer, added. "Timing…*they're* in a different time zone."

"North African?" Steele asked.

"No; *Greenwich* time.[1] We'll work it out."

20th May, near Cantigny, France.

Invited to a briefing for a 1st Division attack, our

first major attack of this war, not counting our

adventure in Flanders. The plans are in place and the

role of the 432nd were unclear, but I had an idea…I

wonder if I am in the same category as these men I

spoke to. Even if I have an upper hand, it feels

incredible…

"There you *have* it, gentlemen," General Bullard, the 1st Division commander, pronounced. "The artillery preparation will last 60 minutes and during the attack will roll in two-minute increments across Cantigny. The infantry will advance behind the barrage until they take the town…"

"And dig in," Steele mused, staring at the intricate bas-relief of the area.

"Of course, *that's* just a formality," General Buck, the 2nd

---

[1] French Colonial units used GMT in WWI for unclear reasons.

Brigade commander, declared. "After *that* barrage…"

"They won't be able to stand up for it for very long," General Summerall, the division artillery commander, smirked. "As much firepower as *we're* putting.…"

"*They've* been shelled by the *best* of 'em, sir," Steele said without looking up from the relief model. "They counterattack because they're *Huns, not* because they're frightened of artillery. Counterattacking is as natural to them as…"

"Colonel, I'd *advise* you to be quiet," Summerall said sharply. "You're getting this brief as a *courtesy*, not as a *requirement*. Your *peculiar* unit…"

"His is the only *proven* machine gun battalion in the AEF right now," Bullard said. "Let's hear from *his* experience."

Summerall glared at Bullard. "Very well, *Colonel*," he said loudly. "Let's hear what *you* think."

"Now…" Steele began, "that's General *Hutier* on the other side, isn't it?"

"*Yes*," Bullard said, surprised.

"He developed the *Stoss* tactics that the Huns have been using since March…" Steele went on…

"How in *Creation* would *you* know *that*, Steele?" Summerall demanded. "*That* intelligence is…"

"*Known* by the higher echelons of the French and British armies, who told *us*, sir," Steele said mildly. "When my company was up on Hill 90…"

"Was *where?*" Summerall sputtered.

"His company did a shift in Flanders; his battalion saved the British Army's heavy guns *and* their next king in March, General Summerall," Bullard said softly. "They're *very fond* of our Colonel Steele up there. Call him *The Anvil* in some circles, because he *falls* on the *Huns* like one, and the *Huns* called his *position* that. So, Colonel, how would *you* prepare for a German counterattack?"

"*Well*, sir," Steele said, not missing a moment, "I've been developing this *idea…here*, north of your ridge… three roads the Germans *must* use to counterattack your Cantigny position come together…*here*. But, if *we*…" Steele spoke for several minutes, gesturing to a part of the bas-relief to the north. They met his presentation with stunned silence.

"Well, Colonel," Bullard said, his face contorted in concentration, "do you have…?"

"You *can't* be *serious*, Bullard," Summerall sputtered. "*This* is utter *lunacy*. You *cannot* expect this…*boy*…to have a plan like *that* which would actually *work*? This isn't a *plan* but a…the Chateau le Aisne Sud," Summerall repeated. "You're going to attack the most fortified single point closest to Paris with a *machine gun battalion* and *cut three roads…*"

"Us and a *French* division, sir," Steele said.

"*What* French unit could *possibly* make this *lunacy* seem, in *any* way, *sensible?*" Summerall spat.

"A division of madmen, sir."

"*Madmen*, Steele?" Bullard grinned.

"Exactly, sir. French North Africans as *crazy* as *I* and my *battalion* are."

28th May, Bois de Aisne Sud, France.

As I do not know what tomorrow will bring, if tomorrow comes for me at all, I leave a record of yesterday. For the first time, I left a note to a loved one who is not of my family, but who I want to be mine…

This morning we saw an incredible show of artillery, and I now know what Verdun must have felt like….

The scout section and the engineers will lead across the foxhole line…They made a mistake when they sent Harris to me…

The Huns centered their lines on the Chateau le Aisne Sud five miles northeast of the outpost line the Huns call Mathilde….

Watching the flashes of the outgoing artillery barrage dance on the wall opposite the doorway of the hut, Steele set his pen down, wrapped up his diary and reached for a sheet of paper, wondering *how* to say what he felt for her...

> *Angie*
> *I've never written like this, but no matter what*
> *happens, you will be in my thoughts, my heart, always...*

He watched the flashes of perhaps *hundreds* of guns, heard the rumblings, sometimes felt the shock waves of the outgoing whiz-bangs putting the rum-jars[1] of the trenches to shame...

> *...I cannot tell you how much I feel connected to you,*
> *even from so far away, even while watching the death*
> *and destruction around me...and I know you will pass*
> *your examinations because of my love for you...*

He found the strap to secure his portfolio, fingered it gently and stuffed his diary, a serial letter to his family, and his note to Angela into the leather case and wrapped the surrounding strap, tying it like a shoe and sliding it into the bottom drawer of his field desk, behind a wooden divider labeled "Personal."

***

"Something to see, Mike," Steele said, watching the eruptions of artillery to the south and west. They stood on a small hillock some two miles behind the forward lines.

"It *is* impressive," Brick agreed. "Just hope it's enough."

"Just hope *we're* enough. Have we heard from Schuhler?" Colonel Etienne Schuhler commanded the 2nd Moroccan Brigade, who would attack on Steele's right/northwestern flank, closer to Cantigny.

---

[1] Crude, large-caliber (up to 12 inch), short-range German trench mortars.

"Just now. He's eager as Hell; makes *me* nervous."

"Never share a trench with someone more courageous than yourself; they might attract snipers or artillery," Steele mumbled.

"Yeah, well, he's got *four thousand* guys braver and *crazier* than us…"

"Inconcievable. Mike, did you ever wonder *why* the French approved this plan of ours?"

"It's occurred to me more than once that they approved it just to show AEF how *foolish* we are."

"Then why do we have an *army's* worth of French guns covering what AEF regards as a diversion?"

"*That* fact doesn't fit my answer," Brick snapped. "Therefore, I *ignore* it and speculate that the French have a surplus of aging ammunition." They cocked their heads towards Cantigny. "*They've* started."

"Yep," Steele agreed, offering his hand. "*See* you, Mike."

"*See* you, Ned."

Steele would go to the front, and Brick would stay behind to supervise the supply and reinforcement of the battalion as they attacked the maw of the German's South Aisne Forest positions.

***

"Autocars and pom-pom Berliets in front, sir," Harris, the sapper/engineer platoon leader, declared. Harris, a middle-aged National Guardsman/road builder from Tennessee, watched with his binoculars. "My sappers are right behind them with *their* Berliets." The area between the German lines and the American/French positions, like any No-man's-land, was strewn with hasty wire entanglements and the wreckage of what had once been there, in *this* case, a farm.

"Sound planning, Lieutenant," Steele sighed, studying the German positions. "Enough material for the job?"

"Fifty logs on each truck, sir," Harris declared. The Army rapidly identified Harris as a leader of men and one *helluva* builder.

"Hope that's enough," Steele muttered. "Where's your additional stocks, Lieutenant?"

"In the *second* wave, sir. We have *five hundred* ready." Pershing plucked Harris out of the Zone of Communications and sent him to Steele.

"Good." Steele gripped his binoculars, watching the barrage slowly lift and start its long roll forward. He studied the two roads across No-man's-land, little more than cratered trails now. Since this part of the front was only three months old, neither side built more than outpost-line positions of hasty holes and connecting ditches. What interested Steele most was the wire entanglements that both sides had put across the roads. With luck, the artillery would damage or shift them. *Without* luck, they would be untouched.

Harris peered at the same roads. "First block on the north road looks…damaged. Second block…*shifted*. South road, first block…destroyed, but so's the road."

"Is this going to work, Harris?"

"I'll build a highway through *Hell* and *Hell-fire* sir." What Steele especially liked about Harris was his cavalier attitude towards obstacles.

"Very well. Let's get *started*. *Head* 'em out!"

As one, the engines started, and the line of trucks rolled slowly forward to the edge of the roads, where a dozen men swiftly moved the first obstacle of barbed wire and logs.

The first of Steele's fifty-four gun barrages began sweeping an area three hundred yards by two hundred, slowly spreading out, then back again. Steele gave a brief shudder as he tried hard *not* to think about what the Germans were hearing: the *bzzz-bzzz-bzzz-thut-thut-thut* from *his* massed machine guns.

Then, the *real* work began.

Legionnaires ran down the north road, a Hotchkiss gun plopping down at the first wire roll. Before the first trucks reached the obstacle, the infantry attacked the wire first with wire cutters to get close to the main concertina wire coils. Then, sappers dropped lengths of Bangalore torpedoes over the bigger wire coils, each topped by great baulks of lumber wrapped with old tires and wire they called Steele Logs. The charges cut the wire in two places, simplifying road clearing.

Not a shot came from the German lines. Legionnaires and sappers shoved the wire aside, and the attack rolled forward.

The *flanking* barrage began, and Steele's gunners shifted *their* fire ahead of the attack.

On the south road, the lead truck took desultory fire from the German line. A Hotchkiss and a pom-pom returned the fire and swiftly silenced the source. As the truck rolled up to the first obstacle, German grenades flew in their direction. Legionnaires found the grenadiers swiftly, dispatching *them* with hand grenades, and for the first time Steele saw rifle grenades fired… their *own*, and *not* those fired at *him*.

But *then* the work became *more* involved.

A crater six feet deep and ten across blocked the road as effectively as a blown bridge blocked a river. But just as men can bridge rivers, so they can fill craters…

Steele watched as men took logs off the truck, hustled them forward, placed them first *in* the hole, then *around* the hole…

Then the *German* artillery started…and *their* machine guns…

And B Company's Hotchkiss guns shifted, finding the German Maxim gunners without overhead cover because, of course, they had just moved out of his *last* sweeping barrages.

Undaunted; unphased, men manhandled logs forward, tossing then rolling them into the crater, seemingly oblivious to the shells and bullets falling among them. One particularly close rum-jar hit within a few yards of the first truck, knocking down several men…

Some got up; others did not. The men kept working and falling. Pom-poms opened fire on German balloons, hitting *one*. One of Steele's howitzers, mounted on a truck-mounted, rotating platform of Peng's design, placed two shells through *another*. A third hastily came down.

Dugan drove his men like a teamster, carrying logs himself over his head. After what seemed like an eternity—but probably less than ten minutes—the lead Autocar rolled over the crater, swaying and sagging. A log truck followed, swaying, dropping more logs in the hole. Bicycles, motorcycles, and machine gun vans followed them…an ambulance stopped to pick up casualties, leaving perhaps three behind.

Then came a platoon of Legionnaires, then *another* machine gun platoon…

And Steele realized *he* had to get moving…

And his barrages, smaller now by one company, shifted again…and overhead Steele heard *bzzz-bzzz-bzzz*….

***

"*A* Company, sir," the bicycle messenger, breathless, handed Steele a note:

>REACHED OBJECTIVE ONE. LINKED WITH ZOUAVES.

Steele paused, listening. "Seven-sevens…C Company?"

"75s," Massie answered. "C Company was headed for Bois Maison…*could* have hit trouble…but…"

"Too *fast*; too *many*," Steele finished. "*Must* be Moroccan guns. Get *this* to B Company," Steele said, scribbling:

>A COMPANY LINKED. REPORT FRENCH CONTACT. C COMPANY STILL MOVING.

He handed the note to a clerk at his elbow and scribbled another note. "Then, *this* to the French guns:"

>FRIENDLY TROOPS IN BOIS MAISON. VILLE MAISON AND BOIS DE ST. BOURGES TO BE OURS BEFORE NOON.

Steele's drive to the Bois de St. Bourges and Ville Maison—halfway to his ultimate objective—met so little resistance he almost felt like he was falling into a trap. "Got a bird?" Steele asked, scribbling a note for AEF HQ:

>BREACHED LINE REACHED BOIS MAISON GOING FOR BOIS DE ST BOURGES.

***

"That clear space there, between the woods," Massie pointed. "Isn't *that*…?"

"Zouaves,"[1] Steele said. "They're *charging* those Hun machine guns." From their vantage point on the road, they looked north by east to observe the advance of C Company, connecting with the French, barraging in front of them.

"*Look* at 'em *come*," Massie mused. "Like Pickett's Charge…"

---

[1] North African light infantry, known for their *elan*.

"*Might* be more like Fredericksburg," Steele said softly, watching scores of men falling before the scythes of the German machine guns…until C Company's guns found them in a fast-sweeping barrage.

"Or maybe San Juan Hill," another voice added. "*Some* of 'em are making those woods…"

"More than *some*," Steele agreed. Fascinated by the horrible scene, he watched as the Moroccans first used their bayonets, then their wicked knives to slash the German gunners and anyone else they found, taking no prisoners. "They're *taking* that line…"

"C Company's right next to them," Massie said.

"To *save* the *Huns*," Steele grinned.

28th May, Chateau le Aisne Sud. [Repeated date; different location, same page.]

Can't [expletive] *believe it…we got here before dark. Captured papers, people, maps, artillery, machine guns, food on the table…Grimes had been moving HQ forward when a seven-seven hit him…But when your attack is going really well, expect an ambush…*

"*How* many?" Steele asked, still stunned.

"*Sixteen* guns," Thorsten grinned like a boy scoring a winning run. "A whole *damn* artillery regiment."

Colonel Hauteclocque, artillery commander of the Moroccan Division, gazed placidly at the array of German guns and the scores of German gunners staring sullenly at their captors. French soldiers were busy hitching the German horses to the guns and limbers to be towed away. "*Colonel* Steele," Hauteclocque said softly in his not-bad English, "you are to be congratulated. Never have I *seen* such a haul of German guns."

"You and me both, Colonel," Steele answered, watching the ragged-yet-proud Moroccans marching by. The Moroccans would advance to the trench lines other French troops occupied the month before, followed by the rest of the French Seventh Army. They expected to reach those lines, some twelve kilometers east of their starting positions, by dark.

"This is the most we have advanced since 1914," Hauteclocque announced. "Between this attack and Cantigny, we will stop the German advance towards Paris *cold*."

"Two divisions stopped a German field army," Steele nodded in agreement.

"And *une* battalion, *mon Colonel*," Hauteclocque added. "*Your* unique battalion of machine gunners."

"I just *happened* on an idea, Colonel," Steele answered modestly.

"An idea General Hutier had some months ago, yes?" Hauteclocque asked with a smile. "I read the same studies as you, *mon Colonel*. If we are to rid France of the *Boche*, we need to adopt their successful methods, as *you* have. *Non?*"

"*Mais oui, mon Colonel*," Steele replied. "*Sic est*."[1]

Hauteclocque smiled indulgently. "*Parlez vous Francais?* Before I *smother* you with my reply?"

"*Un petit peu,*[2] *mon Colonel*," Steele answered. "Some school French and what I've picked up here in the past months. But *Sic est* is Latin, yes?"

"It is, yes, but the French borrow from Latin, as *you* do in *Anglaise*, yes?" Hauteclocque answered.

"*Naturellement, mon Colonel*," Steele answered, watching the marching men, listening to the sounds of gunfire in the distance. "You will take the German guns back…"

"We *will*, yes," Hauteclocque said. "I am Adrien, Colonel," he added, extending his hand. "My son, Philippe,[3] aspires to an army career," Hauteclocque declared. "I tell him never to attack the way the enemy *expects* you to."

"Good advice, Adrien," Steele said. "Call me Ned," then… "Adriene, may I ask you something of a *personal* nature?"

"If you wish," Hauteclocque shrugged, a curious look on his

---

[1] So it is…

[2] A little bit.

[3] Philippe Leclaire de Hauteclocque would be a sucessful general in WWII.

face.

"If a woman calls me my destiny; '*mon Destin*' in French, is *that*, ah…?"

"For a *Breton*, like my wife, you would be the fulfillment of a *prophétie*, ah, you would say…"

"Prophecy?"

"*Mai oui.* When Breton girls come of age, they throw a stone into the sea. The number of times it skips, or the ripples it makes when it sinks, is the number of the young man she is to marry. Four *skips*; the *fourth* young man she *meets* that day."

"Ah. Did she choose *you* that way?"

"*Bien sûr que non*;[1] it's an old superstition." Hauteclocque grinned widely. "Now, I must depart."

"Good luck, Adriene."

"*Bon chance*, Ned," Hauteclocque said lightly, waving goodbye. "Good luck with your *mademoiselle*."

29th May, Bois de St. Bourges.

I walk among the casualties in the aid stations,

making sure no one is suffering more than they have

to. Thorsten's hurt; Grimes is in a bad way; Willis is

out for a few weeks, or months…Again, many dead…I

struggle to feel more and less…[Expletive]!!!

The aid station bustled with aidmen, two of Miller's doctors, three American Red Cross nurses *perilously* close to the front, and a French physician on loan. Steele watched the activities passively, not needing to intrude into Miller's domain. Instead, he moved quietly among the litters, nodding to those in pain, and those who felt nothing.

Then there were the moans and cries. Men called for help, for pain relief, for wives, for mothers…

---

[1] Of course not…

Steele grit his teeth, balled his fists…

"Colonel Steele," a voice called. He turned to look, seeing Thorsten on a litter, his foot heavily bandaged. "Took a piece of hot metal last night…"

"Bad?" Steele asked.

"Doc thinks I'm out of the *war* for at *least* four months," Thorsten sighed, "if not out of the *Army*."

"Well, let's just *hope* you get better." He moved on, seeing at least one runner bandaged up. Then another…and a gunner who won the heavyweight boxing title…and Dugan, his left arm amputated at the shoulder…a loader with a sick father in Indiana…an ammo bearer who boasted he could heft four ammo crates at once, and did…and…"Jack," Steele grinned, "*you* need to stay out of the *way* of those explosions…"

"Yeah," Willis said through the bandages on his face. "Think the burns will make me better looking?" A seven-seven hit a fuel truck fifty yards from where Willis stood.

"Couldn't hurt *that* ugly mug."

"The Colonel is *too* kind."

Steele moved on…there was a loader from Nebraska with a head wound, who enlisted because there were too many mouths to feed at home…there was the best gunner in the battalion with his right hand gone…there was a driver/mechanic with half a leg missing…and Grimes…

The redheaded Major had lost both his legs above the knee. The pallor of his naturally pale skin was now almost as white as the bandages that came up to his chest. He was silent.

"Ned," Miller came up to him from behind. "Something I can help you with?"

"Just having a look, Murph," Steele turned. The bags under Miller's eyes, his pallid skin and a bandaged gash on his cheek were signs of a very weary man. "Can *we*…?"

"Yeah; outside." They proceeded out of the connected tents just as a light rain started. "My surgeon in the rear just reported."

"Wounded?"

"Here, fifty-seven. *Twenty* of them are out of the war for good; the rest *might* make it back in anywhere from two to six months." Miller pulled out a pouch and rolled a cigarette. "From what I hear from my aidmen at the companies, I make the count at *just* over a hundred and fifty total casualties." He took a drag, cocked an ear southwards, and shrugged. "About a hundred will require evacuation. Wonder what 1st Division's count is like?"

Steele listened to the sounds of the battle still raging around Cantigny, and strained for the sounds of the German counterattack on the French in front of Chateau de Aisne Sud. The French 9th Colonial division had joined up with the Moroccan Division the night before, securing that position and blocking the road leading directly to Fontainebleau.

"Can't *say*, Murph," Steele said. "Get some shuteye…"

"I'll prescribe the very same for you, Ned."

***

Finding a quiet corner in the ruins, Steele tried to lie down for rest, leaving Brick in charge for a few hours; he'd done the same for Brick a few hours before…

Bzzz-bzzz-bzzz-thut-thut-thut…

But *rest* would not come; only fitful sleep, with artillery and machine guns and explosions and rivers of blood invading his mind. The wounded he knew rose and fought again, only to be hurt again; the dead fell and died again…

And again…*bzzz-bzzz-bzzz-thut-thut-thut…*

And *again*…a ghastly tableau of horrible wounds and the stench of blood, gas, guts, and smoke…

Until…she appeared, soothed his brow, and he *finally*…

Remembrance Day, 1918, Chateau de Aisne Sud.

Mon coeur…so fair, so fine. So quickly did we become so close…will we ever…?

"Sir," Massie's voice came to Steele, cutting through the shrouds of his sleep, his first *proper* rest in two days. "Sir; telephone. Says it's urgent."

"Yes, all right, Top," Steele sighed. "Who…?"

"Chaumont, sir."

"Give me a minute, Top." Steele pulled his brogans on and shrugged on his overcoat, even though it was warm in his hut, and the memory of those last few moments with Angela was still fresh. "Can you rustle up some coffee, Top?"

"Fresh out of the mess, sir," Massie handed him a can of steaming liquid. "Knew you'd be asking for it…"

"Thanks, Top. Where's…?"

"Orderly room tent, sir," Massie said, then cleared his throat. "Means 'messenger of God,' sir."

"*What* does?"

"*Angela*, sir; the name. Means 'messenger of God.'" Steele looked curious. "You were mumbling it in your sleep, sir. I take it…the name means…*a lady?*"

"Keep that to yourself, if you would, please, Emil."

"I shall *do* that, Ned." He sighed deeply. "Mine's Martha; the name of the lady I dream of. *Her* name means 'the mistress.' Plan to get back to her some day."

"Wife?"

"*Sort* of. We spent *time* together, left her in Nebraska to come here."

"You write?"

"We do. We don't *talk* about the future… I didn't wanna jinx it…but I *might* start."

"NCO's women are…"

"Hard to afford, but *she* owns a *saloon*."

"Ah." Steele sipped his coffee. "Let's get to the phone."

The duty Corporal, dozing lightly at the desk, gave a start when Steele and Massie came in the tent. "Sir," he jumped up.

"*As* you were," Steele nodded. "Where's the…?"

"Sir," the Corporal handed him the receiver, sliding the instrument across the table.

"Steele," he said into the telephone.

"Hold for Colonel Dawes," the voice on the line said. "Colonel Steele," a voice said a few moments later, "we just got word of your fight at Chateau de Aisne Sud. My *God*, man, you have *electrified* this place."

"Just doing what I thought I should, Colonel," Steele sighed into the phone. "*I* thought we needed to *distract* the Huns from Cantigny and…"

"Indeed, you *thought*. The French government is awarding the 432nd the one of the highest honors they give a unit. They hang it on the unit's *flag*. But it just occurred to us that your battalion doesn't even have a *guidon,* let alone a unit *flag*. Do you even have *national colors*, Colonel?"

"Uh…no, sir; not *proper* ones," Steele said sheepishly.

"Well, we can address that from here, I suppose. Does your unit have a motto? Might *help* with the unit colors…"

"Strike *hard*; strike *deep*…"

"Excellent, if odd for a machine gun battalion. I'll see what we can do from here. The old man might want to pay you a visit. Be ready for that."

"Blois, sir?"

"No; *not* you; not *now*. I shall leave you to your Remembrance Day[1] activities, Colonel."

June

1st June, Camp Steele, Étaples.

A depressing meeting with the staff…we're so

[expletive] short of gunners…I need more officers and

NCOs. Pay officers are so [expletive] young…

2nd June, Camp Steele, Étaples.

A note from G…so __that__ bullshit's done…wonder if I

should tell __her__…

The self-mailer popped open easily; she hadn't been interested in privacy; it looked like.

---

[1] Before 1971, Remembrance/Memorial Day was always on 30 May.

Jan'y 5th, 1918
Ned;
You needn't try to care or look for Stan any longer. He died of acute appendicitis at Camp Custer just before Christmas.
My family and I have concluded that this war is just another way for the munitions barons and bankers to make money. Wilson is their stooge, and anyone who willingly fights their war is a fool.
Goodbye,
Georgia Pamplin.
P.S. I only hope Mr. Ford's Peace Ship is successful. We are joining the American Union Against Militarism.[1]
G.P.

"Huh," Steele sighed. "Mike, you heard about this Peace Ship of Ford's?"

"Yeah; saw something in the newspaper Dad sent me," Brick answered. "No one seems to think anything will come of it. Why?"

"Just got...*this*," Steele handed Brick the letter. "Just wondered what that Peace Ship bullshit was."

Brick skimmed the letter. "She a friend of yours?"

"We've been writing," Steele answered. "She asked me to look for her brother."

"Well, I *don't* think you're going to have to write back."

"I guess not. Is *this* one of those 'Dear John'[2] letters?"

"That's what they're *calling* that kind these days." Brick handed the letter back. "Lets *you* off the hook, though."

"How's...? Oh...yeah. Now I don't have to write a 'Dear Jane,' I suppose."

3rd June, Etaples.

Rain...rain...rain...I am summoned to see The

---

[1] The AUAM was the largest US antiwar organization during WWI.

[2] The origin of the term "Dear John letter" is unknown, but probably during WWI. The earliest *recorded* instance was to Ernest Hemmingway in 1919.

Boss…would it be faster by auto? I have never traveled that [expletive] far in an automobile…Rodgers has memorized the train schedules…I wonder if she can make time…?

Another [expletive] letter from G…her memory of me differs from what is real…Di is right…but should I answer?

The summons from Pershing had been perfunctory; almost rude:

> COLONEL STEELE TO REPORT TO AEF HQ AT CHAUMONT AT 9 AM 7 JUNE. SERVICE UNIFORM IS ACCEPTABLE.

That gave him two days to wrap up whatever *trivial* battalion business requiring his attention, and then make the day and a half journey by train from Etaples to Chaumont…or…?

"Sergeant Rodgers: *you* know French roads. *Can* the trip from here to there by auto be done?"

"No reason it *couldn't*, sir," Rodgers said. "The biggest issue, I feel, is fuel. We can't *carry* enough on a touring car. The *roads* are OK *most* of the time. You would have to go *through* Paris any way you *go*…"

"How long would it *take?*" Steele asked. "I gotta decide *soon* to get a *ticket*…"

"*Perhaps* not as long as the train, but…" Rodgers shrugged. "I can't *say* we would not *break down* or run out of *tires*, sir. But if you have an *appointment* to keep with General Pershing, it would be too risky."

"How about we take a motorcycle?" Steele asked. "Dispatch riders run all over…"

Rodgers frowned. "*That's* about four hundred kilometers by road, sir," he said, adding "the suspension on a sidecar would jolt your bones until they rattle. It would be a *most* uncomfortable ride for at a *day* and *most* of a night there *and* back."

"All right, you talked me out of it. I need a ticket and a ride

Wednesday...."

"*Yes*, sir. I can get your ticket this afternoon for the late train from Etaples to Paris on the 5th, that gets in at about 6 on the 6th, then the *morning* train to Chaumont that leaves Paris at 7 and gets to Chaumont in the late afternoon on the 6th..."

"Excellent," Steele said, thinking. "Can you send a *personal* wire while you are at the train station?"

"*Yes*, sir."

Steele scratched out the text.

> WILL PASS THROUGH PARIS 6 JUNE 6 AM STOP MEET ME AT STATION FOR AN HOUR END.

***

Steele checked the letter's postmark that evening, and thought it was curious that, after that *last* letter, she'd write again the *same day*....

> *Dearest Neddie;*
> *Please forgive my last missive, as I was so upset after receiving the news of Stan. He and I were never particularly close, and you and I, after all, have our understanding.*
> *It is my intention to wait for your return with chaste anticipation. I can think of spending my life with no one but you, my <u>dearest</u> Ned. I can hardly wait to hold you in my arms once more, kiss your sweet lips, and gaze into your adorable gray eyes.*
> *Please disregard my last hurtful missive. If you have not received it, my sweet Ned, tear it up before it is too late.*
> *Your loving,*
> *Georgia*

Reading her letter again and again, Steele tried to make any sense of it at all. He glanced into his mirror, assuring himself once again that he had *brown* eyes, not gray. He also strained to recall if they had ever *embraced*, let alone *kissed*. Though his memory of that last summer at home was dim, he was certain they had done neither; he'd *remember* either.

And Steele's "anticipation" was *not* chaste. But should he

answer her, saying he'd lost his heart to another? *Or* say she'd simply lost her marbles? *Or*, not reply at *all* and, *if* they should *ever* meet again, just blame the mail for not answering?

The last option took less energy *and* less stationary.

4ʰ June, Camp Steele, Etaples, France.

The sun is out at last and we are at the British range. We received some of the first Browning versions of the Vickers that fire the .30 caliber standard US ammo we are to evaluate. It is a simplified Vickers with fewer parts but a weak, bolted receiver they call the M1917. Lieut. Peng blew one up in an endurance test. We also got some Colt-made Vickers chambered for our .30 caliber. It is far more robust than the Browning and its receiver and its water system are simpler than the British Vickers. Ask us, and we'd recommend scrapping the Brownings and making more Colt-Vickers.

5ᵗʰ June, Train for Paris.

Wonder if she'll have time to meet...

Gazing out the window at the landscape untouched by battle, Steele, perhaps un-reasonably, prayed he could meet Angela at the Paris station for perhaps an hour the next morning…perhaps longer.

He wondered…hoped…

6ᵗʰ June, Paris.

A brief layover in Paris and a miracle...how fashions have changed...

He saw her near the baggage stacks, gazing around, searching for him. She wore a skirt that *seemed* shorter than Helen's swim dress, and a sleeveless shirtwaist…and her little straw hat…

Their embrace was long, warm and *oh*-so-gratifying—her scent filling his head—with onlookers and passersby grinning and smiling.

They didn't care. *This…was…perfect.*

"*Mon coeur*," she whispered, loosening her embrace, "*mon Destin*, we *need* to…"

"I know," he mumbled, "I just *need*…"

"I do, too. But we can't embrace here on this platform for an *hour*."

"Let's find someplace to walk about," he mumbled. "Been crammed on a bench seat all night."

They hustled through the busy terminal, getting cups of tea from a vendor near an entrance. "Have you heard anything more from your family?" he asked, jostled once again by a passing stranger.

"A letter from Mother," she said, suffering a similar indignity. "She wrote *your* mother; had nothing but good things to say."

"I'm sure Mom would be happy to—"

"Mother *says* so." She downed her tea, setting the cup on a stack of cups on a table. "This was cold."

"Yes," he agreed, finishing his and doing the same. "Someplace we can…?"

"In the *Gare de l'Est*[1] at six in the morning?" she asked. "You haven't *been* here often, *have* you?"

"Just once before. You?"

"Once a *week,* I come with the ambulances to meet the hospital trains."

"Just once a week…?"

"We take turns. Those boys come in *so*…"

"I'll bet." They squeezed their way into a tiny space behind a ticket booth, barely enough for both of them and his baggage. "Did

---

[1] "Station of the East," the main Paris station during WWI.

I *say* that I like your…ah…outfit?"

"You didn't, but thanks. I *cut* the skirt out of a *dress. This* fashion's *trés chic* in Paris now."

"You're *not* wearing stockings…" Ned also noticed other women weren't either.

"There probably aren't *five decent* stockings in the entire Right Bank, and even *those* will have holes. *Most* women are going without because of the shortages. I sacrificed nearly *all* my shirtwaist sleeves to make *underclothes*. Besides, it's so *hot*."

"It is *that*. And *hot* in *here*…"

"Well, I'm not *expecting* to…"

"No. I'm glad you came, though."

"What's the *occasion?*"

"I am summoned to Chaumont."

"What's there?"

"AEF headquarters."

"Are you to be punished?"

"No; Blackjack seems to think I'm a good soldier, likes my advice. Don't ask me why."

"Who's Blackjack?"

"General Pershing."

"Oh." He gave her an abbreviated version of their first meeting in Mexico, and of their other meetings. "So the supreme general in France thinks *you*…I should tell Father."

"Why?"

"Dear heart, as much as we might *love* each other…" He heard little more after that, until she said, "Ned? My *dear* Ned? Did *you*…?"

The tiny space was barely big enough for either of them to turn around, but suddenly he grabbed her with all his strength and kissed her passionately; she did the same.

After several minutes, he mumbled, "no one has *ever* said *that* to me…"

"What?"

"Love."

She smiled brightly. "You shall get *used* to it from me, for I shall never love another as I do you."

"I have *never* loved…I *must* tell you, though…"

He told her about Georgia's letters; she looked thoughtful. "A month ago, someone overheard a ward nurse saying, 'Mr. Wilson's war,' and 'Wall Street banker's war.' *She* was on the next boat home, *dismissed* without a reference."

"Is *that* right?"

"But this *Georgia* sounds desperate. Do you *have* an understanding?"

"She *thinks* we do, but I don't remember discussing *anything* more than writing. She's been *jilted* before." He thought for a moment, then said, "Enough about *her*. Did you pass your examinations?"

"I *did*; all fifty-six of us did. They need nurses *so* badly…"

He looked into her eyes. "About *us*, our…in the hospital…*that* was the *first* time *I*…"

"It was the first for *me* as well. Regrets?"

"None…if *that* was your *first*, you seemed to *know what* you were…?"

"Nurse's training…and women in dormitories get bored *so* easily. *Some* of their stories are *very* detailed and get *quite* graphic. And I am a quick study; grasped the *nuances*."

"Nuances, indeed." She gave a slight giggle and a smile as she reached for his hand. "I imagine they're not much different from the tales swapped in our barracks."

"You've never seen a French postcard?"

"One of those…oh, but not *that* detailed." He looked around. "Can you see a clock from here? My watch is in my bag."

"Yes, it's a quarter to seven."

"We have *half an hour* before I have to…."

"There's *another* train at two that will reach Chaumont at ten tonight, my dear. There is a small hotel just two blocks from *here*. I have a *key*."

"You *know* the train schedule? You took a room…?"

"I can *see* the schedule from *here* and the room's one we use *often* just to get out of the dormitory."

***

He stared out the window, the warm breeze wafting and billowing the thin curtains around. Between the window and where he was on the bed, Angela drowsed peacefully, her breast rising and falling gently. He blissfully thought of nothing but *her* and their last two hours together.

"I *love* you, Ned," she whispered, not opening her eyes. "Now, get some sleep."

"I love *you*, Angie, but I don't know if I *should*. I *have* to meet that train and if I *sleep* too long…."

"Then let's *make love* once more…"

Then, while in the throes of bliss, Ned heard the *BOOM* of artillery, carried on the breeze, embracing Angie with all his might, trying desperately *not* to recall the *bzzz-thut* that haunted his dreams….

***

Patrons crowded the café across the street from the station at midday, keeping the elderly waiters harried. Ned watched another column of French soldiers marching to the station, another string of ambulances and trucks leaving and…several *very* official-looking men arriving in limousines, seemingly in great distress. Civilians in carts and cars, all manner of luggage strapped to them, headed west down the streets.

Angie enquired of a waiter what the commotion was. "The Germans are less than a day away; they've reached the Ainse at the Chemin des Dames. *That* explains all the casualties."

For reasons he could never explain, he was unconcerned. "Shouldn't you be getting back…?"

"I *shouldn't* be *here now*," she said. "I'll get a mild lecture, but they *need* us too much."

"Wonder if my train…?"

"I doubt it would be affected. Chaumont is to the north of there." She smiled at him. "You *have* a room if it *is*."

But…an hour later, they stood on the platform, holding hands, waiting for Ned's train to be called, and hoping that would *not* be....

But, of course, it *was* called.

***

It was nearly midnight when he reached the small hotel in used by most officers visiting Chaumont. A Captain just outside the main entrance looked up from his newspaper. "Good *luck*, Colonel," he said. "Mighty crowded in there. Concierge is on the verge of stacking beds atop each other to make room."

"I'll take my chances." Officers talking, smoking, sharing drinks from flasks crowded the lobby, and Steele wondered if there *would* be a room for *him*. "Do you have a room for Colonel Steele?" he asked the clerk.

"*Colonel*...Steele...ah, *oui, Colonel Steele!*" The clerk pounded the bell, waking a Major snoozing on a divan. A well-worn bellman with one hand and sporting an eye patch appeared. "*Emmène les bagages du colonel Steele dans la chambre 201, Marcel; sans pourboire.*"[1]

"*Oui, monsieur,*" Marcel grunted, shouldering Steele's battered portmanteau. Up four flights of stairs, Marcel opened the door to a single, albeit small, room with a window, dropped Steele's bag on the bed, and made to leave.

"*Monsieur,*" Steele held out a fifty franc note. "*Merci...*"

"*Non, monsieur,*" Marcel said, holding up a scarred hand, "*je ne peux pas...*"[2]

"*Mon camarade,*" Steele held out the note with a small nod and a finger to his lips. "*Merci pour votre sacrifier...*"[3]

"*Merci, mon Colonel; merci...*" Marcel pocketed the note, holding a finger to *his* lips.

7th June, AEF HQ, Chaumont, France.

A few hours with her gives me strength...have I done

---

[1] Carry the bags...without gratuity.

[2] I cannot accept...

[3] For your service...

Distantly, guns boomed…

During a sumptuous meal at a *brasserie* in town, he saw several officers he knew slightly from when he was a Corporal. One Captain recognized him, squinted when he saw his epaulets, then looked away, shaking his head in disbelief.

As Steele waited for his car a few minutes later, the dubious Captain came up beside him. "*Steele*, isn't it?"

"Yes." It was all he could do to keep from adding, *sir*.

"You were a *Corporal* not *that* long ago…"

"I *was*." Again he resisted…but it was easier this time.

"Either you've done *very* well or you'll be *court-martialed*."

"*That's* right."

Pershing's car rolled up, the driver stepping out to open the door for Steele.

The Captain sighed. "You *have* done well…*sir*. Good *day*."

***

"The General will see you now, sir," the Sergeant declared.

As Steele walked in, Pershing stood up from his worktable, looking impeccable, as always, with boots so highly polished one could use them as mirrors if they weren't brown.

"Sir," Steele snapped a salute.

"*Colonel* Steele," Pershing returned the salute with a small smile. "Glad you could make the *time* for me…"

"How could I *not*?" Steele replied, returning the smile. "Can't turn down a summons from the head shed."

"Thank you, Colonel," Pershing answered, "*please* be seated." Steele sat in one of his side chairs; Pershing sat in another opposite him. "Your *father* has been writing letters. He says you *must* be short of everything. Can't that bandit *Willis* find enough men and equipment for you?"

"You *know* Major Willis, sir?"

"There's *damn* few officers in the Regular Army that *haven't* heard of Pirate Jack. And now he's a *Major?*"

"Yessir. He *does* seem notorious. He was wounded last month…"

"Serious?"

"Not very. He gets as much as…I don't know *where* Dad would get *that* idea, sir."

"Regardless, some *very* important people have read your father's letters. Colonel," Pershing said. "And your actions during the emergency in March were, to say the *very* least, exemplary, not to mention last month's fine showing. Your breakthrough battalion is…" Pershing made to stand. "Colonel, I *believe* in this project. And *you* have made it work."

"I appreciate your faith in me, sir," Steele said. "I will do my *very* best to carry out your wishes."

"You have *yet* to disappoint me." Pershing smiled, walked to, and opened a pair of glass-paned doors behind his desk, gesturing, "*Walk* with me."

They paced slowly away from the building into a pleasant, if poorly maintained, garden. Several men stood around outside, smoking; they turned away deliberately. Pershing, his hands clasped behind him, seemed lost in thought. Steele walked alongside, waiting.

"Colonel," Pershing finally said, just as they stopped by a hedge, "I've been thinking of your unit a great deal lately. You have accomplished more with your battalion than entire *divisions* have," Pershing continued. "Yet, you demand so *little*. Your plans are so…*concise*." He stopped, turned to face Steele. "If I didn't know better, I'd say you had a great deal of military experience; certainly more than most of my division commanders. How do you account for that?"

"Well, sir," Steele answered, "I just follow what's in the books, add a little horse sense and some, ah, feel for human nature, and…"

They both looked in the general direction of artillery *rumbling* to the south and west.

"Horse sense," Pershing mused, pulling a cigar pouch out of a pocket, offering a square-ended smoke to Steele. "Understand *you* smoke cigars; *I* prefer cigarettes, but I'll take a *stogie* once in a while."

"Sir..." Steele said, taking a cigar. "Never *tried* one of *these*...they call these cheroots?"

"Yep," Pershing said. "A *little* harsh, but *not* bad. Come from Spain." Steele struck a match on his belt and offered it to Pershing; they puffed their smokes to life. "Knowledge of human nature," Pershing continued, "and you read the books; *everyone's* books."

"Yessir. My dad always insisted that we work with our heads *and* our hands and backs. And knowing how people think, what they'll respond to, and how...*that's* important, too. When I was a *boy* to *home*, managing my brothers and sisters..."

"*Big* family, eh? I had two brothers and three sisters who lived long enough to get names."[1] Pershing gestured with his cigar. "How about you?"

"Four of each, sir."

"My *God*, Steele," Pershing grinned, puffing before tipping his stogie on the hedge. "Quite a brood." He was suddenly thoughtful. "I suppose being older than...*how many?*"

"Four, sir."

"*Half* of 'em *might* give you some insights into people. I was the oldest of *all* of 'em. Maybe *that* gave me *some* skills with people." Pershing looked around briefly; the others in the garden had left. "Steele, I've had British and French officers, now some Americans, say that your battalion *may* be the wave of the future. You're aware, I'm sure, of the German *Sturm* or *Stoss* units..."

"Yessir." Steele tipped his cigar on a hedge; a shower of sparks killed the fire. "What we were up against in March..."

Pershing struck a match, offering it to Steele. "That's *probably* what we're hearing now, from over by the Chemin des Dames..."

"Yessir," Steele said, puffing his cigar back into life. "I could hear *that* fight in Paris. *They're* in a panic..."

"The French *are* frightened, Colonel." Pershing puffed his cigar for several moments, listening to another drumming of

---

[1] Into the early 20th Century, many families didn't *name* children until they reached the age of two, as child mortality was quite high.

gunfire before he put his hands on his hips. "Colonel, we need to beat the Germans back. Once again, I want to use your *battalion* to achieve what none of our *divisions* can: strike *hard* and strike *deep*, as you say."

"Yessir."

"I'm afraid to say that I *must* rush off once again…you'll rejoin your battalion…your replacements are on the way…"

"*Thank* you, sir…"

* * *

Staring into the darkness from the train again, Steele contemplated the course of his life. That Captain got him thinking…without meeting Pershing on the border, without his welding skills…

Despite the telegraph office being swamped, he sent a wire ahead to Paris. An extra hundred francs probably did the trick, though on the *Paris* end…

On the train again, a young man with an older gentleman sat across the aisle from him, the two soldiers next to him, well asleep. A *year* ago, could he have imagined…?

> 8ᵗʰ June, West-bound train and Paris.
>
> I didn't see her at the station. There is much hustle and bustle in Paris, but not as much as before. I went to the hotel, but the room was unoccupied. I don't think she got the wire.
>
> 9ᵗʰ June, Train to Étaples.
>
> I see some French Army trains moving along the parallel track, but not British. I believe the threat to Paris may have passed.
>
> 10ᵗʰ June, Camp Steele, Étaples, France.
>
> Once again [Rest of entry illegible; stain.]

"Gentlemen, we have a great deal of work to do and *not* a lot of time to get it done."

Steele opened the meeting with that all-too-obvious phrase to emphasize the fact that time was *not* on their side. AEF slated the 432nd to help rebuild *two* machine gun battalions while simultaneously rebuilding their own. In a week, the 432nd had received nearly seventy replacements. and not *one* had any machine gun training.

"First thing…I've asked Chaplain Haldane to join us, talk about a memorial for everyone else we lost last month. Chaplain?"

"Colonel," the man said. "We need to make this *very* quick…"

"Of course," Steele said. "Just a benediction should be enough."

"The units haven't been doing much *for* memorials so far; despite our casualties, the training schedules…" Haldane began.

"Let's not spend a lot of time *justifying* it, Padre," Steele mumbled.

"There's one chaplain for every seventeen hundred men in the AEF…" Haldane protested. "I barely have time to *think*…"

"All *right*, Padre, *all right*," George Fore, the new D Company commander, soothed. "Maybe we can help, OK? My company has a divinity student as a platoon leader. Can *he*…?"

"It would *help*, yes," Haldane declared. "If your ceremony isn't *today*; right *now*, then…"

"Very well," Steele said. "Your Lieutenant can say a few words next Sunday, Captain Fore, because everyone's out on the range today. Thanks for coming, Padre…" Haldane stood, somewhat disturbed that he had nothing to do. "Before you go, Padre, I'm sure we'd all benefit from a prayer."

"Certainly. Then, I can hear confession for the next hour," Haldane nodded.

"Major Ishim," Steele answered, "can you guide the padre to the range? We can spare our new Chief of Staff for a half-hour."

"If you can spare *me*, sir," Captain Oscar Maxwell, the new C Company commander, asked, "I'd like to…"

"Sure," Steele sighed. "In fact, let's put this meeting off until after noon chow."

"Better before *supper*," Ishim said.

"Fine. Then let's say 4 this afternoon," Steele nodded, resigning himself to scheduling on the fly…again…

13th June, Camp Steele, Etaples, France.

A pep talk with the men…they ended up cheering me

up…

"Now, we're still using *some* of the good old Hotchkiss guns, but we're promised *more* of the *new* Vickers…*soon*." His exaggerated emphasis on that *soon* raised a chuckle. "But for now, we'll train with *everything*."

The casualty count from Bois de Aisne Sud experience was 219—thirty-seven dead, including Grimes and Captain Moss, commanding A Company, who died of an infection just that morning. *Lieutenant* George Grissom, the 1st Company's former clerk/bugler who just returned from OCS, replaced him.

"We have among us now some unfamiliar faces that we'll have to train to *our* standards…" They had fired 230,000 rounds of 8 mm ammunition and twice as much .303 in three days of combat. That was typical for a battalion in a *week*.

"*Steele* standards," someone in the back shouted. "*Steele standards*," more called. Their vehicles were still being unloaded, and half needed parts or serious repairs.

"To *432nd* standards, fellows; not *just* mine."

"*Same thing*," someone said, to widespread amusement.

"Have it your way. But we still have to be ready to take the field again, they tell me, in *less* than three weeks…"

"*We* can do it, sir," came a shout.

"I *know*…but we *may* have to do it *without our trucks*…" Silence. "AEF says they don't know that they can support *all* our trucks."

"Talk 'em *into* it, sir," came a voice.

"Will if I *can*, men; will if I *can*…We *might* take on more *Lewis* guns…"

"*Not* our kind of gun, sir," came a distinctive voice.

"No, but it arms our ammo bearers to cover the guns from infantry attacks during barrel changes or other stoppages…*and* the *new* Lewis guns *can* use tripods and traversing mechanisms. Their range is that of the *Vickers*…"

"In a *pig's eye*, sir," a voice called. "*Tube's* not long enough…"

"Can't have this discussion here and now, boys," Steele said. "It's not *our* decision, but that of *AEF*…"

"We've *gotta* use 'em, sir," another voice called.

"Or *not*," another answered, to general hilarity.

"All right, you jokers," Steele answered. "At-*ten—SHUN!*"

Walking away, Steele wondered as to just *how* he built such camaraderie without even trying.

July

4th July '18, Bézancourt.

I celebrate another Independence Day working.

Our plan is to attack a place called Étape Du Nord

Blanc in two days, which means Empty Camp of the

North, but I don't know why because there is no

[expletive] camp there. We are supposed to be

supporting the 2nd Division south of us…

"*Half* the gunners have never fired the guns outside the range, sir," Benson declared, his rough hands working against each other. "We're *not* as capable as we once were."

"Are *any* of us?" Steele chided gently. "What's your headcount?"

The lean man consulted a pad. "One hundred twenty-five: a hundred and four present; twenty-one out sick or on detachment."

"Very well. Lieutenant Grissom: A Company?"

"One thirty assigned: one twenty present, ten out sick," Grissom answered, twisting his neck nervously as he often did.

"Captain Maxwell, C Company?"

"One thirty-one assigned: One *ten* present, twenty on detachment or out sick." Maxwell, who Steele regarded as the steadiest of his new maneuver company commanders, answered calmly and assuredly.

"Lieutenant Fore, D Company?"

The 19-year-old boy looked at his list. "One hundred thirteen assigned; ninety answering the role and the rest sick or detached."

"Captain Lorenzo? HQ Company?"

"Two hundred nine assigned; one hundred seventy-nine present; thirty detached or sick." Lorenzo, in stark contrast, was old enough to be most of Steele's men's father.

"*Commandant*? Your Legionnaires?"

"One hundred forty assigned; one hundred thirty answering to the role: ten sick." Haliburton/Haller had a bandage on his left cheek, a still-not-healed wound from May.

"Major Ishim, that adds up to…?"

Ishim had been following with his own report, nodding at most numbers but penciling corrections on some. "Seven hundred fifty-four effectives, sir."

"Lieutenant Majoras: vehicles?"

"We have enough to move the entire battalion plus trains, sir," Frank Majoras, Willis' deputy, answered.

Steele blinked. "We didn't last *week*…*most* of the *autos* were…"

"All top-line, sir," Majoras declared.

"Frank," Ishim grimaced, "*tell* me I will *not* have a bunch of senior officers pounding on my desk claiming *our* autos are really *theirs*."

"I would *never* do *that*," Majoras answered, feigning hurt as if he were Willis' twin. "*Those* vehicles never *had* owners on *this* side of the Atlantic. Besides, *their* count was the same when I *left* as when I *arrived*."

The other officers snickered, choked. "You mean you *traded*...?"

"In a manner of speaking. More like *bartered*. Cost me a case of our best trading whiskey."

"Uh-huh," Steele answered. "Motorcycles? Bicycles?"

"I can answer that, sir," Lieutenant Dennis Ingraham, the new Scout/Survey platoon leader, interrupted. "The scout and courier pool has thirty-one motorcycles, five with side-hacks, and seventy-three bicycles."

"Lieutenant Ingraham has a bicycle and motorbike repair shop back in New York, sir," Majoras said. "He volunteered his services to help me and Lieutenant Peng out. Found *five more mechanics* in the battalion. We're learning to fix German machine guns we got from a 2nd Division patrol..."

"Some *Marines*, sir," Majoras added. "Swapped two bottles of cognac for 'em."

"Might come in handy in the next few days, gents," Steele declared. "The 2nd Division is going into this area *here*, on the Marne. As we've discussed for the past two days, our job is to keep to their northern flank."

"Where's the Moroccans?" Lorenzo asked.

"No Moroccans," Steele said. "Instead, *we* get a battalion of our very own *Marines* to watch *our* flank..."

5th July, Bezancourt.

We have [Page stub.]

[Next six pages torn out.]

[No date; page stub]...[P]*reparations for...*

18th July, Bois de la Bézancourt.

We endure incessant [expletive] *artillery, machine gun fire. Night and day. Gas too. This is harder than*

"We *have* to cut off their movement," Steele said to Massie. Studying the map, he saw a road that joined the two flanks of his zone. "Give me B Company," he said to the telephonist. "Steele here. Plot a two platoon standing/bump barrage on the east-west road northeast of the Bois de Villemontoire, starting in ten minutes."

"*That's…*" the telephone answered.

"Just *do* it." Steele hung up.

"Sir," Massie handed Steele a message from A Company:

HELD UP BY THREE MG. NEED STOKES OR POMPOM.

"*Runner*," Steele called, scribbling a note to D Company:

NEED POMPOM/STOKES AT BOIS DE MARIE.

"*Sir*," Massie pointed to a young Lieutenant, spattered with dust and blood.

"Lieutenant Frederics, yes? C Company?" Steele asked.

"*Yes*sir," Fredricks answered. He had the tired, scared look of someone who had been up for *days* under shellfire…like everyone else.

"What can I do for Captain Maxwell…?" Steele started.

"Captain Maxwell, sir?" Fredricks asked. "*Killed.* Lieutenant Burns sent me to tell you we've reached the Bois de Corneille and we're *still moving.*"

"*Corneille is halfway to the river,*" Steele exclaimed. "Tell Burns well done and keep moving…"

"Sir," Massie interrupted. "If they're in the Corneille, they can look to their left and hit Hill 270 a thousand meters north, where the Boche observers are…"

"Right; good," Steele said. "Turn a platoon towards Hill 270 and put a sweep barrage on 'em, Lieutenant, but keep the main body *moving* to the river."

"Yessir," Fredricks said…but stopped, blinking. "Can you

send a *runner*, sir?"

"Why?" Steele asked, then stopped.

"Sir, *I...*" Fredricks sighed...then collapsed, a large splinter sticking out of his back.

"*First aid,*" Steele shouted, followed by, "*runner...*" as another scared and dirty boy ran in, handing Steele a *startling* note from C Company, scribbled on a corner of a map, of all things ...

REACHED RIVER. OFFICERS DOWN. NAGORSKY.

In the twilight, with mortar bombs falling in the distance, Steele muttered, "high time Nagorsky was commissioned..."

"Yes, *sir....*"

19th July, Marne River.

I can hardly [Rest illegible]

20th July [No location]
Shelling does not stop. Can hardly think...

21st July, Villemontoire, France.
Now I know...Fire and brimstone and a dreadful

scorching wind will be the portion of their cup...[1]

"*Jes*us Christ al*mighty...*" Rodgers stopped the touring car carrying Steele and Massie at the edge of the wood.

They gazed at the road through the woods when they reached it, where a seven-seven battery and two German infantry companies had been marching...

"Even *He* couldn't have saved them..." The three slowly got out of the car.

They surveyed the *results* of Steele's hasty fire mission on this road, meant to cut off the German reinforcement against his left flank.

---

[1] Psalms 11:6.

That it did, leaving *this fly-infested* abattoir…

"Unbelievable." They *slowly* paced towards the killing ground. The sounds of artillery and machine guns that had been so loud just moments before seemed to *vanish* amid the furious *buzzing* of *flies*, and the *screeching* of *rats*….

"You'd *better* believe it." B Company's barrage caught the Germans on the road and tore them apart like, as Pershing saw in Manchuria, tigers in a pit. The barrage also ripped and pounded trees to splinters, turning them into jagged wooden shrapnel.

"It must have been like the *end* of the *world* for them…" Rodgers closed his eyes slowly, standing stock still.

Scores of horses fell in their harness; scores of men died in marching rows when the copper-jacketed hail arrived. Some who tried to find the safety of the woods fell *there*. Many survived that first deluge of death and tried to get away, only to be caught by the barrage as it swept slowly along the road, or to perish, unattended, just outside the curtain of bullets.

"Certainly the end of *their* world…" Massie walked carefully around the beaten zone.

Steele's guns had put barrages into No-man's-land, into trenches, into woods, into bunker lines and seen *those* effects. But never in the *open*…like *this*. Rifle stocks shattered; helmets holed over and over; packs ripped and torn; grenades detonated by the *horrid* torrent of bullets. Caissons *exploded* when bullets hit fuse cases. *Thousands* of missiles pierced the very earth, and tore the turf, the road, and everything they hit into a *hellscape* of little craters amid a forest of *ribs* bleaching in the sun….

"Could never have *guessed*…" Steele blinked over and over, his eyes tearing at the stench of bodies bloating in the summer sun.

Many endured *countless* hits; their bodies reduced to mush amid the ghastly, *infernally loud* buzzing of flies and the *chattering* of rats….

"Neither could *I*…" Massie stopped, staring at a bloody heap….

Even those buried under piles of corpses met their end after their comrades above them became mere meat….

"The aidmen found *seven* still alive." Massie looked away. Even a few taking shelter under horse carcasses found death from above….

Gazing at the scene, Steele wondered, *"how?"*

"They crawled under guns." The barrage decapitated one horse; it cut off all four legs of another. It mangled most of the rest. Massie walked back to the touring car.

A German first aid bag lay forlornly intact in a clear spot in the middle of the road; it's owner…?

"We should detail some men to…." Steele began.

Pigs, birds, dogs, and other animals took advantage of the carnage, a bounty of carcasses. Villagers, looting what they could, frightened some scavengers away.

"Yes…" Massie answered.

"But nothing else *used* this road," Steele said, climbing back into the car.

The barrage had done its job. Three hundred-odd Germans and a seven-seven battery's worth of horses *ceased* to exist, no longer able to return fire on machine guns over three thousand meters away…their *ability* to answer the attack, to seek revenge, *dying* with them…in an eight millimeter *rain* of *death*….

"Let's *go*," Steele sighed.

22nd July, Villemontoire, France.

We have lost fully one-third of our officers in five

[expletive] days, and nearly one half our strength. I

do not know how we can recover as a fighting

unit…Haller's hurt again…and all of E Company are

under a sentence of death…

"So where are we?" Brick asked, coming into Steele's HQ hut. Villemontoire was a ruin, torn and smashed by artillery from both sides.

"How's C Company?" Steele asked. "Is Lorenzo working out?"

"He's an excellent replacement *officer*, but Nagurski runs *that* outfit. Gave him *my* bars as Lorenzo's exec."

"What's their strength?"

"Ninety five on their feet. Might get another dozen out of the hospital in a few days."

"What's E Company's status now?"

"Haller's pretty bad; Salavas took over…"

"Has he got enough *French*…?"

"Eh, he *said* he did."

"What's *their* strength, now?"

"Ah," Brick looked in his notebook. "Ninety-four on their feet; fifteen wounded." He paused. "Lost *thirty nine* this week. One thing, though…"

"Yeah?"

"Our *French* artillery observers want to put *them* in for *Croix de Guerre*."

***

"So, this is *it*, then, Ned?" Ishim said, offering his hand.

"Probably," Steele said. "First Army MG school needs a machine-gun officer and Black Jack said I have to sacrifice my *best*."

"OK, Ned," Ishim sighed. "See you in the next post."

"What makes you think…?" Steele started.

"Because you're *that* good at this, Ned; *that's* why."

August

14ᵗʰ August, Hotel Petite Rose, Paris.

~~Bastille Day~~…it is surprisingly quiet…here for more meetings, more plans, more men if I can get them…I see her again…she has accepted me…

"Ain't this the French Fourth of July?" Brick asked outside AEF HQ. Paris was, for a holiday, remarkably quiet.

"Naw; that's *July 14ᵗʰ*," Major Harry Gowan answered, "but they ain't got a lot of interest in seeing more fireworks." AEF *invited*—not *required*—Steele to sit in on a briefing for the upcoming offensive, the first *large* American offensive of the war. Steele came to plead for more men. Gowan, a replacement for Ishim, came to the battalion from AEF HQ.

Inside, the three elbowed past several junior officers standing outside the big theater, where Harbord and Marshall were standing in front of a large map. "Here," Harbord pointed to a line outside the town of St. Mihiel, "is where we expect to be at the end of the first day."

"We're gonna take *half* that salient in a day?" a voice asked.

"We *are*," Marshall answered. "The Germans are already pulling out..."

"They were pulling out of Belleau Wood, too," another voice said, to much consternation. "They can turn on a *dime*."

"Maybe *then*," Harbord nodded, "but *now* they have the Canadians on their heels up in Flanders."

The meeting went on in a similar vein for another hour. When it broke up, Steele and his men pressed forward, wanting to meet with Pershing or someone who could...

But Pershing had already left.

"Steele," Marshall said sympathetically, "I understand you're shorthanded..."

"More than just *short*, Colonel," Steele sighed. "I'm desperate, nearly 30% short. A spare infantry company wouldn't be—"

"Perhaps we can do *that*," Marshall mused. "There's someone who you'd want to...someone as bold as *you* are who might spare a company. Would *you* like to...?"

"*Lead* me *to* 'im," Steele answered.

***

"Terry Allen," the rangy officer said, "Third battalion, 358th Infantry. Understand you've got a *request*..." He seemed like a homey sort of fellow, not presuming anything because of Steele's slightly superior rank but young age.

"I do, Major," Steele answered, shaking Allen's hand. "I need men..."

"We *all* do, sir," Allen answered. "Colonel Marshall expects I can *spare* some, but I don't…you're a machine gunner?"

"I am, but the 432nd is more *motorized infantry*…"

"Indeed," Allen answered, surprised. "Steele…wait: I've *heard* of you. You did something up north that surprised everyone, *including* the Germans…"

"We *did*," Steele answered modestly. "But I'm running short of men…"

"And you want some of mine?" Allen nodded. "You want my machine gunners?"

"No: I want infantrymen who can work with my *Legion* company…"

"*Legion* company?" Allen asked, startled again. "*French Foreign Legion* company? Yours?"

"Yes; they've been attached to us for some months now. They're my infantry muscle…"

"Well, our *training* has been…thin," Allen admitted. "Just how *many* men do you…?"

"A company…?" Steele asked.

"Huh," Allen said. "Let me *think* about it. I'm in Paris until tomorrow morning. Can I let you *know*?"

"If you *would*…"

"What about…know any good restaurants around?"

Steele named the few that he knew of from his previous visits. "Now, I've been to *brasseries*; I haven't been to more formal…"

"That's fine, Colonel; don't have my dress uniform here, anyway. Are you *free* for dinner?"

"I don't…where are *you* staying?"

***

They walked along the river, arm-in-arm, not speaking. Her uniform dress seemed…loose, but Steele dared not ask about…

"I've lost *so* much weight," she sighed, looking at the sidewalk ahead of her. "This dress *hangs* on me now."

He chuckled. "I was just *thinking* that, but I…"

"Why *is* it that conversations between men and women can't include such mundane things?" she sighed. "*You* remark that my dress doesn't seem to *fit* and everyone around seems aghast. Or, at least, we *know* they *would* if anyone overheard."

"That's so." They kept walking, slowly. "You've been *working* a *lot*..."

"I *have*; six shifts a week, eight or ten hours a shift."

"One day off a week now?"

"Yes, and even *that* changes. I might have Sunday off *this* week, but *next* week I might have *Saturday*, then not *again* until *Friday* or *Sunday* or the next *Wednesday*."

"Hard to plan anything," Steele mused. "I, ah, talked to our surgeon about your staffing last March..."

"Who...?"

"Dr. Miller. He, ah, didn't *think* the hospital was short-handed...even in March..."

They kept walking, not speeding up; not slowing. "Yes?"

"So, that first time I went...on my own, *you* said..."

"You had to be checked for bleeding. I didn't want to wait for a male orderly when I was *just* as capable of..."

"*You* just wanted to see my..."

"*Yes*." She grinned in the shade of her hat. "*You* didn't have the *wit* to protest."

"No. Lucky for you, I grew up in a big household. Girls looking at my privates isn't *that* embarrassing."

"But I'm neither your sister, your mother, or your maid."

"No." They walked on. "Angie, when you said your *family*..."

"It is important before we go *any* further..."

"*How* much further *could* we go?"

Silence. "An *altar*, of course."

Silence. "Is *that* where you *want* to go with *me*?"

"*Yes*," she answered quickly.

"*Shall* we...?"

"I *can't* until the war's over and I can quit the Red Cross. No married woman can be overseas unless their husbands are in the same unit."

"And when shall *that* be?" Steele wondered.

"I should think very soon; sooner than many think."

"What makes you say that?"

"A Canadian officer was in the hospital yesterday. He said they had a breakthrough on the British front last week. 'Beginning of the end' he called it. *Thousands* of prisoners; *hundreds* of guns captured…"

"Can't be over soon enough for me."

"Nor *I*."

***

Staring out the little hotel window, Steele imagined his family's reaction to his letter:

> *…Angela has accepted my proposal of marriage…we wait until after her time with the Red Cross concludes at the end of the war…we don't think it will be long now…*

"*Did* I propose?" he asked.

"As I recall…no," she answered, looking up from her sewing. She was gathering in her already patched uniform dress. "I just said 'yes' when you asked if *an altar* is what I wanted." She paused. "Is it what *you* want, dear heart?"

"It *is*, my dear," he said with conviction. "Should I get on bended knee, like the books say?"

"Perhaps that…but…" she added, putting her sewing down, "*I* always thought that the proposal should come *before* the lovemaking."

"Can't take the *latter* back, can we?"

"No," she agreed, standing up. "But I *think* we should have more on than just *your* trousers and *my* chemise when *you*…."

"I have *suspenders*…"

He reached for her as he dropped to one knee; she stepped closer, tousled his hair while she held his head to her. "Well, more even than *that*. How well do you *know* this officer you want to have dinner with?"

"*Not* well; we just met." He nuzzled her belly, taking in her scent. "But he *seems* like a decent fellow."

She embraced his head to her. "I *have* to finish with my

uniform, then duck back to the dormitory…*what* time did you say? *I* want to make love once more *before* we dine.…"

"Eight. And just a *brasserie*; nothing formal."

"Just as well, for I have *nothing* I could wear to a *decent* restaurant." She cocked her head, listening to the bells chiming. "That's…a quarter past three. Lovemaking first, or sewing?"

***

"He's a fine fellow," she declared, her hand on his arm as they walked along the Seine as a light rain fell.

"He *is*," he agreed. "Even if he said he would only spare a hundred volunteers…it's a hundred more men than we *had*."

"Is that a *lot?*"

"We're about *three hundred* men short of establishment, so, yes, it's a lot for *us*." Along the wide sidewalk, other couples were walking, enjoying the brief respite from the heat brought by the rain. One couple… "Major…Willis?"

"Sir…oh, *sir!*" Willis stopped; Steele and Angela stopped, the dull glow of the setting sun barely allowing identification. "I didn't…"

"Who's your *friend*, Major?" Angela asked. "I'm Angela Gibson," she offered her hand.

"John Willis, miss," Willis said, "and *this* is Miss Monique Claron…"

"*Enchante, Mademoiselle* Monique," Angela replied warmly. "Your work with soldier's families is *famous*…"

"*Merci, Mademoiselle* Angela. *Your* work among the American soldiers and *le midinettes*[1] is *just* as notable…"

"*Merci*. And *this* silent gentleman is Colonel Ned Steele…"

"I am de*light*ed, Colonel," Monique said, her voice smooth and clear. "You, too, are famous among the soldiers, who call you their *anvil*. You know *mon Jacque* well?"

"Well enough to *work* with *your Jack*, yes, Miss Monique," Steele answered. "He's one of my *best* officers."

---

[1] Originally, seamstresses in the great fashion houses. By mid-1918, any French working woman.

"Of course, he's so well known in your Army that he has his own nickname," Monique replied. "*Everyone* knows *Le Pirate*…"

"They do, *indeed*, miss," Steele answered. "I was not *aware* that he'd returned from the hospital. I'm certain he will make up for that oversight very soon. Now; *pleasant* meeting you; *we* shall be on our way…"

"Sir," Willis said quickly, "*Mademoiselle* Monique is helping with our personnel problems…"

"Tell me *later*, Jack, when you report to me and the new chief of staff at the *Gare de l'Est* tomorrow morning at *ten*…"

"*Noon*," Angela purred softly in Steele's ear.

"Noon," Steele said…and the couples stepped off in opposite directions.

A few minutes later, Angela asked, "just *what* was…?"

"It's the senior officer's responsibility to leave first…"

"Not *that*. She's the daughter of a Senator who will soon be a deputy minister of war and she has the *ear* of *Monsieur* Clemenceau.…"

"So Jack's done *very* well *indeed*," he sighed…then mumbled, "*help* us *how*…?"

15ᵗʰ August, Hotel Petite Rose, Paris.

Angie had a bellman take our picture with her

Brownie, and I part with her again…never question

the ways of a supplyman…

After the bellman snapped the pictures, they embraced gently in the hotel lobby, smiling bravely. "Shall *I* write to your family?" she asked. "I must introduce myself…"

"*Mom* would like that," he answered. "She *might* write back, though you'll more *likely* hear from Diane."

"I want to be in the good graces of *all* your family. Do you have an address for Charlie?"

"I *do*, yes. I think he'd *like* that. Al probably told him about you; *they* correspond."

They went out to the street; he in uniform hauling his barracks bag, she in her uniform with her valise. "It eludes me how you put that skirt and shirtwaist in that little bag," he said.

"Roll it tight," she said. "The skirt is smaller than that shirtwaist, and the *chemise* is..."

"And no *corset*," he added.

"Just a brassiere, chemise and underpants," she said. "I'll *never* wear a *corset* again." She looked around. "How *liberating* this war has been for women's *fashions*..."

"How so?"

"The skirts got shorter, and sleeves and stockings went away because of a shortage of materials and labor," she said. "Not to mention *razor blades* for shaving..."[1]

"*That's* so," he said.

"That's what everyone *says*. But it's *much* cooler in this *heat* to go about..."

"*They* may be right. I need to ask...I've seen girl's underthings before, but...those underpants...I've *never*..."

"They're just *very* short bloomers. We like to think we invented them here."

He looked around. "I have to go...*that* way..."

"I have a shift in..." she glanced at her pin-watch, "twenty minutes *ago*...*that* way."

"Yes. I *love* you, Angie."

"Yes, I *know*; I love *you*, Ned. *Please* take care..."

"Same to *you*, my dear."

And, after a lingering embrace...they parted company.

***

"So, Jack," Steele began at lunch, "what kind of 'help' are we getting from your lovely friend? And did you *tell* her you're married?" Steele, Brick, Gowan and Willis met in an *Estaminet* down the street from the train station. They were just an hour from getting on a train back to Etaples.

---

[1] Exactly when modern women began cosmetic shaving is unclear, but ads for feminine shaving products began in the 1920s.

"Of *course*, I told her, Ned," Willis said in his feigned-hurt voice. "*What* do you *think* I…?"

"*We* know you as *Pirate Jack Willis*," Brick chuckled. "So, *out* with it."

"Well," Willis sighed, "Monique has the ear of some *very* important people, and got the French authorities to release American nationals held by the French police for petty crimes into our custody…"

"Yeah?" Steele said, suddenly interested. "How *many?*"

"Three hundred-odd, *she* thought…and we did *nothing* other than talk, walk, drink and eat…."

"If I may be so bold, Jack," Steele asked, "how did you *happen* to *meet* with this young lady?"

"*Well*, Ned," Willis started, "it was like *this*…" Only mathematicians, magicians, or other supplymen *could* follow the exposition that *ended* with…"then *that* Frenchman introduced me to *Mademoiselle* Claron at the charity function yesterday after*noon*. Well, she thanked me for that carload of mutton and asked if there was anything *I* might need that *she* could provide. I said, 'well, I haven't had dinner with a pretty girl since I can't *remember* when,' and *after* dinner we got to *talking* and…"

"So…a carload of mutton got us *three hundred men*…?" Steele sounded incredulous.

"Well, that *and* a case of Irish whiskey for the guardroom at the jail this morning…" Willis said.

"At the *jail*…this *morning*…" Brick repeated.

"Right," Willis said. "I put our new men on cars two hours ago and they'll be in Etaples tomorrow, probably after *we* get back."

"How *many?*" Steele asked softly.

"*Not* three hundred, Ned," Willis said sheepishly. "Three hundred and *twenty-two*. They are in the custody of a squad of French *gendarmes* traveling *with* them, sir." He shook his head. "The *gendarmes* are coming *back* here; we can't keep *them*…"

"What did it cost for *them?*" Gowan asked, slack-jawed.

"A bottle of prewar cognac each," Willis answered.

Steele and Brick looked at each other, shook their heads, and finished their lunch. Gowan, looking confused for a moment, shrugged and went back to eating.

September

"Sir; Major Brick…"

"I'll *come*." Steele closed his eyes tightly, praying that he would *not* see….

Steele walked through the camp behind a medico, trying not to show his fear, his sadness, his *horror* at the illness sweeping his unit. So *many* were sick British soldiers guarded his gates, and food had to be brought in because *all* the cooks but Cohen were sick…and the baker still made biscuits every day….

Now *Brick* was ill…the one remaining officer from Ft. Leavenworth, the one remaining man on *Earth* that he saw every day who he *knew*…

He entered the pest tent behind the medico, the stench of blood and death filling his nose as he donned a gauze mask. A Lieutenant on a pallet of straw near the entrance he could not recognize wheezed and spat up blood as he began a paroxysm of coughing. His skin was blue/black; his eyes were red and wild, unseeing. He had not long to live.

Steele walked past three other such cases before he reached the canvas barrier, the partition between those who would die in days, if not hours, and those who *might* live. No one knew *why* those poor devils on the *other* side did that, but they became what Miller called "blue terrors" in hours after they fell ill. Few of *them* lasted more than a day, and *none* survived two, hacking out their lives so hard some broke ribs.

The medicos stacked those who didn't care anymore in the "dead space," a hasty morgue between two canvas partitions, hoping to create a barrier between hope on the one side and resignation on the other.

Each night, workers hauled the dead away. Weary French volunteers lit funeral pyres every third day to save their own strength and their fuel oil. With everyone in the *world* affected, there was a shortage of coffins and gravediggers.

On the other side of the dead space, a cotton screen enclosed each cot on three sides, facing the aisles. Here, the sick lay quietly, mostly pale, wan, and sweating. Chaplain Haldane quietly blessed patients, himself wrapped in a mask and perspiring with fever.

Steele and the medico found Miller by Brick's cot, scribbling a note on a pad. "Murph; how's the patient?" Brick, breathing hard, didn't recognize Steele; didn't really open his eyes.

"As well as *any* man can be expected to be who has a fever of 103," Miller replied wearily. "Major Brick is our 498th flu patient in two *weeks*, making us *officially* out of action with over 50% sick or dead."

"Hardly a notable milestone," Steele answered quietly.

"The *first* in the *AEF*," Miller finished in the same tone.

"When did *Brick* report?"

"Six hours ago."

"*That* means…?"

"*That* means he's got a good chance of surviving." Miller pocketed his pad. "This…*virus*, I believe it to be…is like nothing I have ever *heard* of. Patients like *these*," he swept his hands across the room, "often survive. Patients like *those*," he pointed to the partitions, "*never* do. Then there's those like, well, the *Padre* there. No, he's *not* well, but he's *nowhere* as sick as those on these cots, and he *won't* get as bad as *those* poor bastards over there."

He stopped. "'Poor bastards,'" he sighed. "They're my *patients* and I disrespect them like *that…*" He sighed. "It comes so *fast.* Warrant Officer Farrell came in feeling unwell at nine yesterday morning. By noon, his fever was 108, and he was spitting blood out of his nose and his mouth. By *three* yesterday *afternoon…*"

"He was *gone,*" Steele said.

"Yes. Sergeant Major Massie is one of those I sent to his *own* cot; he'll recover in a few days. I did some *crude* autopsies, hoping to find something someone could use to find a treatment. I sent some notes and samples to the AEF surgeon-general." Miller stopped again. "If I *had* a microscope here, I might *see* something in that black, ropy *goo* that I extracted from their chests. But…" he shrugged. "Major Willis can't *find* a microscope, and has other priorities. I can only guess what my colleagues or my teachers are thinking now…"

"Is this influenza *that* dangerous?" Steele asked.

"The 1890 strain was *quite* virulent. Oh, there were cases of flu-associated pneumonia, and a few choking on phlegm. But…those…*things* out there…I never saw the like before and hope to *God* I never do again."

"Is it just…?"

"*Some* think it *came* here *from* America…"

25ᵗʰ September, Étaples.

Another nine cases, another three dead from

flu…Rodgers is sick, carrying on…

"Sir," Rodgers asked, as polite as ever.

"Sergeant, have you been handling the paperwork OK, since Sergeant Major Massie got sick?"

"Yessir," Rodgers said. "There *has* been somewhat less of it. I've had to get morning reports from the companies myself. But the daily *hasn't* been going to Paris…"

"It *hasn't?*"

"AEF said to stop for now."

"Ah." Steele looked curious. "You look pale."

"I had the *shivers* last night, sir."

"Take care of yourself, Sergeant."

26ᵗʰ September, Camp Steele.

Big offensive started today in the Argonne... another

five cases, another one dead. Brick's fever is down.

"Major Willis," Steele said, handing over his glass. "What is the status of our vehicle park?"

"We've got all that we *can* into shape, sir," Willis said, pouring another slug of thick wine into Steele's glass. "With Lieutenant Peng and one other mechanic, I figure we're doing pretty damn good with what we've got."

"You're probably right, Jack."

October

10ᵗʰ October, Camp Steele, Etaples, France.

We got orders...

"Sir," the messenger handed Steele a leather folder. "Direct from Chaumont."

"Maybe it's the end of the war," Willis sighed.

The message was terse and blessedly direct.

> LOSSES IN VETERAN UNITS[1] HAVE LEFT THEM WEAKER THAN YOU ARE. APPRECIATING YOUR SITUATION, I HAVE TO ORDER YOU TO JOIN FIRST ARMY AT ST FERMIN.

"Sorry, Jack," Steele nodded. "Order us a train."

------

[1] "Veteran" units at the time of the Meuse-Argonne offensive were those that had fought at least *one* battle before they were pushed into combat; no more than 20% of the total.

15th October, St. Fermin, France.

We are to advance from the old Verdun forts, joining once again with the French on one side and the Americans on the other. There are nearly six hundred men in the battalion now, having taken on the remnants of machine gun companies from divisions which did not fare well in the Argonne and those that have yet to be fully activated...

November

7th November, Near the Meuse River.

For nearly three weeks, my mishmash of a battalion has been breaking in here, sliding around there, always pushing the Huns out of the way or slaughtering them in place. I'm so [expletive] tired I can't think straight. Now, this [expletive] hill we can't even define. Even Harris says he can't build a way around it.

They call us Steele's Anvil at HQ. I feel like I'm being [expletive] hammered, all right.

Nobody wants to be the last man killed in any war. Figured that shit out by now.

8th November, Near the Meuse.

I cannot imagine that Hell would be any worse than this [expletive] place...Hill 90 didn't hold a candle to

Steele put his pen down, rolled it into his diary and peered over the edge of the shell hole, parly protected by the corpse of a dead Hun corporal, and the horse that the Hun once led.

In front of him was the sprawling hill mass, a hellish landscape of crater-pocked mud, riven by collapsed trenches, strewn with barbed wire, and dotted with the blasted remnants of trees, trenches, and people—all of it stinking of gas and rotting or burning flesh, courtesy of the German flamethrowers defending part of *that damned hill.*

Steele was the senior officer as far as he could *see.* The men in the surrounding holes were the only soldiers left at his disposal, all waiting patiently for his decision that would sacrifice *them* for that *infernal hill,* whether in the next hour or the next few minutes.

He heard movement behind him and rolled around onto his back, being sure to keep his head below the edge of the crater. The movement brought the mud-spattered face of General Davis, the 16th Division commander, into Steele's hole. It was Davis's division he'd been supporting/leading for the past three weeks.

Davis leaped across the puddle at the bottom of the hole, leaving a nervous colonel behind. Elbow deep in slime, the General crawled up the side of the hole to where Steele waited, bemused but incredulous. Steele nodded.

"Colonel," Davis grunted.

"Sir," Steele replied.

"What's holding us up?"

"See that hill there?" Davis bellied up to the grisly aperture that

---

[1] Corporal.

Steele had been staring through, heedless of the mess he was making of his uniform. "Hollow as a beehive. *That's* what I'm calling it—the Beehive. Think *that'll* please the folks back home?" Davis seemed unphased. "There's a *cartload* of Hun Maxims in there, and a few flamethrowers. We've tried everyone *else's* plan to get past it. Between the river and the cliff, this ledge is the *only* way forward within our divisional boundaries."

"You're…"

"Ned Steele, sir, 432nd Machine Gun battalion."

"Eh? I've *heard* of you; you're the *Anvil*." Davis extended his hand. "Ed Davis. Pleased to make your acquaintance. Sorry, but there just hasn't *been* time before…" Davis heaved a sigh. "What have you got up here? How would you *take* that beehive?" Davis asked, staring through the aperture.

"Sir, *my* current plan is to wait for those Huns in there to die of old age." Steele waited for a reaction: nothing. "I've got two 75s over *there*," Steele pointed to a ravine to his left, "and a Hotchkiss section, two Vickers sections, a two-inch pom-pom and a one-pounder just ahead of them. Over *there*," Steele pointed to his right, "four Stokes mortars and two Vickers sections. Back *that* way," he pointed to the southwest, "is what's *left* of my maneuver companies—probably *five* Hotchkiss sections, *ten* Vickers sections, and *maybe* a hundred other infantry; so I've got five hundred men still on their feet. Over *that* way," Steele pointed to his right, "is what's left of the 445th Brigade, probably a *thousand* men and *maybe* fifty officers; I've already got *their* machine guns under *my* command. Every man *jack* of 'em's *willing*, but ain't got enough *energy* now to stand in a *chow line*, if we could even *get decent* chow up here. Sir. But…"

"*But*…" Davis repeated, waiting.

"If I had *another battery* of 75s," Steele continued, "a battalion or two of *heavy* guns, and another thousand *fresh* men, I could mask the front *and* the flanks and work my way…," he pointed to the right, "*down* that draw to the *east*—beyond our boundaries— and *up* that ravine *behind* the hill while every Hotchkiss I can get my *hands* on puts a *standing barrage* on *top* of it before all that infantry attacks. But, *sir*," Steele looked straight at Davis, "I ain't *got* another battery of 75s, *nor* a single *solitary* heavy gun, *nor* another thousand fresh men, and my orders are to *strictly* maintain our boundaries. I *could* hammer that *damn hill* with all the machine guns I've got left and throw all the men I can at the front of it, but I'd just be wasting ammunition and lives. So, I *wait*. Sir."

Davis stared at the hill intently for several moments. "Colonel Avery," he finally called behind him. "Can you join us, please?"

The Colonel, whose fastidious uniform was fast becoming *quite* soiled, leaped across the puddle and scrambled up the side of the crater, crouching indignantly in the slippery ooze. Steele saw his disgust, but said nothing.

Davis, still staring through the aperture, spoke slowly and clearly. "Colonel Steele here has a *plan* to take Hill 410. He has called it the Beehive, and that's what *we'll* call it from now on."

"Um, yessir, but *I...*" Steele stammered.

"Since *he* is the senior officer fit for duty in this area, I shall promote him to Brigadier General in the field and place him in *command* of the 445th Brigade and in *tactical* command of this operation, and I don't give a *hang* what *Congress* or *Pete March*[1] or *Black Jack* say about it. Now, *General* Steele, here, you'll need *these*." Davis handed Steele a pair of stars. "Divisional *boundaries* be *damned,* we *must* catch up with the 90th Division's right flank. Your predecessor and his staff are down with influenza. *You* are the *only* officer in this *zone* who even *thought* of a plan to move forward that hasn't already failed. I'll get wires and artillery observers up here within the hour. I can have three French heavy batteries and *another* battery of 75s in position by *dark*. The 3rd Battalion of the 190th Regiment hasn't fired a *shot* yet...that should be at least *six* hundred fresh men; *short* of a thousand, but *there* it *is*. Now, *how soon* can you get your people in position? Is a *night attack* workable?" He stopped. "Can you *do* it?"

Steele didn't hesitate. "*Yes*sir. I'll need to position guides before bringing the 3rd of the 190th and the howitzers up, so not before, say, mid-afternoon. Major *Gowan,*" he called over the General's shoulder.

"*Sir,*" Gowan answered from the back of the hole, the mud and grime doing little to hide his puckered face.

"You're the senior staff officer up here?"

"*Yessir.*"

---

[1] Peyton March, then Chief of Staff of the US Army.

"Would you *like* to be a *Colonel* for a little while? Help me with these stars, please."

Gowan blinked, looked back and forth at the officers. "I'll do what's *needed*, sir," he sighed, removing the silver oak leaves, and pinning a star on each of Steele's epaulets.

"*That's* the spirit, Colonel. Now, tell Major Willis to organize *chow* for everyone up here and I don't give a damn *how* or *what*. Then, organize these men *here* and position them at intervals back to the telephone post. Promote *two* of them to Sergeant and put them in charge of two squads of runners. Tell *our howitzers…*"

***

A light rain started to fall about an hour before dark. Steele, still staring at the Beehive from his hole a thousand yards away, took a moment to think of the miracle he had wrought.

Four connected holes had four telephones and two artillery rangefinders in them, their tripods perilously balanced in the ooze. Nine people, all hopelessly smeared with mud and goo, carried out their respective tasks in English and pidgin French with the quiet urgency of men who had been at war for months, though *most* had only been at it for a few weeks…some for mere *hours*…

Everyone knew the war was ending, but *no one* wanted to be the *last* to die in it.

"All right, gents," Steele said, turning from his reverie. "*Any* questions?"

"Jump-off position is *where*, sir?" A mustachioed Major commanding the 3rd Battalion asked. His men would move to the blocking position.

"Your ravine is about five hundred yards east of the Beehive. My scouts say there are not *that* many obstructions or Hun positions between that ravine and here. Hunker down and launch three green flares when you're in position."

"Prisoners, sir?" Lorenzo asked. He was leading Steele's Assault Group, composed of his battalion's remnants, joined by two pickup companies of infantry from the rest of the brigade. They would directly assault the hill from the front, with twenty Lewis gun teams and two dozen men carrying the new BARs— Browning Automatic Rifles. Lorenzo's polyglot outfit numbered about six hundred. Joining them was that dogged refugee, Savalas, commanding Company E's thirty Legionnaires and hundred attached Americans. He turned down a promotion in his own army to stay with Steele and the 432nd.

"*Take* 'em and strip 'em fast and get 'em out of the way. I'll have no massacres."

The burley Colonel in command of four batteries of French 105 mm howitzers and three sections of 75s asked, "we lift the gas after the first thirty minutes?" They would fire directly at the hill from ranges as short as 600 yards.

"And switch to shrapnel; shoot at any muzzle flashes you see on the hill. The heavy guns in the back will keep firing their usual mix until three *yellow* flares signal the Assault Group is in position. Anything else? No? Then we step off at 6; an hour and ten minutes from now I'll fire the first white flare. *Saddle* up."

They didn't move.

"Gents?" Steele asked. "Is there *anything*…?"

"A little *fast*, sir," the Colonel said, glancing around him at the other officers. "Not *used* to such hasty…"

"Well, it's pretty simple, fellows. *There's* that *Goddamn hill*; we're *here*; we need to *take* that *Goddamn hill* to get *past* it. It's nothing we ain't done before, just unfamiliar terrain, *OK*?"

"Let's get *going*, men," Davis added. "*This* plan is just mad enough to work."

***

"*Three…two…one…NOW!*" Steele fired his Very pistol…and the wet night erupted into a thunderous concert of artillery and machine guns. Steele watched as the lead company of the 3rd Battalion went forward across the field to his right. Overhead, shells and bullets screamed, screeched and sighed. Two machine gun battalions plus Steele's remaining guns hammered the hill as the shells slammed into every inch of the hill mass. Mud, smoke, and explosions seemed to cover the massif.

Still, winkles of muzzle flashes emerged from the chaos.

The bizarre scene, illuminated by explosions, revealed that fire inundated the hill. The smaller machine gun rounds were mostly invisible, except where artillery explosions lit tiny splashes of mud and dirt.

After several minutes, Steele could see muzzle flashes in the ravine, which meant 3rd Battalion was next to the hill and fighting the small German unit there.

Twenty minutes later…three green flares.

Twenty minutes after that…three yellow flares.

And the artillery lifted…and the battle truly began…

9th November, Meuse River.

By God, it worked…we had the hill by midnight

without a major hitch. Nearly three hundred Huns

killed or taken prisoner—at a cost of only seventy-one

casualties for us…twenty-four dead…

"Colonel *Gowan*," Steele yelled into the phone, "*get* your *ass up here* and *pronto*." Steele once again rolled up his diary and stuffed it into his map case.

"Not *his* fault, sir," Massie mumbled.

"I want to know…" Steele started, just as a messenger appeared at his elbow.

"From Captain Lorenzo, sir," the boy said.

> TAKING FIRE FROM ACROSS THE RIVER. LIGHT ENEMY RESISTANCE. CAN SEE BARRACOURT FROM HERE. HAVE 60 PW IN HAND. ADVISE PWS.

"At least Lorenzo learned to be brief," Steele mumbled. Another runner appeared.

> REACHED BARRACOURT BUT CUT OFF BY MG NESTS. HARRIS KILLED. E ATTACKING MG NESTS.

Steele remembered Harris, an energetic, hands-on engineering officer with a can-do attitude. "Take *this* to Captain Lorenzo," Steele scribbled a note:

> SENDING GOWAN FORWARD TO COMMAND ESCORT FOR PWS. HELP E CLEAR ROAD.

"Sir," Gowan said, breathless from his run forward.

"Colonel, you are chief of staff because your expertise is

sufficient for a battalion," Steele began calmly.

"Thank you, sir," Gowan said. "The General is…"

"Now, can you do the same for a brigade?"

"Ah sir," Gowan sputtered, "the brigade already *has* a chief of staff…"

"Yes, but *you're* replacing him," Steele growled. "Doc Miller's medico's lack of transportation is inexcusable…"

"We're short on vehicles of *all* kinds, sir," Gowan offered.

"The medics take *priority*, Harry," Steele said. "Medical care and evacuation are all about hope, and hope is the *foundation* of morale; remember that."

"Yessir."

"You're now chief of staff for both the battalion *and* the brigade, Harry."

Gowan inhaled deeply. "At your *pleasure*, sir."

"It is *indeed* my pleasure, Colonel. Now *get* your behind *forward* and get Lorenzo's PWs out of harm's way…"

9th November Barracourt, France. [Same date;

different location; different page]

Linked again. Met Jake Halford of the 115th Brigade, 90th Division, across the Moselle….There

is always a [expletive] *way…ran into Terry Allen*

again…

"Ned Steele," Steele began, offering his hand.

"Jake Halford," the huge officer grinned. "I've *heard* of you."

"Ain't heard a *thing* about you," Steele answered.

"Just an Iowa farmer in the wrong goddamned place." Halford shook his head. "Two years ago I was a Captain in the Iowa National Guard. Now…my *God*, just *look* at this place."

What had once been a prosperous farming community had become a slaughterhouse. Unburied dead and body parts lay scattered everywhere. Carcasses of horses, cattle, sheep and pigs littered the ruined farms. Broken weapons, pieces of uniforms, and shattered trees lined the roads and trails.

"Yeah," Steele sighed. "Two years ago I was a Corporal in Jefferson Barracks…no, take that back; I was in *Mexico* then…"

"Didn't expect to be *here*, anyway," Halford said.

"Didn't expect *here* to be…like…this."

"Not a sight I'd expect to see on this *Earth*…"

"Or…*anywhere*…"

***

"Major Allen," Steele smiled. "*Pleasure* to see you…"

"Pleasure to be seen, ah, *sir*," Allen said, extending his hand. "You got *stars*, now?"

"For the moment," Steele sighed. "They *say* I'm the youngest General in the Army…"

"Oh, that'll tick off Doug McArthur something *fierce*," Allen declared. "If you plan on a career in this man's Army, you'd better not run into *him* with those stars…"

"Never had the pleasure of meeting *that* officer," Steele said honestly. "Maybe I shall later."

"Anyway," Allen said. "I'm here because I'm to be attached to your Brigade for your attack tonight…"

"Right," Steele said. "We're going to put *you* on the *left*, closest to the river, so we can sweep south and reach the river by dawn…"

"We've been working at night for three weeks," Allen declared. "Maybe we can…"

"Ah, Major," Steele interrupted, looking at Allen's dirty bandage. "You've been shot through the…"

"*Jaw*, yessir. I'm *supposed* to be in the *hospital*, but…"

"Yeah; *you* want to be in on the *end*…"

"As long as I don't get *killed*, yessir."

"Just *cease fire* no later than 11, no matter *what* they do. *Out*." Steele handed the phone to the switchboard operator; the time was 10:59. "*They* haven't stopped shooting yet." A pair of mortar bombs detonating nearby punctuated this statement of fact.

"Maybe it's just a bluff, sir," the operator said. "Ya know, get *us* to stop shooting so they can…"

"I doubt it…*what's* your name?"

"Frazier, sir."

"Frazier, I don't *think* so. Orders came from AEF." Steele listened to the steady beat of rain on the dugout roof. "If it is, though, we'll know soon enough." A long, steady burst of machine gun fire buzzed over their heads. "Sure as Hell *hope* it's…"

Silence…sudden, *deathly* silence filled the dugout. Steele glanced at his watch. "Eleven." He listened…heard *nothing* but the rain.

"Permission to go outside, sir?" Frazier asked.

"*Just* for a moment. We still need someone on the switchboard."

"*Yes*sir." Frazier, an older man—all of thirty, perhaps—slowly stood up from his stool, as if unwinding his body. "Been *on* this damn thing since *dawn*…"

"Step away, then," Steele said. "I'll mind the store for a while."

While Frazier pulled his poncho on, Steele listened and watched the switchboard for any light that signaled an inbound call.

Nothing. Long minutes passed. The rain eased.

Steele picked up the headset, scanned the labels, chose the one that read DIV HQ, plugged in the master, and pressed the button.

"Division," came the answer.

"Steele. *Anything* over there?"

"No; it's all stopped here."

"Can I talk to Davis?"

"Wait."

It was several minutes before a voice came on. "Davis."

"Steele here. Is *this…is* it…?"

"I *believe* so, Steele. I've got nothing from Corps to say different. Are you *seeing* anything, *hearing* anything?"

"To the *south,* some activity."

"There's still *some* offensive activity someplace, I understand. Not everyone *wants* this damn thing to end."

"Well, the rain's letting up here," Steele said. "I'll keep someone on the switchboard…"

"That might just be you and me, Steele. All *my* people want to jump around in No-man's-land."

"So do mine."

"*Hell* with it," Davis said. "*I'm* going to see they don't hurt themselves. I suggest *you* do the same. Make a communications check in a couple of hours. Out."

"Out." Steele took off the headset, set it down carefully. He ducked out of the dugout just as three men—without rifles, helmets, or belts—jumped over the communications sap, turned, and ran towards the front…towards the German lines.

Climbing up the wall of the trench (it had been a German trench before Steele captured it), Steele grappled in the mud and the filth, pushing a coil of barbed wire away before standing up…

Scores of men were atop the trenches, the dugouts, the bunkers, pushing wire away, stacking sandbags for seats. More men lit fires with ammo boxes. A few ventured into the area that would have been No-man's-land just a few hours ago, but now was only mud and shattered trees, ruined buildings and the wreckage of a

German artillery battery caught on a road.

On the other side, gray-clad figures did much the same thing.

Steele looked up at the scudding clouds, saw the disk of the sun high up, felt a breeze on his cheek, a drop of rain on his forehead.

And knew he was alive…but he could *not* cry as much as he *wanted* to.

12ᵗʰ November, Overlooking the Moselle River near

Neuville, Luxembourg.

So it's over, over here…A very odd thing

followed…Matters of mutual interest…?

Bonfires blazed through the night on *both* sides of what *had* been the front. Steele, shaking the mud off his trench coat as he stomped on the duckboards in the little cottage's floor, marveled at the transformation of the fighting front, almost miraculously, from a zone of death to one of tired celebration.

Steele read the note written in a cramped hand:

> *Colonel Grodecki would appreciate a meeting with General Steele to discuss matters of mutual interest. He does not believe such a meeting would violate the terms of the current armistice.*

"How am I to reply?" Steele asked the German Lieutenant.

"I will carry your reply, sir," the Lieutenant answered, his English clipped and precise.

Steele glanced at Massie, who shrugged. He glanced at Captain Branch Dukane, his G2, who nodded. *"That's* who's in charge over there, as of three days ago: Ivan Grodecki."

"When and where?" Steele asked the German Lieutenant.

"The Colonel has arranged a cottage…*here.*" The Lieutenant pointed to a small map. "You may bring whatever escort or guards you choose, sir." He drew a sharp breath. "We are not in *any* condition to fight. The *time* the Colonel proposes is three o'clock this afternoon."

"Tell Colonel Grodecki I'll be there."

∗∗∗

Steele stepped out of his touring car a hundred yards from a small thatched-roof house. Lined up along the road was a group of armed and uniformed old men and boys—the boys younger than fifteen, the men sixty and older. All the boys had dirty faces and empty eyes; most of the old men had gas masks hung around their necks. Both young and old looked both tired and frightened.

It was a short, muddy walk to the cottage; the trail was simply not wide enough for his car. Rodgers walked behind him, his shotgun cradled in his arms.

Outside the remarkably intact structure stood the Lieutenant and another, older man in a clean but worn uniform. Both officers came to attention and saluted Steele. Steele snapped off a salute and offered his hand. "Ned Steele, *Herr Oberst*."

Grodecki smiled broadly, shook Steele's hand and said, "Ivan Grodecki, *Herr General*. Pleased to meet you."

"*Wie geht es dir?*"[1] Steele answered.

Grodecki smiled, answering in English, "as well as a defeated officer *can* feel, *Herr General*. *Try* your German if you wish, but I shall carry on in English, as I need the practice. *Please*." He gestured to a small table and two chairs outside the cottage. "That will be all, Lieutenant. We have some thin brandy, if you like."

"*Bitte*[2]…"

"I won't offer you bread; it is mostly sawdust."

"May I offer you a biscuit?" Steele motioned to Rodgers, who produced fresh biscuits and butter from a gunny sack.

"Oh, *Herr General*, you are too kind," the Colonel smiled. The Colonel poured some red liquid into two glasses, putting the bottle down. "To your *very* good health, *Herr General*," he said, raising his glass.

"To *our* very good health, *Herr Oberst*." They clinked glasses and Steele sipped the liquor; it was even harsher than some of the rotgut his men "liberated" from other battlefields or made in the laundry.

---

[1] How do you do?

[2] Please…

"It is what we have, *Herr General*," Grodecki nodded, putting his glass down. "What we have had for a *year*."

"I've heard stories about turnips…" Steele began.

"The *worst* of them are probably true." Grodecki finished his brandy, took a biscuit from the tin plate and bit in. "*Mein Gott*," Grodecki sighed. "I have had *nothing* like this in *years*. *Vielen Danke*."

"You are quite welcome," Steele answered. "We have more…"

"My men *kill* for such…may I give some to my hurt?"

"Certainly. My baker can *supply* more, if you like."

"I appreciate the gesture, *Herr General*, but *that* would be impractical." Grodecki smiled. "I somehow expected *der Amboss* to be…bigger."

"I'm just a *guy* doing a *nasty* job, *Herr Oberst*," Steele answered with a grimace.

"You do it *well*. The attack on Hill 125[1] four days ago was brilliant."

"Were *you* defending…?"

"My superior was killed there." Grodecki shrugged. "That left *me* in command of the division. Of *other* business: we cannot care for *five* of your hurt soldiers in our custody…"

"I'm not *authorized* to exchange prisoners…" Steele started.

"You are feeding *our* men better than *I* can; this bread is proof of that. I just want to *give* your soldiers back to you."

"Very well. We'll send ambulances…"

"*That* would suit."

"Tell me, *Herr Oberst*, how you learned English?"

"I was a consular officer in England before the war."

"Ah." Steele cleared his throat, concentrating. "*Ich habe Deutsch in der Schule gelernt,*" he said slowly, "*aber ich viele vergessen.*"[2]

Grodecki nodded with a small smile. "It is good *enough*, but if

---

[1] 125 meters=410 feet.

[2] I learned German in school, but I have forgotten much of it.

you don't *hear* it often, your *accent* goes. I have forgotten most of my *Polish* and no Pole would recognize *my* tongue." He sighed. "Our men caper in the zone between us. There are unexploded shells out there."

"We should restrict them…"

"Agreed."

"There's also been some trading between them," Steele said. "I don't know that there's much *harm* other than exchanging *lice*…"

"My men mostly want *food*. My surgeons need medical supplies and something for this damned *Grippe*."

"*Grippe*?" Steele asked.

"You call it *flu*. It has killed many."

"On our side, too," Steele agreed. "That's how I got my star: everyone *else* was down with it. I don't know that we *have* a cure."

"Our surgeons have used morphia to quiet the coughing. They save some that way, they believe."

"Ah. *We* use codeine."

"Yes. Our stocks of morphia are short…"

"I'll see if we can spare some codeine and *other* medical supplies."

"*Very* generous; thank you." Grodecki filled the glasses again. "We're going to be doing this *again*, you know."

"This…what?"

"Fighting each other."

"In America, we want this to be the *last* war…"

"It *cannot*; certainly not *this* one."

"Why?"

"Because we are defeated at *home*, but we are not defeated *here*, at the front. We cannot fight anymore *now*, but, in twenty years' time…" Grodecki shrugged, downed more brandy. "I am *Prussian* and a fifth-generation soldier. They must *crush* us as they have of old before *we* admit defeat."

"You will fight again?" Steele downed his.

"If *Germany* fights, I *must*." Grodecki looked around; skeleton-like boys in uniform watched from several yards away.

"These young men will spawn the children that we will take to war." He offered Steele another drink; Steele held his hand up politely. "These *Gefreiters* and *Feldwebels*[1] will train the boys." Grodecki tossed off his brandy. "And we will fight the Russians *and* the English *and* the French *and* you Americans again."

"But…why?" Steele asked, incredulous at the very idea.

"Because we bled France white," Grodecki declared. "They will demand a humiliating peace and a disarmed Germany." He stared at Steele. "And these *Gefreiters* and *Feldwebels* will be bitter and resentful and find a leader as angry as they; perhaps even a *Gefreiter*."

"You sound very certain," Steele whispered.

"I *am*, my friend." Grodecki stood. "We should meet again, if we can."

"Yes, we should." Steele stood, extended his hand. "*Auf Wiedersehn, Herr Oberst.*"

"Until we meet again, my friend."

22nd November, Near Fontainebleau.

I visited Col. Patton in the hospital; he nearly died…

Walking through the wards, Steele stopped by several of his men recuperating from wounds or the flu, or both. *Most* of the flu had passed. He got to the officer's wing, reading the names one by one, until he came to "Col. Patton, GS." He knocked gently on the door. "Come," came the familiar voice.

"George," Steele said softly. "Heard you stopped some hot metal."

"Ned," Patton grinned. "I *heard* you were…oh, it's *true!* You outrank the *hell* outta me now!"

"Only temporary," Steele declared. "Congress *won't* approve it. Hasn't changed my *disposition* any."

"Glad of that," Patton said, sitting up slightly. "Every time I hear the name 'Steele' these days, I hear about some amazing feat you've managed. I *heard* about that Beehive you captured. Sure

---

[1] Sergeants.

wish I'd been there to see it." He motioned to a chair. "Tell me about it."

"Well," Steele said, sitting. "Not that much to tell. Pretty standard stuff, except for we couldn't go around within boundaries, so we said the *hell* with…."

"Well, I'm sure I'll hear about it later." Patton sat back, wearily. "This damn hip of mine…*ugh.*"

"What happened?"

"Hun MG opened up on us at about fifty yards, caught me in my left hip and nearly ripped my butt off; blew a hole about the size of a silver dollar." Patton shook his head. "About two inches from my butt hole. They say I might have bled to death."

"Sorry, George," Steele said. "I heard your tanks were doing well for a while."

"*Well*, not *good*," Patton grunted. "They aren't *reliable* and they aren't *powerful* enough to be much more than be movable machine-gun nests, when they *can* move. Spend more time being repaired than they do fighting." He sighed deeply. "Then this war *ended* before I could…maybe in the *next* war…"

"I'm sure both your *tanks* and *you* will fare much better in the *next* war, George."

"Think there will be another war?" Patton asked.

"I think we both know the answer to that, George."

***

"They tell us it might be next *year* before we can go home," Angie said. They met in the hospital canteen, a busy place between shifts.

"Since my battalion formed in France, nobody *knows*," Ned answered.

"My parents are coming over at Christmas…"

"With the President?"

"No; Dad wants to see for himself. Besides, they miss Paris."

"Been here often?"

"Every other year before the war." She sighed deeply. "The place has changed so *much*, yet so *little*. I recognize landmarks and streets, but the people…*so* many widows; *so* many orphans…"

"Do you still have that hotel room key?"

"I can *get* it, I think. How long do you have?"

"I can get back to the battalion tonight."

"I *work* until six, but I can find someone to fill in for me."

"Then we would have a few hours."

"And we shall *take* that few hours."

23rd November, Neuville, Luxembourg.

The last Germans left Flanders today. No one fights over Hill 90 any more; now they call it Anvil Hill. Today, for whatever reason, I feel the deaths of so many very deeply now. Death has surrounded me for a year, yet today is the first time I truly feel sorrow for the many after McTee. I cannot explain it.

24th November, Neuville, Luxembourg.

The rain continues…I am ordered to Germany in command a brigade composed of the 432nd and four other MGBs to escort the Germans out of France. For some reason, I feel better; all those deaths now seem justified …I hope my message reaches her…a new lyric is added…

"*These* orders are from AEF, sir," Erskine sighed. "Took me two days to *find* you. Units have scattered to *hell*-and-gone since the Armistice. AEF sends 'em *one* way, *this* Army sends 'em *that* way, *that* Corps sends 'em some *other* Goddamn way…"

"I understand, Sergeant," Steele said. "Congratulations on your promotion. Tell me again why you're not working for me?"

"General Conner said you've got *enough* couriers, sir,"

Erskine said.

"Probably right, Sergeant..." Steele said, reading the top message:

> BRIG. GEN. STEELE TO TAKE COMMAND OF THE FIRST ARMY MACHINE GUN BRIGADE. ORGANIZATION FOLLOWS...

There was more detail in the stack of paper, such as orders of march, routes, dates for rendezvous, and signals on the multiple pages. "Mike, what do you make of this?" Steele handed Brick the bundle.

"Creating a central command for machine guns like they do artillery, I'd guess," Brick answered, handing the stack to Willis. Though he was too weak to take to the field, Brick kept up on *most* of his executive officer duties. "Makes it easier to order all the guns..."

"Three different calibers of ammunition," Willis mused. "Makes *supply* a little touchy."

"With any luck at all, we won't be *shooting* anything," Steele declared. "Well, we've got orders. Gather the maps that came with that and let's get them started."

"Maps into Germany," Gowan said. "Finally getting to *use* mine."

"You *had* maps for Germay?" Steele asked.

"Had 'em since I left Fort Leavenworth for France."

Steele thought, briefly. "Mike, I'll leave you here to command the base camp. You able to do that?"

"I feel stronger every day, Ned," Brick answered, "but...yeah, maybe I *should* be in the rear with the gear."

"Who's the senior *company* commander, Harry?" Steele asked.

"Nagorsky in A Company or Grissom over in C." Gowan answered.

"OK," Steele sighed. "Harry, the 432nd will be *your* battalion and either Nagorsky or Grissom will be your chief of staff *and* exec."

"Me?" Gowan asked. "*Command* the...?"

"About time you stepped up, Harry," Steele said.

"You sure as *Hell* don't want *me* in command," Willis said.

"Nobody's army is ready for *that*, Jack," Steele said, "but you will *also* serve as chief of staff for *this* battalion."

"Here's to hoping you don't need me much," Willis mumbled.

"I'll write a reply…" Steele started, reaching for paper.

"The *only* reply I'm to carry back is 'yessir.'" Erskine sighed.

Steele nodded, paused. "Are you going to Chaumont or Paris from here, Sergeant?"

"Paris, sir."

"Can you carry a *personal* message to the American Hospital in Paris?"

"I *can*, sir."

> *Angie,*
> *I'm ordered to follow the Germans home. I will try to get to Paris as soon as duty permits.*
> *Love,*
> *Ned*

* * *

As they pulled their remnants together at their camp, Steele heard a new lyric:

> *Mademoiselle from Armentieres,*
> *parley-vous?*
> *Mademoiselle from Armentieres,*
> *parley-vous?*
> *Just blow your nose, and dry your tears,*
> *We'll all be back in twenty years,*
> *Rinky, dinky, parley-vous!*

He *hoped* they were wrong….

December

3rd December, German border.

The dispersion of my brigade had reached absurd proportions. I now have MG companies in four

"*Herr General*," Grodecki grinned, saluting before offering his hand.

"*Herr Oberst*," Steele smiled, returning the honors. "We meet again."

"Indeed." They watched Germans march past, over a small stone bridge over an insignificant stream swelled by recent rains. "My division," Grodecki sighed. "Barely three thousand men on their feet."

"You have suffered grievously," Steele said quietly.

"We *have*," Grodecki agreed. "I lost a brother in Flanders, and another in a French prison camp. My youngest sister lost her husband in Russia."

They watched. The Germans were tired; there was no spring in their step. But they did not stop or linger on the bridge. "My friend," Grodecki finally said. "I believe we offered an armistice to keep you from holding a victory parade in Berlin."

"*Möglicherweise haben Sie Recht, mein freund,*"[1] Steele answered.

Grodecki smiled, nodded. "*Richtig.*[2] You have forgotten *little*. I *also* think the British and French accepted an armistice because they did not want that parade to be led by you Americans."

"*Da könnte etwas dran sein.*"[3]

---

[1] You may be right, my friend.

[2] Correct.

[3] There could be something to it.

"*Jawohl*," Grodecki sighed. "Perhaps *too* much."

9ᵗʰ December, Metz, Germany.

As their soldiers march home, they give their people

heart. We share rations with them and they sell us

beer….

The bright winter sunbeams seemed unnatural on the low mountains. Steele and Gowan watched the German troops file past from a street corner in the middle of town. The soldiers carried their rifles slung on their shoulders, their machine guns in horse-drawn carts. Truck after truck, wagon after wagon, followed the marching men. "At least they're better *fed*," Gowan said. "Some of 'em starved before we could…"

"I know," Steele answered, watching the German civilians along the street, hanging out the windows of every building, waving Imperial flags. "Hardly seems like a *defeated* army, does it?"

"Not much," Gowan admitted.

"Will we be able to get ahold of the Kaiser, I wonder?"

"Not if the Dutch won't turn him over."

"That's so. Besides, what would we *do* with him?"

"I hear there's gonna be trials…"

"I heard that too. Maybe Colonel Grodecki is right."

"I *think*, Ned," Gowan sighed, "we both *know* he is. So do the *men*." They watched as *another* young woman ran into the road to kiss a passing soldier. "And that girl there's the *proof*."

A young German man came out of the *bierstube* behind where Steele and Gowan stood, bearing a tray with two steins. "*Vielen danke*," Gowan said, putting a few coins on the tray and taking the steins. Steele reached into his map case and put a can of Maconochie stew on the tray. The young man smiled and bowed away.

"*That* should be his lunch," Steele said.

"I gave him *five* Marks for *fifty pfennigs* of beer," Gowan declared. "His *dinner*, too."

Steele sipped his beer. "A bit *thin*…"

Gowan downed his. "But not *that* bad."

13ᵗʰ December, Metz, Germany.

Following the Germans as they march home

reinforces what Grodecki said. German civilians

regard us with suspicion but not hatred.

23ʳᵈ December, Metz, Germany.

The last Germans left France yesterday. The

Brigade is disbanded; I am reduced to Lieutenant

Colonel and ordered to Paris…Harry will take the

432ⁿᵈ to Fontainebleau.

Volume XIII A
1919

THIS VOLUME EXISTS ONLY IN PIECES; PAGES TORN OUT OF A MISSING binding. There are teeth marks and stains that smell unmistakably of baby upchuck on those we have. Ned's youngest son confessed to having done the deed when he was about a year old.

We transcribed the pages we have, and have verified those contents using the usual collection of outside sources. January is the most complete month and presented here.

January 1919

2nd January, 1919, Hotel Deluxe, Paris, France.
I started this volume because once again I tore out too many pages out of the last one.
I must remember to keep profanity out of in my diaries now.
This place is a staircase or two above Le Petite Rose. My First floor room above the mezzanine is bright and clean, though a bit worn, as big as my kitchen back home. My uniforms still stink of carbolic and phosgene gas, and have more than a few holes. I brought Rodgers and ordered Brick to join me when he can. And the Angie—I can write her name here—is staying here. She and some of her friends who have been here the longest got leave.
As a war hero—or so the press back home calls me—I am a useful ornament to the politicians and senior officers. I have no illusions about what my duties will be here: an overpaid butler to some Washington functionary or politician.[1]

5th January, Hotel Deluxe.
I met her and her friends for lunch. Lovely women. Brick joined us. She is staying up a flight of stairs.

---

[1] Ned's role in Paris is unclear.

Which letter would she have shared? Certainly not the last one. Should I feel flattered or embarrassed? Lunch was as delightful as the company. This evening, we walked around town. I need to know if this isn't a dream. I felt her in my dreams even before she snuck out of her room last night. Wonder if making love is always like that? It is incredible to me how being with her makes me feel alive.

6th January, Hotel Deluxe, Paris.
Even amid shortage, they work hard to maintain a grandiose elegance. I salute their efforts, results and struggle [Illegible.] I notice the chipped crockery and glasses, but I don't mention it to the waiters, as they are already surly.

7th January, Hotel Deluxe, Paris.
I met my new driver, a Sergeant Hughes. We went out to the battalion, saw that the Red Cross has sent the volunteers I asked for to help keep the men clean and amused, and came back safe and sound. Hughes drives a Cadillac Touring car as if it were a baby carriage.
Return of recovered wounded and flu cases from the hospital puts our current headcount to 506 officers and men present and ready for duty. Murph informs me that at least half of the 105 men still in the hospital

will return home and [be?] discharged there.

Dinner with female companions is a long forgotten treat. Mike seems to be a great deal more energetic than he has been. I have to wonder if that malaise so many flu survivors suffer from is permanent.[1]

8th January, Hotel Deluxe, Paris.
A most pleasant diversion; a tour of the Eiffel Tower. Angie, Brick and Angie's friend Harriet [Obscured]

[Date believed to be about 9 January] *I find it hard to believe it was just two months ago we were preparing to attack the last bastions of the Kriemhilde Stellung. I have not heard shooting for nearly two months and yet sometimes at night, I can hear the machine guns rattling in the dark.*

16th January, Hotel Deluxe, Paris.
I have secured the Senator's permission. Now I need her mother's. This is a most daunting prospect. Speaking with Millicent[2]—she insisted on her first name—was unlike any conversation I ever had. My prospects, my earlier relations with women, how much money I had in the bank, all were fodder for her

---

[1] *Encephalitis lethargica* was a long term effect of the 1918 flu. It often lasted for years; some never fully recovered.

[2] Mrs. Millicent Gibson, wife of Senator Branch Gibson.

consideration. But, in the end, she [Rest of entry smudged and chewed]

18ᵗʰ January

Death, death, nothing but death. I am surrounded by death. This has been one of the longest, most grueling nights of my life bar none. But finally I can cry. Dad sent the wire to the Senator,[1] and he had Angie show it to me.

Mama was 38; Di was 23; Helen was 14; Irving was but 12. They died of the flu last October.[2]

I had heard it was bad back home, but not this bad. Flu killed more Americans in three months than the Germans did in a year.

I didn't know how life-affirming being with a woman can be, especially after such news. She is my rock, my buddy like Di was, but of course not like Di was.

19ᵗʰ January, Hotel Deluxe.

Tried to compose a wire home. Didn't know what to say other than 'I'm so sorry', which is horribly inadequate. I wrote so many letters to so many wives

---

[1] Dated 1 November 1918.

[2] Week of 20-26 October 1918. Death certificates dated 23 October: Wednesday. Most Michigan death certificates September-November 1918 followed this practice.

and families. Just didn't know what to say to my own.
I'll think of something later.

22nd January, Hotel Deluxe.
Mike has been doing what I should do with the
battalion, but he's stronger than I am now. His
sister's husband succumbed to the flu in November.
Mike says he barely knew him.

25th January, Hotel Deluxe, Paris, France.
Got a wire from Al, saying everyone else recovered
from their bouts with the flu, except Vanelle. She is
still ill after two months. He also says Charlie is in
Russia. Very puzzling.
Marriage in France requires a civil ceremony; the
church is optional but is often first. I wired home,
saying our civil ceremony will be Wednesday, will do
the church when we get home. Wanted to say
something positive and found it.

29th January, Paris, France.
~~I am~~ _We are_ wed. The ceremony was so brief I
barely knew it took place. We just signed the papers,
and it was done. Mike, Harriet, the Senator, and
Millicent were there.
The hotel put on a magnificent spread. Rodgers and
Willis provided champagne, caviar, sweet
strawberries (where _they_ came from at this time of

year, I shall never know), fresh bread, butter and dozens of roses in our room. General Pershing, Colonel Marshall, Murph Miller, and Angie's other friends from the hospital joined us at the luncheon. Chaplain Haldane gave a lovely benediction. Talbott sent a telegram. So did Lucas, who's a full Colonel now. I wonder how _they_ knew? We took pictures with Angie's Brownie.[1]

30th January, Hotel Deluxe, Paris.
I thought I would feel differently after marriage. All I feel is a sort of sad peace, knowing that Mama, Di, Helen and Irving were with us in spirit, but the others will have to wait for the church when we get home.

---

[1] Film developed in 1997. The images are key to authenticating the diaries.

Volume XIV
1919-1920

I found a yellowed newspaper clipping from the Washington *Times* announcing Ned's marriage to Angie dated a month after the fact in an envelope between in another diary. By the time I found it, the first volume of our transcription of the diaries had hit the press, and we started on Volume XIV.

April

Steele walked along the Rue de Flaubert, admiring the flowers in every shop window, even if the goods were often shabby. He rubbed his bad shoulder, the one he dislocated learning rugby.

As he did every April, when he started a new diary, his thoughts went back to earlier Aprils, *not* so many that he couldn't remember at least most of them. The family christened Irving on Ned's 10ᵗʰ birthday. On his 12ᵗʰ, Ned badly skinned a knee falling off a bicycle. On his 16ᵗʰ birthday, Alan Sr. took young Ned to a burlesque show; he'd done the same with *all* his boys on their 16ᵗʰ. On his 18ᵗʰ, Ned announced his intention to enlist if his father couldn't procure an appointment to West Point.

As he strolled along, he watched a young couple arm-in-arm, the young man wearing a French Army greatcoat. Steele remembered a pretty girl he'd walked out with a couple times before he joined the Army in '14. Then the sound of a bicycle bell startled him…and he looked up…

The sign above the shop window read *Le Bagage avec Benoit*. Alone in the display window sat an enormous steamer trunk covered in leather, with a domed lid at least as large as the trunk itself.

Steele's only *surviving* luggage was his barracks bag and his portmanteau with a broken handle. Angie's battered suitcase had a busted hinge, and her carpet bag had worn through.

"Oui, Monsieur Colonel?" the shopkeeper smiled when Steele walked in, his teeth slightly yellow. "How may I *help* my comrade-in-arms?" His voice was slightly strained; he'd been

gassed.

"Are you Benoit?" Steele asked in French, trying not to stare at the thin man's missing left arm. "Speak slowly, please. Forgive my poor French…"

"*Mai oui, mon Colonel*," Benoit nodded, "I can understand you. Michael Benoit, *at* your *service*."

"First, I must thank you for serving so bravely," Steele answered, glad that Angie drilled him in French every night.

"*Merci*. And I thank *you* for *yours*. Would you like some wine, cheese, perhaps? My *Repaš* is *small*, but…"

"*Mai non, merci*." Steele looked around the dusty shop, scattered with used suitcases and valises. "The trunk in the window," he asked, "*how much* would you…?"

"Ah, *that*…it was a *mistake, mon Colonel*," Benoit said. "The maker's *widow* finished it after the Army *shot* him. She made a lid *much* too large, but *I* have *other*—"

"It's all right," Steele said patiently. "How *much?*"

"For a comrade-in-arms, I *cannot* accept *more* than a thousand francs…"[1]

"A *thousand*," Steele said with mock consternation. "You mistake me for a rich man, *monsieur*. I *cannot* pay more than perhaps *fifty*. On a poor *Colonel's* pay…"

"Ah, yes," Benoit nodded sagely, "I understand. But *I* am but a poor pensioner, *mon Colonel*. I can *perhaps* accept…*five hundred*…"

"And a *noble* pensioner indeed," Steele replied, knowing that his pension was probably the equal to the pay of a Captain in the Regular Army. "I could see going as high as…*one hundred*."

"Ah…*non*, but perhaps…*three hundred*…?"[2]

"Done!"

Benoit grinned, extending his hand. "*Where* shall I have it sent?"

"Hotel Deluxe," Steele said. "Suite 34."

---

[1] About $160.

[2] Just over $50.

"And the name, *camarade?*"

"*Steele…*"

Benoit looked as if he'd met Petain himself. "*You* are '*L'Enclume?*'" he exclaimed,

"The…*what?*" *That* word had *not* been in Angie's lessons.

"*How* you say?" Benoit pounded his fist on the counter several times, then pointed to the spot. "*L'Enclume?*"

"Ah…The Anvil *en anglais*; *oui.*"

"*Colonel*: for a *hero* to France, *two hundred…*"[1]

"Done!"

Benoit wrote out the receipt…*une coffre à vapeur, 200 F…*[2]

May

20th May, Baume-les-Messieurs, France.
Today we had our first parade with our flags and guidon, and our last. I wish there were more of us to see it…At least they want to keep me…Bittersweet farewells are too hard to record…Rodgers has given his notice…We have tickets back…

"*Troop* the *colors*," Steele called.

The battalion watched as the color guard marched the newly acquired 48-star US flag and the newly *made* 432nd Machine Gun Battalion flag in front of every company as if they did this kind of thing every day…which they *had* practiced for three days.

Their unit flag—seen for the first time just two days before—portrayed a machine gun on wheels pushed by a snarling Uncle Sam with the motto in Latin "*percutio, alta rursus,*" on a flowing banner below.

Following the national and unit color guard, Massie and Steele

---

[1] About $30.

[2] The recipt was found in the trunk.

carried the new blue swallow-tail guidon flag, comprising crossed rifles with the name *432 MGB*.

One by one, the adjutants read the orders for the unit's honors: two French *Croix de Guerre* streamers and a *Médaille Militaire*, streamer, a unique Prince of Wales' Own Americans streamer, a unique Belgian *Honore* streamer, and seven American battle streamers.

"Awardees...*post!*"

Twenty-seven people stepped forward to receive (or accept) twelve Distinguished Service Crosses (Rodgers got one), nineteen Citation Stars,[1] twenty-six *Croix de Guerre*, twenty-seven *Legion de Honore*, and five British Military Medals (McTee's brother accepted his). The eldest of Harris' children broke down and wept when he accepted his father's DSC. Steele received a DSC, a *Croix de Guerre*, and a British Military Medal.

"*Pass...*in *review.*"

The small band played the Field Artillery March loudly enough that they could hear it on the other side of the review field, but not *much* louder. Steele and his staff stepped off to lead the parade.

Barely three hundred marched in three blocks that afternoon. Of those who came across on *Euphrates*, there were *seventeen* in formation. Returned for the occasion, the *thirty* survivors of Company E, led by an Italian Sergeant bearing their own guidon, marched at their slow pace behind the rest.

The reviewing officers—Pershing, Liggett, Haig, Foch, and Petain—saluted the battalion's color guard as it passed. A score or more of officers around the drill field, including Talbott, McFadden, and Standhaven, saluted each company as it passed.

Over 1,800 men passed through the ranks of the 1st Machine Gun Instructor Company/432nd Machine Gun Battalion. At its peak strength, after Company E joined, Steele's battalion had 901 officers and men assigned. Nearly 300 left the unit to be instructors, machine gun officers, and NCOs in *other* units. As Steele and his staff closed out the records of the battalion, there were nearly a hundred men still assigned who were in hospitals.

The reviewing stand also had several civilians, including Angie and her family and a host of French, British and Belgian

---

[1] The original Silver Star.

officials.

When *La Legion* detached their men in November 1918, Company E boasted 48 men. Ten had died of the flu. *La Legion* sentenced eight of them to death, after all, but commuted their sentences to transportation for life[1] in recognition of the service they had rendered France. In recognition of the service Haller had rendered France, they awarded him a *Croix de Guerre*... posthumously.

When Steele shouted *"fall out"* at the end of their first and last pass in review, the 432nd Machine Gun Battalion passed into history.

"Three cheers for the *Colonel*," someone shouted.

"Hooray," the battalion shouted...three times.

"That's the *second* time they've done that," Steele muttered to Brick.

"Done what?"

"Cheered me."

"You gave them hope, Ned," Brick answered. "*Now* you've given them something to salute."

"They'll *never* see it again."

"*They'll remember*, though, Ned, and *that's* what matters."

***

As the servers cleared the dessert plates, Angela's father, Senator Coldwell Gibson, said, "well, my boy, my Angel tells me you plan to stay in the Army. Any *truth* to that?" This celebratory repast, planned *without* Steele's knowledge, was a family-only affair.

"I had *planned* on it, yessir," Steele answered, thinking of his men who had their own celebration...elsewhere.

"And you want Angela to follow you around like a *common*..." Angie's mother, Millicent, added. "I didn't raise *my daughter* to be treated like a..."

"*Mother*," Angela interrupted...loudly. "*You* raised me to be an ornament on some other politician's *shelf*..."

---

[1] A euphemism for permanent exile in a penal colony.

"My dear," Steele interrupted. "Don't get into brawls you can't win." To Millicent, Steele merely said, "Angela is a grown woman, Millicent. She can do as she wishes. You *had* to have raised her to trust her own judgement. Why, you let her go off to France, did you not?"

"Not without protest," Millicent grumbled. "Imagine my *daughter* with all those *men…*"

"I voted for this war, Mother," the Senator declared. "My son *couldn't* fight in it, so my *daughter* went to it. I'm just glad she endured.…"

"And endure she did, sir," Steele said. "And endure *I* did. I find the profession of arms to be honorable and…"

"And if that is *your* choice, Edmund, that is your *choice*. Now…" the Senator continued, "I've been asked to give you *unpleasant* news." He handed Steele a message:

LIEUTENANT COLONEL EDMUND A. STEELE, NATIONAL ARMY, IS TO REVERT TO HIS REGULAR ARMY RANK OF CAPTAIN EFFECTIVE 30 MAY 1919, BY ORDER OF THE CHIEF OF STAFF, UNITED STATES ARMY.

"I knew it was coming," Steele said wistfully.

"Look at it this way, my boy," the Senator said. "At least they want to keep you. Now, you're to report to Chaumont on Thursday for *more* orders."

"And *we* must return to Washington," Millicent sighed. "Will you be coming *with* us, Angela dear?"

"I will be with my husband, Mother," Angie answered. "Wherever *he* goes…"

"And right now," Steele said, standing up, "*we're* going to the farewell party for my men."

The Senator merely nodded; Millicent looked distressed, staring at her husband as if to compel something to stop Steele and his wife…

But they left without another word.

***

The balmy wind battered the curtains in the hall windows as Ned and Angie repaired to their room in the chateau the Senator rented for the week. The celebration with the men, maudlin as it certainly was, ended with promises to stay in touch that everyone knew would not be kept. Ishim dropped a note:

> *Sorry I couldn't be there, but the staff is boarding ships now for home. I shall try to stay in the Regular Army, but otherwise will stay in the California Guard.*
> *Stay safe,*
> *Corey.*

Brick and Willis both pledged to *try* to stay in the Army, but they knew Congress would cut every which way to save money and try to forget America's European adventure.

As they approached their room that evening, Rodgers appeared from a side hall. "Is there anything you *need*, sir? Madame?"

"I don't *think* so, Sergeant," Steele answered.

"On Senator Gibson's instructions, I have procured tickets for New York departing on the second of June, sir. They are on the writing table in your suite."

"On *Senator…Father* told you to…?" Angie asked.

"He did, Madam. He knows where you are…ah…"

"Yes, of *course* he does," Steele said wistfully. "What are *your* plans?"

"Senator *Gibson* says he has a place for me." Rodgers answered. To Steele, he smiled. "It has been a *pleasure* serving you, sir, but…"

"A Captain can't *afford* you," Steele answered, offering his hand. "Cedric, it's been a pleasure knowing you and I could not have imagined a *better*…" Steele stopped, looking for the words.

"*Yes*, sir," Rodgers said softly, grasping Steele's hand firmly. "I could not *imagine* a *better*…either." He smiled at Angie, bowed slightly, said, "sir; madam; *pleasant* evening," and walked away.

22ⁿᵈ May, Chaumont, France.

I have my orders…

"Have a seat, Ned," Conner said when Steele reported, pointing to an overstuffed chair in his office. Steele took the proffered seat, wondering what to expect. "The Army, in its wisdom, will keep a core of officers and NCOs to build on when it has to."

"And it will *have* to," Steele said.

"You and I know that better than most others, probably," Conner answered. "The Army needs you at Fort Leavenworth. The School of the Line[1] needs a Machine Gun department, and *you're* going to organize it."

"*Yes*sir," Steele answered.

"The Germans may be licked for now, *but…*"

"They'll be back."

"Yes, *and* the *Japanese…*we've been expecting trouble with them since *Sherman* was General-in-Chief."

"Yeah?" Steele asked. "I thought we were *with* them in this war…"

"Only because they wanted the German possessions in the Pacific, and now they *have* them," Conner said. "They *wanted* New Guinea, but the Australians got there first." He sighed deeply. "I'd expect the next war, maybe twenty years from now, will be with both Germany and Japan." He glanced at Steele. "And we'll be the only country in the world who can fight them both at the same time. Get yourself ready for *that* war, Ned."

"Yessir," Steele answered. "Just blow your nose and dry your tears…" he repeated the last lyric.

---

[1] The predecessor to the Command and General Staff College.

PostScript

I found the guidon, unit flag and streamers at the bottom of the trunk, still flexible. I'd never held a *Croix de Guerre* in my hand; didn't know anyone who had.

There were more diaries, and *pieces* of diaries, and his two memoirs...

On Crest University's Wall of Honor, where the school honors alumni veterans, there's a plaque that reads *Edmund A. Steele, 1938.*

Ned was an alumnus of my *alma mater* and had deposited some diaries *here*, in the Truxton Archive, where we also found his *With the AEF* memoir, and at Camp Penobscott, that he commanded, twice...

Through chance, we crossed paths with a genealogist whose family has a connection to Ned Steele and who supplied the following account.

The Steele Saga

In the year 1050, while on a pilgrimage in Rome, King Macbeth of Scotland *liaised* with a serving girl in his entourage named Sorcha, a member of the Stuart of Bute clan. When it became known that Sorcha was with child, she was married off to a teenage cousin whose father had an estate in far off Ireland.

This long-forgotten incident resulted in a boy—named Mackenzie, which means "son of a great man"—who *could have*, in time, become a claimant to the throne of Scotland. He made his *own* fortune working for William of Normandy, *also* called William the Bastard, William the Conqueror, and, of course, William I, King of England. Mackenzie and his heirs never dared *make* a claim, although their kinsman, by their own *bona fides*, rose to the throne of Scotland *and* England.

Mackenzie had seven half-siblings by his fertile and precociously licentious mother who reached adulthood, as well as nine children of his *own* who made their *own* way in the world. Upon her death in 1101 at the advanced age of 76, Sorcha granted the monks of a Cistercian monastery in Killeen, County Meath on the western coast of Ireland, title to her *considerable* fortune, in part to protect her declaration of Mackenzie's parentage.

Five centuries after Sorcha's *affair* with King Macbeth— intentionally and conveniently forgotten by history—the last of the Stuart/Macbeths, fourteen-year-old Burton Anglim Macbeth, orphaned by a plague, was living near the monks. His fortune, drawn upon on special occasions, had dwindled to but a few shillings. Though he was *far* away from Scotland, for *some* it was *not far enough*.

Charles I—scion of a distinct branch of that same Stuart of

Bute clan from which Burton descended—could not tolerate a lawful contestant[1] to his throne of a United Kingdom of England and Scotland, formed after the death of Elizabeth I. Nor could he afford to encourage the nobles who might recognize such a claim, should the boy have the wit to make one *and* find a patron. So, in 1611, Charles ordered Burton transported to the Virginia colonies for the crime of having had ancestors on the wrong side of the blanket, while simultaneously being *much* too close to the *right* side.

An ironmonger indentured Burton as soon as he stepped off the ship. After five years of sleeping next to the hearth, Burton hammered the first steel of *anything* in North America—a drop-hammer head and shaft. He sold the device for the *handsome* sum of £10 ($1,528.72 in 1997 dollars; a fortune in the colonies) and bought himself out of indenture. In his petition, Burton used the name "Dean," from "*déantóir*"—Gaelic for "maker"—and used the Old English spelling of "Steele," a name given to one who is *hard*. Burton Antrim Macbeth became *Dean Steele—Maker of Steel.*

Dean married four women who bore him six boys and three girls, all of whom reached adulthood. The Edmund Steele in this story is a member of the "Tribe of William," the eldest of Dean Steele's sons, who *liased* with one of *this writer's* earliest ancestors in America, Sinead Colloloy, in 1640.

The scholars transcribing the Steele Diaries are researchers of *the most* diligent energies and talents. Our clan is grateful to them for their unstinting efforts to preserve the diaries and memoirs of one of its most notable members, Edmund Archer "Ned" Steele, United States Army.

Dr. Edward Colloloy, Professor of History and Genealogy,

Southern Michigan College

Fifteen times great-nephew of Edmund A. Steele

---

[1] Sorcha, Mackenzie and their descendents were *known*, but not *acknowledged*—an important distinction.

Historical Notes

The machine gun battalions of World War One are the least-known of all the obscure units in the US Army, including the ordnance and quartermaster units. A full MGB could deliver a division's worth of bullets on a single target for as long as they had ammunition. Unlike the fictional 432nd MGB, the American Army battalions infrequently operated as units until the end of the war.

While motorization of the Army was ongoing during the 1917-18 period, it was never complete. Machine gun units were using mules, horses and men as prime movers right up to the Armistice. Ford introduced the Model T only four years before America declared war; there were *thousands* of them, but not *millions*. Some MGBs were fortunate to have *any* discarded ambulances to move their equipment by the end of the war.

Ned and Angela's courtship was not unusual for the time and place. If she *mentioned* a young man in a wire home, it was significant. Of course, the Senator's remarks about Steele's "good family" were more important to him than to his daughter, but this was the early 20th Century and they expected obedient daughters to…well, Angie wasn't very *good* at obedience.

Women's fashions changed a great deal during the war, especially in France because of material and labor shortages. Because the casualties among men were so great, women of all ages no longer *cared* to hide their legs, and the corset all but disappeared, especially for younger women. Enterprising women made underclothes out of shirtwaist sleeves during the war and ushered in the more sensible foundations that followed in the 1920s.

The Great H1N1 Influenza killed more people than all the bullets, gas, shells and bombs of World War One combined. The disease mostly killed people between the ages of 18 and 40, often within hours of its onset. It may have been responsible, directly *or* indirectly, for up to 100 million deaths worldwide between the fall of 1917, when the first virulent cases *possibly* occurred in England, and January 1922, when the last cases appeared in Australia and Alaska. That Steele's mother and siblings succumbed during the October 1918 Detroit wave would not be unusual, nor would the large numbers of Steele's battalion.

My maternal grandparents survived the flu in Toledo, where Gramma worked for the Red Cross. Grampa *caught* the flu; family legend has it that Gramma turned gray in three days. My mother was born in Toledo in January 1923.

Ned's meteoric rise in the ranks is a complete fiction. There *were* young Majors and Colonels in WWI, but *not* just twenty-two, and certainly no *Generals* that young. His career, his relationship to Pershing, the formation and isolation of the 1st and the 432nd are inventions for the sake of the story. However, during my 27-year US Army career, I *knew of* several versions of Pirate Jack Willis, whose capabilities were *nearly* as legendary. I also knew many, *many* NCOs like McTee and Nagurski and Dugan, and officers like Steele and Brick, Gowan *and* Grimes, fine men all.

Most of the characters in this story are fictional, but some are authentic, historical persons, some of whom you might see again in other Steele Diaries. None of them, of course, ever met the fictional Ned Steele.

As for Ned himself, he has an entire career full of adventures in front of him.

Curtis and Maria, who you met in *The Past Not Taken: Three Novellas,* will be transcribing his diaries and memoirs, and filling in at least *some* blanks with their careful research. How *this* story came about is the subject of *The Persistent Past: The Steele Diaries,* which will appear after *this* story. The last story in the Steele Saga, *Steele's Hammer,* which takes place in World War Two and the Korean War, will appear after *that.*

I hope you will follow along.

www.ingramcontent.com/pod-product-compliance
Lightning Source LLC
Chambersburg PA
CBHW030914300726
48970CB00001B/151